FAKE IT

FAKE IT

Fictions of Forgery

Mark Osteen

University of Virginia Press • *Charlottesville and London*

University of Virginia Press

Printed in the United States of America on acid-free paper

First published 2021

9 8 7 6 5 4 3 2 1

Library of Congress Cataloging-in-Publication Data

Names: Osteen, Mark, author.
Title: Fake it : fictions of forgery / Mark Osteen.
Description: Charlottesville : University of Virginia Press, 2021. | Includes bibliographical references and index.
Identifiers: LCCN 2021008845 (print) | LCCN 2021008846 (ebook) | ISBN 9780813946269 (hardcover ; acid-free paper) | ISBN 9780813946276 (paperback) | ISBN 9780813946283 (epub)
Subjects: LCSH: Literary forgeries and mystifications. | Forgery in literature.
Classification: LCC PN171.F6 O88 2021 (print) | LCC PN171.F6 (ebook) | DDC 098/.3—dc23
LC record available at https://lccn.loc.gov/2021008845
LC ebook record available at https://lccn.loc.gov/2021008846

Cover art: The Forger, Ruth Channing. Aquatint etching, 24" × 18". (Courtesy of the artist)

To my late mother, Lois, who taught me not to lie

CONTENTS

ACKNOWLEDGMENTS

THIS PROJECT has taken me to places and times I never imagined I would investigate. As a specialist in modern and contemporary literature and film, I had no idea, when I began this endeavor, that I would be studying the works of a seventeenth-century female polymath or those of a poetic prodigy of the eighteenth century. But scholars must go where their research takes them, and I am delighted to have met Margaret Cavendish and Thomas Chatterton, as well as all the other writers, filmmakers, forgers, and frauds I've encountered in the course of writing this book. These explorations have provided the kind of rich material—fascinating stories, colorful characters, provocative intellectual conundrums—that would delight and inspire any writer.

But I have not undertaken the journey alone. I owe thanks to the institutions, colleagues, friends, and fellow writers who have furnished research materials, offered advice, and supported my endeavors.

I wish to thank Loyola University for supplying summer research grants and a one-semester sabbatical leave. I am exceedingly grateful to the Special Collections section of the Milton S. Eisenhower Library of the Johns Hopkins University, which provided access to the voluminous, if at times vexing, documents relating to the Ireland forgeries. The Special Collections Research Center at the University of Michigan Library supplied helpful material for chapter 6. My colleagues in the Loyola University Maryland English Department offered useful advice about chapter 7. Friends and fellow writers Scott Allen, Bryan Crockett, and Brian Murray sacrificed their time and eyesight to read and comment on the drafts of several chapters. Jeff Rogers, of Creative Impulse, Inc., provided assistance with the images. I thank all these friends and colleagues for their thoughts and ongoing support.

As always, my wisest and most faithful adviser and partner has been my wife, Leslie Gilden. My debt to her is beyond words.

A SLIGHTLY different version of chapter 3 was published in *PLL: Papers on Language and Literature* 53.4, Fall 2017. Chapter 6 was published in *South Atlantic Review* 85.4, Winter 2020.

ACKNOWLEDGMENTS

FAKE IT

PROLOGUE

Genuine Articles

> The moral life of man forms part of the subject matter of the artist, but the morality of art consists in the perfect use of an imperfect medium.
>
> —Oscar Wilde, preface to *The Picture of Dorian Gray*

A Sexy Crime

"I still consider the letters to be my best work" (126). So writes literary forger Lee Israel in her memoir *Can You Ever Forgive Me?*, which recounts how she fabricated dozens of letters she attributed to Dorothy Parker, Edna Ferber, Louise Brooks, and Noel Coward. Although Israel professes to regret "betray[ing] . . . my community of scholars, a citadel of culture" (122), she feels no guilt about the Parker forgeries, which were "larky and fun and totally cool. . . . I was a better writer as a forger than I had ever been as a writer" (126).

Israel's words capture three important truths about the peculiar form of fraud that is literary forgery. First, she declares explicitly what many forgers come to realize: that faking enables them to fashion a fresh authorial identity. Ron Fortune and Amy Robillard write that forging gave Israel "an opportunity to be truer to who she was as a person and as a writer" (286). More accurately, Israel's forgeries empowered her to *discover* her writerly self. Often forgeries *are* the forgers' best work because the spurious name liberates them from constraining habits and oppressive expectations. In forging texts, they reforge themselves. These writers, like critics and actors, use another artist to ignite their creative fires. The forger attaches herself or himself to that other artist like a flowering epiphyte on a tree. The forged work and persona not only permit the forger to bloom; they may also resurrect or revivify the artist(s) imitated.

Second, Israel's description of the Parker forgeries as "larky and fun" could have been written by any forger or hoaxer, because these activities partake of the spirit of play: forgery is a contest, a performance, often a practical joke. Clifford Irving, for one, admitted that he contrived his scheme to write a bogus autobiography of Howard Hughes as a titanic prank; although he certainly desired the money he earned, he also wanted to test himself and his powers of deception—to win a game against himself and his victims. Third, although Israel's title suggests penitence, the memoir is only part mea culpa: like all forgers, she craves recognition for her scholarship, skill, and savvy. As we will see repeatedly in the real-life and fictional forgeries and hoaxes discussed in this book, fakers are motivated by a paradoxical longing to receive positive attention for the cleverness with which they make themselves invisible. This dialectic between erasure and exposure characterizes all literary and fine-art forgeries and hoaxes. Thus, Israel reproduces several celebrities' letters within the book and then divulges that they are all her work (11): "See how foxy I am!" Even her title is a line she invented and inserted into one of her Parker forgeries (65); that is, the very words with which she asks forgiveness for forging are themselves forged! As she wrote the line, Israel recalls, she "imagined the waiflike Dorothy Parker apologizing for any one of countless improprieties, omissions, and/or cutting bon mots . . . apologizing with no intention whatsoever of mending her wayward ways" (66). The same is doubtless true of Israel.

Before she turned to fraud, Israel's career was foundering: her biographies of Tallulah Bankhead and Dorothy Kilgallen had been successful, but her hasty profile of Estée Lauder flopped, and she rapidly "plummeted from best-sellerdom to welfare" (19). While doing research on Elaine Carrington, she came across a cache of letters from Fanny Brice and stole them; she then supplied postscripts mentioning a gangster (thereby increasing the value of each by twenty or thirty dollars), invented a cousin named Sidney who had found them, and fabricated a deathbed promise that she would not sell other (nonexistent) letters (39–42). During calls to vendors she renamed herself Leonore Carthage and employed her "Smith college alumna voice" to clinch the sales. (She actually attended Brooklyn College [43].) Her motives—poverty, resentment over her lack of success, adulation of famous artists—typify those of the forgers and hoaxers discussed herein. Although Israel avers that the letters' content was the prime selling point, what truly convinced the buyers were the stories she told them. Her background as a biographer had honed her skills as a narrator and gossip, and characters like Uncle Sidney and details like deathbed promises created relationships with her victims: like all good con artists, she took her marks into her confidence.

Indeed, as will become clear in the course of this book, any forgery or hoax is only as good as the stories used to verify its provenance. But not only is a forgery always a narrative; forgeries also function as the seeds of further fictions, which also include the usually mendacious explanations offered by fakers after the fact. Forgeries are kernels from which fictions bloom.

Israel found old paper and rounded up a herd of ancient typewriters to provide verisimilitude. For the Brooks forgeries, she "cobbled together farragoes," blending passages from several letters and changing the language slightly (51). Her forgeries, then, were not exact copies of any extant text; few forgeries are. Rather, her technique exemplifies bricolage, a strategy of assembling fragments employed in much modern and postmodern art and literature. Israel's fakes required sedulous research, a great deal of skill, and a lively imagination. Like all forgeries, they were at once acts of criticism and acts of creation (see Ruthven 171). And like virtually all works of art, they were profoundly intertextual.

After a couple of her Noel Coward fakes came under suspicion and dealers blackballed her, she enlisted an accomplice named Jack Hock. Although a superb salesman, Hock was unreliable and, when he was arrested, blabbed to the FBI. Israel frantically shredded documents and discarded typewriters, but her most important postarrest act was hiring a skillful lawyer. He assured her that her sentence would be light because forgery is "a sexy crime"—one that laypeople and even judges secretly admire (113). He was right: she was sentenced to five years' probation and six months of house arrest but served no jail time. Her experiences also garnered a book contract and, in 2018, a film adaptation in which she is impersonated by Melissa McCarthy. Sexy—and lucrative! (The money she received mostly went to pay the restitution that was part of her plea bargain.)

Not all forgeries are crimes; indeed, of the real-life literary forgers discussed here, only Israel and the Hughes hoaxers received criminal sentences. Art forgers often face harsher consequences, but the slippery real-life forger Elmyr de Hory eluded capture for decades, and the fictional Wyatt Gwyon and Harriet Burden both avoid criminal indictments, though each pays dearly in other ways. But is forgery sexy? Surely! That is one reason why most forgers seem unconsciously to want to be caught. How else can their intelligence, skill, and inventiveness be advertised? Many of us law-abiding types also root for hoaxers, particularly when we do not stand to lose money or pride through our vicarious involvement. Many of us privately wonder whether forgery is wrong. Many of us secretly harbor resentment toward the institutions that (over) value certain artists' works because they are fashionable or because rich people will pay exorbitant sums for them. Many of us nurse a grudging respect for anyone who can gull self-important experts who, we tell ourselves, are probably frauds anyway. We feel schadenfreude when witnessing the credulous get duped: "They had it coming," we think. We marvel at forgers' imitative skill. We smile at their audacity; we smirk at their sometimes ludicrous efforts to wriggle free; we sneer at their and their pigeons' self-deception. And we feel a frisson of righteousness, leavened with a dollop of regret, when they are caught. No wonder art forgery is a perennial theme in fiction, as witnessed not only by the texts discussed here, whose publication dates reach from the 1760s to 2014, but also by very good recent novels such as Michael Gruber's *The Forgery of Venus* (2008), B. A. Shapiro's *The Art Forger* (2013), and Dominic Smith's even better *The Last Painting of Sara de Vos* (2016). The real-life cases and fictions considered here further testify to the fascination forgery holds for artists—and for critics.

Lee Israel eventually garnered the recognition she craved by exposing her self-erasure. Forgeries and hoaxes are, indeed, all about recognition, not merely because they force us to question the provenance of a work of art and judge it genuine or fake, but because they require us to see every work again and try to attach its past to its present. More precisely, they are about misrecognition—identifying something or someone not present. The success of a forgery, one might say, depends on whether the misrecognition is re-recognized. As we examine texts or paintings that we know are, or suspect to be, counterfeit, the awareness of their dubious nature creates a prismatic effect: we watch ourselves scrutinizing them as we ask whether we would have been a believer or a debunker—and as we ask where we stand now. Forgeries urge us to test ourselves, to question our aesthetic responses, to become self-conscious readers or viewers. Suspected or confirmed forgeries induce double vision, placing us simultaneously in two times, enticing us to enter a past that may never have existed. Forgers are time travelers who invite us to accompany them on their journey; hence, forgeries have, writes Anthony Grafton, brought us a "richer sense of what the past was really like" (6). The double vision they engender suits their own dual nature as acts of criticism and acts of creation.

In his study of literary forgery, Nick Groom describes the forger as "a shadow, forging what is already a fabrication, and thereby showing that literature . . . is no less forged than any shadowy literary forgery" (*Shadow* 2). In a similar vein, K. K. Ruthven calls forgery "the 'secret sharer' of literature," its "demystified and disreputable Self" (6, 3). Forged and "genuine" literary works are not Jekyll and Hyde, but Tweedledee and Tweedledum. These twins are joined by a third party, critics, with whom forgers have "been entangled through time like Laocoon and his serpents"; indeed, as Grafton demonstrates, over the centuries, forgeries have "stimulated vital innovations" in critical methods, techniques, and theories (6). Fakes constitute what Georges Bataille would call the "accursed share" of literature and fine art—the element ejected from their restricted economy. Yet the accursed share is what enables that economy to function. As an abject being, the forger is a scapegoat who must be ritually sacrificed to restore what "servile use has degraded" (Bataille 55). This is to say that detected forgeries serve an essential purpose: they lend value to nonforged works, for originality has no meaning without the possibility of imitation. Undetected forgeries, by contrast, undermine the foundations of their field: the existence (perhaps even the possibility) of a perfect forgery (by definition unrecognized) nullifies the myth of freedom, originality, and solitary production that underwrites conventional notions of artistic creation and, in turn, the bases of the art and publishing industries. This is how, as Ruthven remarks, successful forgeries destabilize the "fragile economy of . . . accreditation by drawing attention both to its conceptual shoddiness" and to its expediencies and shortcuts (4). A forgery, he concludes, provides an "indispensable critique of those cultural practices that foster the so-called genuine article" (171).

Fakesmiths

What is a forgery? Umberto Eco defines it as "any text whose actual provenance differs from what it is made out to be" (606). This admirably succinct definition elides too many nuances: for example, it would also encompass plagiarism.[1] But a plagiarist signs her name to someone else's work; a forger signs someone else's name to her own work. A plagiarist seeks credit; a forger (ostensibly) shuns it. According to Groom, a forgery "has no actual source; it conjures the illusion of a source. A forgery of a Picasso would be an original work, but located in Picasso's oeuvre" (*Shadow* 16). Although he is correct about the Picasso forgery, the rest is slightly amiss: forgeries such as Chatterton's Rowley works have an actual source—Chatterton. Groom later offers a more apt definition of a forgery as "an original work within an unoriginal, or rather a pre-existent, context" (70). But that definition would include pastiches, parodies, and counterfeits, and although counterfeits resemble forgeries, differences remain. A counterfeit work is a copy, whereas the vast majority of literary and fine art forgeries are not copies of any work. A counterfeit bill must be a perfect replica of a legitimate one; originality, whether from imaginative embellishment or poor craft, renders it detectable and hence a failure. The most creative counterfeiters, such as Jim the Penman, who hand-engraved his bills, are the ones who get caught. Counterfeit bills are manufactured; forgeries are handmade. The latters' originality resides in the forger's ability to fashion something that *could* have been produced by the named artist. Counterfeit currency does, however, display the signature of a certifying official, which means that all counterfeit currency is forged, but most forgeries are not strictly counterfeits.

Dictionaries both clarify and confound efforts at definition. According to Webster's 11th Collegiate Dictionary, to forge is to "make or imitate falsely, especially with intent to defraud," and a forger is "a person who falsifies, especially a creator of false tales." (By this definition all fiction writers are forgers: see Theses 3 and 7 below.) The *OED* offers virtually the same definitions. These denotations are further complicated by what Barbara Johnson calls the "warring forces of signification" in the word "forge" (qtd. in Ruthven 39): that is, to forge also means simply to make. On the one hand, it refers to the furnace in a blacksmith's workshop as well as to the labor performed there. On the other hand, it designates writing or art signed by or attributed to someone other than its primary creator. Two very different hands are at work in these smithies. Following the intertextual chain back to its source in Greek mythology, we find Hephaestus (renamed Vulcan by the Romans), god of fire and patron of craftspeople, especially blacksmiths. Born parthenogenetically to Hera, he was thrown by Zeus from Mount Olympus, whence he fell for a day until he splashed down in the sea. Nymphs rescued him and, during his exile in Lemnos, he fashioned a magic throne that trapped Hera, whom he released in exchange for a bride, Aphrodite. But the limping deity never quite measured up; he was perceived as a fake god. Nevertheless, he was a skilled, prolific craftsman, at various times fashioning Zeus's thunderbolts, Athena's shield, the arrows of Eros, the chariot of Helios, the armor of Achilles, and even Pandora. Given this history, it is no surprise that forgers are frequently—as in William Gaddis's *The Recognitions* and Orson Welles's *F for Fake*—depicted as sorcerers and alchemists.

"Smith" means "maker"—hence, wordsmith, tunesmith, silversmith—and blacksmithing turns out to be a strikingly suitable synecdoche for creative production. Because the blacksmith fashioned the tools for all other crafts, he was the most important artisan in any village (Bealer 19): without him there would be no hammers, nails, awls, locks, wheels, or horseshoes. The Iron Age would have meant nothing without someone to mold the iron; in that sense, blacksmiths were the material authors of civilization itself (16). The smith lies at the crux of history in another respect: since most smiths used scrap iron as raw material, their craft depended, like that of novelists, painters, and filmmakers (and forgers), on reshaping the artifacts of previous ages (43). Finally, one of the smith's primary skills, welding, is an ideal trope for artistic activity, since it involves joining unlike things together into a seamless whole. The blacksmith, then, perfectly embodies how intelligence and skill can be exercised to create objects both useful and beautiful—by forging. As Grafton shows, the falsifying type of forgery is "as old as textual authority," its first heyday having occurred as far back as the fourth century BCE (8, 10). An awareness of this history suggests that forgery is not merely a sexy crime but a serious, even essential, mode of creative activity. Forgers are fabricators, fablers, fantasizers, frauds, finaglers, flimflammers, and fall guys—fakesmiths.

Autographs

Novelists such as James Joyce and Charles Dickens have exploited the connections between smithing and authoring.[2] But this is somewhat strange, for literary forgeries seem to instantiate Roland Barthes's provocative (if no longer novel) declaration of the "death of the author." In fact, forgeries more comfortably fit Michel Foucault's description of an author as a "principle of unity" (elsewhere translated as "thrift") that "serves to neutralize the contradictions that are found in a series of texts" (128). Ascribing authorship, in his view, is a means of organizing and classifying texts; forgeries and hoaxes, which thwart our desire to link a name on a page with a person, obliterate this taxonomy. Further, Foucault proposes that the "author-function" derives from legal and institutional systems that "circumscribe, determine, and articulate the realm of discourses"; it does not refer, "purely and simply, to an actual individual" (130). In other words, the modern concept of authorship (and creative ownership in other arts) is largely a byproduct of copyright laws. Authors are legal fictions, personae invented to regulate intellectual property. But they *are* fictions: as Christopher Miller comments, "To write is to other yourself, even when writing about yourself" (7). The writer becomes someone else when she turns into an author. Forgeries lay bare these legalities and fictions, while furnishing what Kevin Young calls "a kind of *unauthorized autobiography*" of both the forger and of the ostensible author (256). But there need not even be an auto behind this biography, for the author-function does not require a name. "It is," notes Robert Griffin, a "blank space, which may be signed or unsigned depending on the circumstances" (Introduction 10); it may be ascribed to an imaginary person or to a real person who did not create it. This is where the signature comes in.

What the above definitions ignore is that the essence of forgery lies in the signature. As the notorious (and highly successful) art forger Eric Hebborn once pointed out, "There's no such thing as a fake drawing, only a fake attribution" (qtd. in Keats 105). That is, until a work is mendaciously signed, it is merely a replica, exercise, or pastiche: the signature is what transmutes a copy into a crime. Authorship depends upon the autograph. Thus, the crucial moment for Lee Israel came when she had to sign her letters. To avoid the dreaded "forger's palsy" (shaky lines that would give her away), she devised a "light box" by placing a sheet over a television set so that the light shone through and enabled her to trace the author's signature on the paper (49). Likewise, what certifies art forgeries is not their colors, light, shapes, lines, or perspective; the brushwork that matters most is that of the name.

The signature links mind and body, serving as a tangible token of the signer's presence through the synecdoche of the hand. The signature is, as Peggy Kamuf observes, "supported by immense conventional systems" that allow us to perform operations of "identification, attestation, verification, [and] attribution of responsibility" (viii). A signature is a socially performative act that amounts to a promise: "I am the person who signed this at some specific time." The autograph links moments in time and fuses the self who signed with future versions of that self. The signer becomes a witness to herself, in effect testifying, "I am the same person now that I was then" (see Kamuf viii). In other words, a signature is the metonym of a story as well as a self-portrait. A forgery is a fictional origin story masquerading as a factual one. Yet the signature is also detachable from the instance it designates, meaning that it represents the signer in her absence. In the economic domain, an autograph distinguishes genuine from counterfeit currency and authentic from forged checks or letters of credit. Hence, a false signature, as Peter de Bolla points out, "inserts the possibility of multiple personality, or no identity at all, into the paper-thin circulation of trust in a speculative society," thereby creating "the possibility for the destabilization of self, society and certainty" (73). This is why, as I show in more detail in the first chapter, literary forgery emerged in England concurrently with a credit economy. In this regard, a false signature is politically subversive as well as criminal because it shakes the props supporting all social and economic exchange. A forged literary or art work, then, serves as a metaphor for something larger: a challenge to the network of trust that undergirds civilization. And yet, as Tony Thwaites asserts, a "signature is always close to forgery" (6), because to sign a document is to endorse the idea of an unchangeable self. Indeed, because every person's signature is slightly different from his or her previous ones, each signature is to some extent a "self-forgery" (Schwartz 219). Hence, forged works do not subvert norms so much as expose their fragile foundations.

Misrecognitions

Certain frauds do not require a signature. Hoaxes such as falsified archeological finds or impersonations are not strictly forgeries. To put it succinctly: all forgeries are hoaxes, but not all hoaxes are forgeries. That is, if forgery constitutes "an act intended to trick or dupe," as my trusty Webster's 11th Collegiate Dictionary defines "hoax," then forgeries are a subset of this more general category. The *OED,* speculating that "hoax" is a derivation of "hocus" (thus affirming its magical properties), defines the word as "a humorous or mischievous deception, usually taking the form of a fabrication of something fictitious or erroneous, told in such a manner as to impose upon the credulity of the victim."[3] According to this venerated lexicon, then, a hoax is always a prank or joke. So is a forgery. Yet not all hoaxes are alike, and here Brian McHale has offered some useful distinctions. What he calls "genuine hoaxes" (the quotation marks are his in all cases) are "perpetrated with no intention of their ever being exposed" (236). He places Chatterton's Rowley works and William-Henry Ireland's Shakespeare forgeries (discussed in my first two chapters) in this class. "Entrapments" or "trap-hoaxes," by contrast, are "designed with didactic or punitive purposes in mind": they must be exposed for the lashes to land. McHale cites the Ern Malley documents, which I discuss in chapter 3, as an instance; the fictional Harriet Burden's *Maskings,* treated in chapter 7, also belongs in this camp. Last are "mock-hoaxes," which are "meant eventually to be seen through without any traps being sprung" (236–37). Perhaps a better word for these is "mystifications"; or we may simply dub them misrecognitions.[4] But what is the difference between a "mock-hoax" and an ordinary nom de plume? Are all pseudonyms hoaxes? McHale acknowledges that the distinctions depend on determining the perpetrator's intentions (237). But we do not know whether Chatterton intended eventually to reveal himself as Rowley's creator. And if we interpret his spuriously attributed works as aesthetic experiments rather than as frauds, we might consider them "mock-hoaxes" rather than "genuine" ones. A hoaxer's intentions may also change in the course of the endeavor. McHale's categories thus remind us of the blurry, shifting lines that demarcate the myriad forms of artistic fraud. No matter the type, however, all forgeries and hoaxes rely on misrecognition.

Two real-world literary frauds of the recent past by major novelists exemplify these less heinous brands of mystification. In 1980 Holt, Rinehart and Winston published a book that advertised itself as the "Intimate Memoir of the First Woman Ever to Play in the National Hockey League." Entitled *Amazons,* it was attributed to one Cleo Birdwell—a gorgeous (and, as the story recounts, sexually adventurous) woman whose photo graces the back cover. In a further misdirection, "Cleo" even signed books at public events. The actual authors, it was later learned, were the distinguished novelist Don DeLillo (then less well known than he is today) and his friend Sue Buck. Their collaboration was, as former editor Gerald Howard comments, less a hoax than a "put-on" (59), and as such it worked wonderfully. For one thing, the book is hilarious. It also displays abundant DeLillo signatures—satirical treatments of mass media and sports; witty, crackling dialogue; slightly grotesque characters; incisive anatomizing of male neuroses—without the dread. When a reviewer from Worcester, Massachusetts, noticed these traits and Christopher Lehmann-Haupt repeated the points in the *New York Times,* DeLillo was outed, though he did not reveal the name of his collaborator. (Her identity was discovered after DeLillo's papers were purchased by the Harry Ransom Humanities Research Center.) Even today he does not list it among his published novels and has not allowed it to be reprinted. Birdwell does not live.[5]

Also in the early 1980s, Doris Lessing published two novels under the name Jane Somers; no one but a couple of friends and her publisher knew that Lessing was the author. She later wrote that she employed the Somers pseudonym as an "experiment," a vehicle to escape the "cage of associations and labels" that confined her, and as a way to expose the difficulties that novice writers face (Preface v, vi). The experiment succeeded: not only did "Jane Somers . . . [write] in ways that Doris Lessing [could] not" (vi), but the novel was, as she expected, barely reviewed. Not one reviewer caught on to the deception—which doesn't speak well of their discernment, for both Somers novels feature obvious Lessingisms, such as a diary format; a clipped, no-nonsense voice; and a mildly ironic stance toward the characters.[6]

In these rather benign hoaxes the real author signed the text with an imaginary name. Most forgeries, however, replace the actual creator's name with one that will attract greater attention—a Shakespeare, a Matisse, a Van Eyck, a Howard Hughes, a prodigy, a sensationalist male artist. Hence, we might dub the Somers and Birdwell hoaxes "counterforgeries" because the real author pretended to be someone with a lower cultural profile. Should other forms of fraud, such as impostures, be called forgeries? Not necessarily. All forgeries *are* impersonations, but of a peculiar type: they must involve a signed or otherwise documented certification but do not require the presence of a body. Forgers who employ physical impersonation cross the line from representation to reality, from signature to self; these fakesmiths usually resort to physical imposture to expand the fraud or elude exposure. Impostors are embodied works of art and present themselves as such—artful actors wearing masks that hide, in order to reveal, the truth. Like other forgers, impersonators use false documents to verify their identities and explain their motives, employ artifice to perpetuate their frauds, and eventually lose control of their creations. Such mystifications free their creators from their former personae and from audiences' and publishers' expectations, while earning praise, perplexity and, in some cases, punishment. And they almost always end up expunging themselves. This is the case in Percival Everett's *erasure* and Siri Hustvedt's *The Blazing World:* in the first, a hoax that begins with a parodic pseudonymous novel balloons into physical impersonation when audiences demand to see the author; in the second, male fronts are used to deceive audiences and to confirm the female perpetrator's belief that male artists receive more credit than do females. The presence of a human body, however, changes the valences in the exposure/erasure dialectic by making the invisible visible. The impostor becomes the focal point, attracting the recognition and acclaim that the hoaxer seeks. Ironically, as in the novel *erasure* and in the real-world JT LeRoy hoax of the early 2000s, the impostor steals attention from the originator, thereby erasing him or her more thoroughly. The impostor thus embodies the forger's paradox.

Traces

Are literary forgeries comparable to fine-art frauds? Sándor Radnóti posits that while the "legend of a work forms a primary component of literary mystification," an "autograph manuscript only forms a secondary accessory. It is precisely the other way around in the forgery of fine art" (175). Art historian Nelson Goodman likewise distinguishes between autographic and allographic arts (103). In the former the signature is crucial: a copy is a fraud. In the latter an exact duplication is not deemed inauthentic: copies of a musical score, for example, are not forgeries. It follows that the signature on a forged literary work is of secondary importance, whereas it is primary for, say, oil paintings. Literary works, then, are allographic. But this distinction falls apart upon further examination. The original version and signature on an allographic work *do* matter, as the Chatterton and Ireland forgeries prove. In both instances the original MSS (signed, in Ireland's case, by the bogus Bard) were the only iterations; they were thus autographic.[7] These examples refute Radnóti's contention as well: autograph manuscripts were *primary* elements of those forgeries. Indeed, virtually every thesis advanced below applies equally to literary and to fine-art forgeries and hoaxes.

However, forgeries probably threaten the art industry more than they do publishing, perhaps because there is more money involved. Several theories have thus been advanced to explain why art forgeries are sins against culture. The first, and perhaps most important, is that forgeries violate the "trace paradigm," defined by art historian Thierry Lenain as the hypothesis (taken as a rule) that "every artwork manifests its own origin" (29). This principle also underlies Denis Dutton's contention that forgeries misrepresent achievement, because "reference to origins is a necessary constituent of the concept of a work of art" (181, 182). As Lenain points out, if it were ever admitted that a forger had made a perfect simulation, "the very idea of art would founder" because according to the trace paradigm, "an art object is *nothing but* the aesthetic display of its origin" (242). And yet the perfect forgery must always remain outside of established art history because it is, by definition, undetected. But while the trace paradigm assumes that all forgeries can be exposed, underground history—the kind known to forgers and their audiences—proves this false, as when Elmyr de Hory beheld his own "Matisses" displayed in a Detroit museum. Successful forgeries prove the trace paradigm invalid, and in so doing profoundly threaten the foundations of art connoisseurship and history. The perfect fake is thus the dark double of the masterpiece, with the forger serving as the evil wizard whose magic defeats that of the creative genius.

A second theory holds that forgeries are inherently inferior to "original" works simply because they are imitations. But if even an educated viewer cannot determine by close scrutiny whether a work is genuine, what is the aesthetic criterion used to deem the forged work inferior? As Alfred Lessing points out, "Pure aesthetics cannot explain forgery," for "the fact that a work of art is a forgery" is merely an "item of information" comparable to the artist's age or politics (58, 66). The dismissal of forged works for aesthetic reasons alone is ultimately circular: it assumes the inferiority—and hence, the moral and aesthetic offense—it aims to prove (66).

A third reason is more clearly ideological. Leonard B. Meyer concisely summarizes: "Creation is possible only if there is choice. And choice is possible only if there is freedom" (83). Since forgers are not free, they are not artists. Rudolf Arnheim explains that "in a typical forgery . . . each stroke is separately controlled by the comparison" with a preexisting work or style (236). But this argument does not hold water either. Many nonforged pastiches—works in the style of another artist—are accepted, indeed, applauded, for their originality (Roy Liechtenstein's Benday paintings come to mind), and a few are considered masterpieces. And is it unfree to pen a sonnet? Write a genre novel? Isn't all representational art "unfree," insofar as the artist copies or represents something outside of the work? Arnheim admits that successful forgers "rely on fairly free invention in the spirit of the original's style," producing not slavish copies but "analogies or equivalents" (237). Wyatt Gwyon's forged pastiches of fifteenth-century Flemish masters qualify as such. Like all artists, forgers carefully select materials and make choices throughout conception and production. Meyer's argument discloses the individualist ideology that underwrites art and literary history and their debts to Romantic myths about the creative process.

A fourth explanation holds that forgeries are neither edifying nor enlightening. Meyer argues that a genuine work of art reveals some new aspect of the world; such discoveries can be made only once. Original works have value because they express the fruits of such discoveries (82, 84). Mark Sagoff adds that a painting "advances a theory concerning the way we see things or the way they can be" seen (146). An original painting is an experiment; a forgery is not. But Hustvedt's Harriet Burden designs her *Maskings* hoax to accomplish precisely what Sagoff describes: to remind us that "the way we see things" is inevitably influenced by our beliefs about the artist's gender, sexuality, goals, and history as well as by a period's trends. Her experiment succeeds so well that it fails. Further, as Israel's endeavors remind us, successful forgeries require sedulous scholarship and a strong grasp of a medium's history. They embody the forger's learning: they are the *results* of discoveries. As Lenain points out, a fake is "essentially a product of applied or reverse connoisseurship" (286). As such, fakes teach us about art history by divulging the preferences and prejudices of our own age as well as those of the work's ostensible setting. Hence, art forgeries constitute a form of historical analysis and critique that the industry must repress even as this accursed share allows it to operate.

Lastly, we have what Lenain describes as the "anarchistic solution," which proposes that there is no such thing as an absolutely authentic artwork (30). As Pablo Picasso once remarked to Jean Cocteau, "There are no fakes because there are only fakes." This seems to be Welles's position, as I show in chapter 6. Not surprisingly, few critics and historians have endorsed this view. Welles's contention is too extreme, but the conventional wisdom is also wrong. In this regard, Hebborn, the master forger, presents six axioms that art critics claim to be always true but which are in fact valid only sometimes:

1. The forger will always betray himself by personal mannerisms.
2. The forgery always lacks freedom of execution and originality.
3. A forgery is always of lower quality than the original.
4. Forgeries always reveal the taste of their time.
5. Forgeries only get through in troubled times.
6. Where ocular evidence fails to uncover forgery, scientific examination will succeed. (qtd. in Lenain 301)

Forgers force experts to prove themselves; many fail, as the history of forgery amply demonstrates. Those failures, however, prompt experts to improve their methods, just as Chatterton's forgeries promoted the refinement of historical literary scholarship in England. Yet I find it fascinating that not one of the aestheticians I have quoted mentions that forgeries are a form of theft. A forged work is a bait-and-switch, a shell game in which audiences are asked to find a nonexistent pea. Forgeries are indeed crimes when perpetrated for gain; surprisingly, however, money is not the chief motive for most of the forgers discussed in this book. Ultimately, I agree with Joseph Margolis, who concludes that we can best comprehend forgeries and hoaxes by examining their perpetrator's intentions (160). Forgeries are genuine articles tainted by ungenerous intentions. Likewise, our notions of authenticity are "bound to reflect our shifting interests and the shifting history of our artistic, technological, economic, political, and moral experience" (167).

Let us declare, then, that *a forgery is an artwork, artefact, or document designed to dupe someone that is intentionally signed by, or otherwise officially attributed to, a person, fictional or otherwise, who did not act as its primary creator and who is not the person submitting it for publication, evaluation, or purchase.*

The theoretical excursions above and the investigations below yield fifteen theses. I do not claim that they constitute a complete list of truths about forgeries. The evidence for each one will accrue as we proceed through the chapters. For now, consider them less conclusions than condensations of this book's arguments; conceive of them also as provocations which, like forged artworks and their models, might inspire other writers and scholars to review their assumptions, refine their techniques, and reconsider their objections to the sexily criminal activities and artefacts that we call forgeries.

Fifteen Theses about Forgery

1. Forgeries and other forms of fakery exist in a mutualist relationship with nonforged works: neither is possible without the other.
2. Forgeries and hoaxes foster fresh creative identities in young artists trying to find their voices or styles and in established artists seeking rejuvenation and inspiration.
3. A forgery or hoax is always a narrative, and any forgery or hoax is only as good as the story used to authenticate it. Moreover, forgeries are seeds from which more fictions grow.
4. A forgery always involves a conflict or dialectic between erasure and exposure, as the forger seeks recognition, paradoxically, by becoming invisible. This dialectic explains why perpetrators so often sabotage themselves: most forgers want to be caught.
5. Most forgers believe, or claim to believe, that they are more knowledgeable than experts and are at least as creative and skillful as their models. Hence,
6. Most forgeries are motivated by envy, rage, resentment, or frustrated ambition and usually target specific victims.
7. Literary forgeries and hoaxes demonstrate that all authors are fictional characters and that all creative works are multiply authored.
8. Literary forgeries, which challenge conventional ideas about authenticity and legitimacy, are frequently linked to anxieties about parenthood and paternity.
9. Literary and fine-art forgeries are always deeply intertextual, often profoundly scholarly, and frequently original.
10. Forgeries lay bare the flaws in the Romantic paradigm of the individual genius and the contradictions, hypocrisies, and fictions of the literary and art industries. They challenge the art industry's reliance on name recognition, its adherence to the trace paradigm, and its conflation of economic and aesthetic values. In short: a forgery is a cultural critique.
11. A forgery or hoax is a game that partakes of the spirit of play, performance, and competition. But . . .
12. Like most creative productions, forgeries and hoaxes almost always escape the control of their creators and take on a life of their own.

Forgers are Frankensteins: their offspring are hideous progeny, abjected from the artistic economy and viewed as monsters.

13. Once someone has invested in believing a fake to be real, that person will cling to the belief, even when shown evidence of fraud, especially when the belief is reinforced by other believers: credulity is both persistent and contagious.
14. A successful forgery or hoax is a work of art in which the trickery is itself often the most important and imaginative element.
15. Forgeries violate the norms through which audiences and critics classify works and creators. They are beyond category.

Fake It: Fictions of Forgery investigates a set of fictional forgeries and hoaxes alongside their real-life inspirations and parallels. This book analyzes the fictions surrounding forgeries—both the phony stories designed to authenticate and explain the frauds and the works of art that have inspired and have been inspired by them. The chapters borrow formal ingredients from the texts under discussion: thus, for example, the chapter on *erasure,* a jazz-influenced text, is organized around musical terms; the chapter treating Orson Welles's *F for Fake* uses film terms and structures; the chapter about Siri Hustvedt's *The Blazing World* employs text boxes that mirror the artworks described in the novel. Each chapter develops provocative truths about the process of artistic creation, which emerges as collaborative and imitative rather than individual and inspired; about the force and durability of belief and its resistance to reason; about the conflicts between and conflation of aesthetic and economic values; about the elasticity of identity and authorship; about the human impulses to play, perform, and compete; about the power of narrative as the primal engine of credibility and artistic invention. *Fake It* seeks to illuminate the myriad facets of forgery and imposture by shining a prismatic light on real and fictional lies.

Part 1. Fake Lit: Mockeries

A FORGERY IS A PRISM

According to Ruthven, literary fakes express "creative energies whose power is attested to by the resistance they engender" and display the "disruptive and capricious power of the imagination" even more clearly than those "counterfactual assemblages we call literary works" (3). Ruthven reads literary forgeries as radical experiments that disclose the spuriousness of literature itself. How so? For one thing, canonical literature is founded on a faith in original and unique composition—a falsehood that forgeries and fakes expose by demonstrating that all art is intertextual, imitative, and collaborative. Part 1 explores the relations between "authentic" texts and authors and frauds, between actual forgeries and fictional ones—between real fakes and fake fakes—while plumbing the backgrounds and motives of real forgers and analyzing the outcomes of their experiments. Each of these literary fakes is integrally related to a problem of filiation, inheritance, or parental legitimacy; hence the novels based on them develop parallels between physical reproduction and literary production. In these texts forgers and hoaxers are not merely con artists; they are resurrectionists, raising the dead so we may hear them speak again. Fictions about forgery, we find, often become forgeries themselves and in so doing direct their prismatic light back on readers who believe what they are reading.

A FORGERY IS A SELF-PORTRAIT AND AN INSPIRATION

Modern literary forgery began in the eighteenth century concurrently with the rise of the credit economy and the copyright regime. During this period, as Margaret Russett and others have demonstrated, a permeable membrane separated devices like certain novels' found-manuscript ploys from forgeries such as Chatterton's Rowley works. Romantic poets, whose obsession with authenticity still inflects aesthetic theory, worshiped Chatterton, who inspired authors as different as William Wordsworth, Oscar Wilde, and Peter Ackroyd as well as future literary forgers. The opening chapter, "Thomas Chatterton's Ghosts," begins with Henry Wallis's famous 1856 painting of Chatterton's death, in which novelist/poet George Meredith impersonated the dead teenager. Using the painting as my point of departure, I explore Chatterton's (re)incarnations in his own works and his canny use of forgeries as fuel for his authorial sparks. A ghostwriter, Chatterton fashioned multiple authorial identities both in his forged documents, where he disguised himself as the late medieval monk Thomas Rowley, and in the array of works he produced under various pen names. The ghosts that Chatterton conjured, however, may be less significant than the Chattertonian specters later writers called forth. One of these appeared when Meredith's wife, Mary Ellen, ran off with Wallis. This traumatic event inspired Meredith's first important works: the novel *The Ordeal of Richard Feverel* and his "sonnet" cycle *Modern Love.* Chatterton's specter haunts *Modern Love* through recurrent images of poison and suicide and lurks even more visibly in another poem in the same volume, "The Beggar's Soliloquy," which displays explicit debts to Chatterton's last Rowley work, "An Excelente Balade of Charitie." Here the trail of (re)production meanders from poetic impersonation to fine art impersonation to poetic pastiche. Peter Ackroyd's novel *Chatterton* (1987) adds further layers to this impasto by incorporating a (forged) painting of a middle-aged Chatterton and a plagiarized novel, thereby portraying the poetic prodigy as a spirit who inhabits and influences everyone who encounters his legacy. Chatterton's ghosts enabled him to craft a myriad-minded, multifaceted authorial self; his spirit had similar benefits for those who followed him. By engendering new scholarly methods and spurring enlightening investigations of the nature of artistic creation, Chatterton and his ghosts have made literature a finer art.

A FORGERY IS A PERFORMANCE

Next we investigate the notorious Shakespeare forgeries of the 1790s, in which young William-Henry Ireland fabricated several "Shakspearean" documents in an effort to impress his father and his father's associates. Incorporating the original documents, including the forged play *Vortigern,* into an analysis of the literary politics and family dynamics that impelled the hoax, I argue that Ireland used Shakespeare to fashion a new father—one whose aura let him glow like pale fire—as well as a new authorial identity. The chapter couples this real-life case with Arthur Phillips's novel *The Tragedy of Arthur* (2011), which concerns a rediscovered (but probably forged) eponymous Shakespeare play. Presented as the introduction to Shakespeare's *The Tragedy of Arthur,* the novel is actually a bildungsroman about a fictional Arthur Phillips, his twin sister (an actress), their forger father (also named Arthur Phillips), and their love-hate relationship with the Bard. The play that follows the introduction restages its relationships and refracts those in the Ireland case through metaphors linking paternity, monarchic legitimacy, and literary creation. The chapter's discussions of the introduction and explication of the play are set side-by-side on the page, thereby mirroring the novel's obsession with pairs and twins and enabling readers to choose how to read it. In both the novel and the historical event, Shakespeare stands in for the problematic patriarch, and the documents engender a triangular relationship among the son, the Bard, and the parent.

In each case readers suspend disbelief so as to become collaborators with the greatest poet in the English language. Like the forger, the credulous construct a Shakespeare in their own images. Shakespeare thus becomes a shadow whose name is invoked less as an author than as a symbol of prestige, a synecdoche of fatherhood, and a synthesis of nostalgia, longing, and pride. Rather than holding a mirror up to nature, Shakespeare and his works become a mirror of others' hopes and dreams. Phillips's novel and the Ireland hoax indeed reveal that "William Shakespeare" is always a fictional product of readers' needs. In the end both young authors—young Arthurs—use forgeries to break away from their fathers and achieve self-creation.

A FORGERY IS A MONSTER AND AN EPIPHYTE

The next chapter, "Hideous Progeny," analyzes Peter Carey's novel *My Life as a Fake* (2003). Its premise borrows from a real-life forgery in 1940s Australia, in which two soldiers invented a working-class poet named Ern Malley, composed his works, and got them published—and the editor/publisher convicted of obscenity. Ironically, though both hoaxers later produced several books of poetry, they are best known for the forgeries, which many readers believe to be their strongest work. Carey transposes these facts into fiction by appropriating *Frankenstein* and Mary Shelley's identification of physical and literary progeny. In Carey's version Bob McCorkle, the fake poet "born" on the pages of Christopher Chubb's misattributed *The Darkening Ecliptic,* comes to physical life, obtains a (forged) birth certificate, kidnaps Chubb's daughter, and leads him on a chase across Malaysia. Before McCorkle dies, he leaves a manuscript of his own brilliantly original poetry. Its title? *My Life as a Fake.* This metafictional text, related in layered narratives like *Frankenstein,* epitomizes the imaginative energy that fuels forgeries even as it enacts the truth that all creation involves adaptation, appropriation, collaboration—and fakery. Carey's reimagining of *Frankenstein* also provides a paradigm for all the forgeries in this study, in which the fake becomes a monster that consumes its creator.

A FORGERY IS AN ERASURE AND AN IMPOSTURE

The final chapter in this section centers on Percival Everett's novel *erasure,* which does McCorkle one better: here the physical imposture is intentional. This chapter traces how avant-garde African American novelist Thelonious "Monk" Ellison, infuriated by the success of a racist novel about inner-city Blacks (based on Sapphire's *Push*), writes a parody of Richard Wright's *Native Son* called *My Pafology,* which he attributes to one Stagg R. Leigh. But nobody catches the joke; instead, his hoax text, read as a gritty realist novel, earns a huge advance. Even after he gives it the off-putting title of *Fuck,* the parody becomes a best seller and even wins an award. Monk is forced to impersonate Stagg Leigh, a folkloric figure who is at once an antisocial stereotype and an emblem of liberation. Monk is erased, but through this erasure he becomes . . . himself. That is, the reader realizes that Monk's parody expresses parts of himself—his rage, his sexuality, his "Blackness"—that he has long suppressed. In that sense *Fuck* may be "truer" than the novels written under his "real" name. The chapter also proposes that *erasure* employs a jazz aesthetic practiced through Everett's (and Monk's) riffing on Wright, on the lore of Stagolee, and on the life and works of Monk Ellison's namesake, jazz icon Thelonious Monk. In keeping with the jazz theme, the chapter is organized around musical terms. Smearing the border between forgery and parody, *erasure* reminds us that an author is always an invented persona and demonstrates again that fakery fosters fresh authorial selves and literary forms.

Part 2. Fake Art: Masks

A FORGERY IS A PARADOX

Literary and art forgeries share many features: both require a plausible story about provenance, an explanatory narrative, a talented impersonator, a motivating emotion, and a false signature. Even more than with literary forgeries, the existence of a forged artwork ratifies the copied work's value. As noted above, art and forgery were born and nurtured together; their foster parents were art experts. The dialectic between erasure and exposure that Everett strikingly develops is, if anything, more explicit in art forgeries; thus, fictions about art forgeries repeatedly dramatize the forger's paradox of (mis)recognition. Part 2, then, investigates fine art forgers in fiction and fact.

A FORGERY IS AN ORIGINAL SIN

The most important modern fiction about art forgery is William Gaddis's monumental novel *The Recognitions* (1955), analyzed in chapter 5.

This encyclopedic tale presents a gallery of fakes and frauds, the most prominent being Wyatt Gwyon, who crafts spurious paintings attributed to fifteenth-century Flemish masters because he admires them as paragons of authentic spirituality. That is, he becomes a forger not to make money or to take revenge on experts but to pursue a queer form of aesthetic piety. Inculcated with a puritanical brand of Calvinism, Wyatt eschews originality to seek the perfection possible only in imitation. Through forging he seeks to transcend his own time, which he perceives as a wasteland of corruption, commodification, and counterfeiting. He strives to resurrect those old masters and reconstitute their world, one which, he believes, was charged with the grandeur and gravity of an ever-vigilant deity. Like many real forgers, he and his coconspirator, Basil Valentine, view themselves as conservers of true aesthetic values. For Wyatt Gwyon, then, artifice is a mode of authenticity. By making original copies, he tries to produce what Lenain calls the "nightmare" of art connoisseurship—the perfect fake (234). Only through imitation—which for him means not only studying and copying works but re-cognizing the works' initial cognitions—can an artist conceive immaculately. Only forged works, for him, are truly genuine. After Wyatt stabs his collaborator, burns his forged paintings, and flees to Spain, he takes his aesthetic project to its maximum expression: "restoring" old works by scraping off their paint.

The most significant artwork in the novel is Hieronymus Bosch's circular table painting *The Seven Deadly Sins*. Its shape symbolizes the structure of *The Recognitions* itself, as well as its anatomy of wrongdoing, and provides the centerpiece of Gaddis's moral vision. The question of its provenance becomes crucial, for it represents the "gold" on which Wyatt's aesthetic principles rest. If there is no "gold"—no ideal of perfection and piety that anchors his work and toward which it aspires—then his artistic endeavors, which he conceives as a form of alchemy, are null. *The Recognitions* is thickly intertextual, packed with allusions to mythology, alchemy, art history, and early Christian texts. Moreover, Wyatt's work parallels the procedures of real-life forgers Han van Meegeren, whose "Vermeers" fooled the European art world in the 1930s and '40s, and Jef van der Veken, a restorer who "improved" several Flemish masterpieces. The chapter adapts its structure from the Bosch table, as each section is titled with a color, sin, or painting technique that represents both Wyatt's procedures and his creator's. Gaddis's cavalcade of counterfeits suggests that true aesthetic recognition is as (un)reliable as memory, that fakesmiths are real, if deluded, artists, and that demarcations between the genuine and the fraudulent make little sense in a world of trumped-up emotions, fake products, and phony people.

A FORGERY IS A CULTURAL CRITIQUE

Among the most prolific forgers of the twentieth century, Elmyr de Hory sold scores of his forged paintings for high prices across the United States and Europe. After his frauds were exposed, he recounted his story to Clifford Irving, who wrote a partly admiring book about him. Inspired by de Hory, Irving (with Richard Suskind) fabricated one of the most notorious frauds of the twentieth century: a bogus autobiography of Howard Hughes. A brilliant actor and convincing liar, Irving got away with the scam—until Hughes's disavowal prompted investigators to find holes in Irving's story. Though the fraud was exposed, the de Hory/Irving relationship bore further fruit when Orson Welles, perpetrator of the infamous *War of the Worlds* radio hoax, made his 1974 film *F for Fake*. In this, his final completed feature, Welles emcees an experimental documentary that dramatizes the dubious nature of cinematic reality and the duplicities of art experts, demonstrating how easily filmmakers can fudge reality and smudge the lines between truth and lies. A superior example of postmodernist montage, *F for Fake* simultaneously deconstructs and displays Welles's skill as an auteur and exposes cinema's function as a purveyor of falsehoods. The chapter is structured around film terms and devices—the freeze-frame, the flashback—both to pay tribute to Welles's (and the forgers') skill and to invoke the spirit of play that informs this film and, indeed, all forgeries. This chapter not only brings together three famous fakers; it also widens our critical palette to incorporate cinematic trickery, while highlighting the fact that most forgeries end up being about themselves.

A FORGERY IS A TOOL OF REVENGE AND A MEANS OF RESURRECTION

In Siri Hustvedt's novel *The Blazing World* (2014), artist Harriet Burden—motivated by resentment over the sexism that has stalled her career and fury over her art dealer husband's infidelities—employs three male fronts to present her latest works. In the first she exploits the young male "mask"; in the second the Burdened pair forge a collaboration. The third instance, however, ends in disaster when the "mask," an artist with the cryptic name Rune, appropriates the work and accuses Burden of trying to steal credit. He hoaxes the hoaxer. *The Blazing World* employs what Hustvedt calls "hermaphroditic polyphony," presenting a panoply of voices and texts that includes Burden's journal, reviews by fictional art critics, and friends' and lovers' testimonies, all to illustrate the collaborative nature of artistic activity. The title, borrowed from a utopian fantasy by gender-bending seventeenth-century writer Margaret Cavendish, introduces parallels that accent again the intertextual and imitative properties of all artmaking. To exemplify that thesis, the chapter borrows from the work of Burden (and her models), using text boxes to present profiles of hoaxers and heteronymous artists who shed light on Burden's colossal ruse. Finally, the chapter demonstrates how Cavendish's life and work inspire Burden's final triumph—a gigantic, fecund doll modeled on Cavendish's expansive, multiply gendered, and proliferating worlds.

A sexy crime, a prism, a prank, a provocation, a performance, an experiment, a self-portrait, a paradox, a monster, a sin, a weapon, a cultural critique, a con game, an imposture, an erasure, a resurrection—a forgery may be any of these things, or all of them at once. But it is first and foremost a story. *Fake It* reads, relates, and reframes these stories of falsehood to find within them kernels of enduring truth.

PART I

FAKE LIT

Mockeries

> Yet sit and see / Minding true things by what their mockeries be.
>
> —The Chorus, in Shakespeare, *Henry V*

1

Thomas Chatterton's Ghosts

> This is my formaunce which I now have wrytte
> The best performaunce of my little Wytte.
>
> —Thomas Chatterton, "To John Ladgate"

THE YOUNG man is smiling. Facing us, he sprawls, his head lolling at the edge of the small bed. His tousled red hair on the left of the painting nearly matches the crimson corduroy coat tossed over a chair in the far right. Beside the boy's head rests an open chest filled with papers; scraps litter the floor nearby. His light gray blouse, unbuttoned to his waist, opens to allow his left hand to lie upon his breast; his right hand, nearly lost in shadows, clutches rumpled paper as its knuckles touch the floor. Near that hand, in the center of the frame, an empty vial seems poised to roll. His violet breeches end below the knees, where pale yellow stockings stretch down to at least one black shoe. At the foot of the bed a dark, round table holds more stray paper and a doused candle. Wisps of smoke, perhaps symbolizing the boy's spirit, waft upward from the candle. A half-open window bathes him in dawn's misty light, as it does the spindly rose plant sitting on the sill. In the distance we see a church steeple, perhaps tolling its morning bells (fig. 1). But the boy hears nothing: he is dead. It is no accident that the painting resembles a *Pietà,* for this young man has been sacrificed for art. And yet the satisfied smile suggests consummation: the morning light transfigures him, as if he will soon rise and begin to write.

The painting I've described, Henry Wallis's *Chatterton* (1856), does not depict the real Thomas Chatterton, a poetic prodigy and literary forger who died in 1770 at the age of seventeen, but twenty-seven-year-old poet/novelist George Meredith. This Chatterton—so serenely beautiful in death—is at least as famous as the real-life author who killed himself by ingesting a tincture of arsenic and opium. Indeed, as

FIG. 1. George Meredith impersonates the young forger in Henry Wallis's *Chatterton* (1856). Oil on canvas, 62.2 × 93.3 cm. (Tate Gallery, London © Tate)

Ivan Phillips has pointed out, Chatterton's "tragic corpse has become his most popular work of art" (25). Who was the real Chatterton? It is difficult to say, for countless Chattertons have existed over the two and a half centuries since his demise. Alive, he was a myriad-minded boy whose métier was metamorphoses as he disguised himself with a host of pseudonyms. One of them was that of Thomas Rowley, a fictional fifteenth-century monk and scholar to whom Chatterton attributed dozens of poems and historical documents that he himself had created. There were others: Dunhelmus Bristoliensus, a historian of Bristol, his hometown; Probus, a political satirist; a medieval scholar named Turgotus; a "fallen" woman called Maria Friendless; his own close friend, John Baker; a "sad dog" dubbed Harry Wildfire. As with William-Henry Ireland, who modeled himself after Chatterton two decades later, forgeries and false names brought a new self into being: Thomas Chatterton, author. As John Williams aptly notes, Chatterton and other literary fakers of the period adopted "forgery as a strategy forced upon them by their determination to assert their true identities" (37)—or to discover them.

I have begun with Chatterton's death. But he did not stay dead: he became undead, resurrected by numerous writers who followed him, each one conjuring a Chatterton who served the later author's needs. By 1856 Chatterton had begat numerous avatars: the prototype of tragic, misunderstood genius; a warning about how debauchery strangles talent; a Romantic bard slain by an unfeeling literary world; the greatest British poet since Shakespeare. If during his short life he was a ghostwriter—the author of friends' love poems, the invisible creator of Rowley and his patron, William Canynge—in his afterlife he has become a ghost haunting English literature, influencing and inhabiting those who study his works, an "echo chamber, an imaginary location in which identities merge and voices scramble" (I. Phillips 24). Chatterton's procedures, productions, and motives establish the paradigms for the forgeries discussed herein: the need for a convincing narrative of provenance; the way that forgeries engender further fictions; their intertextual nature; the dialectic between exposure and erasure; forgery's playful and contested spirit; the persistence of belief against evidence; the kinship between forgery and parental legitimacy; their propensity to lay bare the shaky foundations of artistic culture.

Using Wallis's painting as the point of departure, I investigate two of Chatterton's hauntings: the triangular visitations upon Meredith, his wife Mary Ellen, and Wallis, who began an adulterous affair with Mary Ellen not long after the Chatterton painting was completed; and that of contemporary author Peter Ackroyd, whose novel *Chatterton* (1987) playfully portrays Chatterton's legacy by means of a forged painting, a plagiarizing novelist, and a dramatization of Chatterton's final hours. Before introducing these specters, however, we must scrutinize the life and works of this prodigious writer and tease out patterns in his astonishingly varied corpus. Doing so will enable us to trace the intertextual threads that stitch together the fabric of influence and the figures of inhabitation.

A "Boy of Learning and a Bard of Tropes"

> While yet a boy I sought for ghosts, and sped
> Through many a listening chamber, cave and ruin,
> And starlight wood, with fearful steps pursuing
> Hopes of high talk with the departed dead.
>
> —P. B. Shelley, "Hymn to Intellectual Beauty"

Hands

Young Thomas was far from the only forger of his time. As several scholars have shown, eighteenth-century England was the "defining period for modern concepts of fraud" (Baines, *House* 2). Definitions of fraud are inextricably connected to concepts of value, which underwent a "profound transformation" during the eighteenth century (Thompson 1). Forgery became a threat in the financial realm when economic theory and practice abandoned metallism, in which value was thought to reside in the weight of bullion, in favor of cartalism, whereby money was understood as a social fiction founded on faith (Baines, *House* 12). With the emergence of a credit economy certified by handwriting instead of by gold and handshakes, signing a false name to a letter of credit or check became a serious offense. Forgeries undermine what Georg Simmel calls a "supra-theoretical" belief in the economic system and the nation that guarantees it (179); hence, forgery became a capital crime. This crisis of credit went hand in hand with a revolution in concepts of identity. As historian J. G. A. Pocock has argued, "Once property was seen to have symbolic value, expressed in coin or credit, the foundations of personality themselves appeared imaginary or at best consensual: the individual could exist, even in his own sight, only at the fluctuating value imposed upon him by his fellows" (464). The emergence of a credit economy cemented the idea of identity as a phenomenon confirmed by a signature. Because "the self circulated as a name on a document" (Baines, *House* 14), a forgery assailed the social contract itself.

In an age before fingerprinting, the hand, manifest in a signature, was the essential synecdoche of identity, linking intention and action, credit and remittance. A signature at once lengthens and limits the interval allowed for payment. In one sense, the time of signing, the time of reading, and the time of payment fuse because a signature, as I note in the prologue, presumes that the person signing and the person paying are identical, despite the passage of time. However, as Simmel points out, credit transactions open up "a distance whose poles are held together by trust" (480). Like all fictions, a signed document creates an alternate world in which the real person is replaced by a representation that depends on the suspension of disbelief. In other words, it is a narrative, and a forgery substitutes a false story for a factual one. Further, because in signing her name a person also becomes a witness, a cleavage occurs between the signer and the one who verifies the signature. That is, even as it stands for the signer, the signature proves that the payer is *not* the same as the signer, for if she were, she wouldn't need a signature. A forgery both exposes and fills this temporal and ontological gap, thereby becoming a theft not just of one identity but of the very guarantee of stable identity that enables an economy, and hence a society, to function. The ramifications of these changes for literature seem obvious: the author's name is, in effect, a signature pledging that the name on the manuscript (and, by extension, book) truthfully represents the hand of the person to whom it is ascribed. As Nick Groom points out, the eighteenth century was "obsessed with authenticity [and that fact] . . . created opportunities for experimental literature, some of which was called forgery" (*Shadow* 71).

One of these experiments was the disreputable new genre called the English novel. Many early novels came clothed in the garb of history or (auto)biography (Haywood, *Making* 18). Defoe's fictions, for example, posed as factual stories, and novels such as Horace Walpole's *The Castle of Otranto* (1764) used the "shaggy-dog tale of the found parchment" as authentication (Russett, *Fictions* 24). Like some novels (and human impostors), a forgery is a text that lies about its origins. Hence, as Russett has shown, the notion of forgery became the "conceptual measure against which the epistemological experiment of the novel could be understood" (14). But the measurement was inexact for, Radnóti notes, the fact that a story is untrue may be either a literary device or "an act of fraud" or "both of these simultaneously" (186). The line between fiction and fraud was blurry and permeable. Chatterton's Rowley documents exploited these inconsistencies and incoherencies (Haywood, *Making* 72; Russett, *Fictions* 17). Groom is thus right to ask, "Were they really forgeries? Or were they a new form of fiction?" (Introduction 3). Like all forgeries, they were acts of cultural criticism—of the patronage system, of the class system, of the current state of literary scholarship. Thus, comments Susan Stewart, "we see the emergence of imitations, forgeries, and scholarship in a complex interrelation. Imitation arises as a scandal, forgery as a style of genius, scholarship as a cure" (108). Chatterton was skilled in all three modes.

Reliques

> Within the Garret's spacious dome
> There lies a well stor'd wealthy room.
> —Chatterton, "Sly Dick" (composed at age 12)

Thomas Chatterton died before Thomas Chatterton was born: young Tom was a posthumous child, for his father, also named Thomas, passed away three months before November 20, 1752, when his namesake was born. A chorister and writing master, Thomas Senior was deemed eccentric (Kaplan 39). His son, considered dull by teachers, nevertheless manifested from an early age what his doting mother, Sarah, called a "thurst for pre-heminence" (Croft 143). Encouraged by her and by his older sister, Mary, Tom entertained grandiose notions of his destiny. At eight he became a charity pupil at the Colston's Hospital School, where students' blue robes and orange stockings were capped with priest-like tonsured heads, a uniform that would "abet the invention" of Rowley (S. Stewart 115). In July 1767 fourteen-year-old Tom was indentured as a clerk to the lawyer John Lambert. Although the prospects of future greatness seem to have dimmed, Mary reports that he had only a couple of hours of legal business to complete each day, leaving him largely free to "pursue his genius" (Croft 145).

Employed at St. Mary Redcliffe Church, Thomas Senior had explored its muniments room, finding scraps of ancient parchments to use as book covers. Young Tom was fascinated by these materials and later claimed that he had found a trove of papers in a large chest in that room, most of them written by Thomas Rowley, a "secular priest" who lived in mid-fifteenth-century Bristol under the patronage of William Canynge (1399–1474), an actual person who served five terms as Bristol's mayor. Chatterton composed the earliest Rowley works in the summer of 1768. The first to see print was "Bridge Narrative," an imagined account of the construction of the old Bristol bridge, which the shrewd youth sent to *Felix Farley's Bristol Journal* when the new bridge was being dedicated that October.[1] Two local antiquarians, the pewterer George Catcott and the surgeon William Barrett, requested more relics. Chatterton quickly produced two long verse narratives (including "The Battle of Hastings II") and a "vast cargo of antiquarian documents" designed to plug holes in Barrett's projected history of Bristol (D. Taylor xxxvii). Many of the later Rowleys, as I show below, also targeted specific potential patrons. Hence, like the Ireland and Ern Malley frauds discussed later, Chatterton's forgeries engendered a symbiotic relationship between perpetrator and dupes.

Chatterton's output was both prolific and generically promiscuous (I. Phillips 33). The Rowley material includes prose historical documents, lengthy battle verses, dramatic works, journalistic pieces, lyric poems, songs, and ballads as well as drawings and charts. All, of course, were hand-written. The voluminous non-Rowley works include the love poems he ghostwrote for friends, along with the eclogues, dialogues, broadsides, satires, and prose tales to which he devoted most of his ink after mid-1769. For the Rowley works, his major source was Thomas Percy's *Reliques of Ancient English Poetry* (1765), along with samples from Chaucer, Shakespeare, Milton, Gray, Spenser, and others, through which he fashioned a pastiche of Middle English, presenting himself (under various guises) as editor. The pastiches do not bear much scrutiny. For example, although his orthography adds certain letters—usually a final "e" and extra consonants—he was not aware that fifteenth-century readers would have pronounced the vowels differently, nor that when read as Middle English the poems do not scan. Many of Rowley's poems employ rhyme royal with an alexandrine final line—a form that had not been invented in the fifteenth century. Moreover, the boy's attempts to age the documents by brushing them with ochre and soot were far from foolproof, as the smudges smeared when wet. Chatterton biographer E. H. W. Meyerstein dismisses these efforts as "childish bunglings," a "sad array" that would deceive no knowledgeable reader (121); even so, the controversy over their authorship, involving some of England's foremost scholars, boiled for more than five years after Chatterton's death: the Rowley forgeries *did* deceive many reputable antiquarians and critics. Like most of the forgeries discussed in this study, Chatterton's fakes exposed the limitations of expert opinion and the seemingly inexhaustible human capacity for gullibility; eventually, they also fostered sounder literary scholarship.

Onlie begetter

> O Thou or what remaines of thee
> Ella the Darlynge of Futuritie
> Let this my Songe bolde as thy Courage bee
> As everlastinge to Posterytie.
>
> —Chatterton, "Songe toe Ella"

To conjure up, or perhaps dispel, his father's ghost, young Tom summoned other male spirits. As several critics have noted, the early Rowley works define masculinity via a "frictionless series of father-son dyads" in a world nearly bereft of women, presenting a homosocial "vision of parthenogenesis" that anticipates Victor Frankenstein's (Russett, *Fictions* 55). For example, after Canynge's wife dies, he never considers remarrying and instead forges a mutually beneficial relationship of patron and artist/antiquarian with Rowley (the kind Chatterton hoped to generate with Catcott and Barrett [Crane 36]). When Edward IV attempts to coerce Canynge into marrying a noblewoman to thereby solidify his allegiance, Canynge becomes a priest, thus liberating himself from that onerous obligation ("Brief Account of William Cannings," *Complete Works* 54, cited hereafter as *CW*).[2] Louise Kaplan's thesis—that Chatterton's reincarnation of Canynge enabled a "poor but gifted boy to be restored to the position of the artistic son of a wealthy merchant prince" (42), with Rowley as the "poet-biographer-romancer he wished to be" (51)—is persuasive but only part of the story. Given his posthumous birth, Chatterton was left in the "anxious position of inventing his own inheritance" (S. Stewart 149). How better to engender one than with a forgery, which, like a counterfeit coin, relates a tale of false origins? Here, as in the Ern Malley affair discussed in chapter 3, literary production supplants physical reproduction; and as with Ireland's Shakespeare forgeries, the fabricated documents bespeak their maker's anxieties about his own legitimacy. Chatterton's aims even presage those of Joyce's Stephen Dedalus, who replaces his real father with a mythic one while proclaiming his destiny as a "priest of the eternal imagination" who makes the word flesh in his own "virgin womb" (*Portrait* 195, 191). Like Stephen, Chatterton fashioned a new father.

But what kind of father? What kind of man? In the figure of Bawdin, the hero of the early "Bristowe Tragedie" who would rather die than swear fealty to Edward IV, Chatterton defines heroic masculinity as a willingness to perish for one's principles. Yet Bawdin is not the model male in the poem; that role belongs to Canynge. Indeed, although poems such as "Battle of Hastings" are packed with long, repetitive battle scenes that resemble nothing so much as a video game in longhand (they were written by a teenaged boy, after all) and that seem to define manhood traditionally, Canynge's virtues are far from stereotypically masculine. For example, in an effort to spare Bawdin's life, Canynge appeals to the king's softer side:

> Lette mercie rule thyne infante reigne,
> 'Twill faste they crowne full sure. . . .
> But yff wythe bloode and slaughter thou
> Beginne thy infante reigne
> Thy crowne uponne thy childrennes brows
> Wylle never long remayne. (*CW* 9, lines 77–84)

A true king—a true father—is gentle and merciful. His most treasured arts are not martial but filial and artistic; he values culture over conflict, scholarship above swordsmanship. Ironically, perhaps, these sentiments issue from a boy known in Bristol for his "intense dreariness, . . . fiery egotism, . . . abstracted and bitter melancholy" (Meyerstein xv). Rowley and Canynge, then, permitted Chatterton to fill "gaps in his own identity" (Kaplan 101). By fabricating a priest and a father in his massive bildungsroman, Chatterton sires an authorial self.

Ghostwriter

> And where wee kenn somme ishad [scattered] floures besprente
> We take ytte, and from oulde rouste doe ytte clene;
> Wee wylle ne cheynedd to one pasture bee
> Botte sometymes soare 'bove trouthe of hystorie.
>
> —Chatterton, "Letter to the Dynge Mastre Canynge"

While conjuring these specters, Chatterton was also able to "whip up just the right kind of love poetry for [his acquaintances] to present to their lady friends" (Kaplan 57).[3] As the "neighborhood ghost writer," he composed a series of odes to a girl named Eleanor Hoyland for his friend John Baker, who had recently moved to South Carolina. One such poem, "Acrostic on Miss [Eleanor Hoyland]," accents the pains of love through repeated images of stings and, ahem, a "piercing Blade" (*CW* 159). Clever but conventional, these verses display Chatterton's facility with a variety of modes as well as his chameleonic capacity to impersonate.

Most of Chatterton's ghosts were less intimate. And although he aimed to lure patrons, he also sought to elevate Bristol's historical position, to transform it retrospectively from a domain of "meanness" and "mercenary securities" (Letter to Sarah Chatterton, *CW* 561) into a center of patriotism and literary culture. Like Stephen Dedalus, he aspired to "forge in the smithy of [his] soul the uncreated conscience of [his] race" (Joyce, *Portrait* 224). Chatterton's smithy forged fifteenth-century spirits into material objects. That is, the Rowley works are not just poetic texts. Rather, as "complex tactile and visual objects which revolt against print culture" (I. Phillips 26), they include architectural records, lists, drawings, sketches, coats of arms, genealogies, and other materials designed to flesh out Bristol's past. Often drawn from verifiable sources, Chatterton's documents constitute a massive historical novel, an alternative history of the region in which Rowley and Canynge are embedded as prime movers. In the guise of editor, Chatterton writes in a footnote to the "Brystowe Tragedie" that these manuscripts "might possibly throw Light upon many obscure Passages in and help to establish a more Concise History of our Native Country" (*CW* 20). Rowley was the "prism" through which this history could be transmitted (Haywood, *Making* 133). The priest's imagined contemporaries acknowledge his importance, according to "John Ladgates Answer":

> Now Rowlie ynne these mokie Daies
> Sendes owte hys shynynge Lyghte
> And Turgotus and Chaucer live
> Inne evry thynge hee writes. (*CW* 63)

An ideal antiquarian, Rowley visits "all the Abbies and Pryores" to "gather together auncient drawynges ("Brief Account," *CW* 51). Canynge buys these materials from him for generous sums—for example, "Twentie Pounds" (a substantial amount of money in the fifteenth century) for the "Bristowe Tragedie" (54). If only some patron would tender as much for Chatterton's relics! As Nick Groom comments, "Manuscripts were, in effect, paper money" ("*Fragments*" 190); as with paper currency, their value was a function of faith in their origins. Not only, then, is Rowley Chatterton's surrogate as author, antiquarian and editor; his relationship with Canynge models the bonds that Chatterton hoped to form with his patrons.

Stage-Lion of Wronged Love

> They are not ever jealous for a cause,
> But jealous for they are jealous. 'Tis a monster
> Begot upon itself, born on itself.
>
> —Emilia, in *Othello*, 3.4.154–57

Writing as "De Be," in December 1768, Chatterton tried to entice London publisher James Dodsley with "several ancient Poems" by Rowley (*CW* 157). Dodsley seemed a likely target, since he had published Percy's *Reliques,* but the young supplicant received no response. The following February he tried again in his own name and with more potent bait: the verse tragedy *Aella,* which he modestly describes as "perfect," packed with "spirited" language and several "Elegantly Simple" songs. He aims, he avers, to convince the world that monks were "not such Blockheads, as generally thought and that good Poetry might be wrote, in the dark days of Superstition" (*CW* 172). Alas, he continues, the owner of this valuable manuscript will not cede it unless Chatterton tenders him a guinea (*CW* 171). Not surprisingly, this clumsy appeal for money withered on the vine. The play, however, has lived on and is widely recognized, along with the "Excelente Balade of Charitie," as Chatterton's most accomplished work (see Cook 49). Composed in ten-line stanzas of rhyme royal (rhyme scheme: ababbcbcdd), with the last line an alexandrine, *Aella* comes framed by a cast list (Rowley playing the title character) and two verse letters to Canynge, the second containing the lines quoted above justifying the need to rise above the "trouthe of historie." The play thus melds Chatterton's exploration of masculine values with his project of historical revision. The authorial ghost Chatterton conjures here is Shakespeare, specifically *Othello,* which Chatterton uses to dissect the deficiencies in conventional notions of honor and the depredations of sexual jealousy. Othello is revived as the jealous king Aella; Desdemona is reborn as his wife, Birtha; blending Rodrigo and Iago is Celmonde, a knight in Aella's court (Kaplan 91). An "operatic reduction" of *Othello* (Kaplan 92), *Aella* presents a round, unvarnished tale of love and jealousy that displays Chatterton's undeveloped command of psychology as well as his precocious poetic talent and skill at emotional manipulation. As an implausible play written in the 1760s but set before Shakespeare's tragedy, *Aella* is in two senses a preposterous rendering of *Othello.*

On Aella and Birtha's wedding day, the jealous Celmonde brews a plot to put "stronge poysonn ynn the beere" (*CW* 179, l.135) and kill himself with the lovers, but the ceremony is interrupted by news of the Danes' invasion. Aella instantly decides to go to battle, prompting Birtha to lament that he "pryzest mee belowe the joies of fyghte" and to suggest that Celmonde disguise himself as Aella and fight in his place (191, l.423; 192, l.456). (A similar disguise appears in "Shakespeare's"

Tragedy of Arthur.) Aella assures her, "I'm flyynge from mieselfe yn flying thee" (194, l.503), but fly he does. With the unhappy couple offstage, Celmonde soliloquizes, describing honor as a "shadowes shade / A thynge of wynchencref, an idle dreme" (195, l.536–37), echoing Iago's dismissals of virtue as "a fig" (*Othello* 1.3.318) and of reputation as an "idle and most false imposition" (2.3.251–52). After a jump-cut to the Danes, who are preparing for war, we return to Celmonde, who reports Aella's stirring speech to his men and recounts the king's heroism and wounding. Here is Celmonde's chance: "Nowe, Aella, nowe Ime plantynge of a thorne, / Bie whyche thie peace, thie love, and glorie shalle be torne" (209, l.949–50).

Aella hastens home, but Birtha has departed with Celmonde, who has told Birtha that her husband is sorely wounded and will die unless he sees her. In a forest Celmonde attempts to make love to her; she resists; he assaults her; but in the nick of time the Danes, led by Hurra, appear and slay him. Upon learning that she is Aella's wife, they return her to Bristowe unharmed. Meanwhile, Aella, finding Birtha gone, explodes in paroxysms of jealousy:

> Mie race of love, mie race of lyfe ys ronne;
> Nowe rage, and brondeous [burning] storm, and tempeste comme;
> Nete lyvinge upon erthe can now enswote [allay] mie domme.
> (224, l.1292–94)

As with the jealous Othello, "passion, having [his] best judgment collied, / Assays to lead the way" (2.3.188–90). Devastated by the dishonor of his imaginary cuckolding, Aella stabs himself: "Gyffe noblie Aella lyved, as noblie Aella felle" (225, l.1314). Many readers have been "perplexed in the extreme" (*Othello* 5.2.346) by this shocking turn: as Donald Taylor notes, Rowley fails to supply "sufficient grounds for [Aella's] almost immediate suspicion, his jealousy, and his suicide" (137). True. However, Chatterton apparently means to demonstrate that Aella's exaggerated sense of honor is as poisonous as Celmonde's disdain for it. Moreover, as *Othello* dramatizes, what Iago terms "Trifles light as air"—such as a handkerchief—"Are to the jealous confirmations strong / As proofs of holy writ" (3.3.322). Jealousy feeds on itself.

At the sight of her dying husband, Birtha faints; Hurra swiftly relates how they rescued her from the "burled swayne" Celmonde (227, l.1337), reports the would-be rapist's death, and reiterates Birtha's desire to join her husband—tidings that allow Aella to die "contente" (227, l.1354). Birtha declares, "I will make hys grave mie vyrgyn spousal bedde" and expires also (l.1355). Her death seems even less plausibly motivated than Aella's. Yet if the play lacks psychological credibility, it convincingly diagnoses how poisonous are petrified notions of honor and masculine possessiveness, according to which Birtha, as an appendage of Aella, must fall when he falls. Aella would echo Othello's claim that "Naught I did in hate, but all in honour," which only means that he is an "honourable murderer" (5.2294–95). Aella's disbelief in Birtha's honor proves his own lack of it. A more genuine brand of honor belongs to the Danes, who protect Birtha instead of adhering to the cruel dictates of war and whose virtues are not shaken by a rumor.

Infant Author

> The Boy, who Friendless, Penniless, Forlorn,
> Asks thy high favour,—thou mayst call me Cheat—
> Say, didst thou ne'er indulge in such Deceit?
> Who wrote Otranto?
>
> —Chatterton, letter to Horace Walpole

Chatterton's "manufactured antiquarianism," writes Bridget Keegan, "allowed him to hide behind a more authoritative voice than his own to gain access to a literary world from which he would have otherwise been excluded" (214). Rowley and Canynge together composed both a bard to lure would-be patrons and a "beard" for a lower-class boy lacking the education, maturity, and connections that would provide entree into the authors' club. And so the enterprising youth lined up another plump target: Horace Walpole, Lord Orford, who had turned his estate at Strawberry Hill into a museum. His *Anecdotes of Painting in England* had left a hole where the Saxons should have been; Chatterton sought to fill it. Learning that Walpole was preparing a second edition, in March 1769 the teenager sent him a letter along with Rowley's "The Ryse of Penctenyge, yn Englande." In a footnote he praises Rowley's polymathic talents and predicts that whoever patronizes him will place all Englishmen "under an eternal Obligation." Hailed as the "Mecenas of his time," Canynge "happily blend[s]" poet, painter, priest and is "perfect in each" (*CW* 259)—a not-too-subtle suggestion that by patronizing Rowley, Walpole might himself become such a savory blend. When Walpole responded positively a few days later, Tom sent a second Rowleyan tract on painting, recklessly claiming he had found it in that iron chest in St. Mary Redcliffe's muniments room (*CW* 266). This shell landed too close to home, for Walpole had employed the same device to frame *The Castle of Otranto.* Having been advised by his friends, antiquarian William Mason and poet Thomas Gray, that the Rowley works were spurious, he brushed the boy off and wagged his finger, while sniffing that Tom's time would be better spent attending to his legal duties.

Chatterton's reply of April 8 sounds at once self-pitying and defensive: "I am not able to dispute with a person of your literary character. I have transcribed Rowley's poems, &c, &c. from a transcript in the possession of a gentleman who is assured of their authenticity." This claim is not strictly untrue, for Barrett and Catcott were indeed so "assured." Chatterton continues, "Though I am but sixteen years of age, I have lived long enough to see that poverty attends literature. I am obliged to you, sir, for your advice, and will go a little beyond it, by destroying all my useless lumber of literature, and never using my pen again but in the law" (*CW* 271). He did not follow through on that promise, but after May, when he wrote three eclogues and "Elinoure and Juga," he retired Rowley (until his return for a final lap). The wounded youth drafted two versions of an angry letter demanding the return of his MSS before sending a curt third version on April 14. Months passed with no answer. On July 24 Chatterton wrote: "I cannot reconcile your behaviour to me, with the notions I once entertained of you. I think myself injured, sir; and, did not you know my circumstances, you would not dare to treat me thus. . . . An explanation or excuse for your silence would oblige" (*CW* 340). The boy may have had no money, but he clearly possessed an ample supply of chutzpah.

When Walpole finally responded, he asked why Chatterton didn't possess the originals, since he had claimed that he'd sent Walpole transcripts, and pointed out that Chatterton's Spenserisms were anachronistic. Either Chatterton was tricking him, or he was a poor arbiter of authenticity: "The former would show you had little opinion of my judgement; the latter, that you ought not to trust too much to your own. I should not at all take the former ill, as I am not vain of it; I should be sorry for the latter, as you say, sir, that you are very young, and it would be a pity an ingenious young man should be too early prejudiced in his own favour" (*CW* 376–77).

The patronizing tone and insincere self-deprecation inflamed Chatterton's ire, which he had already vented in an (unsent) eighteen-line poem that paints himself as "Friendless, Penniless, Forlorn" and Walpole as a vain toady and hypocrite: Didn't you, Lord Orford, disguise your authorship with a phony tale about a found manuscript? Walpole's worst offenses, however, are snobbery and stinginess:

> Had I the Gifts of Wealth and Lux'ry shar'd
> Not poor and Mean—Walpole! thou hadst not dared
> Thus to insult, But I shall live and Stand
> By Rowley's side—when Thou art dead and damned. (*CW* 341)

His prediction has come true: Chatterton, with Rowley attending, has enjoyed a long afterlife; among Walpole's works, only *Otranto* does much more than collect dust.[4]

Nevertheless, Chatterton doffed his priestly garb. He tried to woo another patron, the pewterer Henry Burgum, by furnishing him with a fake pedigree, but Burgum demurred (see *Account of the Family of the De Berghams, CW* 316–38). Whom should he become now? The literary world offered few models. His "Elegy on the Demise of a Great Genius," written soon after, is less a lament for Rowley than a tongue-lashing of derivative contemporary writers. A parody of elegies, it opens, "Begin my Muse the imitative lay," then goes on to lambaste actual (William Collins) and anonymous poets whose verses recall the howling of cats. When Chatterton recycled most of this poem in "February: An Elegy" (January 1770), he inserted a telling quatrain:

> Now infant authors, mad'ning for renown
> Extend the plume, and hum about the stage,
> Procure a benefit, amuze the town,
> And proudly glitter on a title page. (*CW* 448)

This is a virtual manifesto for the last months of his life, when Tom extended his plume in an almost manic pursuit of renown. But he could not glitter in dull, mercenary Bristol, so he devised another gambit to emancipate himself.

Willful

> For had I never known the antique Lore
> I ne'er had ventur'd from my peaceful Shore
> To be the wreck of promises and hopes
> A Boy of Learning and a Bard of Tropes.
>
> —Chatterton, ["Will"]

In March 1770 Chatterton wrote to Barrett that his own "damn'd, native, unconquerable Pride . . . plunges me into Distraction. . . . I must either live a Slave, a Servant; to have no Will of my own . . . or Die—Perplexing Alternative!" (*CW* 494). He soon fashioned a Will of his own that freed him from those pesky indentures. On April 14 he left his last will and testament, written in "utmost Distress of Mind," where Lambert could find it. Included is a plan to commit suicide the following Sunday (Easter, of course), along with a fifty-four-line poem in heroic couplets that pillories Burgum and praises Barrett while charging that "hardly twenty" in Bristol can even read. His vow to kill himself, he ironically observes, would merely bear out Bristolians' opinion of him, since they "distinguish me by the Title of the Mad Genius" (503). He appends elaborate instructions for his interment and tomb, along with numerous bequests: his "Vigor and Fire of Youth" to Catcott ("being sensible he is in most want of it"), his religion to a dean who habitually falls asleep during worship, and his letters to various "young Ladys," though he adds that they need be under "no Apprehensions from the Appearance of my Ghost for I dye for none of them" (504–5). Even in (sham) despair he manages to be wittily snotty. In any case, the ploy worked: Lambert released him from his indentures.

Through Rowley, Joseph Bristow and Rebecca Mitchell observe, Chatterton "projected his developing poetic identity into a historical universe where he could enjoy successful authorship" (70). Rowley and Canynge had focalized an otherwise diffuse farrago of forms and genres. As Julie Crane notes, "The Rowleyan poetry was peopled with ghosts and spirits, figures either of guile or of need, preparing the ground for their author to merge into his own creation" (36). In raising these dead, Chatterton lifted himself into authorship, but he had drained that imaginary world dry.

London beckoned.

Proteus

"The Authors Face"

> . . . 'twas ordain'd by Fate that I should write
> Spite of the Prudence of this prudent Place
> I wrote my Mind nor hid the Authors face.
>
> —Chatterton, ["Will"]

If Chatterton had actually *been* Rowley, his situation may have been easier to manage, for Rowley's works are all dated (intentionally) before the advent of the printing press. Early modern writers were not always viewed (even by themselves) as privileged components of the production process, and publishers could buy them cheaply—more cheaply than, say, typesetters—or for nothing, if they were subsidized by a patron (Osteen and Woodmansee 8). In the seventeenth century the spread of literacy encouraged publishers to print and reprint works with no concern for authorial rights. Limiting that practice, the Act of Anne (1710), the first copyright statute, fostered a market economy that helped give birth to the myth of the individual genius (Osteen and Woodmansee 9). The result was that Chatterton, like the literary community in general, was suspended between "the patronage-model (as idealized in the Rowley story) and the capitalist market (where the Rowley texts were actually peddled)" (Russett, *Fictions*, 59; cf. S. Stewart 150). He sought to cross this bridge by offering the Rowley works to patrons while also pitching them to publishers such as Dodsley. His career splits at this rift: when he left Bristol for London, he abandoned the pursuit of Bristol patrons to make his name—or rather, many names—in the bustling world of magazines and broadsides.

Chatterton wasted no time in the metropolis: on his first day in London he visited four publishers. Thus began the "sedulous[ ] networking" in what Michael Suarez calls Chatterton's "relentless quest for the contacts and patronage" he needed for success (103, 105). He first adopted the radical Patriot cause spearheaded by MP John Wilkes, writing satires and broadsides under names such as Decimus and Probus, borrowing his style from Junius, Charles Churchill, and Samuel Johnson. Before long he obtained a commission of four guineas to write a "voluminous history of London" (Letter to Mary Chatterton, *CW* 587), and in July 1770 landed another one of five guineas for his burletta, *The Revenge*

(Meyerstein 402). He maintained his ties to Bristol via cheery letters to his mother and sister and bought them gifts with the money he earned. When Wilkes's star sank after his imprisonment, Chatterton blithely switched allegiances: as he wrote to his sister, "He is a poor author, who cannot write on both sides" (*CW* 588).[5] All in all, Chatterton approached authorship with "remarkable inventiveness and acumen," producing eleven works in a little over six weeks between mid-April and late May (Suarez 96–97). The reports from his first landlords, the Walmsleys of Shoreditch, suggest how he sustained this output: the haughty boy barely ate or slept, seeming to them "more a spirit than a real person" (Kaplan 170).

By June he had moved to a garret in Mrs. Angel's house on Brooke Street in Holborn. Meanwhile he composed short fiction in the style of Defoe and Johnson; indeed, his "Maria Friendless Letter," about a fallen woman, was plagiarized from Johnson's "Misella" (see *CW* 594–97; Meyerstein 397). The similar "The False Step," like "Maria" published in *Town and Country* magazine, is "written" by Frances, who loses her virtue along with her inheritance (*CW* 600–4). Although she loves a man named Knowles, her father sets her up with an aged earl; after marrying him, she lives a "kind of negative existence" (603). This phrase might be a good description of Chatterton's own authorial enterprises, for his name does not appear on either of these pieces of sentimental fiction. Likewise, his most accomplished short tale, "Memoirs of a Sad Dog," is attributed to one Harry Wildfire, who inherits, then gambles away, a fortune, romances married and unmarried women, then is hired by a lord to manage his stables. Here Wildfire inserts a jab at Walpole, lightly disguised as "Baron Otranto," a man who, having spent "his whole life in conjectures" (658), mistakes an ordinary headstone for "the third runic alphabet of Wormius" (659). After more financial scrapes and another marriage, Wildfire hits bottom: he becomes a political writer (661). This genial picaresque yarn, like the other stories, fits comfortably into the conventional fiction of the period, which may explain why they quickly made their way into print. ("Sad Dog" was published in *Town and Country* in July.)

In the wake of the innovative and ambitious Rowley works, don't the London efforts seem disappointingly derivative? Don't the "forgeries" seem more original than the originals? Had the author's face that Chatterton so assiduously cultivated decomposed into that of a hack, his persona devolving into a "negative existence?"[6] Not entirely. The London pieces possess a sprightly energy and display Chatterton's boundless capacity for invention—and imitation. Indeed, what Chatterton's writings, both Rowley and non-Rowley, reveal most strongly is a gift for impersonation. In London he replaced Rowley, D. B., John Baker, and "Dopnal Syrric," author of "Godred Crovan"—the authorial masks of Bristol—with the au courant disguises of Probus, Decimus, Maria, Frances, and Harry, but Chatterton seemed unable to compose without a costume. As Meyerstein observes, "Though afire to have his name blown about, not a single printed attribution by him stands signed with it" (324). The dialectic between recognition and invisibility that typifies all forgeries operates forcefully here: Chatterton needed to erase his name to make his name. Given the connection between self and signature outlined above, one might conclude that he had no identity at all. But in fact, his authorial self was flexible, fluctuant, light-handed. His works remind us that all authors are fictional creations, verbal masks that may have little in common with the living person who extends his quill. Like other impostors, Chatterton became his "own mother and father" (S. Stewart 145), collaborating with his conjured ghosts to create a protean authorial self. Paradoxically, he begat himself as author by remaining invisible—foreshadowing Dedalus's God-like artist who dwells "within or behind or beyond or above his handiwork, invisible, refined out of existence" (Joyce, *Portrait* 189). Chatterton was a ghost before he died: he could come forth only by vanishing.

Pilgrim

> Now giving and taking's a proper exchange,
> Like question and answer: you're both content. . . .
> If Charity's Christian, don't blame my pursuits,
> I carry a touchstone by which you're tried.
>
> —Meredith, "The Beggar's Soliloquy"

One theme solders a link among these diverse personae, welding the Rowley/Canynge forgeries to London writings such as "Sad Dog." It is also the ethical foundation of Chatterton's oeuvre: the charitable use of wealth. Susan Stewart contends that Chatterton's canon constitutes an "ongoing critique of materiality—particularly an attack on money," and that he sought to use Rowley as a means of circumventing the capitalist marketplace in Bristol (152). This is only partly true: as we have seen, he was shameless in seeking patronage. Nevertheless, through Canynge, Chatterton indicates that the accumulation of wealth is pointless, even immoral, unless it is used for beneficial purposes such as building or improving churches, patronizing the arts, and helping those in need. As Kaplan observes, "Canynge's central ethical principle" is "the benevolent use of riches" (65; cf. D. Taylor 149–50). Thus, for example, in "Yellow Rolle," Canynge replies to the king, "You dyspende Heavenne to gette Goulde but I dyspende Goulde toe gette Heaven" (*CW* 65). Conversely, in poems such as "The Gouler's Requiem" (a gouler being a usurer), Canynge condemns the thirst for gold as both inhuman and ineffective, as the gouler finally recognizes: "Inn thee [gold] I all mie Joie and goode dyd wase, / Botte nowe to mee thie pleasaunce ys ne moe, / I kenn not but for thee, I to the Qwood [Devil] muste goe" (*CW* 291). Against greed Chatterton proffers a gift economy in which parties exchange not to best but to befriend one another and where obligations remain implicit and flexible. This is for him, as for Meredith's beggar, a "proper exchange." Walpole's worse failing, in this regard, was that he wasn't Canynge.

Chatterton's most significant treatment of this theme is the last Rowley poem, "An Excelente Balade of Charitie," which he submitted to *Town and Country* in July 1770.[7] A retelling of the Good Samaritan parable in seven-line rhyme royal (each last line, again, an alexandrine), it opens with an evocative description of a hot day and an impending thunderstorm—"'Twas now the pride, the manhode of the yeare"—during which a "hapless pilgrim" waits near St. Godwin's convent (*CW* 645). As rain begins to fall, the abbot passes, dressed in a gilt-edged robe and wearing shoes a lord would envy: "Full well it shewn he thoughten coste no sinne" (647, l.54). The pilgrim asks for alms; the abbot spurns him: "None touch mie rynge who not in honour live" (l.67). Chatterton again condemns false honor as a cloak for vanity. As the rain increases, a monk dressed in plain, clean gray happens by. Hearing the beggar's request, he loosens his pouch and tenders a coin: "Here take this silver, it mae eathe thie care; / We are Goddes stewards all, nete [nought] of our owne we bare" (648, l.81–84). He even strips off his undergarment and hands it to the mendicant to help him stay dry.

Most critics concur that the "Excelente Balade" is Chatterton's most accomplished short poem, not least because its faux-medieval orthography and setting suit its action and theme. It concisely conveys Chatterton's—or is it Rowley's?—disgust for hypocrisy, mistrust of authority, and obsession with reviving and repurposing ancient stories and tellers. This time his resurrection is truly brazen, for the revivified narrator here is none other than Jesus of Nazareth, who relates this parable in Luke 10:30 in response to the question "Who is my neighbor?" Like the Canynge documents, the poem endorses an economy of donation without hope of remittance—a gift that counters the market economy of exploitation and ruthless impersonality. Although the ballad fits Chatterton's long-standing ethos (and made his work more marketable), many read it after his death as a *cri de coeur* from a young pilgrim reduced to loneliness and penury in an unforgiving metropolis, a symptom of depression, and an omen of his impending suicide. Others have applauded it as a welcome return to Rowley's authenticity after the hackwork of the first London months (see Cook 5). But it may have been written a year earlier and hence had little to do with his death. We do know that he met his demise a few weeks later.

Which brings us back to Wallis's painting.

A Noble Insanity

> Thy sunken eye, thy haggard cheek it shews,
> The quick emotions struggling in the Face
> Faint index of thy mental Throes,
> When each strong Passion spurn'd controll,
> And not a Friend was nigh to calm thy stormy soul.
>
> —Coleridge, "Monody on the Death of Chatterton" (1790)

Written when he too was a scholarship boy, Coleridge's poem crystallizes the picture of Chatterton that pervaded the literary world for decades after his death: a genius who killed himself in despair and hunger after being rebuffed by shallow, unfeeling publishers and snubbed by the self-satisfied Walpole. This is the mythic Chatterton who inspired Romantic poets. As Kaplan puts it, he "had been abandoned, and he let himself die" (235). For evidence, readers cite a line from Chatterton's "The Unfortunate Fathers" (written in January 1770): "Suicide is sometimes a noble insanity of the soul" (*CW* 445). But that sentence resides in a letter written by a character in the story: it is far from a personal confession. Recently the consensus regarding Chatterton's death has shifted away from suicide toward accidental overdose. Many scholars now believe that Chatterton was "handling himself very adeptly in

London" (Groom, Introduction 9) and earning a decent living (Suarez 100). Richard Holmes was likely the first to argue that Chatterton died accidentally after ineptly self-medicating for a venereal disease, probably syphilis, for which one of the most common (albeit dangerous and ineffective) treatments was a tincture of arsenic and opium—the very mixture that killed the young bard.[8] In *Chatterton*, Peter Ackroyd shows how the overdose might have happened: the drunken teenager, confused about the proper ratios, ingests too much arsenic. In any case, the deathbed scene likely bore little resemblance to Wallis's beautifully serene tableau. Chatterton's final throes probably resembled those of another literary figure, Emma Bovary: violent convulsions, racking abdominal pains, compulsive vomiting, bloody diarrhea, a purplish anoxic face, and a slow, agonizing death.[9]

The young man was not smiling.

In the ensuing years, as more of Chatterton's works came to light and his fame spread, contemporaries blamed Walpole for the youth's suicide, even though their correspondence had ended several months earlier.[10] Walpole felt compelled to defend himself in a letter to William Bewley, a defense that he enlarged in a letter to John Broughton, editor of *Miscellanies in Prose and Verse* (1778), the edition of Chatterton's works where Walpole had been attacked. In the Broughton letter Walpole famously links literary and financial forgery: "All of the house of forgery are relations; and though it is just to Chatterton's memory to say, that his poverty never made him claim kindred with the richest, or most enriching branches, yet his ingenuity in counterfeiting styles, and, I believe, hands, might easily have led him to those more facile imitations of prose, promissory notes" (qtd. in Baines, *House* 162). I have noted how the two forms of forgery are related conceptually, but Walpole's slippage from literary faking to financial crime is too facile, for there is no evidence that Chatterton ever contemplated forging financial documents. Rather, he used his texts as counterfeit currency. In any case, Walpole, like virtually everyone else, was ambivalent about Chatterton, describing him alternately as a "consummate villain" and as a "complete genius" (qtd. in Baines, *House* 162, 163). Fittingly, this author of the first Gothic novel was haunted by Chatterton, who seemed to him a person of many and shifting faces—"bookish, a natural genius, a criminal, an imaginative forger, a poor boy"—descriptions that "recur throughout Chatterton's afterlife" (Cook 91).

Genius

> Far from the reach of Critics and Reviews
> Brush up thy Pinions and ascend my Muse
> Of Conversation sing, an ample theme
> And drink the Tea of the Heliconian Stream.
>
> —Chatterton, ["Conversation"]

Chatterton's mother and sister also painted different versions of Tom to the numerous callers who visited them, "shrewdly rearranging the facts" depending on who sought his manuscripts (Kaplan 41). One such visitor was Rev. Herbert Croft, who in July 1778 persuaded Sarah and Mary to lend him (for a guinea and a half) several Rowley works and all of Thomas's letters. Croft (who was the Walmsleys' landlord) kept the materials for months, then used them for a lengthy digression in his sensational epistolary novel *Love and Madness* (1780), where a hundred-page biography of Chatterton—complete with letters, poems, and analysis—interrupts his account of events leading to James Hacking's murder of his lover. The Chatterton documents were a scoop, and Croft's sympathetic treatment of him as a misguided and misunderstood genius had a powerful effect on later biographers as well as on would-be forgers such as William-Henry Ireland, each of whom added his own "prejudices, romantic fantasies, [and] wishful thinking" to his predecessors' errors (Kaplan 251).[11] Croft's novel sparked the mythmaking that awarded Chatterton an "iconic place in the late eighteenth- and nineteenth-century cultural imagination" (Bristow and Mitchell 79) and helped to dispel the predominant early image of Chatterton as a "dreadful libertine, a syphilis-ridden profligate" (Kaplan 191).

Croft argued that Chatterton wrote all the Rowley works, but not everyone agreed. Indeed, the Rowley Controversy "dominated large sections of the periodical press between 1777 (when Thomas Tyrwhitt published the first edition of Chatterton's works) and 1782" (Cook 93). It proved to be one of the key cultural debates of the period and eventually fostered new standards in criticism and scholarship while also "launching the posthumous career of Thomas Chatterton" (Groom, Introduction 4). Actually, Catcott had begun burnishing the boy's reputation as early as 1771, when he brought Samuel Johnson and James Boswell to the muniments room, although the visitors remained unconvinced that Rowley had existed. By April 1773 Oliver Goldsmith had become a Rowleyan (i.e., one who believed Rowley had written the works attributed to him); antiquarians such as Jacob Bryant also joined the Rowley camp. Among those on the other side was Thomas Percy (whose verdict of forgery came in September 1773 [Rogers 130]); on the fence (at first) was Thomas Warton, editor of an influential history of English poetry. Soon allegiance to Rowley became a "metonym for rebellion" against the literary establishment (Lolla 159). But the Rowleyans faced a dilemma: they had to claim that the boy was not talented enough to have written the works but was smart enough to have understood their worth and transcribed them (Bristow and Mitchell 63). To judge him a genius, that is, they had to recognize him as a fraud: yet another of forgery's paradoxes. Oddly, then, it was the anti-Rowleyans who held Chatterton in the highest regard. Percy, for example, deemed him "one of the greatest geniuses that ever existed" (qtd. in S. Stewart 120), and even Edmond Malone, who definitively debunked the Rowley materials in his *Cursory Observations on the Poems Attributed to Thomas Rowley* (1782), opined that Chatterton was "the greatest genius that England has produced since the days of Shakspeare" (qtd. in Rogers 138). Maria Grazia Lolla remarks that many of those involved did not want the controversy to end, being "more interested in arguing and pursuing research" than in answering the authorship conundrum (157). Although most literati, including Warton, eventually concluded that Chatterton had forged the Rowley writings, the deeper conflict involved what should be called genuine scholarship. The result was a blossoming of new methods that combined the historical attention of the antiquarians with the aesthetic sensibilities of the literati.

Somewhere the young man was smiling.

Daemon

> Now rest, too hapless Chatterton, whose strain
> My bosom warms while singing Bawdin's fate;
> Yet shalt thou live! Nor shall my song be in vain
> That dares not thine, but dares to imitate.
>
> —Ann Yearsley, "Elegy on Mr. Chatterton," 1787

Yearsley's poem, addressed to Chatterton's "neglected shade," imagines him as a "joyless Youth . . . quickly hurl'd / From Hope's fair height, to

Death's unlov'd embrace" (l.15–16). The boy's ghost even speaks of his agony. This rendering of Chatterton as a victim "killed by a haughty lord and neglected by . . . society" (Fairer 235) prevailed among the Romantic poets who followed Yearsley, blotting out the enterprising aspirant, the precocious lyric poet, the sly opportunist, the sedulous student, the fiery pamphleteer, and the hack fiction writer. Haunted, like Yearsley, by what they believed to be his pathetic suicide, they invoked Chatterton as a "daemon"—not a demon but an attendant spirit like, say, Hephaestus (Groom, *Shadow* 193, 190). He embodied a warning. Thus, Wordsworth famously alludes in "Resolution and Independence" to the "marvellous Boy, / The sleepless Soul that perished in his pride" (43–44). (This poem also borrows Chatterton's rhyme royal.) A slightly different Chatterton served as a muse. To these writers his "tragic devotion to his art was untainted by material ambitions," never mind his relentless pursuit of patrons and pennies (Keegan 211). None of these specters bears much resemblance to the shrewd, headstrong young man we have come to know.

Wordsworth's marvelous boy is the one lying on Wallis's bed. But Wallis's painting was far from the only visual representation. The first one appeared in 1782 as an engraving in *Westminster* magazine; it was distributed as a memorial handkerchief entitled "The Distressed Poet, or a True Representation of the Unfortunate Chatterton" and presented him as a "victim to his pride and poverty!" (R. Holmes 254–55). The so-called "goggle ey'd portrait" of 1797 (fig. 2) shows a boy with long, unkempt hair, a "genius on the very edge of madness" (256). The similar frontispiece to John Dix's biography, published in 1837, pictures a large-eyed child who seems about ten years old (fig. 3). Nobody knows what Chatterton actually looked like; the overlarge eyes in these "portraits" signify his supernatural qualities. Edward Orme's *Death of Chatterton* (1794, fig. 4) likely served as model for Wallis. Orme's Chatterton, his eyes open and a look of suffering on his visage, lies in the opposite direction from Wallis's; to the left a woman (Mrs. Angel?) and a child enter the room and gaze at him. This work, which also includes an open chest and a desk with a doused candle, depicts the garret as dark and shabby, with peeling paint and plaster. Similar is Francesco Bartolozzi's engraving, in which the poet rests on the bed, head right, light streaming from a window to reveal his agonized face, while rats feed below (fig. 5). Its resemblance to a prison cell is reinforced by the legend: "And ah! Let

Fig. 2. The "goggle-ey'd" portrait of Chatterton: a "genius on the edge of madness." Artist unknown, late eighteenth century. Line engraving, 15.9 × 11.4 cm. (© National Portrait Gallery, London)

Fig. 3. This is how Chatterton was depicted in the frontispiece to John Dix's biography (1837). Unknown boy engraved as Thomas Chatterton, by Nathan CooperBranwhit, after William John Alais. (© National Portrait Gallery, London)

FIG. 4. Edward Orme's *Death of Chatterton* (1794) likely served as model for Wallis's painting. Print on paper, 40.7 × 50.4 cm. (© Trustees of the British Museum)

Pity turn her dewy eyes / Where gasping Penury unfriended lies." Chatterton is a pathetic victim, propelled to suicide by an unfeeling world. In none of these is the young man smiling; in that regard Wallis's rendition is novel.[12] These visual representations reinforce the second part of thesis 3: that forgeries are seeds from which multiple fictions bloom. As Holmes puts it, "Chatterton first forged himself and then was posthumously forged by others" (253).

Chatterton's dying plant bore many flowers: fatherless boy, ghostwriter, self-begetter, opportunist, con artist, pilgrim, madman, victim, genius, presiding spirit. His daemon would not be banished. Dozens of articles, as well as plays, novels, and poems, were published about him in Victorian England.[13] Throughout the era he served as "both a spectre of ruin and an imposing seer" (Crane 37). He was neither of these for Robert Browning, whose essay on Chatterton (1842) draws heavily from Dix's melodramatic biography to defend the boy from imputations of immorality (Smalley 110). Browning hypothesizes that Rowley allowed the boy to gain more traction in the literary world while also protecting him from criticism. Browning views Chatterton's departure

FIG. 5. Francesco Bartolozzi's engraving depicts Chatterton as pathetic victim driven to suicide by an unfeeling world. Unknown man called Thomas Chatterton, by Francesco Bartolozzi, after Raphael Lamar West. Stippled engraving on paper, 11.3 × 14.2 cm. (© National Portrait Gallery, London)

for London as a "gallant and manly" effort to free himself from the "slavery" of Rowley and of his patrons (120). If Chatterton had really wanted to be a forger, he remarks, the boy's arrival in London would have been the "white minute for discoveries" of new relics (132). Instead he wrote under many names and forms: "Any thing but Rowley!" (130). Browning's Chatterton is less victim than valiant adventurer, not a half-mad genius but a young poet like many others, forcing his way into the literary world by inventing characters and giving them a voice—much like the young Robert Browning, author of *Dramatic Lyrics* (1842) and future author of *Dramatis Personae* (1864). Haunted by Chatterton, Browning remade the youth into a version of himself; the boy's death helped to fertilize his own aesthetic growth.

This is also what happened with George Meredith. But Meredith did not write an essay on Chatterton; instead he became him.

Hiding the Skeleton

> Unnatural? My dear, these things are life:
> And life, some think, is worthy of the Muse.
>
> —Meredith, *Modern Love* XXV

Like the work of his Pre-Raphaelite compatriots, Wallis's *Chatterton* possesses a sentimental, dreamlike quality (Gaunt 176), its details carefully chosen for their symbolic properties. The subject's "pride is conveyed by his fashionable clothes," while "the smoking candle and the fading rose evoke the passing of time and the passing away of a spirit" (Oliver 84). It also alludes to medieval and early modern paintings by Van der Weyden, Michelangelo, and Rubens that depict Christ in the arms of His mother (Cieszkowski). More important for my purposes, the painting is a "point where four very different lives meet and overlap" (Cieszkowski)—a nexus of influence and interaction between eighteenth- and nineteenth-century cultures and between "genuine" and "forged" art, a kernel of energy from which multiple vectors flow.

Chatterton made a big splash. John Ruskin deemed it "faultless and wonderful: a most noble example of the great school" (qtd. in Cieszkowski). Pre-Raphaelite maven Holman Hunt gushed that "the cruelty of the world towards poor Chatterton . . . will never henceforth be remembered without recognition of Henry Wallis" (qtd. in Clingham 50). He was right: the painting fixed "the figure of the boy poet in the Victorian imagination: languid, auburn-haired, and refined" (Crane 28); it also occasioned the "resurgence of academic interest in Chatterton in the 1850s and '60s" (Cook 201). So popular was the painting that when it was exhibited in Manchester in 1857, it had to be guarded by policemen (Oliver 84).[14]

Twenty-five years old (eight years younger than Mary Ellen Meredith) when he completed *Chatterton,* Henry Wallis was the son of a wealthy architect. He favored works with a literary theme, as in his *Dr. Johnson at Cave's the Publisher* (1854), and in several paintings he depicted a young Shakespeare. He never again matched the popularity of the Chatterton oil, though he came close with *The Stonebreaker,* a powerfully expressive portrait of a collapsed quarry worker, finished the following year. Diane Johnson notes that in biographies of Meredith, Wallis figures as a malevolent shadow who "appeared at an inopportune moment to seduce Mrs. Meredith, father a child on her, and vanish like an incubus at her death" (103). In fact, he supported his illegitimate son throughout his life. But his relationship with the Merediths permanently altered the direction of his career: after giving up painting in the early 1860s he traveled around the globe and became an authority on ceramics, publishing important volumes on Italian majolica and other early modern ceramics. He never married. Little information is available about Wallis, who lurks at the penumbra of this artistic seance. One thing is clear, however: Chatterton's ghost reshaped his artistic persona.

The son of a Portsmouth tailor who went bankrupt, George Meredith was ashamed of his background. In a striking coincidence, just before his eighteenth birthday he, like Chatterton, was apprenticed to a solicitor, in this case Richard Charnock (Lindsay 30). Like young Tom, he arrived in London as a teenager, bubbling with ambition and energy. Tall and athletic, with curly auburn hair, young George was handsome but callow. He met his future wife through the *Monthly Observer*, a literary magazine that Charnock funded and to which Mary Ellen, then he, contributed. Until very late in their marriage he was an artistic failure. But if *Chatterton* was a dram of toxin for the Merediths' marriage and for Wallis's life as a painter, it was a tonic for George's writing career.

A Disappointed Inkstand

> She can be as wise as we,
> And wiser when she wishes;
> She can knit with cunning wit,
> And dress the homely dishes.
>
> —Meredith, "Marian"

Mary Ellen came from an estimable literary family: her father, the novelist Thomas Love Peacock, was a good friend of the Shelleys, and their circle "preferred advanced females" (D. Johnson 27). A clever, beautiful young woman (fig. 6), she justified her father's conviction that "girls could be as strong, as spirited, as intelligent and learned as men" (D. Johnson 46). She was also acerbic, moody, and afflicted with kidney disease. Six years older than Meredith, she met him after her first husband, Edward Nicolls, died while trying to rescue a sailor whose boat had capsized. Although the Nicollses' marriage lasted only two months, the couple produced a daughter, Edith. Meredith met Mary

FIG. 6. Henry Wallis's pencil drawing of Mary Ellen Meredith (1858). Pencil on paper, 22 × 25 cm. (Image © Ashmolean Museum, University of Oxford)

in 1846 and was immediately smitten; he is reported to have proposed to her five times before she finally accepted (Jones 51). Although her father didn't care for Meredith, he nonetheless attended the wedding of the twenty-one-year-old groom and twenty-seven-year-old bride on August 9, 1849.

The marriage was initially a brilliant success, as the couple together produced literary works as well as a son, Arthur. In June 1849 Mary Ellen published a poem, "The Blackbird," in which the title avian loses his mate; a "loveless prisoner," he sings a lament to all who come near. Meredith loved the poem so much that a few years later he revised it and published it along with his own poetic gloss (Meredith, *Poems* 74–76; the poem is alluded to in *Feverel* 205). At this point she was more successful than her husband: his 1851 collection of poems flopped, while a cookbook she had coauthored sold well (D. Johnson 81). To make matters worse, this artist of cuisine was wed to a man with such terrible digestive problems that the Peacocks' friend Thomas Hogg dubbed him "The Dyspeptic" (82–83). Mary eventually grew exasperated with her husband's refusal to find a paying position. Once she sent him for an interview, but he "forgot," wandered off, and came home jobless: he was determined "not to take a position which he felt would break down his resistances to an oppressive world" (Lindsay 78). His first novel, an Arabian-themed fantasy called *The Shaving of Shagpat* (1855), won favorable reviews but few readers. In 1854 Mary posed for Wallis's painting *Fireside Reverie,* which was accompanied by a Meredith quatrain that ends, "She, that by the fire so gravely dreams" (D. Johnson 90). Mary Ellen's dreams were increasingly not about her husband. She kept a commonplace book where she transcribed favorite passages; its selections reveal guilt that she no longer loved George and show a longing for "a higher morality in which love and independence had a place—in which people were not bound legalistically to other people" (107). The couple quarreled frequently and bitterly. High-strung, hot-headed, strong-willed, each one an "incomparable wielder of the rapier of ridicule" (qtd. in Austin 138), they "sharpened their wits on each other," remembered Edith (qtd. in D. Johnson 94).

And then came *Chatterton.*

Rapid Falcons in a Snare

> Like sculptured effigies they might be seen
> Upon their marriage-tomb, the sword between;
> Each wishing for the sword that severs all.
>
> —Meredith, *Modern Love* I

No one knows how or precisely when Mary's affair with Wallis began, but in the spring of 1856 (after the painting was completed), Mary invited him to stay with her and George upon Wallis's return from France. That Christmas George wrote to a friend that Mary was residing at Blackheath—not with him. By the spring of 1857 she was traveling to Wales with Wallis (her father recommended which waterfalls to visit) and then moved to a cottage in Clifton, near Bristol (Chatterton's hometown), where, on April 18, 1858, she bore a son named Harold. Meredith was listed as the father, but there was no doubt in anyone's mind that Wallis was the child's real father: the birth certificate was not exactly a forgery but certainly a fraud. (Later Harold took the name Felix Wallis.) Then the couple dashed off to Capri—perhaps for a lark, but more likely to improve Mary's health, which was again declining as a result of kidney disease and many pregnancies and miscarriages. Young Arthur Meredith stayed with the Nicolls family, but by the time Mary returned, George had taken the boy and refused to give him back. Not only had

Mary lost her son; she had returned alone. The conventional view is that Wallis abandoned her, but it is just as likely that they simply "went underground" (D. Johnson 133).[15] What is certain is that Mary Ellen became seriously ill and that, until very late in her illness, her husband (they never divorced) refused to let her see her son (Jones 88). By this time she was living alone, unable to care for Harold/Felix. In October 1861 she died; neither Meredith nor Wallis attended her funeral. On her headstone is this versanelle by Tennyson:

> Come not when I am dead,
> To drop thy foolish tears upon my grave,
> To trample round my fallen head
> And vex the unhappy dust thou would'st not save.
> There let the wind sweep and the plover cry;
> But thou, go by.

Meredith was loath to talk about her or the circumstances of their separation, and when he did speak his recollections were graceless and unforgiving. The man was not smiling. For example, in a June 1864 letter to his friend William Hardman, he writes, "To say that she approached madness without being quite mad is to express her mental and moral character. She dallied with responsibility, played with passions, rose suddenly to a height of exaltation, sank to a terrible level. And was very clever" (*Letters* 1:262). In old age his memory was even more self-justifying: "She was mad, you know. . . . A mistake, a sad mistake. No sun warmed my rooftree" (qtd. in D. Johnson 97).[16] Thus did he exculpate himself—this man who became renowned as a protofeminist. Biographer Mervyn Jones argues that the experience deepened Meredith's "sympathy for women," a theme that "resounds as a *leitmotiv* through all his novels" (94). This is not unfailingly true. It is true, however, that Meredith channeled his jealousy, rage, and pain into his art, especially into *Modern Love* and *Richard Feverel.* The ghost of Chatterton presides over this real-life story: had Meredith not posed as Chatterton, Mary and Wallis would likely never have had their affair. But we would not have *Modern Love,* one of the most important poetic cycles of the nineteenth century, nor would we have *Richard Feverel.* Indeed, Meredith's impersonation was as fruitful as Chatterton's: although the painting and its aftermath poisoned the Merediths' marriage, it nurtured the writer who became George Meredith. To bring about that resurrection there had to be sacrifice, but this time it was neither the forger nor his impersonator; it was Mary. It was as if the painting passed to her the Chatterton bargain, which stipulates that one may give birth to an author, but only if someone dies.

Love's Ghost

> 'Tis morning: but no morning can restore
> What we have forfeited. I see no sin:
> The wrong is mixed. In tragic life, God wot,
> No villain need be!
>
> —*Modern Love* XLIII

The fifty poems of *Modern Love*, first published in 1862, chronicle a marriage that strongly resembles the Merediths'. The poems, which Meredith called sonnets, are sixteen-line lyrics, numbered but untitled, and arranged in four quatrains (abba cddc effe, ghhg).[17] The third-person narrator sets the scene in the first nine poems, retreats, allowing the husband's voice to take over (although the two perspectives blend at times), then returns at the end. The elusive narrative presents waves of attraction and separation in a "ceaseless discovery of fluctuations" (Lucas 26) alongside a battle for dominance that neither party can win (Kozicki 144). The wife, referred to as "Madam," has had an affair, which the husband learns of in a letter he finds (XV); they host a dinner party at which they pretend everything is fine. The husband takes a blonde lover ("Lady"), and the two women meet (XXXVI), after which the husband and wife try to make up (XLII). They have a frank talk and seem to reconcile, but the wife disappears and then commits suicide by taking poison (XLIX). Her death is the locus of Chatterton's haunting: as Jones notes, "Suicide by poison had a significance for Meredith reinforced by the Chatterton picture, by reading *Madame Bovary* and by his own description of Clare Forey's suicide" in *Feverel* (93). But whereas in Chatterton's life and Wallis's painting the subject ingests poison, in *Modern Love* (and in *Feverel*) the toxin is transferred to the wife: women, real and fictional, are the sacrificial victims.

Modern Love employs a complex set of image clusters involving eyes, silence, knives, and stone. More important for our purposes are repeated tropes of poison, venom, snakes, and serpents, which are introduced in the first sonnet and recur until the wife consumes the fatal draft in the next-to-last poem (see Barr 284). As Elizabeth Wright pointed out many years ago, the wife's death by poison is foreshadowed in the first poem's lines, which refer to drinking "the pale drug of silence" (I.10; Wright 4). Like *Aella, Modern Love* is deeply indebted to *Othello:* in all three works sexual jealousy impels lovers to act irrationally and results in one party's death. I am not contending that in these poems Meredith was directly influenced by Chatterton's verse drama; I propose, rather, that the texts are entwined through the intermediary of Shakespeare's tragedy. Although the lovers "ape the magnanimity of love" (II.15), their marriage is a fraud, in retrospect rendering their signatures on the marriage license invalid. All these elements, but particularly the poisoning motif, invoke the shade of Chatterton.

In the second poem the narrator remarks that each lover "sucked a secret, and each wore a mask, / But, oh, the bitter taste her beauty had! / He sickened as at the breath of poison- flowers" (4–6). Soon she sends a message displaying "hypocrisy designed: / She treated him as something that is tame" (V.3–4). In the next poem the husband, after kissing her, wonders about the "price of blood-drops, as I know, / For whom the midnight sobs around Love's ghost." Inwardly, he asks, "What's the name? . . . the new name thou hast won" (i.e., her lover's name), while they sit by the fire, laughing (VI.7–8). Poem IX elaborates on the toxin motif as she looks up at him and "from her eyes, as from a poison-cup, / He drank until the flittering eyelids screened"; he compares her body to an "intoxicating grape" (11–12, 15). Images of poison and serpents recur in XXVI, where love, first likened to an eagle, metamorphoses into a "subtle serpent," and he believes that she must "bear all the venom of his tooth" (l.8, 16). The serpent insinuates itself into poems XXXII and XXXIII, the latter of which alludes to Raphael's painting *St. Michael Striking down the Demon;* by poem XXXIV the serpent has shed its skin and assumed a new guise; now both lovers' eyes "dart scrutinizing snakes" (9): the venom does not issue from an outside source, but from the couple themselves.

Sonnet XV is the nexus for the Chatterton and *Othello* allusions as well as a turning point for *Modern Love* as a whole. Entering his wife's chamber, the husband notices how "low / Hangs that abandoned arm toward the floor" (1–2): she lies in the same position that Meredith/Chatterton does in Wallis's painting. Indeed, she seems inhabited by the spirit of Chatterton (as rendered by Wallis) when the husband thinks,

"Sleep on: it is your husband, not your foe. / The Poet's black stage-lion of wronged love, / Frights not our modern dames:—well if he did!" (4–6). Contemplating her "waking infant-stare," he scans her handwriting in a letter to him, then reads "another letter lately sent. / The words are very like: the name is new" (15–16). This letter is, alas, *not* forged: it is proof of her affair. Pauline Fletcher, tracing this poem's allusions to Shakespeare's tragedy, argues that the husband constructs his wife's infidelity out of "trifles light as air," thus becoming a "super-subtle Venetian" more akin to Iago than to Othello (91, 97). Au contraire. A love letter from one's spouse to another lover is scarcely a trifle. Yet the wife apparently does not fear that he will find it as the "black stage-lion" espied the infamous handkerchief. While the husband appears to eschew Othello's violent reaction, the allusion to the Chatterton painting, with her in the dead boy's position, implies that he has already mentally murdered her. We may imagine him echoing Othello's question

> Was this fair paper, . . .
> Made to write "whore" upon? . . .
> I should make very forges of my cheeks,
> That would to cinders burn up modesty,
> Did I but speak thy deeds. (4.2.71–72)

This marriage is dying; the letter is the poison cup.

Meanwhile, they pretend that all is well. Sonnet XVII finds them playing hosts, but their guests "see no ghost," as with "sparkling surface-eyes" the couple performs a "most contagious game: / HIDING THE SKELETON, shall be its name" (4, 6–8). The corpse of their marriage, like Chatterton in Meredith's works, is invisible but pervasive. In XXXV the game changes its character when the husband recalls how

> At Forfeits during snow we played, and I
> Must kiss her. "Well performed," I said: then she:
> "'Tis hardly worth the money, you agree?"
> Save her? What for? To act this wedded lie! (13–16)

Forfeits is a guessing game, the forfeits being the actions a losing player performs as punishment.[18] This husband's punishment is to kiss his wife! But he is an experienced game player. For example, in XX he finds a "wanton-scented tress" from a previous lover and wonders "if for those times I must ask charity / Have I not any charity to give?" (15–16). It is hardly just to blame her for an affair when he has not been faithful himself. Instead of accepting this truth stoically, he decides to seek a lover as a "Distraction," even while recognizing his course of action as the devil's snare (XXVII.1, 10). Sometimes, however, he is more witness than player: when his wife and his lover meet and compliment each other, he "stand[s] amazed" at their skillful dissembling (XXXVI). Soon he asks, "Can I love one, / And yet be jealous of another?" He vacillates, fearing that his "old love may be alive" and has "seized [his] nursling new love by the throat" (XL.15–16). Caught between wife and mistress, he can commit to neither; it is as if the dying marriage, like rotten fruit, taints everything that touches it.

In Sonnet XLIII the husband visits the shore, seeking to "dig Love's grave." But nature offers no relief. Gazing at the ocean, he beholds breakers "dart their hissing tongues high up the sand": the serpentine imagery, with its hint of poison, has migrated from the lovers to the natural world. Realizing that "no morning can restore / What we have forfeited," the husband parses blame and, in the lines that form the epigraph to this section, decides that "the wrong is mixed," that the finger of guilt points at each of them, that both are "betrayed by what is false within." No evil serpent is seducing an innocent victim; it is in their nature—and perhaps in human nature—to love more than one, to engage in hypocrisy and deception.[19] The couple walk along the shore, "parley" (XLVI.1), and seem to forgive each other. Opening their "inmost hearts," they drink "the pure daylight of honest speech. / Alas! That was the fatal draught" (XLVIII.8). Instead of a welcome air-clearing followed by make-up sex, the honest dialogue only spurs further alienation: the wife tells him he may go to the Lady, then vanishes. The voice now switches back to the third-person narrator, who tells us that the wife believes "his old love had returned" (XLIX.3). That night she calls him to her bed: "'Now kiss me, dear! it may be now,' she said. / But Lethe had passed those lips, and he knew all" (15–16). She has poisoned herself.

The young woman is not smiling.

"Thus piteously Love closed what he begat!" begins the final sonnet. "These two were rapid falcons in a snare, / Condemned to do the flitting of the bat." Indeed, "each applied to each that fatal knife": whereas Aella stabs himself, these lovers (metaphorically) stab each other. Given the biographical context, many critics contend that Meredith could have been much crueler to the wife, that her offenses "pale" beside his "merciless excoriation of his cruelties and stupidities" (J. Holmes 531). On the other hand, Diane Johnson argues that Meredith wrote the poem "in a mood of self-vindication, for it would be read by people who knew his personal history"; thus, having the wife "magnanimously" kill herself is "sheer wish-fulfillment" (208). It is true that only the wife dies; despite the husband's and narrator's apparent even-handedness, her suicide cannot help but seem a vindictive act of proxy revenge by Meredith. In any case, Wallis's *tableau morte* influences the poem, as evidenced by its recurrent images of poison, culminating when the wife kills herself. Perhaps Chatterton's forgeries are themselves the poison; as we have seen, forgeries are deemed toxic by the literary establishment. The painting is also reproduced in the scene in which she becomes the Chatterton figure, building on the hint of femininity in Meredith's impersonation. Unlike Chatterton, she dies for love, but for art too, because *Modern Love* distills grief and rage into a mixture that, however poisonous for Meredith's fictional and real wives, was a revivifying elixir for him.

The Soul's Ordeal

> For I am not the first who found
> The name of Mary fatal!
>
> —Diaper Sandoe, *The Ordeal of Richard Feverel*

Alan Barr aptly observes that *Modern Love* "juxtaposes, largely to subvert and expose it, the courtly, sentimental, relatively static (lyric) mode of the sonnet tradition with the narrative, often satiric or ironic, . . . realistic characteristics of the novel" (289). Meredith was writing such an ironic novel while Mary Ellen was conducting her affair: *The Ordeal of Richard Feverel.* In it Sir Austin Feverel rears his son according to a rigid system, one element of which is a profound mistrust of women. Why the misogyny? Because Sir Austin has undergone the same experience that Meredith did. As the narrator tells us early in the novel, this story is "by no means new. He had a wife, and he had a friend" (9). The friend, Denzil Somers, a "sort of poet" who writes under the name Diaper Sandoe (9), entices Lady Feverel to, well, touch "his guitar in her chamber" (10). Although Sir Austin forgives him, "the woman he could not forgive," for she has "blackened the world's fair aspect for him" (11).

Consequently, Sir Austin's features become a "flexible mask" covering his pain (11).[20] He tries to hide the skeleton, but it keeps escaping from its tomb to lodge in his mind: he imagines his estranged wife as a "phantom" mocking him, and the memory "seized and convulsed his heart, and filled its unforgiving crevices with bitter ironic venom" (111). As in *Modern Love,* a toxin affects both lovers.

Indeed, *Richard Feverel* is, in part, a study of how bitterness poisons a soul. Sir Austin believes that women are "our ordeal. Love of any human object is the soul's ordeal" (162). The system by which he raises Richard is, as Meredith stated in a letter, Sir Austin's "way of wreaking revenge" (*Letters* 1:40). But in seeking to restrain and protect his impetuous son, he succeeds only in making him defiant and setting him up to fall in love with the first lovely young woman he meets. In depicting the dangers of bitterness, perhaps Meredith worked through his own feelings of betrayal. Or maybe not: when Lady Feverel reappears in chapter 39, Richard takes her away from Sandoe, who has metamorphosed into a "decrepid butterfly chained to a disappointed inkstand" (364). "Poetic justice had been dealt to Diaper the poet" by Meredith the novelist (365), who punishes him as he likely wished he could have punished Henry Wallis, ripping his lover away and leaving him alone in his old age. Lady Feverel fares no better. She returns just as the married Richard becomes involved with the (married) seductress Bella Mount, and his guilt over the affair indirectly causes his wife's death. Indeed, the two unfaithful women are virtually identified, injecting a creepy oedipal subtext to Richard's affair. As Richard's mother is for Sir Austin, so Bella, called "Bella Donna," is the dram of poison for Richard (358). Although the women are not the only lovers to suffer, they bear the brunt: Richard's ingenuous wife Lucy succumbs to "brain-fever," and his cousin Clare, secretly in love with him for years, dies by taking poison after marrying a man she doesn't love. These punitive inventions may have helped Meredith purge his rage, but they indicate the lingering presence of the Chatterton painting (and Chatterton's death) in Meredith's life and art.

A Proper Exchange

> Helpless and ould am I alas! and poor;
> No house, ne friend, ne moneie in my pouche;
> All yatte I call my owne is this my silver crouche.
>
> —Chatterton, "An Excelente Balade of Charitie"

That presence is even more palpable in a poem that Meredith published in March 1861 and republished alongside *Modern Love.* "The Beggar's Soliloquy" amounts to a gloss on, or riposte to, "An Excelente Balade of Charitie." We know that Meredith read Chatterton's poem, for he quotes its sixth line—"'Twas nowe the pride, the manhode of the yeare"—in an 1883 letter to Louisa Lawrence (*Letters* 2:700). Despite its title, Chatterton's poem is not a ballad, but Meredith's is, employing the conventional iambic tetrameter in octave stanzas (ababcdcd) throughout. As in Chatterton's poem, a beggar waits outside a church, but Meredith's pilgrim, unlike Chatterton's, seems happy with his lot. Echoing Sir Austin Feverel, he avoids women, deeming them nothing but a "plateful of vanity pepper'd with vice" (V, 155). He also despises stingy shopkeepers: "The poor and the rich in giving agree: / Your tight-fisted shopman's the Radical mean" (VIII). Most importantly, the beggar's ethos, expressed in stanza XI, presents a pithy (if self-interested) argument for charity, explicitly stating what is implicit in Chatterton's poem:

> Now giving and taking's a proper exchange,
> Like question and answer: you're both content.
> But buying and selling seems always strange;
> You're hostile, and that's the thing that's meant.
> . . . . If Charity's Christian, don't blame my pursuits,
> I carry a touchstone by which you're tried. (157)

He recalls a girl in London who tendered him a shilling, which he promised to repay "in a better sphere," like the priest in Chatterton's poem who awaits his reward from the saints. Unlike her, the churchgoers exiting the sanctuary "hate chaps to beg": church attendance allows them to give lip service to the creed of loving one's neighbor (158).

Meredith's and Chatterton's poems each use a beggar to attack hypocrisy. In both, mendicants are moral touchstones, yardsticks for the values that many apparent Christians fail to enact. Both poems also posit a gift economy in opposition to mercantile exchange. Whereas in the latter, parties calculate benefits versus costs and aim to balance accounts, in the former, the exchange cements a personal connection in which repayment may be postponed indefinitely. Although Meredith seeks a comic effect and Chatterton accents pathos, both poems champion charity as the most genuine currency in the moral economy. Only such true coin permits a "proper exchange." The other exchange here is intertextual, between a dead poet and a living one, in which Chatterton, in effect, dies to give birth to Meredith's authorial self. *Richard Feverel* and *Modern Love*—Meredith's first mature novel and his finest work as a poet—reach a higher plane of literary achievement than he had previously attained. Both issued from the umbra of Chatterton's death, as portrayed by Wallis and enacted by Meredith.

One of Mary Ellen Nicolls's articles for the *Monthly Observer* was a meditation on death, written in French and published in January 1849, before her marriage to Meredith. In light of her subsequent suffering and early demise, its sentiments seem at once prophetic and pathetic. Yet her attitude is neither: it is Romantic, recalling the philosophy underlying poems such as Wordsworth's "We Are Seven." She writes, "We see that in nature, all death is birth," and this is true for human souls (qtd. in D. Johnson 74). The same axiom may apply to artists. Chatterton's writings were peopled by ghosts, both of those who lived in flesh and of those who lived only in ink. Those specters inspired him; he, in turn, inspired writers who followed. Likewise, the deaths chronicled here—Chatterton's actual death and his painted one, as well as those of Mary Ellen and the women in Meredith's works—fostered the birth of new selves. Chatterton lived on as a muse and presiding genius for those who wrote in his wake. Meredith, who "died" as Chatterton, was resurrected as a better author (though probably not a better human being). The sacrifice of his old self, of his marriage and his spouse, germinated his mature works and gestated a new author: the esteemed Victorian novelist, George Meredith. Was it worth it?

Resurrectionists

Patchwork

> To *live,* then *die,* man was not *only* made.
> There's yet an awful something else remains
> Either to lessen or increase our pains!
>
> —Chatterton, "Impromptu on the Immortality of the Soul"

Wallis's *Chatterton* also midwifed Peter Ackroyd's *Chatterton,* a witty, illuminating novelistic meditation on artistic creation and the relations between fact and fiction. As he states in his preface to Nick Groom's edited volume *Thomas Chatterton and Romantic Culture,* Ackroyd aims to place both Chatterton and himself within a tradition of those who have employed a "mixture of historical styles as a form of ludic comprehension of the past" (2). The novel presents Chatterton as what Laura Savu terms a "spectral trace" (126) occupying a "paradoxical" condition of "absence as presence" that typifies his position in Romantic and post-Romantic literary history (J. Williams 36). Fakery and fraud abound in Ackroyd's novel, as the story encompasses a forged portrait, spurious documents, at least one plagiarized novel, and a set of bogus artworks. Ackroyd cleverly weaves in quoted and misquoted phrases and sentences, challenging readers to guess which are original and which are borrowed, engaging us in "an impossibly expansive and entertaining game" (Westerman 354): his own version of Hide the Skeleton. In so doing, notes Savu, he presents novel-writing and life-writing as palimpsests that dissolve "the boundary between historical fact and imagined fact, between the historical figure and the invented one" (106). Animated by the spirit of forgery, Ackroyd presents faking as a form of play or challenge; by layering together different periods and various forms of fraudulence, he indulges in his own brand of fakery.

What happened to George Meredith happens in this novel to an unpublished twentieth-century poet named Charles Wychwood: he *becomes* Chatterton. Hoping to sell an old book on eighteenth-century flute playing at an antique shop, Charles encounters a portrait depicting a middle-aged man holding manuscripts in his left hand, his right hand hovering over four quarto volumes (Ackroyd, *Chatterton* 11). The subject's eyes bear "an expression of sardonic and even unsettling power" (11), and so, despite a warning that "there is death on that face!" (12), Wychwood trades the flute book for the painting. While cleaning the painting at home, he licks his finger and jokingly tells his son, Edward, that he is "eating the past"—an apt description of Ackroyd's method—then feigns death, lying "with one arm trailing upon the carpet" (15). A bit later he testifies to feeling as though "he had become the painter" (22): he both impersonates Chatterton and "creates" him. His friend, librarian Philip Slack, identifies the painting's subject as Chatterton and the books as Chatterton's *Kew Gardens, The Revenge, Aella,* and *Vala* (23).[21] But wait: didn't he die as a teenager? Not if the painting is genuine, for it is dated 1802, when Chatterton would have been fifty years old. This conundrum compels Wychwood to seek more Chatterton materials and eventually to become possessed by the spirit of the young forger.

The boy poet lurks at the margins of the novel's action in the figure of a red-haired youth who appears on the street when Charles collapses (47) and as a denizen of Slack's library (72); he also shows up as a shadow in St. Mary Redcliffe church when Charles travels to Bristol (54). There Charles reads an inscription bearing the lines from Shelley's "Hymn to Intellectual Beauty" that begin "While yet a boy I sought for ghosts." This is what Chatterton did—and what his successors have done by reading and reconstituting him. (No such memorial exists in reality.) A pamphlet there reads: "Chatterton knew that original genius consists in forming new and happy combinations, rather than in searching after thoughts and ideas which had never occurred before"—a quotation from George Gregory's 1789 biography of Chatterton (Ackroyd 58). Also in Bristol, one member of a gay couple hands Charles a stack of Chatterton manuscripts to spite his lover, a man named Joynson, the descendant of the (fictional) first publisher of the Rowley poems. These documents fuel Charles's quest to know—to *become*—Chatterton.

Other artists soon get involved. One of them is Harriet Scrope, an elderly popular novelist who, unable to make progress on her autobiography, enlists Charles as her ghostwriter (40). A more appropriate position cannot be imagined, for he is, in an important sense, already a ghost, and Chatterton is ghostwriting Ackroyd's novel. Her writer's block is caused by a dark secret: she is a plagiarist, which Slack discovers when he comes across two nineteenth-century novels by one Harrison Bentley. Both novels are about fraud and impersonation: in *The Last Testament* a scholar discovers that a renowned poet's final works were actually written by his wife; *Stage Fire* features an actor who believes himself possessed by the spirits of dead Shakespearean actors (69).[22] In Harriet's rendition of the former, entitled *The Finer Art,* the poet's secretary forges the poems; the artist in the second novel is not an actor but a poet haunted by the spirits of dead writers (69). After publishing her first novel, Harriet felt bereft of ideas. Using *The Last Testament* as "support" (102), she wrote *The Finer Art.* Gaining confidence, she borrowed only the beginning of *Stage Fire* for her next novel, because "the experience of employing a plot, even though it was the invention of some other writer, had liberated her imagination" (103). As with forgers, so with this plagiarist: faking enables her to fashion a more inventive authorial persona.

Philip too once tried to write a novel but gave up when he realized it was just a "patchwork of other voices and other styles" (70). The description fits the novel we are reading, testifying to Ackroyd's thesis that originality is irrelevant and perhaps impossible, that all authors are patchwork figures, all texts intertexts. Literary creations are depicted here, as in virtually every text discussed in this study, as Frankenstein's monsters; in this formulation all authors are possessed by their predecessors.

Philip disinters another dusty tome, a memoir with art plates. One of them reproduces the Chatterton monument picture and states that Meredith, "with thoughts of self-murder after his wife's desertion, sat in the gloomy environs of St. Mary Redcliffe." He had purchased a vial of mercury and arsenic, but as he prepared to swallow it, he was halted by a young man's "hand laid upon his wrist" (70). Meredith's arrested suicide never happened, but this imaginary incident advances Ackroyd's portrayal of Chatterton's possessive power, as does a succeeding scene when Charles renews his acquaintance with a college friend, Andrew Flint. Though a successful novelist, Flint believes himself a hack and has embarked on a more reputable literary project: a biography of George Meredith. Yet he agrees that Meredith, like Shelley and Coleridge, "got it all from Chatterton" (77). And so did William Blake, according to another antique volume Philip discovers. This monograph, written by one Professor Homer Brillo, proposes that Blake was profoundly influenced by Chatterton (72). Presumably the good professor thoroughly scoured all available documents to mount his argument, which is also Ackroyd's: all texts are ghostwritten.

Forging the Forger

> Arise now from thy Past, as from the Dust that environs thee.
>
> —William Blake (fictional), as forged by (the fictional) Chatterton

Part 2 begins with a confession. Among the materials Charles procures from Joynson is a manuscript memoir allegedly written by Chatterton in which he proudly admits to having fabricated the Rowley works as part of his grand "Miracle": bringing "the Past to light again" (83) and reuniting the living and the dead (85). "This musty stuff," he recalls assuring his mother, "will make our Fortune." Yet for him the forgeries are mostly a delightful masquerade, a play in which he is a "strolling Player and this Chamber is [his] Theatre" (86). Why would such a talented lad resort to faking? Because, he avers (echoing or foreshadowing the comments of scholars such as Browning), anything he produced in his own name would have been "despised and neglected" (87). The masquerade continued in London where he was "young Thomas Chatterton to those I met" but "a very Proteus to those who read my Works" (89). So far the fictional Chatterton sounds very much like the self-dramatizing young man we've come to know, but now Ackroyd performs his own magic trick, introducing a fictional publisher named Joynson, who has detected the boy's forgeries and offers him a proposition: fabricate new works by other poets. Why, protests the proud prodigy, should he "stoop to *imitate* . . . the Verses of Poets much inferior to me?" Answer: "You cannot eat or drink Pride." Chatterton can prove his superior talent by "doing their Work better than ever they could" (91). Thus begins a scheme that will change the face of English literary history: Chatterton will sign his pastiches with the names of Gray, Akenside, Churchill, Collins, and, yes, Blake. He will be not only the "greatest forger in history" (94) but the most prolific and protean poet who ever lived. The confession is, we learn later, a fake—a forgery of a forger—which only makes it more Chattertonian. (Recall that the boy crafted a spurious will to wriggle out of his indentures.) Charles and Philip believe in its authenticity. Just as, according to Joynson, Chatterton has "other Authors within" him, so Chatterton hides within other authors (90).

Charles's wife, Vivien, is uneasy about her husband's Chatterton fetish. She has experience with forgeries, being employed at Cumberland and Maitland's art gallery, whose owners have learned of a trove of new paintings by the recently deceased artist Joseph Seymour. When Seymour's assistant, Stewart Merk, brings them to the gallery, however, he confesses that he painted them all himself: these are Merk's works (114). The canny Merk (short for Mercury?) points out that Seymour's recent death will add value to these creations. The gallery owners agree to sell them as genuine Seymours. This plot turn is far from implausible; in later chapters I examine the symbiotic relationship among art forgers, dealers, experts, and owners in which forgeries enhance the value of nonforgeries while lining the pockets of all involved. But this scheme is not as secret as the plotters hope: Vivien tells Harriet that the paintings are fake, triggering in her a craving to procure the portrait and the Chatterton papers.

As Charles struggles to write the introduction to his edition of the Chatterton texts, he finds himself able only to reproduce sentences he has already read or heard. Worse, every biography of the young bard depicts a "quite different poet: even the simplest observation by one was contradicted by another, so that nothing seemed certain." "If there were no truths, everything was true"; or, to put it another way, nothing was true (127). Moreover, Charles's Chatterton fixation is so dominating his life that his son warns, "Can't you see he's trying to hurt you?" (129). Because young Edward believes that Chatterton is alive, Charles brings the boy to the Tate Gallery to view the Wallis painting. As they stand before it, Charles seems to fall into the picture: suddenly it is he lying there "with his left hand clenched tightly on his chest and his right arm trailing upon the floor" (132). When he informs Edward that the model was George Meredith, the boy triumphantly proclaims, "So he's not dead yet!"

Here we are again, gazing at Wallis's painting.

A Model Poet

> The awful shadow of some unseen Power
> Floats though unseen amongst us.
>
> —Shelley, "Hymn to Intellectual Beauty"

Among the most illuminating elements in Ackroyd's postmodernist patchwork are the scenes depicting the Merediths and Wallis that begin in part 2. In the first scene the two men prepare to create the famous painting while exchanging ideas about aesthetics. Meredith proposes that art is "just another game" and hence "the greatest realism is also the greatest fakery" (139). For Wallis, however, there is no reality except "in visible things." Mary's entrance darkens the scene, for it is evident that she does not respect her husband, who jokes, "I am a model poet, at least. I am pretending to be someone else." Unamused, she remarks that she finds him "more natural on paper" than in person. "So I am a forgery but my writing is not?" She answers, "You must ask your looking glass that question" (141). The banter barely conceals her disdain while divulging that Meredith's compulsive clowning poorly masks his feelings of inadequacy. Wallis too realizes that their play is "in earnest" (143). (Ackroyd may have borrowed this scenario from *Modern Love.*) Reality and performance are not opposites: performance produces and educes real emotions; life imitates art.

Preparations continue as George jokes around, pretending to choke: "The poet has taken poison!" Wallis remarks, "You are Chatterton to the life" (155). But it is Wallis who seems possessed by the boy's spirit: Meredith declares, "You *are* a Resurrectionist, Henry. You can bring the dead to life" (156). Wallis here anticipates Orson Welles and Gaddis's Wyatt Gwyon, for whom fakers and forgers are sorcerers. Wallis revives Chatterton in order to kill him—and thereby bring him back to life again, just as Chatterton resurrected William Canynge through the medium of Rowley. But whereas Wallis believes only in what he sees, Meredith believes only in what he reads. For him, Chatterton's Rowley "has more life in him than any medieval priest who actually existed. . . . [N]o one had properly understood the medieval world until Chatterton summoned it into existence." Meredith proposes that the artist *creates* the world and that is why this painting "will always be remembered as the true death of Chatterton" (157). He may be right, but that scarcely enhances his real life, in which his death as Chatterton becomes a catalyst for the death of his marriage. It is as if the painting breaks through its frame. Soon Mary tells George she is leaving him (172). Serendipitously, they browse through some old paintings in a shop, among which is the portrait of the middle-aged Chatterton. Mary perceives George's future face in it. "What do you think, Mrs. Meredith," he asks; "Is he the original or merely a model?" (173). Chatterton, in the portrait, watches as their marriage dissolves. We do not know if he is smiling. Equally haunted, Wallis predicts that his work will show that Chatterton is not dead, for his painting has been "infused with the soul of Chatterton," a "soul that had not yet left the body" (164). Though it will "take on a different life as another painting in a world of painted objects," it will never be *merely* an object. "Neither he nor Chatterton could now wholly die" (170)—nor will Meredith *as* Chatterton. They are all resurrectionists.

If only they could help Charles, who collapses in a restaurant and wakes believing he is Chatterton. In his death throes he reenacts the Wallis painting, inhabiting the boy's corpse, sprawled in the Holborn garret. Charles dies, his position mirroring Chatterton/Meredith's in the painting (169) and placing Edward in young Tom's condition—a fatherless boy (Westerman 351). At Charles's funeral the Bard of Tropes is present: Vivien detects the "lineaments of a human face" in the X-ray of Charles's brain (179). Disgusted with everything Chattertonian, she gives the documents to Harriet, who already has the portrait.

A Finer Art

> Since we can die but once what matter it
> If Rope or Garter Poison Pistol Sword
> Slow wasting Sickness or the sudden burst
> Of Valve Arterial in the noble Parts
> Curtail the Miserys of Human Life
> Tho' varied is the Cause the Effect's the same
> All to one common Dissolution tends.
>
> —Chatterton, "Sentiment"

The above lines form one epigraph to part 3 of Ackroyd's novel, much of which is devoted to imagining Thomas Chatterton's final day on earth. He was correct that we all end up equally dissolved but wrong that the method of death matters not: if Chatterton had succumbed from a streptococcus infection, it is doubtful that the Romantics would have made him their guiding star. In Ackroyd's telling, Tom's mood on that August day is ebullient and enthusiastic; he feels so exhilarated living in a garret above the city that he completes an elegy and a satire before eight a.m.! When he tells his friend Daniel Hanway that he fears he has caught the clap from his landlady, Hanway informs him of a "kill-or-cure" treatment—arsenic mixed with opium—which Chatterton procures from an apothecary, fibbing that he needs the tincture to treat stomach cramps (195). He assures the druggist that he has no intention of committing suicide, though for the sake of debate he quotes the line from "The Unfortunate Fathers" (suicide as a "noble insanity of the soul"). Afterward the apothecary recounts this incident, "with appropriate embellishments, to anyone who cares to listen" (197). Chatterton's mood sinks after an encounter with an intellectually disabled boy he finds standing before a ruined house. He gives sixpence to the boy, who says his name is Tom. "Better to give him arsenic," Chatterton thinks, "than to leave him undefended against this harsh world" (210). The boy will be "always known as Tom" (211). Here is another Chatterton avatar representing an element in his makeup: the poor child alone in the metropolis, a version of the pathetic victim imagined by the Romantics. A besotted evening with Hanway raises our Tom's mood again, and on the way home, he invents some verses that, invoking "Songe to Ella," forecast his afterlife:

My syllables, the remnants of antiquity
Will come back as shadows of posterity
Let this my song bright as my vision be.
As everlasting as futurity. (216–17, italics in original)

Ackroyd crosscuts repeatedly between these scenes and the twentieth-century events in the wake of Charles's death. These montage-like juxtapositions imply parallels: as Chatterton buys the drugs, Harriet brings the portrait of the middle-aged Chatterton to the gallery. Her act "kills" him again, for Cumberland and Maitland immediately determine that the painting is a fake: the hair is wrong, the furniture shown wasn't in style until the 1830s, and, most definitively, another face is detectable beneath Chatterton's. Harriet suggests, however, that a good forger could solve these problems—at once indicating her awareness of the Merk forgeries and appealing to the owners' greed (201). They agree to leave it to Merk, who detects that "the face itself seemed to have acquired the characteristics of three or four different images" (205). In other words, the painting embodies the protean nature of its subject: though forged, it is a genuine Chatterton. In the same spirit, Merk pledges to produce "the best fake you ever saw."

This discovery means that the Chatterton documents are also forged; hence, Vivien and Philip decide to return them to Joynson, back in Bristol. Joynson confesses that his ancestor, Chatterton's publisher, contrived the entire scheme. Wounded that the young poet had accused the publisher of buying up his work and abandoning him, Joynson, after Chatterton's death, fabricated the confession to "repay him in kind, to fake the work of a faker, and so confuse forever the memory of Chatterton; he would no longer be the poet who died young and glorious, but a middle-aged hack who continued a sordid trade with his partner" (221). Motivating Joynson's forgeries are the same passions that inflame most of the forgers discussed in this book: indignation, envy, greed, and a self-righteous (and self-deluded) belief in their own talent. Meanwhile, Merk works on the painting. After a solvent exposes the previous paintings, a catastrophe unfolds: the face dissolves, becoming "two faces, one old and one young," and then the entire painting bubbles, cracks, burns, and peels apart (228). As the painting melts, so, in the interlaced sections, does young Chatterton as the arsenic performs its lethal ministrations: he vomits, defecates down his leg, and inwardly shrieks, "I am being melted down" (227). He suffocates, bucks, convulses, and flies out from his body.

The young man is not smiling.

When young Edward goes to view the Wallis painting one last time, it seems "even more real . . . than before," and as he gazes at it, the painting seems to move and metamorphose: a breeze stirs the rose plant, two people enter the room, covering their noses and mouths, and the young poet bears the face of Edward's father (229). The vision consoles him, for he knows that his father "would always be here, in the painting. He would never wholly die" (230). Yet when he hears that the forged portrait has been destroyed, Edward exults, "Chatterton's dead!" (230). His spirit has passed to another person, this time Philip Slack, who now grasps that "there is no real *origin* for anything" (232). Pure originality is a chimera and all works are patchworks. These scenes suggest that the ghost of Chatterton is not merely a fatal miasma; it possesses a transfiguring power that permutes an object made of oil and canvas, of too, too solid flesh, or of paper and ink into something as everlasting as futurity. How? By inviting viewers and readers to believe in a reality beyond the mundane such that those perceiving it become cocreators and may even be inspired to fashion their own imaginative constructions. This is what happens to Philip, who decides that he can write a novel after all. It is the one we have been reading. Thus does *Chatterton* circle back on itself: Philip has been the implied author all along. Of course, lurking behind him are not only Chatterton, Meredith, and Wallis but Peter Ackroyd, the talented tailor who has stitched together these fragments, reincarnated and impersonated all three artists. He too has been inhabited by the spirit of Chatterton, forging a palimpsest not in paint but in print.

Despite its postmodernist trappings, Ackroyd's novel endorses the age-old maxim *vita brevis, ars longa.* Yet the cult of originality is challenged and choked not only by Chatterton himself—whose "fakes" were originals and whose "originals" were copies—but also by Meredith, whose imagination, kindled by his impersonation of a dead poet, permitted him to become a living poet. The veneration of originality is subverted by all the artists in the novel—plagiarist, forger, pasticheur—and by Ackroyd himself, who weaves together fiction and fact, present and past, to dramatize the power and range of artistic influence and possession. The tripled visions he presents imitate the multiple temporal layers engendered by all forgeries. Chatterton too dwelt among the ghosts he created or resurrected, breathing life into specters; his own "ghost" is doubled-edged, requiring a sacrifice that empowers other artists and nurtures other lives. Just as the prodigy's ghosts enabled him to craft a multifaceted authorial identity, his specter did the same work for those who followed. His forgeries engendered new scholarly methods, inspired later authors, and prompted enlightening investigations of the creative imagination. Chatterton's ghosts have made forgery a finer art.

The boy himself stars in the novel's final vignette. Dying, he finds himself flying back to St. Mary Redcliffe, where he views Rowley's tonsured head, passes a young man on the staircase, and quotes Wordsworth's as-yet-unwritten lines about poets in their youth ending in "despondency and madness" (233). But he is neither mad nor despondent; he is delighted, for he knows he "will live forever." When his body is found the next morning, "Chatterton is still smiling" (234).

2

"What King Forged I?"

FATHERS, FRAUDS, AND THE WORKS OF WILLIAM FAKESPEARE

> If there be nothing new, but that which is
> Hath been before, how are our brains beguiled,
> Which, laboring for invention, bear amiss
> The second burthen of a former child!
>
> —Shakespeare, Sonnet 59

An idle nineteen-year-old law clerk, seeking to gratify his Bard-besotted but unfond father, is blessed with a brilliant idea: What if he were to discover and present the patriarch with a documented signed by his idol? Papa might even praise the boy! Fortuitously, the lad finds such a document, then another, and then more; he even unearths a heretofore unknown Shakespeare play entitled *Vortigern.* His father is beside himself with pleasure. More than two hundred years later, a novelist, the son of a Bard-loving father, opens a safety deposit box where he finds a quarto edition of a lost Shakespeare play entitled *The Tragedy of Arthur.* The son, who professes not to like Shakespeare's work, is charged with proving its provenance and publishing it. Why not the father? Because he is in prison for forgery.

The first scenario, which took place in late 1794, was one of the most notorious frauds in literary history: the Ireland forgeries, a series of documents allegedly written and signed by Shakespeare but actually created by a teenager, William-Henry Ireland.[1] Although the boy eventually confessed, his father, Samuel, maintained until his dying day that the documents were genuine. The second occurs in *The Tragedy of Arthur* (2011), a novel by Arthur Phillips. That volume presents a 250-page "introduction" by Arthur Phillips, followed by the play—credited to Shakespeare. The "also by" page enumerates other works by Phillips and by Shakespeare. The title page reads "*The Tragedy of Arthur,* a novel by Arthur Phillips." Is this the same Arthur Phillips who has written the introduction? Is it a play or a novel? We are further confounded when we turn the page to find a preface, written by "The Editors of Random House," proudly proclaiming *The Tragedy of Arthur* to be a newly discovered play by Shakespeare, first published in 1597 and verified by a roster of eminent scholars. Yet the introduction—actually a bildungsroman about Arthur Phillips—avers that the play is a fake. What in the Globe is going on?

The two cases, one real and one fictional, smear the lines between those two domains, as forgeries always do. Beyond forgery, the two share a good deal. Each one revolves around a relationship between a father and children, invoking parallels between literary and familial provenance and disclosing anxieties about legitimacy and inheritance. In both instances the fakes are prompted by a longing to be loved, but whereas William-Henry Ireland began creating his forgeries mostly to make his father happy, *Arthur*'s play, if it is a forgery within its novelistic world (a question to which I return at the end of this chapter), was created to enrich the children and to vindicate the father's genius. In both instances William Shakespeare stands in for the problematic patriarch, and the son's disposition toward the documents involves a triangular relationship among him, the Bard, and the parent. In both cases (as in *My Life as a Fake* and *erasure*), the wayward child is analogous to the illegitimate literary creation. In both instances—as in most of the texts discussed herein—forgery becomes for the offspring a mode of self-formation and a means of fabricating an authorial identity.

Both forgeries succeed, at least temporarily, because people *want* to credit the Shakespeare documents: readers suspend disbelief in order to become collaborators with the greatest poet in the English language. Indeed, both believers and forgers build a Shakespeare in their own images; in that sense, the believers are also forgers. Through believers' imaginations, Shakespeare becomes a shadow, or a ghost like Chatterton, whose name is invoked less as an author than as a symbol of prestige, a synecdoche of fatherhood, and a synthesis of nostalgia, projected desire, and pure hubris. Rather than holding a mirror up to nature, Shakespeare and his works become a mirror of others' hopes and dreams. Phillips's novel and Ireland's hoax suggest that "William Shakespeare" is always a fictional product of readers' needs. Since we know so little about him, each reader creates her own Shakespeare, turning the Bard into what Joyce in *Finnegans Wake* calls an "epical forged cheque" with which we pay ourselves for our devotion (181).

These forgeries' credibility depends less on forensics than on faith, because, as I posited in the prologue, a forgery is only as successful as the stories that accompany it (see thesis 3). In this respect, forgeries are collaborative creative and research projects, of which the documents form only one part. The Ireland and Phillips examples demonstrate again that authorship, like paternity, is a legal fiction, that we invent our fathers and our authors by believing in their creative powers. The Ireland case and the Phillips novel dramatize this book's major themes: the dialectic between the desires for recognition and invisibility; the propensity for forgeries to inspire further fictions; forgeries as products of scholarship and test cases of intertextuality; the persistence of belief in the face of confounding evidence; the complexities of authorial identity. The two sets of forgeries also raise questions more peculiar to their circumstances: How does one know who his/her parents are? Are literary and physical parenthood truly analogous? Is there really any significant difference between illegitimate and legitimate authorship (and parenthood)? How do authorial identities change with the times? These real and fictional frauds bear out Ruthven's assertion that forgeries display a "'disruptive and capricious power'" to destabilize "the fragile economy of literary accreditation by drawing attention both to its conceptual shoddiness and [to] the expediencies that characterize its operations" (4).

Becoming the Bard

> Never did I before blame nature's work
> But now I fain wou'd quarrel with her hests,
> For that in me, she caus'd a lack of years;
> Else had these prayers, these blessings all been mine!
> To have a crown and kingdom at command
> Is but as dross; but thus to have them come
> Might from their airy beds the angels draw
> To taste the joys of this our mortal earth. . . .
>
> —Uter, in *Vortigern* (3.2) by "William Shakspeare"

> . . . the stain of birth
> Was ne'er forgot nor ne'er forgave in me
> No matter I upraised a glorious realm.
>
> —King Arthur, in *The Tragedy of Arthur* (5.3.14–16), by "William Shakespeare"

Bardolaters

Deism may have been the principal Protestant creed among late eighteenth-century English intellectuals, but another faith grew beside it: Bardolatry. Thanks largely to the distinguished actor and theatrical impresario David Garrick, Shakespeare emerged from a century and a half of near eclipse to become the guiding light of English letters. By the 1790s a market had boomed in Elizabethan literary relics—cups supposedly carved from a mulberry tree that had grown in Shakespeare's yard, swatches of fabric from Ben Jonson's vest. The veneration of the past also infected the theater where, in Jeffrey Kahan's words, "if it wasn't old, it wasn't good" (21), and if it was Shakespeare, it was gold. Although Shakespearean pastiches abounded, most older plays, including Shakespeare's, were abridged for accessibility or bowdlerized to suit the period's notions of propriety. In one notorious "improvement," *King Lear* was altered so that Cordelia survives (Kahan 23). Few people had read or seen an Elizabethan or Jacobean play in its originally published form. As Kahan observes, Shakespeare was the "phantom of the playhouse"—always present yet never really there (28). Even so, the enigmatic glover's son had become an icon of English culture, attaining a stature well beyond that of mere mortals: he was always "The Matchless Bard." In this atmosphere the discovery of Shakespeare's papers would be "the literary equivalent of the Crown Jewels" (D. Stewart 2).

The Samuel Ireland household was a temple of this religion. A prolific and popular travel writer and collector—as well as a tireless self-promoter and social climber—Samuel possessed numerous relics, including one of those mulberry cups and a favorite chair allegedly hewn from the same tree.[2] Nightly he read Shakespeare's works aloud to William-Henry and to his daughters Jane and Anna Maria, interrupting frequently to gush about the MB's glorious language and gigantic wisdom. His son he deemed a lazy dimwit: William-Henry had languished at several prestigious schools and had come half-awake only after being exiled to a private academy in France, where he had at least grown fluent in French. William-Henry's elder brother, Samuel, had died as a small child, yet his father insisted on calling the surviving son "Sam," as though William-Henry were the one who had perished (D. Stewart 6). There was no Mrs. Ireland; a woman called Mrs. Freeman, born Anna Maria de Burgh, served as housekeeper and manager. Although she was probably the mother of the three surviving children, she had previously been the mistress of the notorious libertine John Montagu, the Fourth Earl of Sandwich, who had sired children everywhere and (it was rumored) left Mrs. Freeman a fabulous parting gift of some L12,000—about a million dollars in today's American currency—as well as babies (see D. Stewart 13; Grebanier 270–71). Is it any wonder that the Irelands entertained doubts about the boy's paternity?[3]

Bogus

For a short period, however, a different author supplanted Shakespeare as evening entertainment: Herbert Croft, whose novel *Love and Madness* was a best seller. Based on a real murder case from 1779, it presents a protagonist named Mr. H., who kills his ex-lover in a fit of passion.[4] It was not this portion that riveted the Irelands; it was the long digression about Thomas Chatterton. As I outlined in chapter 1, Croft's book was both a literary and scholarly coup, providing for the first time a plausible chronology and bibliography of Chatterton's Rowley works, sympathetically presenting his motives and arguing that he was unfairly vilified. William-Henry was dazzled by the tragic young poet, seeing in his story similarities to his own condition: Chatterton had no father; William-Henry's disdained him; both were believed to be dullards; both worked as law clerks (D. Stewart 52). W-H wrote an acrostic poem to Chatterton and, according to his *Confessions,* envied his fate (11). William-Henry Ireland was probably the first author haunted (or inhabited) by Chatterton's ghost. Chatterton certainly influenced his orthography, for the Ireland forgeries employ eccentric spelling similar to that of Chatterton's forgeries, though not that of the Elizabethan—or any other—period. Croft's novel may have inspired William-Henry's forays into fraud, or perhaps the spark was the Irelands' visit to Stratford in 1793, where a farmer jokingly (and falsely) proclaimed that he had just destroyed a bundle of papers bearing Shakespeare's name—much to Samuel's chagrin. His appetite whetted, the elder Ireland intimated that he would "willingly give half his library to become possessed even of [Shakespeare's] signature alone" (*Confessions* 45; cf. *Authentic* 7). W-H now grasped how he might at once glorify his poetic idols and gratify his eager father.[5]

The young man had been imitating signatures for some time and speculated that if he copied one in earnest, he "might occasion a little mirth, and shew how far *credulity* would go in search for antiquities" (*Authentic* 3, emphasis his). And so he crafted a letter presenting a book to Queen Elizabeth, using vintage paper, remaking the seal by reheating and cooling the wax, and rubbing soot on it to conceal the difference. The ink, however, was poor, so bookbinder Thomas Laurie's assistant supplied an ink that turned brown rapidly. W-H showed the letter to his father, who "thought it genuine" (*Confessions* 40). This was a practice run; what he really needed was a Shakespeare relic that would, writes Bernard Grebanier, "at one stroke banish the cloud of illegitimacy, cancel the years of disappointment over his unfitness as a scholar, and . . . cause a warm spring of love to gush from his father's heart" (71). Purportedly "for mere frolick and diversion," the boy copied Shakespeare's handwriting on a mortgage deed recording a transaction involving him, fellow actor John Heminge, and one Michael Fraser and his wife (*Authentic* 7). W-H showed it to his father on December 16, 1794. At this point, William-Henry insisted, he aimed only to give his father pleasure and had "no intention whatever of attempting anything further" (9). But when he witnessed his father's delight and, perhaps more significantly, noticed how much attention the document attracted from curiosity seekers and the intellectuals his father ached to impress, he couldn't help himself: "Urged, partly by the world, and [his] own vanity," he persisted in his scheme (9).

Samuel wanted more. More he got: his son "discovered" a 1589 promissory note from Shakespeare to John Heminge pledging payment of a five-guinea debt in return for his "great trouble" in some business at the Globe (which did not exist at the time). The boy signed it with his left hand, which became a problem later. William-Henry was not aware that no promissory note from Shakespeare's day had ever been found (Grebanier 82). But no matter: the people he had targeted believed in it. Realizing he needed a convincing story of provenance, W-H invented a wealthy but imaginary personage he dubbed "Mr. H.," who had kindly granted him access to a massive trunk wherein he had found the documents. Mr. H. wanted to remain anonymous and desired no monetary reward; as a gentleman, he didn't wish to be pestered by questions and collectors. Samuel and his growing flock of gulls were satisfied.

William-Henry was not. It had long been whispered that England's National Poet might have been a closet Papist. The young forger could deflect this scandal by fashioning a document attesting to the Matchless

Bard's Protestantism.[6] Using the same eccentric spelling, the boy improvised the Bard's Profession of Faith, making sure to employ "many capital *double-yous* and *esses,*" which he had learned to copy from Shakespeare's actual signature (qtd. in Grebanier 91, italics in original). He proffered this document to his father on Christmas Eve. Near the end of its heartfelt and fulsome plea for God's mercy, W-H "Shakspeare" offers what he believes to be a powerful culminating image: "Forgive O Lord alle oure synnes ande withe thye grete Goodnesse take usse alle to thye Breaste O cherishe usse like the sweete Chickenne thatte under the coverte offe herre spreadynge Wings Receyves herre lyttle Broode ande hoveringe oerre themme keepes themme harmlesse ande in safetye" (S. Ireland, *Miscellaneous papers;* Grebanier 91). In the Beginning was the Bird! Could anyone read that final sentence without cackling? Yet some readers did not cry "fowl": eminent educator Samuel Parr, for instance, who examined the document and listened to Samuel read it aloud (as Will trembled with trepidation), was dazzled: "Sir, we have many very fine passages in our church service," he declared, "and our litany abounds with beauties; but here, sir, is a man who has distanced us all" (*Authentic* 16).

Nor did William-Henry find the image risible. Indeed, in his *Authentic Account,* he admits (ostensibly seeking to absolve his father of blame) that he was the forgeries' "onlie begetter." Similar humblebragging characterizes many of his writings about the affair and sheds light on what drove the boy to such extreme, even farcical, lengths. In his *Confessions,* for example, he inserts several speeches from his later Shakespearean pastiche, *Henry the Second* (168–75), as evidence of his talent. While W-H was fashioning Shakespeare as an aspiring but pious eighteenth-century gentleman who "paid [his] way," as Joyce's Mr. Deasy might say (*Ulysses* 25), he was also using Shakespeare to remake himself, to invent an improved William-Henry Ireland—not a ne'er-do-well law clerk but a budding litterateur. As other distinguished persons began to express their delight, it was easy for the impressionable teenager to believe that he had indeed unearthed the works of a literary genius—one named William-Henry Ireland. Will, though a novice fakesmith, was learning to forge himself. And so, "fired with the idea of possessing genius to which I had never aspired," he fell into what he calls the "gilded snare" that caused so much unhappiness (*Confessions* 69).

Believers

By early 1795 Samuel Ireland had turned his home into a museum of Shakespeareana. Some of the leading lights of English letters paraded through his Norfolk Street house, examining the papers and expressing belief in their authenticity: poet-critic Joseph Warton; Francis Webb, secretary of the College of Heralds; prominent critic James Boaden, who had helped expose the Chatterton forgeries; and, foremost among them, James Boswell, who, after perusing the documents, fell to his knees and cried, "How happy I am to have lived to the present day of discovery of this glorious treasure—I shall now die in peace." Then he kissed the papers (Kahan 83). None of these illuminati was a Shakespeare scholar, yet their blessing lent the papers a potent imprimatur. There were four people who could have blown the whistle at any time: bookbinder Laurie and his assistant; a chambermaid who frequently witnessed William-Henry committing his illicit deeds; and fellow clerk and would-be actor Montague Talbot, who had interrupted W-H in the act and then became a coconspirator. Not one of them spilled the beans. But why did the others believe? First, because belief is like a virus: it spreads more easily in groups (see thesis 13). When the men perused the papers together, the desire not to be viewed as a philistine overruled their skepticism. Second, because William-Henry's forgeries, which seem ridiculously transparent from a distance of two-hundred-plus years, came equipped with a compelling story: a mysterious trunk owned by a secretive, wealthy man who, for unknown reasons, trusted the lad with his treasure. The tale combined intrigue, class snobbery, and the thrill of sharing secrets. The Believers became a self-fashioned elite: believing made them bigger. Third, confirmation bias also played a part; as Doug Stewart puts it, "All the forgery does is suggest a plausible story. The forgery's victims see to it that the story comes true" (57). As in every forgery and hoax discussed in this book, the hoaxed collaborated with the hoaxer: thus, as Kevin Young aptly observes, victims "serve as the hoax's midwife, handmaiden, and ghostwriter" (209). Fourth, the piecemeal nature of the discoveries promised more juicy tidbits about the elusive Swan of Avon. Perhaps most of all, the papers provided a blueprint for self-invention. These men wanted to believe because doing so made them—and William-Henry—coauthors with Shakespeare. Like the Matchless Bard himself (in *The Winter's Tale*) and the artists in Ackroyd's *Chatterton*, they fancied themselves resurrectionists. Thus they failed to notice that Shakespeare's handwriting varied from document to document or to remark the similarity of this orthography to Chatterton's, and they raised not an eyebrow at the suspiciously convenient (and implausibly capacious) trunk that, as if relocated from St. Mary Redcliffe church, began to spew out Shakespearean documents like a printing press possessed by a poltergeist.

Bettering the Bard

William-Henry promised to show the full text of *Vortigern,* produced a series of financial documents involving the actors who had allegedly performed it, then fabricated a letter from Shakespeare's patron, the Earl of Southampton. These documents were verified as original—and original they were (Grebanier 106). Three other documents merit attention. The first responded to the sense of dissatisfaction surrounding Shakespeare's will, discovered in 1747. Why did the playwright leave only his "second-best" bed to his wife, Anne Hathaway? Was he unhappily married? Holding a grudge? Stingy? W-H now served as marriage counselor (or perhaps matchmaker), writing a love letter from Will to Anne conveying profound affection, complete with poem and lock of hair. He later claimed that the letter was "done to strengthen the authenticity of the papers" (*Authentic* 15), but he also wanted to impress the Believers and firm up their faith in the provenance of the play he was drafting. Both letter and poem are atrocious, and not just in their spelling. A single stanza of the latter should suffice:

> Is there inne heavenne aught more rare
> Thanne thou sweete Nymphe of Avon fayre
> Is there onne Earthe a Manne more trewe
> Thanne Willy Shakspeare is toe you. (qtd. in Grebanier 110)

This is doggerel, no doubt, yet Boaden found it full of "the utmost delicacy of passion and poetical spirit" (qtd. in Grebanier 111).[7] Why "Willy" would possess a letter he had already sent to his wife, along with his own hair, was not explained. (The balding Bard would have been wise to treasure every tress.) Emboldened by this success, W-H crafted an even more shocking document: a friendly letter from Queen Elizabeth to Will S. When Edmond Malone turned his gimlet eye to the Shakspeare Papers (as they were called, without the first "e"), this text most aroused his ire: he devotes nearly one hundred pages to dissecting its single paragraph. Indeed, the young forger stumbled here. For one thing, the letter mentions that Lord Leicester accompanied the queen to Hampton, but Leicester died in 1588, when Shakespeare was a twenty-four-year-old nobody who had yet to write a single play. Why would the Queen take notice of an unknown actor? And it was addressed to the Globe Theater, which had not yet been built and, in any case, was never on the Thames, as the letter indicates. Yet the Believers swallowed this royal repast whole. Why not, then, go ahead and forge a play?

Not just any play: *King Lear.* And while you're at it, why not improve it? After all, like so many of Shakespeare's dramas, it contains a good deal of "ribaldry" unworthy of the Matchless One. Young Ireland decided to "make alterations where [he] thought the lines beneath" the MB (*Authentic* 18), where actors had apparently altered his immortal words. He made other improvements as well. For example, many readers had raised a brow at Kent's brusque departing lines: "I have a journey, sir, shortly to go; / My master calls me, I must not say no" (5.3.321). Willy I. would better Willy S.:

> Thanks Sir butte I goe toe thatte unknowne Land
> Thatte Chaynes each Pilgrim fast within its Soyle
> Bye livynge menne mouste shunnd mouste dreadedde
> Stille mye good masterre thys same Journey tooke.

And so on (see S. Ireland, *Miscellaneous papers* 6–7). Ireland's MB also appended a headnote begging his readers not to blame him for the liberties he had taken when he had "deparretedde" from "Masterre Hollinneshedde" (Grebanier 118). Never mind that Shakespeare had blithely "deparretedde" from Holinshed whenever a play's exigencies required it, nor that he seemed to care not a whit about future readers (and did not even try to get the plays published).

Meanwhile, William-Henry composed what he hoped would be the first of many masterpieces, the tragedy *Vortigern,* handing the final pages to his father in April 1795. W-H now began to advocate (he *was* a law clerk) for himself, forging letters from Mr. H. praising William-Henry's wisdom and talent: "No *man* but your *son* ever wrote like *Shakspeare.* . . . If your son is not a second Shakspeare I am not a man" (qtd. in D. Stewart 118, italics in original). The boy's self-delusions, as well as his touching desire to impress (and best) his father, are palpable here. The Ireland family members busied themselves copying, pruning (it was too long for the stage), and improving the play, which W-H had been unable to revise, having been forced to deliver the pages as fast he could scribble them.[8] Negotiations with Richard Brinsley Sheridan, manager of the Drury Lane theater, soon became mired in financial disagreements. All the talk of money prompted a worry: What if a Shakespeare heir were to surface? All that work for nothing! The motives for William-Henry's next creation, then, were admittedly mercenary: to "stop all claims whatever to the papers" aside from his own (*Authentic* 23). His remedy? Forge a Will to forge a will.

Bequests

On June 12, 1795, William-Henry presented his father with a deed of gift signed by Shakespeare, dated 1604. According to the deed, every person who has ever read, witnessed, or performed a Shakespeare play should say a prayer of thanks to the man who rescued the apparently bibulous, hydrophobic MB from drowning. On some undated occasion, the MB, "toe merrye throughe Lyquorre," fell into the Thames, upon which a companion swiftly doffed his jerkin and jumped into the water, saving the Swan from a watery demise. That person's name? William Henry Irelande (S. Ireland, *Miscellaneous papers;* Grebanier 145–47). So strong was Shakespeare's gratitude that he bequeathed to his rescuer and descendants the rights to several of his plays. This document neatly deflected any rival claims to the copyrights of *King John, Henry IV,* and *Henry V,* as well as to W-H's recently discovered *King Lear.* It was a shame that in 1604 *King Lear* hadn't yet been written, but nobody noticed. Like all forgeries, this one bears a tale of false origins, but the origin story isn't merely that of the document: it is also the forger's. As Grebanier points out, William-Henry, "fairly well convinced of his own illegitimacy, is here giving himself an imposing genealogy" (147), meanwhile shoring up his family's finances for the foreseeable future. What could be more elegant?

A little too elegant, perhaps. Yet few questioned it; even William-Henry was astonished that the Believers had bought this bogus bequest. In that same packet was an even more explicit document, dated 1611, in which Will I., correcting Will S's damnably real 1616 will, bequeaths the rights to several plays to friends and associates, along with rings for his wife and daughter. (He forgets that he has two daughters.) Of course, he also mentions the very love letter that William-Henry had recently "found." Fakespeare makes Heminge his executor and distributes sums to various friends. His most generous bequest, however, is to "that Chylde of whome wee have spokenn butt who muste notte be named here"; this person receives more than £287, along with the rights to eight plays and another that was "neverr yett Impryntedd called Kyng Vorrtygerne," and to any further plays the Bard might write (S. Ireland *Miscellaneous papers;* Grebanier 170). The will contains numerous blunders, but the most obvious one is this: Shakespeare knew that the rights to his plays belonged to the companies that produced them. Incomprehensibly, then, he donates plays he does not own to those who already own them. (Malone notes this error in *An Inquiry,* 290.) This is indeed "'Will' in overplus!" (Sonnet 135). Perhaps readers' minds were clouded by the revelation that Shakespeare had begat a bastard, for this news opened the door to further intriguing possibilities. Maybe Heminge had raised the child. And if so, perhaps the elusive Mr. H. was his descendant! Young William-Henry was now writing an "overheated romance novel" (D. Stewart 126). But here the infant author outsmarted himself: if the illegitimate child owned the rights to *Vortigern,* then unless the forger could create a link between the child and the Irelands, William-Henry had just cut himself out of the profits of his own play! Sloppy errors aside, willful William-Henry had now fabricated two Wills: Shakespeare and himself.

Bodings

By that fall some members of the press were questioning these all-too-convenient discoveries. The *Morning Herald* began to publish Henry Bate Dudley's mock-*Vortigern* (before the play had even been staged). Montague Talbot, pressed to help his friend, wrote an account of dealing with the mysterious Mr. H. that, unfortunately, contradicted W-H's story. Young Ireland improvised well enough to smooth over these ruffles, but these exigencies prompted Samuel to publish, on December 24, 1795, the *Miscellaneous papers and legal instruments under the hand and seal of Shakspeare,* an impressive folio containing facsimiles of all the Shakspeare Papers. In his self-justifying preface, Samuel writes that he has "courted, he has even challenged, the critical judgement of those, who are best skilled in the Poetry and Phraseology of the times in which Shakspeare lived," and he cites numerous antiquarians who have "testified in favour of their authenticity" (1). Although the volume cost a steep four guineas—what a working man earned in two months (D. Stewart 101)—it sold out quickly. Crisis averted, but only temporarily.

A more serious one occurred on December 30 when attorney Albany Wallis marched into the Ireland home with a document displaying the real John Heminge's signature; it looked nothing like William-Henry's forged one (*Confessions* 88). W-H contrived a desperate remedy, dashing to his office (where he kept his forgery materials) and returning with a new document and a new story. It seemed that when William-Henry informed Mr. H. of the Heminge signature, the man readily produced a second document bearing a signature like the real one. Brandishing this new document, W-H explained: there were *two* John Heminges in Shakespeare's circle, a tall and a short one, the tall one associated with the Globe, the short affiliated with the Curtain Theater. Short John had signed the document that W-H had forged, Long John the real one (Grebanier 182–83; D. Stewart 155). Wallis credited this cock-and-bill story. The young forger had raced to his office, fabricated the new document, invented the explanation, and returned home in a mere seventy-five minutes. Wallis was convinced that nobody could have pulled off such a stratagem in so brief a time (*Confessions* 93). One has to admire the boy's velocity along with his audacity.

But Fakespeare's bacon wasn't saved. In January the *Telegraph* published a mock letter from "WILLIAME SHAEKSPERE" TO Beenjaammiinnee Joohnnssonn" (dated 1658) and a few weeks later George Woodward published *Familiar Verses from the Ghost of Willy Shakspeare to Sammy Ireland* (D. Stewart 157–58). Former Believer Boaden had crossed to the other side, and in his January 1796 *Letter to George Steevens, Esq.*, he presented a satirical poem about the Shakspeare Papers, pointing out the absurdities of the spelling and noting that in some of the "corrected" lines the MB had suddenly forgotten how to count to ten (Grebanier 186). Worse, *Vortigern* was earning less than unanimous praise. Sheridan, for example, commented that Shakespeare "must have been very young" when he wrote it (*Confessions* 139), and the theater's manager and leading actor, John Philip Kemble, doubted its authenticity. One consequence was a drastic reduction in the promised financial rewards: the Irelands would receive only ££250 (about £10,000 or $15,000 in today's money) and a share of the box office receipts—not paltry, but not the mother lode Samuel had envisioned.

Blast

The negotiations and delays in writing the *Vortigern* manuscript had pushed the premiere back to April 2, 1796. (Sheridan had vetoed Kemble's impish suggestion that it be staged on April Fool's Day.) Yet nothing had been heard from Edmond Malone, the most distinguished Shakespearean of the day; he had not even visited the Ireland home to view the documents. His silence seemed curious, but he was working in private. He finally published *An inquiry into the authenticity of certain miscellaneous papers and legal instruments* on March 31, just two days before *Vortigern's* premiere. His assessment was devastating, lengthy (more than four hundred pages), and unequivocal. The Shakspeare Papers are fake, he announces at the outset, and he promises to demonstrate "beyond a possibility of doubt, that not a single piece in this collection was the production of Shakspeare, or of the other persons to whom they are ascribed" (7–8). Since William-Henry had sedulously used paper from the period (tearing pages from books, ensuring that they lacked watermarks), Malone adduces examples of orthography, phraseology, handwriting, and chronological data to obliterate the Papers' validity.

Almost one hundred pages are consumed with his detailed devastation of the Queen Elizabeth letter. Malone cites examples from a multitude of late Medieval and early modern texts to debunk the documents' "laboured and capricious deformity of spelling" (68–69). He lists usage mistakes, points out the errors about the Globe and Shakespeare noted above and, after comparing the letter's handwriting to Elizabeth's true hand, concludes that the Ireland letter is a "manifest and bungling forgery" (111). Why did this one document so enrage him? Patriotism. Faking Shakespeare is one thing; forging Her Majesty's correspondence is tantamount to treason!

The other documents seemed to have been scripted by a "drunkard or madman," particularly those ascribed to Heminge, whose handwriting inclines alternately to the right and left, as no real person's would (137). (W-H signed some with his left hand and some with his right.) And would Shakespeare have misspelled his own name? He always signed himself "Shakspere," never "Shakspeare," as the forgeries have it (120). Malone mercilessly assaults the Southampton letters, in which Fakespeare both addresses the earl improperly and tells him what he already knows.[9] He mocks the "sickening," "namby-pamby" Hathaway letter and poem for referring to cedars before they had been introduced in Britain (164, 162) and derides the Profession of Faith's absurdly beneficent chicken (201).[10] Regarding the will, Malone, citing the mistakes mentioned above, declares that "the thickest Cimmerian darkness" is "bright sunshine compared with the vapid nonsense and impenetrable obscurity of this fabrication" (276). What about the plays? "Life is not long enough to be wasted in the examination of such trash" (305), albeit not too short to sneer at Kent's "corrected" speech in *Lear* (309).[11] Malone refutes the claim that there are too many documents for a forger to have written in a single year and ridicules the hokey oaken chest. The Papers, he concludes, are a "clumsy and daring fraud" perpetrated by someone ignorant of Shakespeare, English theater history, and the English language (352–53).

Ouch.

Later—too late—Samuel rebutted Malone in two volumes (*Mr. Ireland's Vindication* and *An Investigation*), where he managed to score a few points about usage but lacked convincing responses to Malone's dissection of the anachronisms, handwriting, and other egregious errors. The desperate dad also issued a handbill on the day of the performance condemning Malone, which only widened the distribution of his adversary's message (Kahan 179). William-Henry himself was puzzled, even a little flattered, that an eminent scholar required four hundred pages to destroy a forgery he deemed so crude (*Authentic* 26; *Confessions* 189). Did Malone's exposé make a difference? It likely appeared too close to the premiere to do much damage. Few people had time to read it, and those who did probably showed up anyway, though their attitudes had doubtless shifted toward the skeptical side.[12]

The stage was literally set for the premiere of *Vortigern*. But Malone's condemnation was only one of its many problems. Sarah Siddons, the famous actress who had agreed to play Vortigern's wife, Edmunda, had bowed out; poet laureate Samuel Pye, who had contracted to write a flattering preface, instead produced an equivocal one that was withdrawn. (A neutral one was provided by James Bland Burgess.) Kemble detested the play and had (perhaps intentionally) miscast several parts, giving a comic actor named Phillimore the role of the Saxon warlord Horsus and a Mr. Dignum, cursed with a squeaky, high-pitched voice, the part of a baron. These elements contributed to the play's ultimate failure. But its own flaws were obvious, even to a rowdy crowd that had gathered less to witness a new Shakespeare play than to enjoy a public spectacle.

"Boisterous and High Sounding Words"

Why *Vortigern?* Like many of Shakespeare's genuine plays, it is a tale of ancient Britain found in Raphael Holinshed's *Chronicles,* a copy of which resided in the Ireland library.[13] Moreover, John Hamilton Mortimer's painting *Vortigern and Rowena* was displayed in the Ireland home; W-H cites it as his primary inspiration (*Authentic Account* 20; *Confessions* 133), while expressing astonishment that nobody noticed the unlikely coincidence that this particular play had miraculously shown up in the capacious chest (*Confessions* 134). Like many novice authors, William-Henry Shakspeare relied on imitation, and *Vortigern*'s plot is a fairly skillful Shakespearean pastiche. Like *Richard III,* it is a story of illegitimate succession in which Vortigern, awarded half the kingdom by King Constantius, plots to murder him (as in *Macbeth*); though plagued by doubts, he calls on the forces of darkness to assist him. Also as in *Richard III,* Vortigern assigns two men to execute the deed, but one is unwilling, so the other kills both his crony and the king. Vortigern now schemes to murder the rightful heirs, Constantius's sons Aurelius and Uter, and to arrange his own daughter Flavia's marriage to a man he has chosen instead of to Aurelius, whom she loves.[14] Flavia cross-dresses, for no apparent reason, to find Aurelius, who has gone to war to reclaim the kingdom. Meanwhile Edmunda goes mad (shades of *Hamlet* and *Macbeth*) and the Fool (like Touchstone, among others) offers some (not very witty) quips. Vortigern's son Pascentius goes into hiding, renting a forest cottage and residing there with his sister. A worried Vortigern hires Saxon mercenaries, who encounter his children and Aurelius. Despite Pascentius's slaying of the Saxon Horsus,[15] the good guys (Aurelius et al.) lose the battle. At the victory party Vortigern spots the Saxon lord Hengist's daughter Rowena and is immediately smitten, proclaiming her his new queen. Poor Edmunda! Revolted by their father's crimes, Pascentius and his brother Catagrinus defect (as in *King John*). After losing the ensuing battle, Vortigern wants to die but, unable to find anyone to kill him, fights on. After Vortigern's sons are reunited with Edmunda, the king learns that Rowena has taken poison. Vortigern then delivers a Hamletian soliloquy in which he considers the meaning of death. Though he fights ferociously, he is taken prisoner, but just as Aurelius is about to slay him, Flavia intercedes; her father is spared and Aurelius becomes king.

The author, barely twenty years old, with no experience and scant talent, concocted the play in two months. Is it any wonder that it's not much good? The pacing is clumsy, the plot confusing, the characterizations thin, and the verse pedestrian at best. *Vortigern* also contains too many speeches telling us what we have just witnessed. But if it is not nearly as good as Arthur Phillips's Shakespeare play (discussed below), it is not as pitiful as one might expect. Indeed, in a few spots the Easily Matched Bard commits poetry. For example, William-Henry's lyrics to the play's three songs (one sung by Edmunda) are not bad at all, and the queen's confused speeches are affecting. In act 5, scene 2, Vortigern's remorseful indecision is nicely expressed, as he contrasts his despair to his former self-assurance, and recalls, "When thou didst cry, I strove to stop thy mouth, / By boldly thrusting on thee dire ambition, / Then I did think myself indeed a god!" (63). The finest lines in the play occur in 5.1 when Vortigern contemplates death. As he recalls the faces of his victims, their eyes seem to

> Wrench from off my brow this sacred crown
> And make me too a subject like themselves;
> Subject! to whom? To thee, O sovereign death!
> Who hast for thy domain this world immense;
> Church-yards and charnel-houses are thy haunts,
> And hospitals thy sumptuous palaces,
> And they wouldst be merry, though does chuse
> The gaudy chamber of a dying King.
> O! then thou dost ope wide thy hideous jaws,
> And with rude laughter, and fantastic tricks,
> Thou clap'st thy rattling fingers to thy sides;
> And when this solemn mockery is ended,
> With icy hand thou tak'st him by the feet,
> And upward so, till thou dost reach the heart,
> And wrap him in the cloak of lasting night. (64)

The image of death's crawling, icy grip is truly chilling. But then, it is borrowed from Shakespeare's Mistress Quickly. Unfortunately, too, the muffing Bard mixes the metaphor when the cold fingers suddenly hold a warming cloak. Even at his best, Will Ireland's heat is a pale fire.

More importantly, perhaps, several speeches evoke the forger's own situation. For example, Uter's lament for his youth, used as my epigraph, rings true—as it well might, since it expresses its author's frustration at being underestimated. In response to this speech, Aurelius wishes

> That so my heat amazed brain might work
> Thoughts suiting more this vast immensity
> O most expanded, O most fertile mind!
> When thou would'st copulate with thoughts like this,
> Thou art mere nothingness; or when the lips
> Do pour forth boisterous and high sounding words,
> They back again to the poor mortal brain,
> And scoff at thy presumption. (3.2, p. 33)

This sounds like nothing so much as the writer's attempt to invoke his recalcitrant muse, with a sidelong apology for his presumptuousness. In Vortigern's hubris we may read the youthful author's realization that he has been caught in a self-made trap. Perhaps most of all, the play dramatizes William-Henry's resentment toward his father (as Vortigern) and his wish that Samuel might recognize his son's worth and capitulate to his greatness. As often happens in forgeries, the forger hints at the fraudulence of his own work. And like all literary forgeries, *Vortigern* is a self-portrait, a work whose subject is, in part, its own spurious provenance.

Burial

Unruly audiences were common in eighteenth-century theater, and this capacity crowd was in high spirits. This wasn't just a play; it was a resurrection! The throng behaved itself throughout the first two acts: the songs were a success, and many applauded or wept at Edmunda's mad scenes (D. Stewart 180–81). But the mood began to shift when, in act 3, the squeaky-voiced Dignum commanded shrilly, "Let them bellow on!" eliciting titters. An even more uncomfortable moment transpired at the end of act 4. Playing the just-murdered Horsus, Mr. Phillimore lay right where the drop curtain landed, so that his legs rested on the audience's side while his upper torso reposed unseen behind the curtain. After a few moments of waiting, he laboriously heaved himself up, groaning all the while.[16] From this moment on, the crowd "gleefully waited for new signals for mirth" (Grebanier 219). A blatant signal sounded during Vortigern's death speech. This was the moment Kemble had been waiting for: he strutted around, mugging and milking the words for bathos. His delivery of the line "When this solemn mockery is ended," in what William-Henry describes as "the most sepulchral tone of voice possible," seemed to refer to the play being acted (*Confessions* 157, where W-H misquotes the line). The crowd erupted in "rude laughter" that lasted for ten minutes. When the mirth finally subsided, Kemble repeated the line "with even more solemn grimace" (157). Few heard the remainder of the tragedy, for a near-riot had broken out: a drunken MP named Sturt, who had loudly defended the play throughout, seized a stagehand and put him a headlock, before being pelted with oranges (Grebanier 223; D. Stewart 184). Willy's masterpiece was buried "under an avalanche of derision" (Grebanier 227); the Irelands' reputation accompanied it into the tomb.

Vortigern is bad, but that does not fully explain the audience's reaction. As Pye pointedly asked, "How many persons were there in the theatre that night . . . who, without being led, could distinguish between the merits of *King Lear* and *Tom Thumb?* Not twenty" (qtd. in D. Stewart 187). Group dynamics were also at work: if the actors had taken the play seriously, the audience might have been bored but may not have booed: like the Believers, the Booers rode a bandwagon. Astoundingly, W-H professes pride in his accomplishment, writing that "the world praised many parts, but said it was uneven, having the same errors as are usually found in many of *Shakspear*'s plays, it was generally thought superior to the worst of his plays and much inferior to his capital one's [sic]" (*Authentic Account* 21, italics in original). He even claims that his humiliation did not "lessen the satisfaction I felt in having at so early an age wrote [*sic*] a piece which was not only acted, but brought forth as the word of the greatest of men" (26). W-H had forged Shakespeare, but Shakespeare had also forged him—into a playwright. His response helps to explain why, after *Vortigern*'s flop, The Matched Bard produced a list of forthcoming "discoveries." But he could not hold out much longer: pressed by Samuel to introduce him to Mr. H., W-H confessed to his sisters, to Wallis, and, finally, to his father. Samuel didn't believe him. Mr. H.'s fulsome letters had not persuaded him that W-H was bright or industrious, and he knew the boy was not capable of writing *Vortigern*. At Wallis's urging, W-H signed an affidavit confirming his authorship; Samuel scoffed. (See *Confessions* 256 for the affidavit.) To credit the confession, he would have to admit that he had been deceived by a dullard.

Incensed by his father's obstinacy, William-Henry left home, abruptly married a woman he barely knew, and made a pilgrimage to Bristol, where he interviewed Chatterton's sister and visited St. Mary Redcliffe church. On December 12, 1796, father and son met, but Samuel still refused to believe that his son had forged the documents. That *Vortigern* and the Shakspeare Papers were fakes was now commonly accepted, yet many believed Samuel to have been the perpetrator.[17] Ostensibly to absolve his father as well as to apologize, W-H published (against Wallis's advice) his forty-three-page *Authentic Account* shortly thereafter. Alternately abject and self-justifying, the author asks readers to regard the forgeries as the conduct of "an unthinking and impetuous boy," rather than that of "a sordid and avaricious fabricator instigated by the mean desire of securing pecuniary emolument" (n.p.; he inherited his father's pompous prose style). At the conclusion, he offers three declarations: that his father did not know the papers were forged; that he himself was their only begetter; and that any publication verifying their authenticity is a lie (43). So says the confirmed prevaricator.

It didn't work. The *Monthly Mirror,* for example, charged that the ill-written prose in this "contemptible" document proved William-Henry incapable of forging the Papers. The *Morning Chronicle* cleverly asserted that "W. H. Ireland has come forward and announced himself author of the papers attributed by him to Shakspeare; which, if *true,* proves him to be a *liar*" (*Confessions* 269). Many readers assumed he was protecting his father, and the young man's apparent self-sacrifice is strongly tinged with pride: "I am the sole author of documents and a play that fooled the world! But I am so very sorry." Short of money in 1805, he published the lengthier *Confessions,* which ends with a list of seven excuses: 1) he did not intend to injure anyone and 2) did not in fact hurt anybody; 3) he did not do it for money and 4) did not benefit financially from the forgeries; 5) the Believers are to blame for their own gullibility; 6) he was just a kid (he subtracts two years from his actual age, claiming to have been only seventeen); and 7) he was persecuted because others felt embarrassed (*Confessions* 301–2). Although numbers 5–7 are true, obviously William-Henry did injure his father and himself, and he did receive *££*90 for *Vortigern.* He also earned money from publishing the *Confessions.* As with the Ern Malley forgers, William-Henry Ireland became notorious for the Shakspeare Papers, which were far more famous and widely read than any of the sixty-seven other titles (plays, poems, Gothic novels, ghostwritten biographies) he produced in a literary career that stretched into the 1830s. At times he even reforged his own forgeries, recopying *Vortigern* and other documents and selling them as the originals (Kahan 205–7)! Actually, Ireland's forgeries created two authors named William. Indeed, the story of his forgeries is an unconventional *Künstlerroman,* a coming-of-age tale in which William Ireland uses William Shakespeare as an instrument to find his vocation. In that regard, he was little different from many other aspiring writers—or from most forgers.

Bastard

At what point did William-Henry move from seeking to gratify his father to trying to gull him? The two motives were likely intertwined from the start. Their relationship was troubled. Samuel was cold to the boy and for years had promised a "great revelation" that probably concerned Will's parentage. The son was likely convinced of his own illegitimacy. That would explain why his father had never married Mrs. Freeman and why W-H could never please the patriarch, and it would provide another reason for Samuel's ceaseless social climbing. The dead brother added to the problem: William-Henry could only be, at best, a counterfeit of the lost son, a copy of a copy (Kahan 119). He was, in his own mind, a human forgery. Indeed, W-H's probable illegitimacy furnishes a striking parallel to Vortigern's accession (and to the plot of *The Tragedy of Arthur*) as well as a motive for his fakes. By *becoming* Shakespeare, the budding author could at once make his father proud of him and build a replacement father—a better one—named Will. The forgeries also wrote another proud papa into existence: Mr. H., the praiseful pater William-Henry so desperately craved (see Kahan 118). Not only did he create these fathers; he controlled them. He made this happen as a bastard writing bastard texts.[18]

For many of his later works William-Henry Ireland understandably employed a nom de plume. Groom argues that the Shakespeare forgeries unfairly cast a shadow over W-H's more estimable later productions. Not merely a fraud, Ireland was, Groom argues, a "radical *bricoleur,*" a kind of postmodernist *avant la lettre* who employed pastiche (Gothic novels, *Vortigern, Henry the Second*) and impersonation to craft an authorial identity (*Shadow* 221). Kahan has also sought to rehabilitate Ireland, having edited his works and overseen a production of *Vortigern* staged in 1997 at London's Bridewell. He ruefully notes, however, that the reviews were all negative (224): two centuries have not improved it. However we rate his later works, there was one person William-Henry never won over: his father, who insisted to his dying day (in 1800) that the Shakspeare Papers were authentic. His son viewed this recalcitrance as an insult, and he expresses his pain and resentment in a trilogy of poems written in 1803: "The Bastard," "The Bastard's Complaint," and "Reply to the Bastard's Complaint." These poems divulge his motives more baldly than do his prose accounts. Here, for example, are key lines from "The Bastard":

> Alone thou stand'st, a wretched Bastard born,
> Go, let thine acts thy friendless name adorn. . . .
> May Bastards, tho' bereft of friend and name
> Feel in their breasts eternal thirst of fame!

The speaker's plight is even more abject in "The Bastard's Complaint":

> In vain I claim a father; none is near;
> In vain I weep; no mother dries the tear.
> By these denied, by parents thus forgot
> Who shall commiserate the Bastard's lot?

And in "Reply":

> Thou know'st no father's love, no mother's sigh,
> No kindred but the fost'ring power on high,
> By one neglected, and the other's shame,
> Thy sole inheritance the Bastard's name. (all qtd. in Grebanier 288–89)

Like King Arthur in *The Tragedy of Arthur*, the text to which we now turn, the stain of William-Henry's birth was "ne'er forgot nor ne'er forgave," no matter that he upraised a glorious realm. But for a few months the Friendless Bastard had become the Matchless Bard. By reinventing his literary fathers, he, like Vortigern, was able to think himself, if only briefly, a god.

Pale Fire

> The sun's a thief, and with his great attraction
> Robs the vast sea; the moon's an arrant thief,
> And her pale fire she snatches from the sun:
> The sea's a thief, whose liquid surge resolves
> The moon into salt tears: the earth's a thief,
> That feeds and breeds by composure stolen
> From general excrement: each thing's a thief:
> The laws, your curb and whip, in their rough power
> Have uncheck'd theft.
>
> —Timon, in Shakespeare's *Timon of Athens*, 4.3, 439–47

> I see in every sinew and thine eye
> Thy testimony's proof: thou art my print.
> I know these lineaments as if I peered
> Into a glass of other years. . . .
>
> —King Arthur to his false son, Philip, in *The Tragedy of Arthur*, 4.4.40

The family relations in *The Tragedy of Arthur*—both novel (i.e., the introduction) and play—mirror those of the Irelands. One might suspect that Phillips wrote *The Tragedy of Arthur* as a contemporary gloss on the case, but Phillips has stated that he had not read about the Ireland forgeries until he was well into the research for the novel (Reilly interview 4). Yet the parallels are striking. Again we witness a vexed father-son relationship; again a (probably) forged play that experts certify as genuine; again a son writes a book justifying his behavior after the fact. Again a sibling (the fictional Arthur Phillips's twin sister, Dana) vies with her brother for their father's affection. Like *Vortigern*, Phillips's play and novel concern legitimacy and succession; in the novel, however, the father is the forger and the son is first a believer and then a debunker who, contracted to write an introduction to the newly discovered Shakespeare play, instead denounces it as a fake.[19] Both works are bildungsromans in the guise of forgeries in which youthful protagonists invent themselves by winning and then rejecting—while inadvertently emulating—the father and father surrogate, William Shakespeare. The children use Shakespeare as a tool both to win their parents' love and to forge themselves as artists (thus bearing out Theses 2 and 8).

The Tragedy of Arthur troubles the distinction between fraudulent and legitimate creation. Its narrator pretends to be the author and, as in a forgery, dares us to determine where reality ends and fiction begins. *The Tragedy of Arthur* is signed by Arthur Phillips. But which one? Is this author the person of the same name portrayed in the novel? The novel includes a play, also called *The Tragedy of Arthur,* attributed to Shakespeare, but written by Arthur Phillips. Which one? Obviously, the play is a faux forgery perpetrated by the real Arthur Phillips. But in the fictional world, the play was probably written by the narrator's father, also named Arthur Phillips. In a sense, then, *The Tragedy of Arthur* is a double forgery, for both play and novel mislead readers about the identity of their creators. The introduction is also a fake, in that the real Arthur Phillips is not identical to the narrator and implied author. If the play was "really" written by the parental Arthur, readers confront a puzzling series of involutions that induce us to ask whether an author's—or an Arthur's—identity can ever be pinned down. (Remember thesis 7: all authors are fictional personages.) By means of this Timonian tangle of thefts, imitations, and borrowings,[20] Phillips suggests that all fictions are forgeries, fraudulent documents that purport to be about real people, narrated by characters who do not exist, about events that did not happen but pretend to be real. Ultimately, however, the novel vindicates the Senior Arthur Phillips's contention that forgers are true makers of wonder.

Paratexts

The preface to *The Tragedy of Arthur* presents what follows as an introduction to Shakespeare's previously lost play, first published in 1597. This astonishing discovery, the editors announce, is the "first certain addition to Shakespeare's canon since the seventeenth century" (vii). They also boast that "there is now no notable voice in Shakespearean studies who questions" its authenticity, and list several scholars who have certified it, including the coeditor, fictional Professor Roland Verre (from the root *ver* or "truth"). Anyone reading past the first few pages, however, will understand that the play's provenance is far from certain. The editors also declare that the play displays The Matchless Bard's "unmistakable imagination and language" (viii). It does not. Indeed, the assurance with which the editors trumpet their achievement indicates the opposite of confidence, and their bold pronouncements are contradicted by the "brief" (250-page) introduction. The editors' preface is followed by a facsimile of the title page featuring the name "W. Shakespere." The novel, then, is a mock mock-hoax, a half-missed mystification. The paratexts thrust us into a game of shadows that resembles the one in Vladimir Nabokov's *Pale Fire,* a classic twinned text also involving a posthumous work (John Shade's 999-line poem) and an editor's eccentric, self-exposing annotations. *The Tragedy of Arthur* is a shade of Nabokov's waxwinged text, in which the false azure of its windowpane, I propose, becomes a mirror for both narrator and reader. Like Nabokov's novel and like other forgeries, *The Tragedy of Arthur* commits literary "criticism by other means" (Ruthven 171), coupling a satire of the Shakespeare industry and modern Bardolatry with a family romance—two romances, in fact—all of which require the reader to split into two minds, one suspending, the other sustaining, disbelief.

As with *Pale Fire,* readers wonder, "How do I read this thing?" The editors urge us to "plunge directly into the play" to allow "Shakespeare to speak for himself" (ix). If we do that, we may approach it with eyes untainted by Arthur Phillips the younger's undermining introduction, which encourages us to view it as a Shakespearean pastiche authored by his father. Yet reading the play first strips away a great deal of necessary background about its origins and resonances with the family romance traced in the introduction. Reading the introduction first poisons the well of authenticity but permits us to appreciate Phillips's multilayered irony. Having read it both ways, I recommend that one read the introduction first and, while reading the play, flip back to key passages in the introduction. In any case, one must read in two directions at once, a fitting enterprise for a novel that advertises its own preposterousness. To mirror Phillips's strategy, my discussions of the introduction and play appear side by side; readers may choose for themselves how best to read them.

Patrimony

"I have never much liked Shakespeare," narrator Arthur Phillips (the younger) begins (1). His antipathy is a reaction formation, for the Phillips household, like that of the Irelands, worships at the MB's shrine. Arthur Sr. begins reading to Junior and Dana when they are six years old. (Phillips's demurral notwithstanding, this idea

Pastiche

Early in the introduction, Phillips quotes Milan Kundera's *The Curtain,* which imagines a contemporary composer who crafts a sonata in the manner of Beethoven, one so brilliant that, if it actually were Beethoven's, it would count among his greatest works. But no matter how magnificent the creation, seems to have been borrowed from the Irelands.) Once an aspiring painter, Arthur Sr. now crafts phony coupons, pictures, and documents, including a voucher that he uses to treat his kids to a fancy dinner (17). He once faked a draft notice so that a rival for his sweetheart's affections would travel to North Carolina only to learn that he hadn't been called up (41). Perversely justifying an art forgery in court, Dad boasts, "Thanks to me, its value swelled a thousandfold": "Don't say I didn't make something!" (11). Many critics, including myself, would agree that forgery is creative making. And as the novel proceeds we come to understand that, in his own way, Arthur Sr. is a creative genius.

Yet Senior's explanation of his forgery as merely taking advantage of "an uneven distribution of knowledge between buyer and seller, just a market inefficiency" is disingenuous (10). Junior translates: his father forged a signature on a drawing as well as a "long, very supportive, typed and aged provenance," thereby "transubstantiating the small picture, temporarily, from anonymity to Rembrandtivity" (10–11). Senior imagines himself as a priest or wizard whose aim is "to astonish. To add to the world's store of precious possibility" (20). An escapade in which he enlists the ten-year-old twins to secretly create "alien" crop circles on farmland leaves Junior delighted that his father has "given him (and the world) a glimpse of something hidden," a realm of transformation and magic—a midsummer if signed by a contemporary composer it would be "laughable. At best its author would be applauded as a virtuoso of pastiche" (12). Many postmodern novels—including *Chatterton, My Life as a Fake, erasure, The Blazing World,* and *The Tragedy of Arthur*—employ pastiche. Still, one needs extraordinary audacity to imitate Shakespeare, and not only because he stands atop the mountain of literary achievement. A pasticheur must deftly employ the unfamiliar idioms of Elizabethan English, master iambic pentameter (and know when to switch from verse to prose), craft complex characters, and pace the action expediently (*Vortigern* being deficient in these latter two qualities), among other challenges. By these criteria, *The Tragedy of Arthur* is a triumph. It proceeds swiftly to a strong climax, portrays a despicable but complex villain in Mordred, presents themes—the nature of monarchy and legitimacy, the relations between fathers and children, the hero's maturation—typical of Shakespeare, and compellingly depicts its conflicted protagonist. The language, however, is shallow Shakespeare: its iambs rumble along regularly, rarely altering the meter for rhythmic effect, emphasis, or thematic resonance (as Shakespeare does) and seldom employing caesuras. As Phillips's imaginary scholars point out and as someone reading, say, *Richard III* would notice, the Shakespeare of 1597 is a far more adept versifier than the author of *Arthur,* whoever it is. The night's dream. "This may be," he recalls, "the closest I ever felt to him" (21). As with the Irelands, so with the Phillipses: forging solders familial bonds. Later Junior admits that his father's frauds "made the world more wondrous" and inspired his own choice of vocation (55). Most of Dad's scams are, however, less wondrous, such as the "grubby little tax dodge" he executes by fashioning bogus coupons so his friend, grocer Chuck Glassow, will get a tax credit (55). No wonder Junior eventually shouts, "Fuck his magic!" (51). Junior is self-aware enough to note that in the "Shakespeare" play King Arthur also attempts to be "unlike his father," Uter (also the name of Vortigern's son), who raped a nobleman's wife (58). (King Arthur is the product of that forced union.) Junior comments that King Arthur, a "charismatic, charming, egocentric, short-tempered, principled but chronically impulsive bastard," resembles his father (9). He neglects to note that this description applies to himself.

Fraternal

Growing up in Minneapolis, Arthur and Dana are Minnesota Twins whose existences seem modeled after Shakespeare, whose work "teems with twins" (e.g., in *Twelfth Night* and *The Comedy of Errors;* Shakespeare was himself the father of fraternal twins). The Phillips kids are but one of many sets of doubles in the novel: the two fictional Arthurs, forger and fictioneer; dual novelists (real and fictional) named Arthur Phillips; mirrored play's language echoes that of the early Shakespeare's as a marching band resembles a madrigal.

Certainly, *The Tragedy of Arthur* is better than *Vortigern.* What complicates our response is the introduction, which frames the pastiche with a charge of forgery, so that it is not just novelist Arthur Phillips penning a Shakespeare pastiche; within the novel's world, it may be a pastiche masquerading as a genuine article. The gap between a forgery and a pastiche is filled by a signature: To whom is the work attributed? In keeping a straight face, as it were, about *The Tragedy of Arthur,* Phillips narrows this gap. Where does experiment end and fraud begin? (This is also a question for Everett's Monk Ellison.) All three significant eighteenth-century literary forgeries—Chatterton's, Ireland's, and their predecessors, the Ossian works of James Macpherson—employed new literary techniques to present original works (and attributed them to someone else). Like their works, *The Tragedy of Arthur*—novel and play—erodes the distinction between the authentic and the fraudulent, the original and the imitation. If, as the cynical Timon (and the self-justifying Arthur Phillips Sr.) holds, everyone steals, including Shakespeare, why do we condemn certain thieves and celebrate others? How may a writer convey the paradoxes of pretense and capture the fictions of forgery? Phillips does it by embodying both Arthur Phillipses in the play's protagonist and by making

Arthurs in the narrator and the play's king (as well as the real author and the king). The play and the introduction also form a complementary pair. Through these dyads, the novel suggests that authentic and forged texts are twins and that the Bogus Bard is a fraternal twin to the Matchless One, an author who, like Chatterton, acts as a Hamlet-like specter haunting all Shakespeare forgeries.

Sister and brother share many interests and loves—including Shakespeare, at first. Thus, when Arthur is roughed up after defending his sister from accusations of lesbianism (she does turn out to be gay), she quotes Sonnet 57, then reads him act 2, scene 2 from a 1904 quarto edition of *The Tragedy of Arthur*—ostensibly an heirloom handed down from their great-grandfather (26–27)—in which King Arthur exhorts his troops by describing England as a virgin to be defended (292). Afterward, Junior decides that Shakespeare is "okay" (27).

Pretenders

Before long the twins diverge, not least because Arthur flounders in search of an identity while Dana is "already . . . her own true self" (44). But her "true self" is a mask: she becomes an actor, one who utters someone else's words while performing as a different person. In short, she is a pretender. In college she adopts a potent new persona that enables her to fight her father "on his own terms and hit him where it hurt[s]" (63): she becomes an anti-Stratfordian,

sure that the questionable text is itself about faking.

Feigned

The Tragedy of Arthur, like many Shakespearean histories and tragedies, concerns monarchic succession. Arthur, the product of Uter's rape of the Earl of Cornwall's wife (and therefore a bastard like W-H Ireland), is reared by the Duke of Gloucester far away from court and his father's incessant wars with the Saxons. While acknowledging that Arthur was "only lent" to him (1.1.85, p. 266), Gloucester realizes that Arthur's character is a judgment on his fatherhood:

weaving an elaborate theory that would transform every Shakespeare play into a forgery and the Matchless One into a moon shining reflected light. She proposes that Edward de Vere (the Earl of Oxford) and his lover, an unknown Jewish poet named Binyamin Feivel, contrived to write the sonnets and plays and assign them to an obscure actor.[21] The scheme would give young Will a chance to "play a better version of himself and . . . win great fame" (66) on the condition that he sign an affidavit after each forgery attesting that he did not write it. But the sham author had his own will: once he became a legendary playwright, Willy balked at continuing to play the front and viewed the affidavits *themselves* as forgeries designed to destroy his reputation (71). After Oxford's death in 1604, the Mendacious Bard burned the affidavits (72).

Dana, like W-H Ireland, even invents a genealogy for herself, determining that Feivel's descendants changed their name to Phillips and that her favorite plays (including *The Tragedy of Arthur*) were all written by her ancestor. She imagines that Oxford and Feivel agreed to reveal the fraud later and pledged that all the monetary rewards would fall to the heirs of the one whose plays elicit the most royal command performances over the centuries. Dana thus convinces herself that she will inherit $9 million in 2014. Junior rightly views her fable as part of a larger delusion in which the "authenticity of *Arthur* [is]

> On me will lie the blame an he's not
> meet
> The censure is on Gloucester's
> weary duke.
> . . . What king forged I? All England
> will be judge. (1.1.95–98, p. 266)

Arthur is not a true king—yet. Like the introduction, the play is a coming-of-age story akin to the *Henry* trilogy but within a single drama. Given their shared qualities as "charming, egocentric, short-tempered, principled but chronically impulsive" bastards (9), it makes sense that Rex's maturation mirrors Junior's: King Arthur also acts rashly, disguises himself as someone else, falls in love impetuously, and at the end partially but painfully redeems himself.

The young king's internal conflicts appear early in the play when he disguises himself as a swain to woo a shepherdess, to whom he intimates that he "bleeds remorse" for a man such as he might have been, spending "his days in chambers, closets, armor. I had fled by breakfast were I that cursed prince" (1.2.77–79, p. 271).[22] He doesn't want to be king, nor does he feel worthy. Mordred, the son of the Pictish king, Loth, has no such qualms: as the "deathsman of repose" (1.2.10, p. 273), he is disgusted that Arthur might presume to sit on the English throne (1.3.66, p. 276). Sick of war, Mordred's father restrains him. Certain English nobles agree with Mordred, but the new king has superstition on his side, having been born on St. George's Day, April 23, which is also Arthur Junior's tightly bound . . . to the authenticity of her father's love for her. She could not afford to believe that he could have lied to her about Shakespeare" (74). Dana clings to this "screw thee" to Papa until the end of her college years at Brown. Violating his probation, Arthur Sr. shows up at her graduation (instead of at Junior's), which sends him back to prison and Dana into a mental breakdown. Once reconciled with her father, Dana recants her theory.

Then the twins reverse positions: she becomes a confirmed Bardolater, he a Shakesatheist. A similar binary in the play dramatizes King Arthur's self-division: he both wants and does not want to be king. Indeed, he believes himself a pretender. Likewise, Junior is correct in his otherwise sophistical argument that Shakespeare serves as a mirror where readers and audiences project their own desires and fantasies and see them reflected. Hence, Dana's Shakespeare is her father as wonder-worker; Junior's Bard is a domineering fraud.

Nonetheless, they live together in New York after college, Dana landing acting jobs and Arthur writing copy for an ad agency. As an actor and a huckster-cum-fiction writer, the twins embody two elements of the forger's personality. His father's son despite his defiance, Junior uses a quotation from *The Tempest* to sell Absolut vodka and an excerpt from Sonnet 6 to tout, of all things, a sperm bank. But when Junior journeys to Minnesota to help his father defend himself in a new indictment (for birthday.[23] The doubters' views are echoed by Mordred's messenger, who derides the young aspirant as a "bastard with no right to throne" (1.5.111, p. 283). Though they too entertain doubts, the English nobles bristle at this insult and carve on the poor courier's forehead the words "Arthur Rex" (1.5.195, p. 286), the same words Junior finds tattooed on his penis after his besotted blackout. In each case the name is both a putdown and a challenge: prove yourself worthy. Is Arthur more than a randy upstart? A faint echo of a real king? In a soliloquy at the end of act 1, King Arthur questions his fitness, worrying that he embodies his sire's violence and that his "monstrous getting surely cursed the land" (1.5.24, p. 288).

> What king was he to spawn such
> king as I?
> . . . I bear his blood, his wit, his
> faults, his sin,
> Save he did crave a kingdom for
> his own,
> While crown unsought now
> perches up on me. (1.5.34–37, p. 288)

Which Arthur is speaking? It could just as well be Arthur Phillips Jr., trying at any cost *not* to become his forger father. King Arthur—like Arthur Jr., William-Henry Ireland, and Thomas Chatterton—is desperate to prove himself to the surrogate fathers who surround him. Like them, King Arthur becomes himself by becoming someone else.

forged lottery tickets), the dismayed dad accuses him of using the MB for mercenary ends and, more damningly, of not "*making* anything" (84, italics his).

Young Arthur spends most of his spare time seducing women—or trying to; he and Dana even place bets on who can first bed the women they select. One such adventure leads to a prickly denouement in which Arthur awakens after a drunken blackout to find himself with a permanent reminder of his losing wager: "ARTHUR REX" tattooed on his penis (88). In the play these same words are carved on the forehead of an unfortunate Saxon courier who calls King Arthur a bastard (286). Thus, the dick joke has a point: in both play and novel, the male member is a synecdoche of power and legitimacy as well as the bone of contention with regard to inheritance. Indeed, both Arthur Rexes act as though their willy, not their will, is king, letting the wrong head do much of their thinking.

An infatuation with a woman in London prompts Arthur to quit his job and accompany her to Venice. In a letter Dana suggests that he is following the dictates of both his willy and, unwittingly, of his Willy: as a Jew in Venice, a Romeo intent on being free of his family, he is "already unoriginal." She quotes the lines from Sonnet 59 that serve as my epigraph ("If there be nothing new . . . : 10–11). Even in his unoriginality Junior imitates Shakespeare, who "plundered like a madman from everyone" (112).

Arthur eventually winds up in Prague, where he remakes himself—by replicating his past, marrying a woman named (not Dana but) Jana and siring twin boys. His father's congratulatory letter conflates his son and the fictional Rex: "Arthur, his wandering and resistance complete, has taken a wife and accepted his crown" (114). Emerging Arthur becomes an emerging author: he publishes his first novel and sends it to his father, who swaps it for cigarettes. Dana writes, "The half-made man . . . comes to his wizardly father for approval, for his freedom to become fully human. Sound familiar, Caliban?" (117). Every action Junior undertakes seems stolen from the Bard, as if he were a moon snatching pale fire from the sovereign sun. Arthur Junior can only be, like the play's king, a pretender.

Pigeon

When Junior returns to Minnesota to help his father make the transition from prison, Senior drops a bomb in the form of a text. First he flatters his son with words Junior has been waiting for decades to hear—"You make wonders, Arthur"—then intimates his great plan to "do something together" (132). He gives Junior the key to a safe deposit box inside of which is a 1597 quarto edition of *The Tragedy of Arthur*, by "W. Shakespere." Junior is skeptical: "My father, of all people, a forger, owned and had kept hidden for decades a real 412-year-old document? No.

Fledgling

King Arthur rises to the occasion on the eve of battle by delivering the stirring peroration to his troops with which Dana consoled her traumatized brother. Even this speech, however, shows the fledgling king groping for the proper tenor, as he offers two inapt tropes—first comparing the Picts to boys hiding behind their mothers' skirts (2.2.20, p. 292) and then to boys who must be taught to "decline and conjugate hard words" (2.2.29, p. 293)—before arriving at one that arouses them, literally, by picturing York as a virgin who needs to be protected and then penetrated

Empirically disproven by everything I knew about him" (143). But Arthur wants to believe, to see himself and his father as "partners in something unprecedented, earthshaking," an enterprise that might both treat the world to a true wonder and permanently mend their relationship (149).

Dad urges Arthur to subject the text to every possible test. He explains that it will fix the twins and their mother for life (with money "honorably gained!"), while rewarding Junior with fame that his novels could never bring (151). Plus, "You will be collaborating with him!" (152). This is the delusion that blinded the Ireland Believers: credulity made them cocreators with a genius. Arthur Sr. goes even further, puffing up his son in a manner that William-Henry Ireland could only dream of, telling Arthur he is "more of a creator than [Shakespeare] was" because, unlike the Bard, Arthur truly *is* matchless, having "made things from nothing" instead of "merely" adapting and expanding existing sources (153). Junior will now borrow genius from the sun called Shakespeare! After the first blush of pride fades, however, young Arthur's skepticism returns, and he asks his father where he obtained the play. His elaborate story is compelling, for the father has taken to heart thesis 3: that a forgery is only as good as its authenticating story.

In 1958 Senior was hired by a wealthy man living in a big country house (his name is not Mr. H., but it might as well be) to make a replica (2.3.32, p. 293). "Suddenly everyone starts to nod and grip their hilts, if you know what I mean," Dana comments (28). The exhortation exposes the gap between Arthur's experience (these troops have never conjugated a Latin verb) and those of his men. How can Arthur be both a sovereign and one of the guys?

His ambivalence may explain his decision to order Gloucester to masquerade as King Arthur in the next battle. But when the English win the battle, Gloucester looks like a shirker, the shining glory he earned now glittering on Arthur's brow. Gloucester sourly notes that

> Deception 'pon deception preys and fats
> Itself, the stronger to deceive anew.
> 'Twas ever thus, but now is Gloucester's name
> All shard bestrewn, so Arthur's fledgèd name
> Might tower up to all the world's esteem. (2.7.14–18, p. 305)

Gloucester is a forgery of a forgery, as well as the surrogate father of an unsatisfactory son. Viewing Gloucester from inside a friar's costume, Arthur imagines the duke as king and then speaks the lines that, for one scholar, prove the play's authenticity. Envisioning how his subjects might perceive him, the king realizes that

> Imperfect is the glass of others' eyes
> Wherein we seek in hope of handsome glimpse

"for insurance purposes, perfectly legal" (until the man tries to sell it with the fake signature), of a small painting in the man's collection (156). On his shelves were several volumes of sewn-together quartos, one of which held four plays by Shakespeare, two by Jonson, and the apocryphal play *Mucedorus.* Thumbing the tome, Senior discovered an eighth play not mentioned in the table of contents: *The Tragedy of Arthur.* The patron was a boor who never read his own books, so Senior simply ripped *Arthur* from the pack and smuggled it out. The owner had not known it was there and thus "suffered no loss. There isn't even a word for what happened to him." Junior replies, "Yes, there is. That's stealing. It's a word. In English" (158). Thrilled to think of the Bard and himself as "secret chums" (159), Senior was even more elated after his diligent research uncovered no mention of the play anywhere (160, 163). (He forged the "1904 edition.") In short, he possesses the *only copy of an original, undiscovered Shakespeare play.* It's an "oil well. A gusher. A field of gushers" (163).

As forgery narratives go, this one is better than most. Moreover, it confirms thesis 9: that good forgeries are works of assiduous scholarship. Yet an unbiased witness would find the tale fishy. What was the wealthy man's name? Wouldn't he know what was in the volumes he had so carefully sewn together? And wouldn't there be at least some mention of the play, considering that four hundred years of

> Yet find dim shapes, reversed and
> versed again,
> Which will not ease our self-love's
> appetites. (2.7. 32–35, p. 306)

People see in others their own hopes embodied; believing makes a fiction true (see thesis 13). Thus, to Gloucester's disgust that "by gross deception came this victory / Your men believe you led them into war," Arthur blithely responds, "An if they believe, then so I did" (2.7.73–75, p. 307). By believing him a king, they make him one. After all, a king is not a person but a symbol, an imaginary being, a synecdoche for subjects' collective aspirations and dreams. All kings are, in that sense, pretenders. The speech also describes the play in which the king resides, which is in many respects about its own fraudulence—it is Shakespeare "versed again." Moreover, the lines describe the author's position, as Arthur Phillips the character and novelist (or Arthur Phillips Sr., the forger) watches his own life refracted in the play, "reversed and versed again." Here, as in *Pale Fire,* a text is not a window on the world but a cracked mirror in which one witnesses oneself coming to life. This imagining, even if impelled by egotism or false faith, frees one for what Senior would call "wonders." Far from covering the face, a mask reveals it: the lie exposes the truth. In that respect, we may say that all literature is a species of forgery—and that is its wonder.

Shakespeare scholars have combed over every detail of his life and work and that lost plays such as *Cardenio* are named many times? Junior buys it, nonetheless. Why? Because he wants his father to love him; because he is seduced by the prospect of being the MB's collaborator (which would make him matchless too); because he is excited by the research involved and already knows Shakespeare's works well; because, after publishing four novels, he is bereft of inspiration; because his sister believes in the play's authenticity. Senior knows that he himself can't touch it: "My career is ideally suited to make my word on this useless. 'Read all about it! Convicted forger discovers Shakespeare play!' I would sink him. . . . [W]e have to do this for him" (164)—for Shakespeare, but also for *him*, Arthur Sr. Nor, he admits, does he have the talent to tiptoe into "the Fakespeare bog" even if he wanted to. "I could never write anything as beautiful as this play. I am a faker, in every way" (168–69). Junior is thus the *only one* who can make this happen. These reasons are potent, but, young Arthur ruefully notes, "Like all good pigeons, I took on most of the work of conning me myself' (136).

He also cons himself about Petra, Dana's new romantic partner, with whom he becomes infatuated. Reading *Arthur* by her side, he is aswim in fond fantasies, imagining himself as the character in *Two Gentleman* who "loses his mind and madly pursues the hero's beloved" (141) and later

Fond

Rejecting his violent bloodlines and believing that "the glory of a king is weighed on a scale / By what prosperity his kingdom joys," not by how many wars he fights, King Arthur shows clemency for the prisoners of war—much to Cumbria's dismay (2.8.9–11, p. 310). The latter is proven right when these Saxon warriors return and pillage English settlements. Cursing himself, Arthur orders all remaining prisoners slaughtered, including Mordred's brother Calvan. Then he errs again, eschewing Gloucester's carefully arranged, politically advantageous marriage to a French princess once he is reintroduced to Guenhara, the sister of his old friend Constantine (recalling Vortigern's sudden infatuation with Rowena).[24] He recalls "feigning" being king as a boy, implying that his real crown is also a costume, that he is more player than king. In fact, he seems to be as much in love with his own former self as with Guenhara. King Arthur's infatuation thus mirrors Arthur Jr.'s for Petra: he loves her not for who she is but for what she shows him about himself. Arthur Rex is Arthur Jr. versed and reversed: whereas Junior loves his sister's friend, the king loves his friend's sister.

Guenhara too inverts her assigned roles: she miscarries twice (not her fault, of course, but the queen's job is to produce an heir) and dominates the uxorious Arthur, who allows her to rule over a feminized court preoccupied with romantic intrigues. Cumbria complains that they "play at manliness" envisioning Petra as the character in *Twelfth Night* who falls in love with a female twin dressed as a man and then transfers her love to the male (175). Petra's love, he fantasizes, will shape a "better version of me." And so, he hopes, will *Arthur.* Belief, as noted in thesis 13, is a "virus" that replicates itself in groups (143); hence Petra and Dana's credulity about the play rubs off on him, even as he asks them to play devil's advocates. Whereas Arthur looks for signs of forgery everywhere, Dana takes "any oddity as proof that it must be authentic" (166): Shakespeare is a mirror of expectations, a vehicle for wish-fulfillment. The deciding hook comes in Dad's final email from prison, informing his son he is dying. Junior vows to "do anything to make it right and to hold tight to every love and opportunity and moment that remained in his life and in mine" (169).

Fever

Arthur Jr. marches boldly into the bog. The first scholar he consults notes that a rival company produced two Arthur-themed plays around 1597, and Junior loves the portrait of Shakespeare as a working writer in a competitive group—like a member of an ad agency or baseball team (173). Nor is he discouraged when he realizes that his advance will amount to many times his earnings for his novels. Junior peruses academic volumes (whose authors include several actual Shakespeare scholars), reads Holinshed and Malory, studies theatrical practices, bones up on "Shakespearean forgeries (3.3.25, p. 333) and at the end of act 3, scene 3, he wonders whether he should "play regicide / As shallow Arthur has too long played king," but eventually decides against it (3.3.85–86, p. 335). The final line of his speech is Arthur Jr.'s "smoking verb," the match that immolates his belief in *Arthur*'s authenticity. The two stories here converge: just as Junior becomes convinced that *Arthur* is a forged play, so Cumbria (and perhaps King Arthur) is convinced that Arthur is a forged king. Cumbria persuades Arthur to name Mordred as his successor if Guenhara bears no child. He agrees, as does Mordred, who plans to "implant a prince ourselves to hold our claim / And with her womb prove Mordred's right to rule." Meanwhile he will act "as a vengeful brother ought" (4.3.36–37, 41–42, p. 346). If Arthur wants to turn everyone into pretenders, Mordred will play his part. The events of the Phillipses' story are reversed again: Arthur Jr. has acted as a vengeful brother, turning against his father's play and betraying his sister by sleeping with Petra. If, as Dana maintains, the play is "about" Arthur Jr., then he is both hero and villain, performing both as Arthur Rex *and* Mordred.

Players

Young Arthur also mirrors Philip, a teenager who suddenly appears in act 4 claiming to be King Arthur's son by a York seamstress named Elizabeth—another bastard. Gloucester scoffs at his "cozenage," but, miraculously, the king accepts it (or pretends to), speaking the lines that form the

(Ireland)"—as the real Arthur Phillips no doubt did when writing this novel. "It was a measure of my fever—money-hungry, lust-breathing, fame-thirsty, guilt-fueled, daddy-pleasing—that I enjoyed all of it" (171). He discovers in its theme of monarchic succession further evidence of its authenticity.[25] Most convincing are the play's autobiographical resonances: Hamnet Shakespeare died in 1596, and *Arthur* is "manifestly about lost fatherhoods & lost childhoods" (183). In other words, it is about him!

A parade of pedants troops through the apartment where Senior, finally out of prison, resides. One scholar suggests that the play was written no later than 1595, that it "*pops* like him at many moments," and that its hero is suitably complex (190). An expert on paper announces that "the hardest fact any forger has to overcome is a simple truth: every object contains the history of its own making," but he boasts that modern forensic science can't be fooled (197).[27] Two new developments complicate this orderly cavalcade. Dana bitterly quarrels with Petra, and Arthur, ostensibly coming to Dana's aid, ends up having sex with her lover. During this ignoble betrayal, Dana stars in a production of *Two Noble Kinsmen.* And then Arthur Sr. dies. Junior's self-serving eulogy praises him as an "original" who "lived for art and wonder" but "wasted himself in the least exalted, least wondrous escapades one could imagine" (200). Yet Junior still nurses three "articles of faith": that his father loved him; that second epigraph to this section. This "prince" is Arthur's "print," his mirror image—a metaphor that explicitly connects King Arthur's belief in Philip to Arthur Jr.'s initial belief in *Arthur.* An incredulous Gloucester interrogates the king, commenting that the boy probably came "hoping for a coin, / And you'll emboss his face on every one" (4.4.75–76, p. 349). Instead of receiving a sovereign, Philip may become one. Perhaps Arthur knows the boy is counterfeit and clings to him for that very reason, since he feels himself a fake. In any case, after the king exits, Philip delivers a soliloquy in which he admits to being a fraud, noting that Elizabeth gave birth to a child the same day Philip was born, but that boy—perhaps Arthur's actual bastard son—died recently.[26] Philip is an actor, a forgery of a forgery.

The appearance of a Player King at court thus seems fitting, and when the PK meets Mordred, the former assumes that the Pict is also a thespian. And he is: an actor pretending to be Arthur's ally. After Mordred dismisses the Player King as a "malapert, to current king," the PK puns that "such currency is compassed by the art" (5.125–26, p. 354). These coinage tropes extend the parallel between performance and counterfeiting. Just as counterfeit coins require the faith of the exchangers to acquire value, so dramatic art requires belief to work its magic. Mordred's subsequent assumption that Philip is a pretender furthers the idea that a monarch, like a forger, is *always* an actor. For he can win Petra without hurting his sister; and that the author of *The Tragedy of Arthur* is William Shakespeare. These three trees are "one and the same, connected under the soil" (201). He soon discovers that the branches are rotten.

Fakespeare

While cleaning out his father's effects, Arthur finds an index card on which is scrawled "explain Arthur in York"; next to an arrow is written "Cumbria backs away," and below that is a line with scansion marks: "When Righteous men would stand aloof" (202–3). The line seems to be a draft of the final words of act 3 (335), when the Earl of Cumbria decides to scuttle a plan to assassinate the indecisive King Arthur. Immediately envisioning this card as the "smoking verb" (205), Junior feels sick, not only because the play is a fake but also because "the death of *Arthur* meant the death of Arthur's love all the way back" to the son's childhood. He feels as if "a spell has worn off" (204), like Bottom waking to find himself wearing an ass's head. The ingenious backstory now becomes simpler: his father faked the 1904 edition as a test, selected an Elizabethan printer with no heirs as his "publisher," found authentic paper, wrote the play himself, then created the binding. Simpler, yes, but more plausible? Not really. Arthur's mother notes that "there were barely libraries in those prisons. Somehow he's concocting sixteenth-century ink?" (206). And was Senior, a Bardolater but no bard, capable of Arthur, however, the costume never quite fits, and in a soliloquy before the final battle, he questions how his story will eventually "fill a stage." He imagines future historians condemning his rashness but argues that "the stain of birth / Was ne'er forgot nor ne'er forgave in me, / No matter I upraised a glorious realm" (5.3.14–16, p. 359). In peacetime he might have escaped the "shame that I have failed to be myself" (line 24). It is as if William-Henry Ireland were speaking. Arthur, separate from his royal identity, chafes at the duality, just as Arthur Phillips Jr. vainly seeks a genuine identity while immuring himself in illusions. If Arthur Sr. is the play's author, these lines amount to a self-portrait of man who tried to be an artist and a good father but could never assume either mantle comfortably. His true nature was to be a fake.

Mordred, having kidnaped Philip and Guenhara, offers to swap them for the English throne. But then Mordred's troops attack. Enraged, Arthur slaughters Mordred's ambassadors. A desperate Philip confesses his fraud, but the executioners don't believe him, and he is murdered along with Guenhara. The stricken Arthur fights on, albeit disgusted that he has become his murdering father (5.5.36, p. 367). Likewise, despite his lifelong efforts not to be *his* father, Arthur Phillips Jr., by publishing this play, becomes a twenty-first-century Hamlet carrying out his dead father's wishes. King Arthur's dying words express his fervent wish—the wish, indeed, of all writing a play that could hoodwink Shakespeare scholars? How did he contrive, in the 1970s, a forgery that would defeat forensics tests that didn't yet exist? Ignoring these questions, Junior resentfully imagines Dad dying with a smile on his face: not only has he duped his desperate son, but he has "fooled everyone." Like W-H Ireland, he managed "to feel like he's Shakespeare. As good as Shakespeare" (207).

A will complicates this battle for Will. Senior leaves a quarter of his estate (including the money from *Arthur*) to Mary, Dana, Arthur, and Chuck Glassow, shrewdly stipulating that the bequest be nullified if Junior or anyone else tries to discredit the play. Believing that Glassow's presence clinches the fraud and that its discovery would destroy his career ("Nobody reads Clifford Irving's novels anymore"), Arthur prepares to joust: "I refused to resemble my father in any way. . . . I was not going to let him get away with it, even if it cost me $10 million" (212). Dana disagrees, though her defense—"You didn't notice that it's about you?"—seems to bolster Junior's case (213). The play, she declares, is a gift that represents "his love for you." If it is a forgery, "he forged it for you." And what does Junior have to lose? If it's not a forgery, he is "a dick," the idiot who will go down in history as the one who couldn't recognize the MB; if it is a forgery, he is still a dick, because he will have dismissed this tangible sign of his father's love just so he can be right. Young Arthur is "the first person ever to suffer from a double oedipal complex, and one of [his] dads is four forgers—"To be some other man than what I am!" (5.5.49, p. 367). With all pretenders dead, Constantine (named, Junior believes, after an attorney who sent his father to prison) accedes to the throne and unifies Britain.

Is *The Tragedy of Arthur* a forgery? As a drama attributed to Shakespeare but part of a novel written by the Arthur Phillips whose smiling visage graces the dust jacket and who lives "in New York with his wife and two sons" (we don't know if they are twins), it is at least a mock forgery (or fake mystification). As such, it is a forgery *and* a pastiche, one inspired by the same motives that impelled the hapless William-Henry Ireland: to *become* the Bard. But are we to believe that the play has been forged by Arthur Phillips Sr. (or someone else), or should we accept it as a (fictional) play by Shakespeare?[28] If the latter, as Dana points out, Junior is a fool too blinded by resentment of his felonious father to see the truth; he publishes his folly for all the world to witness. If Senior is the author, however, the play is more resonant, for in this light it displays—as in a cracked looking glass—the fictional author's perceptions of himself, his career, and his family. According to this reading, Senior is King Arthur: a self-deluded would-be visionary, a poor actor who has never fit the roles of father and provider. If so, then Philip of York is Arthur Jr.—a liar who lucks, briefly, into destiny. Yet King Arthur also mirrors Arthur Jr., and if Senior is the author, we now understand that he is a wise father who knows his own hundred years old" (214). Calling her brother a "bastard" (215), Dana even suggests (as Kahan does with the Ireland forgeries) that other family members—her mother, herself, all of them together—wrote the play (216). She appeals to his generosity ("Couldn't you let him win this last one?"), his greed, and his vanity. (She claims to prefer his writing to Shakespeare's.) But Junior will not budge and emails his editor that he is backing out. The editor plausibly points out that the index card could be mere study notes, but having crossed the Avon, Arthur has planted himself on the other bank.

Too late. A massive marketing campaign (featuring t-shirts with Mordred's self-description as "the deathsman of repose") has already been launched, along with online contests, trips to Stratford, tweets, and tchotchkes. Although one of Dana's cohorts claims that the play's "texture is all wrong," picking out several "dead giveaway" phrases, he cannot compete with the growing chorus of experts who deem it authentic (222). (The "giveaway" lines all turn out to be Shakespeare's.) One scholar does point out, as noted above, that this poet who "finished his sentences at the ends of his lines" is not the Shakespeare of 1597 (235). But the linguists matter less than the lawyers who threaten Arthur with a breach of contract suit. If he reneges, no money will be forthcoming to him or to his family, and they will issue the book anyway—and sue him for damages. Arthur must publish or perish.

child to be someone who, precisely by trying *not* to become his father, becomes him. If it is a forgery within its fictional world, the play embodies the "anarchist" theory of creativity according to which everyone steals. Either way, through imitation and theft the Arthurs become authors. They strive for originality, but author Arthur Phillips achieves it—by faking. And so, in his own misbegotten manner, did William-Henry Ireland. In becoming Shakespeare, each one becomes an author and thereby becomes himself. Whoever that is.

Problem Play

Although some of Arthur Jr.'s misgivings about the play are the offspring of principle, he admits that vindictiveness motivates him just as much (212). Yet his sour attitude bears stringent intellectual fruit in the form of insights about forgers. One is the dialectic between erasure and exposure outlined in thesis 4: the forger is the only artist whose success depends on *not* being recognized (239). Fooling the world confirms the forger's greatness, as William-Henry Ireland (and Elmyr de Hory and Clifford Irving) believed. But what good is that? Junior grasps that forgers want to be caught in order to broadcast their brilliance. Forgery, he comprehends, is "paradoxically arrogant and self-effacing," at once a "plea for attention and an ashamed desire to be invisible" (228). We have seen how this conflict worked on William-Henry Ireland: the ridiculous contrivances that he used to camouflage his forgeries may have been motivated by a secret desire to be unmasked. Often the only one capable of grasping the forger's ingenuity is the victim. And sometimes that victim wants to be duped. Hence, Arthur realizes, a forgery prompts us to ask ourselves, "What actions or thoughts out there are like mine—are *me*—even though I've never done or thought them?" (229). This is the meaning of the lines from *Arthur* quoted above, which refer to seeking a "handsome glimpse" in the "imperfect glass of others' eyes" (2.7.32, p. 306). A forgery allows believers to bask in the weak glow of a reflected sun.

These desires probably also propel the phalanx of philologists who endorse the play's authenticity. In his interview with Reilly, the flesh-and-blood Arthur Phillips voices disgust for the "mystical reverence" with which Shakespeare is perceived (5), and here he pokes fun at this cult. Yet Phillips's satire of the "Shakespeare industrial complex" (4) is too facile. These academics talk about "loving" the MB, but there is little rigor in their investigations, despite the forensic expert's braggadocio. They offer speculative biographical connections (*Tragedy* 238) or resort to impressionistic responses about characterization (235), but they never dissect the poetry, which gives itself away in the first pages. In the real world, it would take a Macdonald Jackson or a Brian Vickers about five minutes to determine that *The Tragedy of Arthur* is a fraud. Still, both the fictive and the real Arthur Phillips are correct about scholars' sometimes compromised motives. As Junior remarks (and as we have seen with the Ireland and Chatterton forgeries), "Once they wager their egos, they never quit" (238; see thesis 13).

Arthur Jr. has wagered *his* ego on Petra and is delighted when she informs him that she is pregnant (he is the father) and that she wants to keep the baby. How fitting: a bastard child of Shakespeare lovers will be born beside a bastard text. "This fixes everything. It's *authenticating!*" (240), he gushes, thus identifying literary and physical creation. His giddy mood deflates when Petra tells him that Dana has committed suicide. But once he arrives at her apartment, a living—and livid—Dana opens the door. She mocks her brother's fantasy that she would step aside and leave him with Petra and child. "Because you're such a great husband and father? You can't even think of something consistent with the characters" (247). What shall the wayward boy-man's punishment be? They select one from the Bard's works: he will reenact *Love's Labours Lost*. And so Arthur is banished for a "twelvemonth," must publish *The Tragedy of Arthur*, and must "divest [himself] of [his] precious reputation and self-love." He must tell the truth in his introduction so that every reader—and there will be millions—can judge him along with the play. His sentence *may* end after all three judges have read the book (250–51). Harsh? Probably. Yet we may detect in it a hint of W-H Ireland's humblebragging—the satisfaction of portraying oneself as the world's greatest villain. As an ending to the novel, however, it is neither comic nor tragic. Unlike the play, the introduction is, Junior decides, a "*problem play*" (255, italics his). In any case, the Phillipses cannot escape from Shakespeare: their lives, like those of Ackroyd's characters and those in the play itself, are ghostly stencils of works written hundreds of years ago. The play adds another layer, another shadow, another set of twins, to this impasto, as if the modern-day characters are pale reflections not only of Shakespeare's but of Fakespeare's light.

3

Hideous Progeny

FORGERY, *FRANKENSTEIN*, AND PETER CAREY'S *MY LIFE AS A FAKE*

> Now I find that once more I have shrunk
> To an interloper, robber of dead men's dream,
> I had read in books that art is not easy
> But no one warned me that the mind repeats
> In its ignorance the vision of others. I am still
> The black swan of trespass on alien waters.
>
> —Ern Malley, "Durer: Innsbruck, 1495"

> I beheld the wretch—the miserable monster whom I had created. He held up the curtain of the bed; and his eyes, if eyes they may be called, were fixed on me.
>
> —Mary Shelley, *Frankenstein*

ONE SATURDAY afternoon in October 1943, Lt. James McAuley and Cpl. Harold Stewart, poet/soldiers stationed in Melbourne, Australia, decided to play a trick on Max Harris, the youthful editor of *Angry Penguins*, a literary journal that championed modernist poetry. Using only the books they had at hand—a complete Shakespeare, Ripman's *Pocket Dictionary of English Rhymes*, the *Concise Oxford Dictionary*, a book of quotations, and a report on mosquito control—they crafted a series of poems that they attributed to an imaginary figure named Ern Malley. After crumpling the paper and staining it with tea to evoke Malley's tortured drafting, they sent three poems and a letter from Ern's equally fictitious sister, Ethel, informing Harris that the twenty-five-year-old Ern had recently died from Graves' disease and had left his work with her. Immensely impressed, Harris replied to Ethel that he wanted to publish the poems and wished to see more of Ern's output. Ethel duly sent a book of seventeen poems entitled *The Darkening Ecliptic*, along with a preface outlining Ern's aesthetic principles. Harris published these writings in June 1944. Within two weeks the hoax was exposed, and McAuley and Stewart penned a letter explaining that the trick was a "serious literary experiment" aimed at discrediting modernism, which had led to the "gradual decay of meaning and craftsmanship in poetry" (*Ern Malley's Poems* 7, hereafter cited as *EMP*). Not long afterward Harris was arrested, tried, and convicted of publishing "indecent" material in the Malley poems.

Many literary historians, especially Australians, are familiar with this version of the incident. But like all fakes, the Malley forgeries are enveloped within stories—one meant to authenticate the fake and at least one more designed to explain and justify the perpetrators' motives. As I show below, the second story is also partly fictional.

One night in June 1816, eighteen-year-old Mary Godwin had a "waking dream" (Shelley 24). Charged, along with her lover, Percy Shelley, and his friends Lord Byron and John Polidori, to write a ghost story, she had struggled to discover a topic. Out of her nightmarish vision arose the image of a "pale student of unhallowed arts kneeling beside the thing he had put together" (24). She saw the being stir and the creator awaken: "Behold the horrid thing stands at his bedside, opening the curtains, and looking on him with yellow, watery, but speculative eyes" (24). Thus did she conceive *Frankenstein,* according to her preface to the 1831 edition. At the end of that preface, she writes, "I bid my hideous progeny go forth and prosper. I have an affection for it; it was the offspring of happy days, when death and grief were but words" (25). Mary Godwin Shelley's wish for her patchwork novel identifies literary creation and physical creation—a striking association from a woman who had, by 1831, borne four children and watched three of them perish. It was as if her literary offspring might compensate for her babies' deaths.

In 2003 Peter Carey married the Malley and Shelley stories. The issue of this unlikely alliance is a novel about forgery, monstrous creation, and kidnaping told, like *Frankenstein,* via embedded narratives. As if to acknowledge its second-hand status, Carey titled his novel *My Life as a Fake* (hereafter *MLAF).* The Ern Malley affair seems tailor-made for an author long fascinated by liars and frauds (e.g., Herbert Badgery, the extravagantly lying narrator of *Illywhacker*). Carey's brainchild exemplifies the absurdities, complexities, and provocations of literary forgeries and the fictions they inspire and raises challenging questions about authorship, parenthood—particularly the parallels between literary and physical creation—and the power of writing to shape identity.

Carey's frame narrator is Sarah Wode-Douglass, editor of the *Modern Review,* who, in 1985, recalls being lured to Malaysia thirteen years earlier by a family friend: elder poet and best-selling novelist John Slater. In Kuala Lumpur she met an Australian named Christopher Chubb, who told her a complicated and frankly incredible tale. In the 1940s Chubb, angry at having his poems rejected by David Weiss, editor of the journal *Personae,* invented a (deceased) working-class poet named Bob McCorkle and his sister, who sent to Weiss McCorkle's book, *The Darkening Ecliptic.* Chubb even fashioned a photo of McCorkle by cutting and pasting images from a magazine (his efforts further reinforcing thesis 6). Weiss published the poems, enthusiastically announcing the discovery of a genius, but was soon arrested and tried for obscenity. So far, aside from the number of hoaxers, the story follows the Malley affair closely. Enter Frankenstein, or rather, Frankenstein's creature: a tall man calling himself Bob McCorkle interrupted the obscenity trial and soon semi-accidentally killed Weiss. A few years later, McCorkle kidnaped Chubb's adopted daughter, Tina, and led him on a chase across Malaysia. Then McCorkle died, leaving behind his own hideous progeny—both a scarred daughter and a manuscript of brilliant poems written on bark paper. Ultimately Chubb was killed and Sarah, despite her obsessive pursuit of the McCorkle magnum opus, never obtained it.

In revisiting the most famous literary forgery of the twentieth century, Carey perpetrates a different sort of mystification—we might call it a mock forgery—by enlisting *Frankenstein* and expanding Shelley's (and Malley's) metaphoric link between physical reproduction and textual creation (see thesis 8). The result is more hideous progeny—a textual body formed by stitching together fragments of other textual bodies. Carey's novel indeed suggests that all literary works are fakes that nonetheless thrust themselves, like Frankenstein's creature and Bob McCorkle, into the real world, where the creator loses control of them (thesis 12). Far from endorsing Foucault's definition of an author as the "principle of thrift in the proliferation of meaning" (ed. Harari 159), *MLAF* suggests that authorship fosters proliferation and that forging never ends.

The Ern Malley poems differ from Ireland's Shakespeare forgeries, in which The Matchless Bard's name was used to garnish the teenager's clumsy work, and from Chatterton's medievalist excavations, in which Rowley and Canynge became surrogate fathers and instruments of authority and self-formation. But all three attribute a written document to an author who did not, in fact, create it. In this respect, it matters not whether the sham author be an entirely invented character (Rowley, Malley); a quasi-mythological, albeit formerly existing person (Shakespeare, Stagolee); or an equally mythologized living person (Howard Hughes). As I suggest in the prologue, the signature, which links mind and body as well as the time of signing and the time of reading, serves as a tangible signifier of an author's (former) presence. Recall de Bolla's observation that a false signature "inserts the possibility of multiple personality, or no identity at all, into the paper-thin circulation of trust in a speculative society," thereby creating "the possibility for the destabilization of self, society and certainty" (73). Such multiple personalities and destabilizations occur, I propose, not only in the Malley forgeries but also in *Frankenstein* and *MLAF*. Carey's novel further suggests that human selfhood is brought forth, for better or worse, by writing and storytelling but that such identities are always unstable and metamorphic. A forgery is a masquerade authorized by a signature that emerges from what Ruthven calls "dispersed" authorship (92). As noted in the prologue, a forged work is part of a larger imposture—the impersonation of an artist or author. Most such impersonations remain in the realm of representation: the impersonation is literal, meaning written, not physical. But when forgers or hoaxers supply a body, they render the forger's spectral presence tangible, making visible what was invisible, raising the stakes, and crossing the line from inscription to incarnation. However, the physical presence of the impostor does not liberate the forger from entrapping paradoxes; indeed, as *MLAF* and *erasure* (discussed in chapter 4) dramatize, that body instead replaces the author's, making his or her expungement even more complete.

Black Swan

> If this be the norm
> Of our serious frolic
> There's no remorse.
>
> —Ern Malley, "Sonnets for the Novachord"

"Literary forgery is criticism by other means," writes Ruthven, who concludes that hoaxes "release creative energies not yet domesticated by those cultural conventions which legitimate literature as a social institution"

(171, 199). His description fits the Malley poems, which Michael Heyward has called "the most decisive piece of literary criticism ever produced in Australia" (293). Throughout the affair and its aftermath, McAuley and Stewart insisted that their aims were literary, not personal. Nevertheless, Max Harris, a student at the University of Adelaide who had burst onto the scene as a champion of modernism with *Angry Penguins*, seemed to them as plump a target as a flightless bird, and Cassandra Pybus has shown that envy of the precocious Harris motivated the fraud (143–44). But Harris wasn't entirely credulous: he sent the Malley poems to Adelaide Professor J. I. M. Stewart, who found them "derivative" and "incomprehensible" but did not detect a fraud; Harris's coeditor, John Reed, deemed them marvelous. After Harris's encouraging reply to Ethel, she filled in Ern's biography: he had been a mechanic, then sold insurance, but died unknown and unpublished. Along with the seventeen poems comprising *The Darkening Ecliptic*, she forwarded Ern's "Preface and Statement," a manifesto packed with proclamations such as "Every poem should be an autarchy" (*EMP* 23; the line is plagiarized from Herbert Read).[1] Both the preface and the biography—that of an unpolished, working-class genius—appealed to Harris's sensibilities. Fancying himself Max Brod to Malley's Kafka, he forged on with publication.[2]

McAuley and Stewart weren't merely pranksters: though only in their mid-twenties, both were published poets. Something of a prodigy and renaissance man, McAuley played accomplished jazz piano and had steeped himself in European poetry, particularly the French *Symbolistes*. Stewart had studied Jung, translated Mallarmé, and later became a Buddhist (Heyward 48, 65). They agreed, however, that modernism was a sham and proclaimed in their public statement exposing the hoax that it "rendered its devotees insensible of absurdity and incapable of ordinary discrimination" (*EMP* 7): their claims bear out thesis 5. Yet they must have meant for Harris to realize eventually that he had been gulled: no exposure would mean no humiliation, in which case the jape would have no point. The Malley forgeries thus exemplify McHale's "trap-hoax," one designed "with didactic and punitive purposes in mind" (236). To rub it in, they claimed to have "deliberately perpetrated bad verse," selecting awkward rhymes from Ripman and pilfering the opening lines of "Culture as Exhibit" from a US officer's report on draining mosquito breeding grounds (*EMP* 8). They also nonchalantly declared that they had written the Malley poems in a single afternoon (8). Their rules?

They would muster no coherent theme but present only inconsistent hints "held out as a bait"; they would take no care with verse technique; and the poems would imitate "the whole literary fashion" of European modernism (*EMP* 8). Ruthven comments that literary forgeries "disturb the societies in which they are produced . . . in ways resented by the guardians of cultural institutions" (2). In this case, however, the self-appointed "guardians" were the ones creating the disturbance. What were they guarding against? The incursions of cosmopolitanism. As Brian McHale observes, a "nationalistic subtext" runs through this hoax (242) as it also did in James Macpherson's Ossian poems, in Chatterton's Rowley works, and, to a lesser degree, in the Ireland forgeries.

Should we believe their account? Probably not, for David Brooks has demonstrated that this story is nearly as fictional as Ern himself. First, their claims of spontaneity and rapid composition are "undermined by a number of factors," including the insertion of the Dürer poem, which McAuley had written earlier and shelved (Brooks 70). They also used, or remembered, numerous other works in addition to those they listed, including several by T. S. Eliot, Ezra Pound, Stéphane Mallarmé, Dante, and Keats, among others (Brooks 240). Their professed disgust for modernism also seems suspect, given that McAuley had written a master's thesis on the *Symbolistes* a few years earlier, and Stewart had completed a book displaying the influence of Hart Crane, Mallarmé, and Rilke (Lloyd 22). Brooks thus argues that the Malley poems were the issue of McAuley's internal struggle, a "dark night of the soul" from which he emerged with a scathing contempt for his former self (19). Ern Malley was a composite image of the hoaxers' former poetic personae. Yet their procedures were, Philip Mead notes, quintessentially modernist, as they employed found materials and aleatory methods reminiscent of the same Dadaists they scorn in their statement (Mead 117; *EMP* 9).[3] The poems, then, are wrapped in a package of falsehoods: not only is the story of Ern and Ethel a fiction; the second, self-justifying story is at best misleading and at worst mendacious—a part of the hoax. Their justification exemplifies thesis 3: that forgeries are the seeds from which fictions (here we may call them "lies") blossom.

Soon after the hoaxers pretended to come clean, a police detective named Vogelesang arrested Harris for obscenity, having deemed certain lines in Malley's poems "indecent." "Boult to Marina," which glosses some scenes in Shakespeare's *Pericles* (written with a coauthor) and contains a suggestive pun about standing "Boult-upright"; and "Sweet William," which refers to an "unforgivable rape," were the main targets, but the poems were indicted as much for obscurity as for obscenity (Heyward 237). The September 1944 trial was a farce, with the prosecution arguing that the poems were nonsense while at the same time claiming that their meanings were clear—and immoral. Literature professors J. I. M. Stewart and Brian Elliott testified; although the latter had expressed admiration for the poems, the two agreed that parts of *Darkening Ecliptic* were "indecent" and "distasteful" (Heyward 169, 253–54). Ultimately Harris was convicted of publishing indecent material, fined £5, and forced to pay more than £21 in court costs.[4] McAuley and Stewart, though "embarrassed and appalled," faced no criminal or civil charges (Heyward 261). Despite its absurdities, the trial raises questions that Carey's novel develops: Who is responsible for a work of literature? Is the author its sole "parent," or do other parties--editor, publisher, reader—serve as cocreators (see thesis 7)? Does a literary work, like a child, take on its own life once released from authorial control (see thesis 12)?

> It is necessary to understand
> That a poet may not exist, that his writings
> Are the incomplete circle and straight drop
> Of a question mark.
>
> —Ern Malley, "Sybilline"

McAuley and Stewart end their public statement thus: "The writings of Ern Malley are utterly devoid of literary merit" (*EMP* 9). Many readers have disagreed. For one thing, *The Darkening Ecliptic* succeeds brilliantly as parody, cleverly alluding to various modernists and mimicking their styles (Heyward 184–85). In a piece included in the 1961 edition of the poems, Herbert Read points to the poems' "effective use of vivid metaphor" and "subtle sense of rhythmic variation" (*EMP* 10); Brooks concludes that the Malley poems are "glorious, luxurious, sensical, profound" (243). Even venerated figures such as Kenneth Koch and John Ashbery have found much merit in them and have published their own "Malley" poems.[5] These critics argue that Malley's work exemplifies "a successful experiment in collaborative writing" (Mead 116), a prime instance of Ruthven's "'dispersed' authorial practice" (92). As with *My Pafology* in Everett's *erasure,* so here: the misread parody unintentionally elevates the intended target and escapes the authors' control.

Robert Hughes suggests that the hoaxers "reached inspiration by the side door of parody" (305), but years later McAuley maintained that the controversy was really a "quarrel over the nature of inspiration," and gamely tried to distinguish between "pseudo-inspiration"—which is a "surrender to irrational forces" without the "sovereign power of the shaping intellect"—and genuine inspiration, which is an "action of the whole man" (*EMP* 15, 16). But he and Stewart *did* shape *The Darkening Ecliptic* with their intellects, as the numerous allusions and clever parodies demonstrate; hence, the poems are genuinely inspired according to McAuley's own definition. And indeed, despite its weird words and awkward rhymes, *The Darkening Ecliptic* shoots off sparks of brilliance. Moreover, it coheres through motif and theme, the most pervasive being Malley's nonexistence and the hoax itself.

This is never better expressed than in the complexly layered, ekphrastic opening poem, "Durer: Innsbruck, 1495," a gloss on Albrecht Dürer's early painting *Innsbruck Seen across the River Inn,* in which the town's buildings are reflected in ghostly fashion in the river before them (fig. 7). The speaker envisions the painting behind his closed lids and finds the town "real," but then understands that Dürer had already grasped that art cannot capture reality but only copy it, that the water's reflective powers anticipate his own representational art. The painting is thus a third-order representation that seeks to depict both the real town and its reflection in the water. The speaker's creation, therefore, is fourth-hand, a copy of a copy (the painting) of a copy (in the water) of the actual town.[6] More broadly, the poem implies that all modern art must acknowledge its belatedness—and it does so cleverly, through its symbiotic relationship to a previous work. Trumpeting its own lack of originality, it tests the notion that all art involves forgery or imitation—and embodies it, since the poem, written earlier by McAuley, is itself a kind of fake fake.[7]

There are further indications, such as the lines from "Sibylline" quoted above, that a fraud may be afoot.[8] For example, "Palinode" alludes to an "ancient forgotten ruse / And a natural diversion" (Brooks 312). "Boult to Marina" imagines a dialogue between the pimp Boult and the lost daughter Marina derived from Shakespeare's *Pericles.* But that play was a collaboration with another playwright, probably George Wilkins. Attributed to Shakespeare in the Quarto but not written solely by him, *Pericles* is a semiforgery, and the hoaxers likely selected it for this very reason.[9] In "Petit Testament," the speaker, though admitting failure, allows that it is "something to be at last speaking / Though in this

FIG. 7. Albrecht Dürer's *Innsbruck Seen across the River Inn* (1495) shows the town's buildings reflected in the river before them. Watercolor. 12.7 × 18.7 cm. (Photo: Erich Lessing/Art Resource, NY)

No-Man's-language appropriate / Only to No-Man's-Land" (323). Who speaks "No-Man's-language"? A person who doesn't exist. But there is another answer, which I offer below.

One might also read these lines as the *cri de coeur* of an unrecognized poet. A prime reason for his despair is the sense of belatedness introduced in the Dürer poem. McAuley and Stewart use artful allusiveness to develop this theme (as in thesis 9). Thus "Sweet William" addresses Blake, "Boult to Marina" and "Young Prince of Tyre" refer to *Pericles*, and "Colloquy with John Keats" opens with a line echoing Pound's "A Pact": "I have been bitter with you, my brother" (Brooks 320).[10] This speaker admits that they "are as the double almond concealed in one shell," a line that simultaneously figures Keats and Malley as twins and intimates that the speaker is really two people. This double-voicedness, as Lloyd points out, pervades the volume (28).[11] For example, the two "Night-Piece" poems present twin sensibilities working through the same material: lovers near a pond hearing frogs and a splash, viewing iron birds over a gate, feeling melancholy. The first has a world-weary, Eliotic tone, as well as some sesquipedalian diction ("umbelliferous"); more objective, the second version eschews such grandstanding and conveys an atmosphere of desolation and loss in neo-Symbolist fashion. Elsewhere, the text battles with itself, its "creeping disjunct minds" ("Young Prince of Tyre" 319) forming awkward juxtapositions and forging clunky language yet fostering provocative tensions. In short, the collaborative composition enhances the volume's effects.

This doubling effect couples with the poems' portrait of the lovelorn artist as a young man. In this sense, the letters, biography, preface, and poems are parts of the textual body of Ern Malley, a "haphazard amorist / Caught on the unlikely angles / Of an awkward arrangement" ("Palinode" Brooks 312). The "arrangement," however, is likely not with an imaginary lover but between the hoaxers. In their statement McAuley and Stewart admit that they "gave birth to Ern Malley" (*EMP* 8), and as Ern takes shape, the poems conflate literary and physical reproduction, bodies, and texts. For example, "Sonnets for the Novachord" equates poems with "loaves and fishes" (305); "Culture as Exhibit" compares humans to "wraiths and wreathes of tissue-paper" and depicts the speaker as a bookworm who "chewed / Back-numbers of Florentine gazettes." Those words are now incorporated into his textual body (316). "Petit Testament" confesses that "we shall never be that verb / Perched on the sole Arabian tree" (322): through a miraculous metamorphosis, bird becomes word. In the final lines of "Petit Testament," the speaker describes a pelvis that "explodes like a grenade" and likens himself to a thistle that "puffs its full seed upon the indicative air." The metaphor is itself an exploding seed that weds words and weeds, physical reproduction and literary production (323). We may thus read *The Darkening Ecliptic* as the offspring of two minds colliding and converging in what Wayne Koestenbaum describes as "a way of discharging language in a masturbatory *folie à deux*" (8).[12] Ern is ejaculated into existence through textual intercourse. In this sense, the production of Ern Malley, undertaken without sexual congress with a female, resembles Victor Frankenstein's creative process.

McAuley and Stewart tried to fail; they failed. Ross Chambers aptly concludes that the hoax worked "for the very same reason that it fizzled, which is that . . . the pseudo and the real thing are not so easily distinguished" (40). Thus, although Malley remains the "black swan of trespass on alien waters" (Brooks 304), by the conclusion of *The Darkening Ecliptic* he has announced himself to our ears, paradoxically, by describing his failure to be heard. In this respect, the Malley poems—like *Frankenstein* and *My Life as a Fake*—are about their own creation. Indeed, *The Darkening Ecliptic* could have been titled *My Life as a Fake.*

The last line of "Petit Testament"—the final line published in *Angry Penguins*—reads "I have split the infinitive. Beyond is anything" (323). "Beyond" *was* almost anything, for the hoax yielded consequences that far transcended what McAuley and Stewart could have envisioned. As years passed Malley, like Jack's beanstalk, grew and grew, becoming a symbol of Australian culture as potent as Phar Lap or Ned Kelly. Malley's presentation of himself as dwelling in "No-Man's-Land" resonated with Australians, who viewed themselves as living in a "fake culture, . . . [as] defenders of the butt-end of Europe in a land they did not understand" (Heyward 19). Moreover, the poems have undergone canonization (Mead 116), partly because Australian poets such as John Kinsella and John Tranter have advanced the legacy of this imaginary being whom

FIG. 8. Sidney Nolan's *Ern Malley* (1973) depicts the imaginary poet as a misshapen monster. Oil on hardboard, 122 × 122 cm. (Gift of Sidney & Cynthia Nolan, 1974, Art Gallery of South Australia, Adelaide; © Art Gallery of South Australia 744P27)

they perceive as "a patron saint of experimental verse" (qtd. in Page, n.p.). In 2006 Tranter published "The Malley Variations," ten poems that place *The Darkening Ecliptic* in dialogue with authors such as Allen Ginsberg, Gertrude Stein, and Louisa May Alcott (!). Quotations from *The Darkening Ecliptic* sporadically flash through the gloaming. For example, "An American in Paris" contains the line "I have I found you, my brothel" (Brooks 357), which not only echoes the opening lines of "Colloquy with John Keats" but sets up a five-way conversation among Keats, Pound, Malley, Tranter, and Henry Miller (according to Tranter's online notes). This dramatization of belatedness and multiple authorship is in the very spirit of Malley.

Other Australian artists have found inspiration in the poems. Ian Kennedy Williams's novel *Malarky Dry* (1991) depicts a "real" (nonpoet) Malley.[13] Sidney Nolan (an associate of the *Penguins* group) created a series of Ern paintings in the 1970s in which Malley seems monstrous, half-made (fig. 8). In the 2000s Garry Shead fashioned a group

FIG. 9. In *Petit Testament II* (2005), Garry Shead places Ern in a coffin as a woman in the foreground reads a book, perhaps *The Darkening Ecliptic*. Etching, 24.5 × 31 cm. (© Garry Shead)

of etchings to accompany the poems (fig. 9). And in 1976 composer/lecturer/broadcaster Peter Tahourdin created *Ern Malley: A Dramatic Testament,* a musical piece for narrators, tape, soprano, baritone, and chamber ensemble.[14] The strongest evidence of Malley's importance, however, is this: although McAuley and Stewart each went on to publish several books, none has become as famous as *The Darkening Ecliptic*—nor, many argue (Tranter and Elliott among them), as effective.[15] The tricksters ended up trapping themselves; and Harris, who became a prosperous bookseller and republished the poems with his own glosses, got the last laugh. Like Frankenstein's creature, Ern became an unkillable monster who forever haunts his heedless parents.

Epiphyte

> A new species would bless me as its creator and source; many happy, excellent natures would owe their being to me. No father could claim the gratitude of his child so completely as I should deserve theirs.
>
> —Victor Frankenstein, in Shelley, *Frankenstein*

Mary Shelley identifies Frankenstein's creation of the monster with her own creation of the novel, writes Chris Baldick, such that "both its composition and its subsequent cultural status mim[e] the central moments of its own story" (30). That is, like Victor Frankenstein (and the Malley hoaxers) Shelley lost control of her creation. *My Life as a Fake* both literalizes her identification between literary and physical creation and adopts *Frankenstein*'s (and the monster's) structural design. As many critics have noted, Shelley's novel is "patched together from numerous textual sources" (MacFarlane 342; Ketterer 15), including Coleridge's *Rime of the Ancient Mariner,* Erasmus Darwin's field notes, Wordsworth's "Tintern Abbey," Marlowe's *Dr. Faustus,* the writings of Rousseau and Locke, and especially *Paradise Lost,* which she was rereading during the novel's composition.[16] Her method, that is, mirrors her protagonist's: assembling an assortment of fragments. Sandra Gilbert further asserts that Shelley's "principal mode of self-definition . . . was through reading" (41). Victor Frankenstein, it follows, errs by "brooding upon the *wrong* books" (e.g., Cornelius Agrippa); likewise, his creature, whose library is limited to Plutarch, Goethe, *Paradise Lost,* and an overheard translation of *The Ruins of Empire*, "must have been parented, if at all, by *books*" (Gilbert 49, 53, emphasis hers). Barbara Johnson thus concludes that *Frankenstein* is about "the experience of writing *Frankenstein*" (7). If so, Victor Frankenstein is a barely disguised representation—a misrecognition—of his "parent," an author who, according to Shelley's preface, "can give form to dark, shapeless substances, but cannot bring into being the substance itself" (23).

Mary Shelley, too, had difficulty bringing her authorial self into being. As Susan Eilenberg reminds us, *Frankenstein* was first published anonymously (167), with Shelley dedicating it to her father without acknowledging their filial relationship, as if she, like Ern and her creature, had no parents (177). She also employed manifold versions of her own name in letters, inserting and removing her father's, mother's, and husband's surnames seemingly willy-nilly; in at least one case she signed herself "Marina"—the name of the lost daughter in *Pericles* (170–71). She thus presents herself alternately as a composite, like the monster—a "multiple, a crowd, . . . a family" (182)—and as nobody at all. She passes this condition of anonymity or polyonymity to her hideous creature, who is called many things in the novel but is never given a name.[17] Now let us reconsider the question I posed above: Who speaks in "No-Man's-Language"? Answer: Frankenstein's creature, whose efforts to speak himself into existence are all mediated (hostilely) by Frankenstein and the sea captain Robert Walton: their authorship appropriates his. In Shelley's self-effacement, then, we find not only an identification with her stitched-together monster, but also, writes James Carson, an "incipient critique of the individualistic notion of originary creativity" (436) and an allegiance to the kind of dispersed authorship exemplified in *The Darkening Ecliptic* and *MLAF*.

Her self-portrait thus welcomes other collaborators. These included her husband, who impersonated her in the preface (Eilenberg 178) and contributed about four thousand words to the novel (Ruthven 92), mostly to intensify its stilted diction (see Mellor 14–15). Their collaboration went in the opposite direction as well, for Mary Shelley's second-most-famous literary progeny was the poet Percy Shelley. After he died, she became her husband's editor, issuing unpublished works, gathering his essays, and changing his image from that of atheistic libertine to what Susan Wolfson calls "Christlike idealistic martyrdom" (203). As Wolfson writes, "Editor Shelley authorizes herself as the textual producer/recreator of poet Shelley," putting him together from fragments just as Frankenstein does in building his creature (196). In the process, she also put herself back together after the deaths that ravaged her family: resurrecting Percy revived Mary as well and allowed her to solidify an authorial identity (205). Yet these facts evoke the same questions that Carey poses in *MLAF:* Who is the "parent" of a text? The initial writer? The editor? The publisher? The reader? All of the above (thesis 7)?

Extrapolating from these phenomena, Carey's novel implies that all literary creation is collaborative and forever unfinished and that such creations have more than one life. It does so, first, through characters and events that parallel *Frankenstein*'s. Here is a (probably incomplete) list of features borrowed from Shelley's novel:

1. A patchwork creature comes to life and develops hatred for its creator.
2. The creator refrains from explaining his creation to others, thereby incurring more damage.
3. The story unfolds through embedded narratives told to a frame narrator.
4. The creature recounts his story to his creator but gets little sympathy.
5. The creator forms a complex love/hate bond with his creature, then pursues the creature with malicious intent.
6. Both creator and creature die at the end.
7. A theory of creativity, self-formation, and parenthood emerges, along with a warning about the perils of irresponsibility and obsession.[18]

Christopher Chubb's wild tale-within-a-tale, related in segments while he works as a bicycle mechanic (the same trade that he and the Malley hoaxers gave to their fictional poets), thus reenacts Frankenstein's narration to Walton, with Sarah playing the auditor's role. Sarah also mirrors Margaret Saville, Walton's sister and the recipient of his letters (and of all the embedded narratives), as well as the Great Assembler herself, Mary Shelley. Sarah even resembles Frankenstein's creature, as someone who would prefer to stay in her room and peruse *Paradise Lost* (*MLAF* 11) and whose identity is formed through reading. Ultimately, as I show below, she inhabits the role of Frankenstein himself—at once author and product of her creation. Hideous progeny proliferate: not only are McCorkle and his poems the "children" of Chubb, but so is Tina, Chubb's (probable) daughter, whom McCorkle kidnaps and raises. Although we are never sure if McCorkle is the fabricated poet come to life or a mad genius who has borrowed McCorkle's name, the point is that "giving birth" to him *literarily* gives birth to him *literally.* The final offspring is *My Life as a Fake* itself: Carey reincarnates Frankenstein's monster as he reforges the Malley forgeries.

MLAF thus typifies what David Cowart has termed a "symbiotic" text: one that appropriates characters and plot lines to retell an earlier story from a different point of view or with an updated setting (4–8). Examples include Carey's own *Jack Maggs* (1998), which reimagines the life of Magwitch, the convict in *Great Expectations.* Such texts further demonstrate the collaborative properties of literary production. They also seem to fit Groom's description of a forgery, which he likens to "an impostor—or even a parasite" ("Original" 6). But whereas a parasite harms its host, symbiotic texts engage in a mutualism that benefits both (see Cowart 4). That is, the "guest" text gains value from readers' familiarity with the "host" text even as the earlier, host text is afforded new life and reopened to fresh insights. This is the case with *Frankenstein* and *MLAF*—and perhaps with most literary forgeries (thesis 1). Late in his novel Carey offers a related metaphor for such intertextuality—that of an epiphyte, a plant that grows from the body of another plant without harming its host (237). Such works are, like the Malley poems and other forgeries, at once literary creations and literary criticism, Frankensteinian quilts fashioned of fragments torn from a myriad of sources. Ghostwritten texts, they are, like forgeries, haunted by the shades of preexisting textual bodies.

To Mould Me Man

> Like you I sought at first for Beauty
> And then, in disgust, returned
> As did you to the locus of sensation.
>
> —Ern Malley, "Colloquy with John Keats"

John Slater lures Sarah Wode-Douglass to Malaysia by exploiting her contradictory feelings for him, a suave but undependable father figure with whom she has a quasi-incestuous, though nonsexual, relationship.

Similarly, as she hears and transcribes Chubb's story, her emotions careen wildly from disgust over his exploitation of Weiss to pity for his losses to a grudging admiration for Chubb's endurance. Her critical faculties are no more reliable. Trusting only her pulse rate (*MLAF* 27) as the true measure of a work's value, she declares that one "cannot really counterfeit a voice" (26). Has she never heard of the dramatic monologue? In any case, Chubb's description of McCorkle's post-*Ecliptic* poems prompts "covetous emotions" in her (65). She will even endure Chubb's lengthy, convoluted yarn if that's what she must do to get them. Sarah envisions herself as Coleridge's Wedding Guest, unable to tear herself from the glittering eye of this "*grey-beard loon*" (39, italics in *MLAF;* see also 114). Mesmerizing eyes embody the power of narration throughout *MLAF,* while also alluding to the optic bond between Frankenstein and his creature displayed in the lines that serve as Carey's (and my second) epigraph. Like the Guest and Walton, Sarah needs to hear this tale. Why? Because she too is a fraud. Less than halfway through the novel, Slater disabuses her of a long-held belief that her mother drowned herself after Slater rejected her. (A mother's early death is another trait Sarah shares with Frankenstein and Mary Shelley.) Suddenly she grasps that "misconstructions" had "made [her] who [she] was" (133). Who she is is a closeted lesbian whose longtime lover, Annabelle, remains married to a man. One ironic result, then, of Sarah's immersion in this maze of lies is her discovery of a truth: she is a fake, a misconstructed being like Frankenstein's creature.

John Slater, erstwhile enfant terrible, legendary womanizer, and author of *Dewsong* (dismissed by Chubb as "overripe Dylan Thomas" [109]) has become rich and famous for writing popular novels and in his sixties retains a louche grandeur. Sarah initially views him as the "incarnation of deceit" (4), but as he recounts the McCorkle hoax, she starts to trust him. Yet he too is a fake and a forger. Just after the war, McCorkle, burning to legitimize himself, approached Chubb demanding a birth certificate; Slater, then working for MI5, fabricated one for him. In this sense, Slater is as responsible for authoring McCorkle as Chubb is, each of them having brought him into existence through writing.[19] The knowledge that Sarah and Slater, each of whom narrates at times, are fakes at once undermines our faith in their credibility and emphasizes Carey's thesis that all creation involves collaboration and chicanery.

> . . . alack,
> That monster envy, oft the wrack
> Of earned praise
>
> —Gower, in *Pericles* 4.l.11–13

Christopher Chubb is, or was, a nasty fellow—a sore loser, a snob, and, according to Slater, a "leech" (35). Chubb, of course, contends that Weiss was the fake (31) and that he, Chubb, has always been a lover of truth (38). Like many real-life forgers, as noted in thesis 6, he was motivated by both envy and a belief that *he* was the true guardian of aesthetic virtue. Defending his "savage jest" (72), he quotes McAuley and Stewart's dismissal of modernism and maintains that he meant no harm to Weiss (38).[20] He also boasts of cobbling together the photo of McCorkle from parts of three different men, building an immense creature with a "huge powerful nose and cheekbones, great forehead like the bust of Shakespeare." He "chopped him up and glued him. . . .What resurrectionists we were-*lah*" (51).[21] (He mirrors Cerimon, the sorcerer in *Pericles* who brings Pericles' wife Thaisa back from the dead [3.2], as well as Ackroyd's Meredith, Wallis, and Charles Wychwood.) But when Chubb volunteered to be prosecuted with Weiss, he says, the latter accused him of wanting to share the glory and asserted that McCorkle's poems were beyond Chubb's capabilities (52). Weiss may have been right, for Sarah finds the poems Chubb has written in his own name "priggish, self-serving, snobbish," lacking McCorkle's wild, "nasal passion." "If this was his 'real' poetry," she concludes, "I preferred the fake" (86). For Chubb (and for Carey) authenticity requires fakery.

An episode involving Chubb's ruined suit (which Slater pays to have repaired) interrupts his story and sheds light on his current condition. In fact, Chubb changes his "suit" several times in the novel—the man who began adulthood as a promising poet has become, in turn, a pariah, an insurance copywriter and salesman, an indicted murder, an outraged parent, an abject exile and bicycle mechanic, and a self-defender. He is a shapeshifter, a patchwork persona; the suit is merely his current costume. But he is stuck with it, for the tailors in his district refuse to serve him: "He not a person," one explains, but a vampire who will "drink your blood until you grow weak and die" (119, 120). For them Chubb, not McCorkle, is the parasite. The suit episode reinforces the sense that Chubb has vanished into McCorkle's penumbra, for as his creature thrusts himself into prominence, Chubb grows thinner and thinner, as if being devoured by an internal worm. The forger's dilemma—that conflict between exposure and erasure outlined in thesis 4—has engulfed him.

In Chubb's account Weiss was essentially Max Harris, a handsome young impresario of the literary vanguard.[22] But Weiss was as confused as Chubb, on the one hand maintaining that Chubb couldn't have written the McCorkle poems and on the other accusing him of enviously hoaxing him (62). All Chubb would ever be known for, he asserted, is the work of McCorkle. Alas, the same is true of Weiss, for the McCorkle poems have placed them in an epiphytic relationship. Hence, after Weiss's death Chubb witnessed a grotesque irony: lines from McCorkle's (Malley's) "Petit Testament" were used as Weiss's epitaph! Just as ironic: the only person truly capable of appreciating the cleverness of Chubb's hoax was now dead (57). Chubb needed Weiss, and when he died the brilliance of his prank was eclipsed.

> Did I request thee, Maker, from my clay
> To mould me man, Did I solicit thee
> From darkness to promote me?
>
> —Adam, in *Paradise Lost* 10.743–45

Partway through Weiss's obscenity trial, a massive man with "wild dark eyes and black, shoulder-length hair" burst out angrily, "Ask the author, you fucking philistine" (*MLAF* 59). It was as if, writes Chambers, "Frankenstein's monster was declaring himself to be Frankenstein" (41). McCorkle here personifies "the *textual* subject produced by readerly authority" (39, italics his), embodying how characters and texts become independent of their initial creators. Recounting McCorkle's narration, Chubb recalls hearing him quote the *OED*'s definition of "publisher": "One whose business is the issuing of books, . . . one who undertakes the printing or production of copies of such works" (75). McCorkle was outraged by this denotation, but it shrewdly captures the publisher's tripartite roles as creator ("issuing"), copier, and killer (or at least undertaker), roles shared, Carey suggests, by every party in the creative process. Weiss apparently agreed, for when Chubb reminded him that he was the actual author of the McCorkle poems, Weiss responded, "Doesn't matter. . . . I am his publisher" (52)—that is, his cocreator. McCorkle then told Chubb that he broke into Vogelesang's residence, scalped him, and declared, "I would take any amount of skin and hair for the cause of poetry" (78).

Yet McCorkle also insisted that Weiss "was like a mother, for he had brought me into the world, had given me life, had stood by me" (78). Upon breaking into Weiss's home, McCorkle recalled that he exclaimed, "I am your author, Mr. Weiss" (81). And then comes a pivotal moment in the novel (Ashcroft 35): McCorkle recited "Durer: Innsbruck, 1495" to Chubb just as he had earlier recited it to Weiss. Voiced by this "wild man" (*MLAF* 81), the poem was remade: "This was and was not the poem Chubb had written. . . . This lunatic had somehow recast it without altering a word. What had been clever had now become true, the song of the autodidact, the colonial, the damaged beast of the antipodes" (82). By reading the work, McCorkle author(iz)ed himself: he became a creator whose offspring was Bob McCorkle. The scene reopens the question of who is responsible for a literary work. A writer produces words, but unread they lie dormant on the page. An editor cuts the umbilical cord, wraps up the product, and places it in hands of the publisher. The publisher midwives its emergence into the world of other books and "issues" it to others. And the reader, like a foster parent, adopts and reshapes the work with each reading or recitation. Conversely, as McCorkle's proclamation indicates, the writer also authors the publisher, creating him/her as such by placing the progeny in that person's hands. As with Frankenstein and his creature, each party engenders the other. McCorkle and Chubb were both brought forth by *The Darkening Ecliptic;* Sarah desires a similar delivery.

Into the story comes Nousette Markson (whose real name may be Mary Morris), an artist and photographer who seduced Chubb in the hoax's aftermath and who, between 1945 and 1952, changed her occupation five times and her nationality twice (145). She knew she could trust Chubb not to spoil her secrets, for, she reminded him, "you are a fake yourself" (91). Imagine Chubb's surprise, then, when Nousette introduced him to her good friend—a large man named Bob McCorkle. "You see, my darling," she announced to Chubb, "you are not a fake at all" (94). Throughout McCorkle's narration his "piercing dark eyes" held Chubb in thrall as he demanded a birth certificate, then recited the lines from *Paradise Lost* quoted above (which are also *Frankenstein*'s epigraph [94–95]). Paradoxically, this piece of paper proved that McCorkle was *more* than a piece of paper. As noted earlier, McCorkle's certificate, created by John

Slater, was a forgery, yielding an identity as fraudulent as Ern Malley's. Yet it inscribed McCorkle into existence: writing forged and ratified the connection between name and body. "He wants to be Bob McCorkle," Nousette advised Chubb, "let him be Bob McCorkle" (95).

But Bob wanted to author more than himself. After Nousette was impregnated—probably by Chubb, but possibly by Slater—she bore a child named Tina. Like Frankenstein (and Monk Ellison) she didn't want her offspring, and Chubb adopted the baby, despite having no idea how to rear a child. So why was he not relieved when, a week after he took in Tina, McCorkle broke into his house and kidnaped her? "You never gave me a childhood," McCorkle charged (151); holding the infant, he declared, "This is a childhood" (153). Echoing Frankenstein's hideous being, McCorkle demanded "justice" (152); Tina would be his vehicle. The bastard text come to life abducts the bastard child; as in *The Tragedy of Arthur* and the Ireland forgeries, questions of legitimacy apply both to literary and physical creations. Alas, Chubb now faced the liar's plight: nobody believed his claim that the baby was kidnaped, especially not by a person whom they all knew to be a figment of Chubb's malicious imagination. Though he was acquitted of murder, Chubb's life was destroyed. But whose daughter *is* Tina? The novel's identification of literary and physical creation implies that, like a text, a child may have multiple "authors." The remainder of the novel translates Chubb's ambivalent desire to "own" McCorkle and his literary offspring into a quest to recapture Tina.

Hantu

> I am no viper, yet I feed
> On mother's flesh which did me breed.
>
> —*Pericles* 1.1.65–66

In the last third of the novel, intertextual progeny multiply along with the narrative layers. This embedding mirrors *Frankenstein*'s complicated structure. For example, beginning in chapter 11 of Shelley's novel, the creature relates his history to Frankenstein, who conveys it, much later, to Walton; Walton, in turn, writes the story and sends it to his sister, Margaret Saville. The implied reader, then, is the sister of the frame narrator, and thus the model relationship between teller and auditor is that of siblings. A sibling would be a sympathetic auditor—unlike Frankenstein, who briefly empathizes with his malformed product but ultimately refuses to build him a mate. In *MLAF* Chubb narrates his story in pieces to Sarah, who later assembles the fragments. She thus blends the roles of Walton and Margaret Saville, serving as Chubb's "collaborator" (204). Indeed, as Chubb talks, Sarah begins to feel as if *she* were his creature and he her surrogate father. (He is even mistaken for her father by a hotel employee.)

Chubb's story is a composite affair. Slater and Tina fill in gaps, and Chubb relays McCorkle's words as well as the experiences of a bizarre character named Mulaha the poisoner whom he encountered during his pursuit of McCorkle. As in *Frankenstein,* characters are doubled or even tripled: Mulaha is Chubb's alter ego, another man whose existence has been narrowed to a single overpowering emotion—in his case, fury—thereby transmogrifying him into a monster (189). ("Mulaha" means "temper.") Because of a war injury, one of Mulaha's eyes had turned sideways—a synecdoche of his emotional injury and cyclopean rage as well as of Chubb's own cockeyed creativity. This single eye is as captivating as McCorkle's pair, and it seems to trap Chubb into agreeing with Mulaha that McCorkle must die.

McCorkle's kidnaping of Tina also replays a plot element in *Pericles,* in which Marina, the title character's daughter, is stolen by pirates and sold into a brothel. Moreover, the relationships among the various creators and their offspring resemble the venomous kinship between the play's King Antiochus and his daughter, described in a riddle (two lines of which I've quoted above) that Pericles solves early in the play.[23] That is, Chubb's "son" hated him, and Chubb wanted to kill his first "child" to protect "his" second. Yet when he briefly wrested Tina away from McCorkle, she called Chubb a *hantu,* or demon, and screamed for her real father—McCorkle (*MLAF* 203). If one were to adopt a common interpretation of *Frankenstein* in which the creature enacts Victor's unconscious desires, one might conclude that McCorkle kidnaped Tina because Chubb didn't really want her and that McCorkle carried out Chubb's desire to disappear. His etiolated condition in 1972 bears out this reading, as does his insistence that he "could never, *ever,* have made [McCorkle's later] poem" (164, emphasis in original). But in 1972 he wants the poem back, perhaps so that he can verify his own existence and thereby get credit for McCorkle's works, and he wants to enlist Sarah as accomplice.

After an arduous search, Chubb found Tina and McCorkle and had them brought to a jungle lord, who soon became convinced that Chubb was the kidnaper and set him adrift on a raft to die; he was rescued by another jungle lord, who also soon decided that Chubb was the kidnaper.[24] A chastened Chubb returned to Mulaha, who had constructed a booby-trapped package to mail to McCorkle; by touching a poisoned nail upon opening it, he would expire on the spot. But when the time came, Chubb merely stabbed the giant ineffectually in the buttock. Clearly Chubb did not want to kill his creation; he only wanted to, um, pierce him in the rear end. (The homoerotic elements in *Frankenstein* and the Malley hoax are clearly at play here.) Chubb should have felt free. But no: McCorkle "had become part of [him]" (249). Author and text have brought each other into being. Thus, a year later, when he received a letter from McCorkle explaining that he was dying in Malaysia from Graves' disease—the disorder given to Ern Malley that responds readily to iodine treatment—he brought the necessary drugs to Kuala Lumpur.

Entering the sick room, he beheld, like Frankenstein, "the wretch—the miserable monster whom I had created. He held up the curtain of the bed; and his eyes—*wah!* what eyes—were fixed on me" (252). As McCorkle lay dying (from leukemia, it turns out), Chubb reassumed the parental role, as if, like Frankenstein, he suddenly "felt what the duties of a creator towards his creature were" (Shelley 94). Raising McCorkle "like a damned lover in my arms," he felt as if he were "holding [his] own vital organs in [his] hands" (*MLAF* 254). McCorkle's "terrible" eyes elicited Chubb's promise to care for Tina and McCorkle's common-law wife, Mrs. Lim, after he died (255). McCorkle said to Chubb, "We are one, you and I" (256)—"the double almond concealed in one shell," as Malley's (or McCorkle's) "Colloquy with John Keats" puts it.[25] Then he handed him the book he had been writing since leaving Australia (256). Its title? *My Life as a Fake.* This poetic confession of fraudulence has, paradoxically, made McCorkle real. Yet Chubb still refuses to believe that Tina could have loved this loathsome "tapeworm" who stole and fed off her (254): "He was a user and a thief, yet tears were shed for him. My role was to be his cause of death" (258). As in *Frankenstein,* a creator is also a killer. In making and unmaking McCorkle, Chubb unmade himself.

Sparagmos

> O'er bear the shores of my mortality. . . .
> O, come hither,
> Thou that beget'st him that did thee beget.
>
> —Pericles to Marina, *Pericles,* 5.1.193–95

During the breaks in Chubb's narration, Sarah finally sees McCorkle's photo (and those piercing eyes) and glimpses the cover of his book, "grey and wrinkled like the bark of a tree" (209). The glance reaffirms her determination to possess it at all costs, as if she too has become a *hantu* scheming to kidnap McCorkle's progeny. In 1972 Tina, speaking to Sarah in her shrine to McCorkle, gestures toward the books crowding the shelves and explains, "This is our family. . . . Bob McCorkle is the tree-*ah* . . . [W]e are the roots. These poems are the flowers. . . . When that old man [Chubb] steals this book, he has broken the flowers from the tree" (231–32). Tina's words aren't merely metaphors, for the three of them fashioned the book's paper from bark and plants they gathered throughout Malaysia. Earlier Sarah had witnessed Chubb holding McCorkle's book and noticed that "both book and hand seemed to be related parts of the same creature" (225), as if the volume were literally made from skin. Whose? Perhaps Tina's, for when she bares her flesh to Sarah, her scars seem as "dense and as widely distributed as those on a rubber tree" (233). Apparently, McCorkle truly believed that "any amount of skin and hair" should be sacrificed for poetry: Tina "gave everything" to make the book (234). And so did Mrs. Lim (limb?). As she recalls in another embedded narrative, in 1960 (the year of Malaysia's independence), after she joined the pair as they collected bark and leaves to make paper, they encountered assassins who slashed Mrs. Lim with machetes, leaving livid scars across her body and face. All this for a book! And now these thieves want to steal it. Can we blame her for protecting it so fiercely?

Under the suspicious eyes of McCorkle's minions, Sarah at last reads McCorkle's *My Life as a Fake.* She is stunned. "Whoever he was or had been, Bob McCorkle was indeed a genius. He had ripped up history and nailed it back together with its viscera on the outside, all that glistening green truth showing in the rip marks" (235). As a body comprising elements of himself, Tina, Mrs. Lim (and Chubb), McCorkle's book literalizes Shelley's and Carey's (and Malley's) identification of physical and literary creation: they all conjugate that verb on the tree. They are also parts of Malaysia. "To say that the poet had attempted to create a country may sound simply glib, until you understand that this is exactly what he has done," Sarah concludes (235). McCorkle succeeds in doing what James Macpherson and Thomas Chatterton merely attempted. No longer writing in "No-Man's-Language appropriate / Only to No-Man's-Land," McCorkle has forged himself and his new country with words. What are these words worth? "What price would I put on a Shakespeare sonnet?" Sarah wonders. "How much for Milton, Donne, Coleridge, Yeats?" (243). What is the value of art and how is it determined? This is a key question for all forgeries and their fictions. Sarah's answer is that the book is "worth being born for" (235). But is it worth killing or dying for? That is what she must now decide.

Mrs. Lim recalls repaying McCorkle's kindness by giving him a gigantic orchid (237). This epiphyte provides an apt metaphor for McCorkle's and Carey's works. We might read the trope as a further expansion of Tina's metaphor, in which Bob is a tree. But since he is a creature of Chubb, McCorkle is not the tree (that would be Chubb) but the epiphytic plant that grew from it; his book and his daughter are the flowers. Similarly, Carey's book, grafting together *The Darkening Ecliptic* and *Frankenstein*, blossoms into a new epiphytic flower, while doing no harm—indeed, reviving—its germinal texts. And McCorkle, by providing Chubb with material for his story and a reason, however perverse, for living, brings him back to life, begetting him that didst him beget. What resurrectionists they are!

> For Books are not absolutely dead things, but doe contain a potencie of life in them to be as active as that soule was whose progeny they are; nay they do preserve as in a violl the purest efficacie and extraction of that living intellect that bred them.
>
> —Milton, *Areopagitica* 3

And what murderers! After Chubb promises Sarah that he will procure McCorkle's book for her, she follows him to his house, where she instead finds the women wounded and Chubb dismembered, lying in a puddle of blood (263). The women claim that thieves killed him and stole the book, but actually they murdered him to protect *My Life as a*

Fake. Chubb's fate is cruelly ironic: the man who assembled McCorkle from fragments has been disassembled in an act of "*sparagmos*" (265). The scene recapitulates the moment in *Frankenstein* after Victor decides not to make his creature's companion: "The remains of the half-finished creature, whom I had destroyed, lay scattered on the floor, and I almost felt as if I had mangled the living flesh of a human being" (Shelley 148). Staring at the carnage, Sarah, blood literally on her hands, realizes that her effort to kidnap McCorkle's book has caused Chubb's death (263). No longer Margaret Saville, she has become Victor Frankenstein *and* his murderous creature. Left with "a wound that would not heal," Sarah sees herself as one of those "sad friends of Truth" in Milton's *Areopagitica,* searching for the mangled body of Osiris (22–23). The truth, too, has been "dismembered and scattered" (265). And so, since 1972 she has been re-collecting the parts of this "horrid puzzle" (265), imitating Shelley, Frankenstein, Chubb, and McCorkle (and the Malley hoaxers) as she composes her work and herself from leftover bits and pieces. While Chubb's fate may be poetic justice, McCorkle's *My Life as a Fake* remains in his shrine, now as foul to Sarah as Mrs. Lim's "disgusting giant orchid" (266). But Carey's *My Life as a Fake,* likewise an epiphytic orchid blossoming from the trunk of earlier texts, has fully sprouted.

Sarah is haunted by Chubb, and her book—also called *My Life Is a Fake*—has been ghostwritten by McCorkle and Chubb. Similarly haunted is Carey's novel, ghostwritten as it is by Ern Malley, Mary Shelley, Harold Stewart, and James McAuley. Who, then, is the author of Bob McCorkle and his works? Chubb is and is not: he admits he could not have written McCorkle's later poems, and the poems in his own name cast doubt even on the authorship of *The Darkening Ecliptic.* McCorkle makes *The Darkening Ecliptic* his own by reciting it and verifies his authorial powers with his later creations. Sarah admits that she is Chubb's collaborator, and Slater forges McCorkle into existence with a birth certificate. Tina and Mrs. Lim give McCorkle their love, gather and create his paper, and sacrifice their bodies. In short, they are all coauthors. Carey's novel is similarly collaborative, as he fashions *his MLAF* by marrying fictions, facts, and forgeries, enlisting multiple narrators and retold tales to consecrate the ceremony. Yet in another sense, the book is, like *Frankenstein,* anonymous: the possessive pronoun in the title refers to so many characters that, like Shelley's hideous progeny, it seems to have no author at all. *The Darkening Ecliptic* was, of course, really written by McAuley and

Stewart; in that sense, Carey too commits forgery by attributing their poems to Chubb/McCorkle. Hence, as Robert MacFarlane observes, the novel shows that "under careful scrutiny, the apparent opposition between 'making' and 'faking' collapses into near-identity," that fakery is "a necessary condition of literary creation; and that repetition is the first making and plagiarism the unoriginal sin" (345). Authors, that is, are never sole creators: a work may be set down by one or more writers but upon "birth" becomes an orphan, a bastard reared by myriad foster parents—editors, publishers—then nurtured and reshaped by readers and critics. In this sense, then, as thesis 7 proposes, all literary texts are the products of collaborative breeding, epiphytes clinging to the tree of literature. And yet, like that orchid, they bloom.

The same is true of human identity. Mary Shelley's "creation" of Percy Shelley, and Chubb's and Slater's (and Sarah's and Carey's) authoring of McCorkle and of their own histories remind us that we human beings write, speak, and read ourselves into new identities. In that sense all authors are fictional characters who must be resurrected and remade, like Frankenstein's creature, by imaginative readers. It matters not whether the name on the cover matches the one on the birth certificate, because authors forge our existences through the words that we leave or inspire others to leave. Like sorcerers spelling ghosts, we bring the dead back to life so they may speak to us. Yet we are also murderers: as Sarah realizes, the quest to make is inextricable from the urge to destroy, to cross out and rewrite old stories and personae and forge them anew. Epiphytes blossoming from the tree of words, authors and forgers are all robbers of dead men's dreams.

4

Fuck It

PERCIVAL EVERETT'S FAKE BOOK

> A genius is the one most like himself.
>
> —Thelonious Monk

> What a bold man he must be:
> With his forty-four and his Bowie knife,
> never hesitate to take your life.—
> Oh, everybody talk about Stackerlee!
>
> —D'Arcy Fanning, 1918

Prelude: Straight, No Chaser

"No, BUT if you hum a few bars, I'll fake it." This sentence is a punch line, but many who tell the joke don't really understand it. Using a melodic fragment ("hum a few bars"), an incomplete set of chords, or some combination of the two, an experienced jazz musician can approximate just about any requested number—that is, "fake it." Such situations led to the rise of "fake books": compilations of lead sheets (the melody of a song plus chord symbols) that gigging musicians use to broaden their repertoire. These, in turn, gave way to the so-called real books—handwritten anthologies compiled by jazz musicians who did not pay royalties to the composers. Technically illegal (and riddled with errors), they were nonetheless stocked by music stores (often under the counter) and purchased by musicians with nods and winks. Eventually, they were supplanted by legal, royalty-paying, correctly transcribed real books that, ironically, help musicians to fake it. To fake it, then, is to improvise, although the term retains a whiff of sly inauthenticity.

Jazz pianist Thelonious Monk, composer of "'Round Midnight" and many other classics, heard Miles Davis's group perform the song at the Newport Jazz Festival in 1955. On the drive back to New York, Monk told Miles that he had played the tune incorrectly. A heated argument ensued, in which Davis insisted that people liked his version better than Monk's and accused the latter of jealousy. Monk got out of the car and walked all the way to the ferry while the others drove to Manhattan (Kelley 190). In Monk's eyes, Miles was faking it—performing a tune without knowing it well. Monk was surely right about the chord changes, yet many jazz musicians prefer Davis's version, which raises the questions: Who is the real author of a song, the composer or the performer? If everyone gets it wrong, are they really wrong?

This incident and these terms provide a prelude to my discussion of Percival Everett's *erasure* (Everett's preferred spelling) in which an "experimental" novelist named Thelonious Ellison—who goes by the name "Monk"—is brought up short by a glance at Juanita Mae Jenkins's *We's Lives in da Ghetto,* a bestselling novel (inspired by Sapphire's *Push)* written in Black dialect (African American Vernacular English, or AAVE) that stereotypes African Americans as ignorant victims and abusers. Outraged by its success, he hastily pens a parodic novella called *My Pafology,* narrated by nineteen-year-old criminal Van Go ("Go") Jenkins and attributed to one Stagg R. Leigh. Monk's fake book—a pastiche of Richard Wright's *Native Son* and *Push,* among others—offers its own pernicious stereotypes: Go has four children by four different women, cares for none of them, and lives on the outlaw fringe of society. To Monk's surprise and chagrin, *My Pafology* is purchased for a large sum by a major publisher. As events unfold, he finds himself impersonating Stagg Leigh; the ironies mount when Monk becomes a judge for a book award and his parody, retitled *Fuck,* wins. The novella is Monk's "fuck you" to *We's Lives,* to the pop-culture locusts who have swarmed on it, and to the industry that has deemed his own latest novel unpublishable. But if they don't know they're being fucked, who is the victim? And who has the last laugh? Not Monk: as with Christopher Chubb, Monk's hideous progeny consumes him.

Monk Ellison embodies the plight and potentialities of the forger and literary fraud. Although he dismisses *Fuck* as a "so-called" novel (*erasure* 208), his protests aren't entirely convincing because he craves erasure *and* exaltation, anonymity *and* recognition. Like Chatterton and Chubb, he uses imitation and impersonation to free his imagination and to forge a new writerly persona: *erasure* reminds us again that an author is always an impersonation, a mask (theses 2 and 7). And as all writers realize but forgeries demonstrate most clearly, a book is never only what its author believes it to be; once "born," it takes on a life of its own (thesis 12 proving true again). *Fuck* and Stagg R. Leigh become Monk's Frankenstein creatures, turning on their master and pursuing him relentlessly until they subsume him. These now-familiar patterns gain heft and complexity through their imbrication in African American history and culture, several of whose major works Monk and Everett cite and rewrite.

Jazz plays a prominent part in this history and culture. I propose, indeed, that *erasure* employs a jazz aesthetic that emerges from, and transforms, the blues impulse as defined by Ralph Ellison. Although no music is "heard" in the novel, Everett nonetheless plays jazz by signifying—a form of revision and parody that Henry Louis Gates Jr. famously defined as a paradigm for African American literature—on canonical and noncanonical texts and by means of his provocative treatment of identity, improvisation, and imposture.[1] This juxtaposition of intertextual appropriation and jazz performance converges on the trope of riffing, which refers both to the melodic patterns commonly used in jazz and blues and to a spoof or parody. My subtitles, borrowed from those of Thelonious Monk's compositions, indicate *erasure*'s jazz aesthetic; the "solos"—vignettes from the musician's life—suggest parallels between the two Theloniouses. It makes sense, I argue, to think of *erasure* as an extended musical composition complete with riffs, verses, bridges, and solos (cf. J. Brooks 1049). Indeed, because Monk and Everett summarize earlier texts and revise them, *erasure* constitutes a jazz fake book in prose.

Riff: Think of One

> You got to *dig it* to dig it, you dig?
>
> —Thelonious Monk to saxophonist Steve Lacy, 1960

erasure is not Percival Everett's only foray into dispersed authorship. Similar tactics pervade his novel *Percival Everett by Virgil Russell* (2013), in which an elderly father and his son trade stories that are embedded within and comment on the story in which they reside. Everett does not always identify the teller, and the stories tend to converge or stop abruptly, engendering what Roland Barthes calls a "writerly" text—one that forces the reader to create connections, fill in gaps, and actively participate in generating meaning. Eventually a fairly straightforward narrative about the father's escape from his assisted living facility emerges, but it remains uncertain who Virgil Russell is and why the author's name appears in the title. Like *erasure, Virgil Russell* reminds us of Michel Foucault's apothegm that an author is not an "actual individual" (ed. Bouchard/Simon 130) but a name through which we "characterize the existence, circulation and operation of certain discourses" (124). Everett's works, in which he sometimes shows up as a character, as if to imply that the author has been composed by his text, traffic in such circulation. Far from yielding unity or thrift, however, his authors proliferate wildly. Such multiplications are implicit in Foucault's definition, because authors produce not just their own work but "the possibility and the rules of formations of other texts" (131). Barthes, the subject of Monk Ellison's academic paper, similarly describes a text as "a multi-dimensional space in which a variety of writings, none of them original, blend and clash" ("Death" 146). This sentence describes *erasure*, which, in the guise of Monk's journal, incorporates his impenetrable conference paper, fragments from a novel-in-progress, thoughts on fishing and woodworking, the embedded novella *My Pafology* and other stories, quotations from *Invisible Man*, and Monk's CV.[2] For both theorists, and perhaps for Everett, originality is a chimera, since all texts are intertextual and constantly under revision. For Barthes, however, it is the reader who "holds together in a single field all the traces by which the written text is constituted" ("Death" 148). This is our task with *erasure.*

Monk Ellison faces the perplexing truth noted in my prologue: that a person who becomes an author generates a second self, an alter ego who accompanies (and sometimes overwhelms) her physical identity—and may betray it. Indeed, if all texts circulate and recirculate, it follows that all texts are multiply authored (thesis 7). What does this mean for the person whose name appears on the cover and who expects to earn money and fame from a book? This question is complicated by forgery. Recalling Groom's argument that the "literary forger is a shadow, forging what is already itself a fabrication, and thereby showing that literature . . . is no less forged" (*Shadow* 2), we understand that the shadows in Monk Ellison's case are multiple and overlapping, consisting not only of the Black artists whose work he plunders and parodies but also of Van Go Jenkins, Stagg Leigh, and their avatars. Monk is *over*shadowed by his creations—erased by his own pencil. His calculated attack on the literary establishment and racist popular culture awakens him to the fact that his life and career have been built on falsehoods, that his true identity may be that of a fraud. More broadly, Monk's hoax epitomizes Ruthven's point that "literary forgery is not so much the disreputable Other of 'genuine' literature as its demystified and disreputable self" (3)—its Van Go Jenkins, its Stagg R. Leigh. If Monk's furious "fuck it" fails in its initial purpose, it does prove him right about the publishing industry. Like Harriet Burden's *Maskings* experiment, Monk's hoax succeeds so well that it fails.

Riff: Work

> You rehearse every time you play on your instrument.
>
> —Thelonious Monk

Everett has resisted being identified primarily as an African American novelist, and his wildly eclectic oeuvre—Westerns, mysteries, satires, coming-of-age fictions, metafictional texts, revisions of classical myths, and diverse story collections—is difficult to classify. Still, several of his works have explored themes of racial authenticity, identity, performance, and the "African American experience," a phrase that *erasure* mocks. For example, the eponymous protagonist of *I Am Not Sidney Poitier* (2009) enjoys the fruits of wealth because his mother invested in Turner Broadcasting in its infancy; Not Sidney maintains a close relationship with Ted Turner and need not hold a job.[3] That freedom allows him to undergo a series of picaresque misadventures involving racial humiliation that, the reader soon (or not so soon) perceives, are all pastiches of Sidney Poitier movies. For instance, after Not Sidney is arrested and jailed in Alabama, the prison bus crashes, leaving him handcuffed to a white inmate: it's a riff on *The Defiant Ones* (1958). Not Sidney attends Morehouse College, where he enrolls in a course on the philosophy of nonsense taught by . . . Percival Everett.[4] There Not Sid finds a girlfriend, Maggie Larkin, who brings him to meet her color-conscious parents, wannabe whites whom Not Sid ultimately tells off, albeit not before receiving oral sex from Maggie's sister or before the reader realizes they are reenacting *Guess Who's Coming to Dinner* (1967), its liberal white parents lightly shaded.[5] Near the end Not Sidney informs a woman in Smuteye, Alabama, that his name is Sidney Poitier (183). Although Everett implies that the "real" Poitier embodies white folks' notion of a good Black man, Not Sid's travails enable him to grow into what Poitier also represents: decency, nobility, fortitude. At novel's end Not Sidney is given a Lifetime Achievement Oscar and delivers a speech that ends with words he desires as his epitaph: "I AM NOT MYSELF TODAY" (234). Or is he? Has he betrayed himself or become himself? Has faking it made him real? Is the author of this pastiche Percival Everett (who is also not Sidney Poitier) or the many writers and directors who made those movies? Authorship seems irretrievably scattered in Everett's cinematic fake book.

The vagaries of authorship and the erasures of African American history figure heavily in *A History of the African-American People [Proposed] by Strom Thurmond* (2004), an antic satire Everett cowrote with James Kincaid. The ludicrous title project is initiated not by Senator Thurmond—a dyed-in-the-wool segregationist who fathered at least one child with a Black woman—but by his unhinged aide, Barton Wilkes, who enlists the fictional Everett and Kincaid to be the senator's ghostwriters.[6] Channeling Thurmond, Wilkes sends Everett and Kincaid source material aimed at proving that slavery, racism, and Jim Crow were not all that bad. The duo dutifully read the racist texts and even interview Thurmond, who comes off as charming but clueless and, yes, bigoted. The project is scuttled when Strom offends his ghosts, yet the unwritten history presents themes similar to *erasure*'s. For example, although Thurmond writes not a single word, he is regardless the fake book's author as well as, in one sense, the author of the satire about him and his (nonexistent) book, because the ghostwriters capture Thurmond's voice in the excerpt from "Thurmond's" history presented within the novel's fictional world; moreover, the (real) authors put words into Strom's mouth during his imagined conversations with their fictional avatars. There are multiple Thurmonds as well as double Everetts and Kincaids. In other words, the real authors are characters in a novel in which they are the "real" authors of a nonexistent (and falsely attributed) book. For Everett an author is less a principle of unity than a seed from which multiple fictions and creators sprout.

Riff: Played Twice

> Everybody is influenced by everybody but you bring it down home the way you feel it.
>
> —Thelonious Monk

The Thurmond novel's pointed statements about the erasure of African American history and the stupidities of the publishing industry appear in *erasure,* made more specific via multiple allusions to canonical African American texts. Monk's surname, for example, nods to the author of *Invisible Man,* to which Everett alludes throughout *erasure.* Monk also acknowledges that *My Pafology* is a parody of *Native Son,* with Van Go playing Bigger (or perhaps Littler) Thomas. These intertexts have been analyzed by several critics.[7] Less recognized is how *erasure,* written by an author who once worked as a jazz musician, employs a jazz aesthetic. One element of this aesthetic is intertextual appropriation, a tactic integral to the origins of bebop. This style—the foundational form in modern jazz—emerged in the early 1940s during jam sessions in Harlem nightclubs where musicians traded solos over standard tunes they knew by heart. To record these tunes, however, would require the musicians or record companies, many operating on shoestring budgets, to pay royalties to the composers. To avoid these fees, the musicians improvised new melodies over the harmonies ("changes") of those chestnuts. Thus "How High the Moon" molted into Charlie Parker's "Ornithology"; "Indiana" metamorphosed into Miles Davis's "Donna Lee"; "Sweet Georgia Brown" was relocated west to become Monk's "Bright Mississippi"; and the Gershwins' "I Got Rhythm" got remade countless times in tunes such as Monk's "Rhythm-a-ning." Because the courts determined that harmonies cannot be copyrighted, these so-called contrafacts, and the fake books that reproduced them, proliferated.[8] The authorship of these songs is irretrievably multiple. Are these jazz artists mere copycats? Is George Gershwin's reputation diminished or augmented by such appropriations? Just as Thelonious Monk signified on canonical musical texts, so his literary namesake pilfers from and parodies canonical literary texts. That is, *My Pafology* is a contrafact on *Native Son:* it sings a new melody over *Son*'s "harmonies" as Monk riffs on Wright.

Gates writes that signifying always "entails formal revision and an intertextual relation" (51), and the process figures prominently in "jazz performances and in the play of black language games . . . [as] a mode of formal revision"; it is thus often "characterized by pastiche, and, most crucially, it turns on repetition of formal structures and their differences" (52). Both *erasure* and *My Pafology* reiterate formal structures (such as TV appearances) and fit Gates's definition of jazz improvisation as a dialogue with African American history (63–64). That is, Everett intends readers to recognize the allusions to *Invisible Man, Native Son, Push,* and the Stagolee legends even if (or because) his characters do not. And if Monk's novella lampoons Wright and Sapphire, it also acknowledges their priority and preeminence. As with Jelly Roll Morton's variations on Scott Joplin's "Maple Leaf Rag" (Gates's example), *erasure* and its embedded texts do not "'surpass' or 'destroy'" their precursor texts so much as they "complexly *extend[ ]* and trope[ ] figures present in the original" (63).[9] Michael Jarrett further suggests that jazz improvisation, so often intertextual and collage-like, functions as "a kind of musical satire" (343). He calls this "trope" (strategy) "satura," stemming from the same root as "satire," which once denoted a medley or hodgepodge (344). As a satire that incorporates multiple embedded texts and forms, *erasure* constitutes a jazz text.

Jarrett goes on to remark on how "jazz discourse has repeatedly concerned itself with . . . erecting and policing real/fake distinctions" (346): the overarching theme of jazz discourse is authenticity. This theme is central to *erasure,* not only because Monk Ellison has always believed he is not "black enough" (2) but also because one of his objections to *We's Lives in da Ghetto* is that its educated, middle-class author has never lived in one. By that measure, *My Pafology,* praised for its "realism" but written by an upper-middle-class professor, is inauthentic. Everett and his readers understand, however (as his protagonist does not), that *My Pafology* expresses elements of Monk's character and beliefs that he does not recognize. He has never known himself. Thus, the novel indicates that authenticity is an inadequate measurement of artistic achievement because an author's intentions, whether "genuine" or not, are always overshadowed by readers' perceptions of a work. Just as Miles Davis's version of "'Round Midnight" became the real one when it was reproduced in fake books, so *My Pafology* escapes Monk's intentions as it enters the marketplace and becomes "real." As we have seen, literary forgeries and hoaxes challenge notions of authenticity: although "inauthentic," they often stem from or nourish artistic impulses indistinguishable from those of "authentic" art. One of those impulses and procedures is the creation of a mask.

I have argued elsewhere that two formulas typify most jazz fiction. The Tragedy of Misunderstood Genius depicts an artist driven to depression or death by self-destructive habits and a philistine industry and audience that fail to support him. This paradigm sometimes overlaps with a second formula, the Romance of Style, in which an avant-garde or vernacular artist and her work are vilified but end up either crushing or being crushed by a more popular, diluted form ("Blue Notes" 6, 38–39). *Erasure* blends these formulae: the misunderstood Monk is driven to depression and rage and then blotted out by his pen name; his avant-garde art is ignored, criticized, and then supplanted by his parody, which becomes a bestseller because it is misrecognized. These stereotypical patterns do, alas, typify the lives of some real jazz musicians, including that of Monk's namesake. Glimpses into the biography of Thelonious Monk reveal a kinship between the two artists and flesh out *erasure*'s jazz aesthetic.

Solo: Nutty

Even among jazz musicians, Thelonious Sphere Monk (1917–82) was regarded as eccentric; late in life he was diagnosed with bipolar disorder. In his manic phases he would pace for hours, sleeplessly walk the streets or talk incessantly; the longer, more frequent lows meant withdrawal, paranoia, and spells in which he would stare emptily into space and not respond to questions. During one such episode he reportedly spoke to no one for months. In the late 1950s critic Marshall Stearns dubbed Monk the "Greta Garbo of jazz" (Kelley 191). Around that time, Monk was prescribed Thorazine. (His dosage eventually peaked at an elephantine 2,500 mg daily.) But even early in his career he was thought enigmatic: in a 1948 letter in Down-Beat, *Lorraine Lion (wife of Blue Note Records founder Alfred Lion and, later, owner of the Village Vanguard jazz club) remarked on the "aura of mystery" surrounding him, concluding, "It's impossible to put the strangeness of his characteristics into writing" (qtd. in Kelley 131). While John Coltrane soloed during one 1957 gig, Monk stood up and began a "peculiar little spinning dance, elbow pumping up and down on each turn, with an occasional stutter step allowing him to glide left and right." Critics described the dance as "a spectacular example of modern performance art" (Kelley 231), but his fellow musicians perceived it as a way to conduct and goose them to swing harder. Similarly, his wit and humor were often mischaracterized as signs of madness; he spoofed this image by titling one tune "Nutty." His other titles—which range from the eponymous ("Monk's Mood," "Thelonious") to the arcane ("Epistrophy," "Crepuscule with Nellie")—also include a few, such as "Think of One," and "Ask Me Now," that are jesting responses to the question, "What's the name of this tune?"*

Verse: Brilliant Corners

Everett presents *erasure* as Thelonious Ellison's journal, to be read after his death. At the outset he describes his musical tastes (Aretha, Charlie Parker, Mahler) and his profession as a fiction writer. He is careful to note that he is also a "son, a brother, a fisherman, an art lover, a woodworker," this last mostly because of the "shame it caused my mother" (1). Throughout his life Monk, like his namesake, has felt like an outsider, frequently being told that he isn't "*black* enough," and that his novels fail to convey "*the African American experience*" (2, italics in original). "I don't believe in race," he asserts. But others do—and there lies a problem: American society maintains rigid notions of what it means to be Black or white, who qualifies for each category, and how artists should position themselves within these binaries. Monk tries to ignore these constructs and is currently working on a novel that treats a "critical text by Roland Barthes, *S/Z,* exactly as it treats its so-called subject text which is Balzac's *Sarrasine*" (6). That novel is unlikely to become a best seller. One suspects, in fact, that Monk does not really care for his own work, just as he does not know or love himself.

Everett reproduces Monk's academic paper, entitled "F/V," in all its jargon-laden glory. Here is an example: *"And so we come to dismantling of the endeavor as the endeavor of the text at hand, Sarrasine, not being chosen as a model at all, but accepted as one treated in a way which in turn is a model for the treatment of other texts, as is this text"* (17, italics in original). Everett has characterized the paper as "incredibly obtuse . . . [and] nonsense" (Mulholland interview 30), but beneath the obfuscation lies an explanation of Everett's method: a parody of Barthes, it borrows Barthes's methods to demonstrate that any text can be parodied and thus dismantled.[10] This murky manifesto manages to offend several members of the Nouveau Roman Society, who hate Monk (also a member) because he has had the temerity to publish a realist novel, *The Second Failure,* and thus earn the epithet "mimetic hack" (18). Another member, a white woman named Linda Mallory, pesters Monk for sex. He treats her with barely concealed disdain and displays a self-absorbed and superior attitude toward most everyone else.[11] Monk's brilliant corners inadequately smooth his feelings of inadequacy and alienation, his chronic feeling that "I didn't belong" (21).

Solo: Thelonious

Monk's music was also considered weird. Although he was a cofounder of bebop, he received less credit for it than cohorts Parker and Dizzy Gillespie, perhaps because Monk's pervasive use of whole-tone harmonies (augmented chords and dominant sevenths with flatted fifths) and his credo that a solo should acknowledge the melody rather than merely play over the changes went against the grain. His piano style accented percussiveness and employed a staccato attack at odds with jazz's dominant legato phrasing. Monk's compositions also defied convention and categories, ranging from the very simple—"Blue Monk" is a blues that doesn't even bother with the IV7 chord—to pieces such as "Four in One" or "Gallop's Gallop," which present substantial challenges for even elite musicians. Monk's music, with its dissonances and surprises, is all sharp angles—"brilliant corners," as one song title has it.

Verse: Blue Monk

Browsing in a bookstore, Monk Ellison finds one of his own novels filed under African American studies, even though the novel in question, *Persians,* has nothing do with African Americans; the dust jacket photo does the classifying for him.[12] "That fucking store was taking food from my table," he responds indignantly (28). He then reads the opening page of a nearby novel, *We's Lives in da Ghetto,* a runaway bestseller by Juanita Mae Jenkins, about a fifteen-year-old Black girl and Juneboy, her brother with Down syndrome: *"My fahvre be gone since time I's borned and it be just me an' my momma an' my baby brover Juneboy. In da mornin' Juneboy never do brushes his teefus, so I gots to remind him"* (28–29, italics in original). "I . . . thought I was going to throw up," Monk recalls. "It was like strolling through an antique mall, feeling good, . . . and then turning the corner to find a display of watermelon-eating, banjo-playing darkie carvings and a pyramid of Mammy cookie jars" (29). As offensive as its racist stereotypes (perhaps more so) is that Jenkins has received three million dollars for movie rights.

A review of Jenkins's novel summarizes its tale of "*typical Black life*" (39). Its narrator, Sharonda Johnson, pregnant with her third child by a third father, lives with Juneboy and their drug-addicted mother. After Juneboy is killed in a drive-by gang shooting (what else?), Sharonda turns tricks to earn money for dance classes. After being discovered by a Broadway producer, she rises to the top and buys her mother a house, but her "*limitations catch up with her*" and she falls from grace. At the end she is trying to raise money to get her babies back. Praised for its "*haunting verisimilitude,*" the novel is said to portray the ghetto "*in all its exotic wonder*" (39). If this encomium weren't enough to drive Monk nutty, he learns from his agent, Yul, that his own latest novel has been rejected again. While conceding that his work is "*masterfully written and constructed*" the editor asks, "*who wants to read this shit? It's too difficult for the market. But more, who is he writing to?*" (42, all italics in original). Yul summarizes: "The line is, you're not black enough" (43). He then mentions *We's Lives* and, though agreeing that "it's shit," notes that "it sells. This is a business, Thelonious"—words often spoken to that other Thelonious. In both cases, economics erase aesthetics.

Watching an interview with Ms. Jenkins on the *Kenya Dunston Show* (i.e., *The Oprah Winfrey Show*), Monk learns that the author attended pricey Oberlin College and visited Harlem once for all of two days (53). Her apparent inauthenticity infuriates him as much as her book's terrible writing and racist stereotypes. Dunston reads an excerpt and gushes, "Girl, that is some writing, right there." (One is tempted to add, yes, that is some *awful* writing.) As Brian Yost points out, in placing economic success above literary quality, Jenkins imitates Sharonda's prostitution (1328). Any political content is vacated (Murray 737) as value collapses into exchange value: if it won't sell, it's not worthwhile. These conditions, mirroring those of the fine art world depicted in *F for Fake,* are ripe for forgery.

Riff: Ugly Beauty

> CONCREET JUNGLE
> it's a prison days
> we live in
> at least me
> I'm not really free
> baby, Mama, HIV
> where I wanna be where i wanna be?
> Not where I AM
>
> —Precious Jones, *Push*

We's Lives in da Ghetto is a parody of *Push* (1996), a novel by Sapphire (née Ramona Lofton) that chronicles the emergence of its narrator and protagonist, sixteen-year-old Claireece Precious Jones, out of abject poverty and abuse into literacy and self-respect. *Push* sold well at its first printing and returned to the bestseller list upon the 2009 release of Lee Daniels's movie adaptation, *Precious.* Both novel and movie have been praised for their "gritty realism" ("Sapphire's Story") but have also come under fire for reinforcing stereotypes about inner city life and Black males (Larkin 126–27). Precious is pregnant with her second child, and her life is, if anything, worse than Sharonda's. It's not bad enough that her first baby has Down syndrome (and goes by the unfortunate name of "Mongo"); compounding her misery is that both children's father is none other than her own father, Carl. Where is her mother? She is right there—abusing Precious, whom she treats as a household slave and accuses of stealing her man. Laying it on even thicker, Sapphire makes Precious HIV positive, a dire diagnosis in the late 1980s, when the novel is set. Lesley Larkin, who has analyzed the kinship between Everett's parody and Sapphire's novel, has described Precious—obese, unschooled, victimized yet voicing prejudices—as a "physical embodiment of negative stereotypes" about Black women (133), and calls both parents "cartoonish" in their exaggerated sociopathy (137). Their counterpart is the Sapphire figure, a teacher named Blue Rain who patiently pulls Precious out of abjection by teaching her to read and write. If the parents are cardboard villains, Blue Rain is a plaster saint.

Push merits some of Monk's (and Everett's) contempt. Yet it is difficult not to root for Precious. She experiences moments of striking self-awareness, as when she opines that aptitude tests "paint a picture of me an' my muver—my whole family, we more than dumb, we invisible" (30). (Precious may not have read Ralph Ellison's novel, but Sapphire certainly has.) However, as Precious rises to literacy and gains confidence, the novel becomes repetitious. Almost as offensive as its stereotyped characters is its presumption that African American readers must be spoon-fed didactic empowerment sermons instead of presented with complex characters and situations. Indeed, the novel's aims and reception bear out Everett's critique of the publishing industry in his article "Signing to the Blind" (1991), where he complains that "our readers are white. Black people do not buy books. We are at the economic mercy of a market which seeks to affirm its beliefs about African-Americans" (10). *Push* and *We's Lives* offer such affirmations: aimed at providing middle-class white readers with conscience-soothing pathos (and bathos), they permit them to pity poor Black people while eliding systemic racism with tales of individual overcoming. The ghetto looks exotic to these literary tourists, and books like *Push* pander to them; while purporting to challenge prejudices, they reinforce them.

Clearly, however, Everett not only read *Push* but also borrowed parts of it for *My Pafology.* Thus, for example, Precious writes, "I have to say sometimes I hate my muver. She don't love me" (*Push* 34). Monk's Van Go Jenkins similarly attests, "I thinks about my mama. I hate her. I loves her" (*erasure* 80). Precious laments that "all my life I been outside of circle" (*Push* 62). Doesn't Thelonious Ellison say virtually the same thing? Further, as Larkin notes, *Push* and *erasure* "share a surprising number of formal and thematic strategies," including a treatment of stereotypes and the use of postmodernist devices (128–29). But the differences are stark: whereas Sapphire replicates clichés to serve a one-dimensional plot, Everett employs stereotypes self-consciously, not merely to dispel them but also to demonstrate how even a thoughtful, affluent Black artist like Monk can be snared by them even as he sneers at them.

Solo: Well You Needn't

Thelonious Monk's reputation for eccentricity did not aid his career. Indeed, he became notorious for showing up for gigs late or not at all, for performing briefly and then vanishing, or for sitting taciturnly on stage while letting his sidemen play every solo. Offstage, the police treated him as just another Black junkie. And so, after an August 1951 bust for heroin (the drugs probably belonged to his friend, pianist Bud Powell), Monk lost his cabaret card—essential for working in New York. That was the first of three times he experienced this crippling punishment. As a result, like Monk Ellison's fiction, his music was underappreciated for decades. He didn't work regularly or receive due recognition until 1957, when he drew plaudits and large crowds during a six-month stay at New York's Five Spot Café while performing in a quartet with tenor saxophone star John Coltrane.

Bridge: Monk's Point

> You already know how to play. Now play wrong and make *that* right.
>
> —Thelonious Monk to drummer Ben Riley, 1964

Monk Ellison's personal life is just as demoralizing as his writing career and equally full of erasures. His sister, a physician who provides abortions to low-income women, is murdered by a "pro-life" zealot. His brother, Bill, has recently come out as gay, thereby forfeiting his wife, children, and much of his medical practice. Their once formidable mother is succumbing to dementia, and her decline may render their longtime family servant, Lorraine, destitute. Monk is forced to take a leave of absence from his teaching position to help care for his mother. When he applies for an adjunct teaching job, we are permitted to peruse his CV. Of the four published novels listed, by far the most successful is the ironically titled *The Second Failure,* his sole "realistic" (always written with scare quotes) effort, about a "young black man who can't understand why his white-looking mother is ostracized by the black community" (61). Monk professes to hate it. He would protest that it compromises his artistic vision, but a more probable reason for his abhorrence is that the novel touches on his own uncomfortable relationships with his parents and his race. Yul asks him to produce another like it.

In this mood of fury, resentment, and envy—the same emotions that impel most forgers and hoaxers (thesis 6)—Monk sits down to write. Recalling "passages of *Native Son* and *The Color Purple* and *Amos and Andy,*" his hands begin to shake, and he hears people outside shouting "*dint, ax, fo, screet,* and *fahvre!* And [he] was screaming inside, complaining that [he] didn't sound like that." Then he imagines a man asking what he is doing. Out of his mouth comes, "Why fo you be axin?" (61–62). And so Monk begins "a book on which I knew I could never put my name."[13] *My Pafology* is his "fuck you" to Juanita Mae Jenkins, Kenya Dunston, and the publishing industry; it is also a "fuck it" to his career as a literary novelist.

Riff: Four in One

> Oh, that bad man,
> O cruel Stagolee.
>
> —"Stack O' Lee Blues," by Mississippi John Hurt

With *My Pafology* Monk aims to call publishers to account for their greed, to pillory pop culture mavens like Kenya Dunston for pandering, and to prove that a real artist can toss off something like *We's Lives* with minimal effort (thesis 5). These aims qualify it as one of Brian McHale's trap-hoaxes, "designed with didactic or punitive purposes in mind" (236). For the parody and its skewer to penetrate, Monk must reveal his authorship at some point, yet it is not clear how or when he conceives of this moment transpiring. Instead he merges with his alter ego, coming to realize, as Russett notes, that "fictions create their authors, rather than vice-versa" ("Race" 360). *My Pafology* fits into the history of African American fakes alongside bogus "nonfiction" narratives such as *Autobiography of a Female Slave,* written by a white woman named Mattie Griffith.[14] Like Ireland's forgeries, *The Tragedy of Arthur,* and the Ern Malley poems, *My Pafology* is a bastard text, as illegitimate as Van Go's four children, a cuckoo chick with a fake foster parent; like the Ireland and Phillips fakes, it is *about* fatherhood and masculinity (see thesis 8). Indeed, as a spoof of *We's Lives in da Ghetto* (itself a parody of *Push*) and an extended riff on *Native Son*—a *Native Grandson,* if you will—*My Pafology* is three-dimensional parody, and we might add a fourth dimension if we surmise, as I do, that Everett also means to satirize Monk Ellison.[15] It thus exemplifies Gates's definition of signifying, inasmuch as it "entails formal revisions and an intertextual relation" and is "characterized by pastiche" (51–52). Monk uses his blues to play jazz.

Although Everett frames *My Pafology* as inspired by Monk's indignation, Everett first wrote it as a stand-alone text in reaction to *his* frustration at seeing dust jackets refer to an "authentic black story" (George interview 13). Everett thus channels Monk's outrage to pose significant thematic questions: What is a fake book? What is a "real" author? Can a parody deliver themes of which the author is unaware? How does using a pen name change an author and his/her work? Are all creative works Frankenstein monsters? Other questions more germane to African American culture accompany these: What is a "real" Black man? Is he someone like Van Go, all testosterone and nervous energy? Like Thelonious Ellison? Like Thelonious's conservative physician father? A cat like Monk?

Or perhaps it is Stagg R. Leigh. The pseudonym designates a figure who has cast a long shadow over African American culture and folklore since the late nineteenth century. The countless Stagolee stories and songs all derive from an incident in 1895 in which St. Louis tavern owner and pimp Lee Shelton, known as "Stack," murdered one Billy Lyons in an argument over a hat. Shelton's trial the following year yielded a hung jury, but his second trial brought a twenty-five-year prison sentence (Brown 21–34). Long before he was paroled in 1909, Stack Lee was commemorated in songs; over the decades, according to Cecil Brown's indispensable study, he was transmogrified from murderer to folk hero. Stagolee's rejection of the law, romantic love, pity, gratitude, and special consideration for women, exemplify the so-called "bad nigger" (Brown 201, 180). Van Go Jenkins is a riff on Stagolee. And just as Stagolee evolved from criminal to (anti)hero, so Van Go elicits from many readers a contempt tinged with admiration.

Riff: Felonious Punk

> Caught the old lady bent over shovelin' coal
> Put twelve inches up her hole.
> Four little devils runnin' around,
> Hollerin, "Mother, mother, stop him 'fore he fucks us all."
>
> —"Stacklee in Hell"

Narrated by nineteen-year-old Van Go in AAVE, *My Pafology* begins with a dream in which Go's mother calls him and his sister Tardreece "human slough" (i.e., castoffs, or morally degraded); the dreamed Go stabs his mother "cause I hate her. Cause I love her. Cause I hate her. Cause I ain't got no daddy" (*erasure* 65). His motto is "the world be stinkin, so why not me?" (65). The four children Go has sired (none of whom he supports), named Tylenola, Dexatrina, Aspireene, and Rexall (who has Down syndrome like Mongo and Juneboy), point to the pervasive drug culture in which Go scrapes out a living while mocking poor Blacks' alleged penchant for naming their children inappropriately.[16] While the names are obviously meant to be comic (one of Go's dreamed children is called "Pastischa" [82]), they also bespeak the narrator's social role: as Chauncey Ridley observes, Go is a toxic drug in the social system (101). Like Precious Jones, he is a walking stereotype of inner-city youth: greedy, idle, lustful, and eventually a rapist and murderer (Larkin 148). Expelled from school, Go spends his days hanging out at the pool hall with his homeys and committing small-time crimes. A person less like cerebral, middle-class Monk Ellison would be hard to imagine.

But Go has moments of self-analysis, one of which occurs after he argues with Rexall's mother, Cleona, who aspires to be a nurse: "There be two lil' niggers in my head. . . . Nigger A say, Be cool, bro, who know you ain't gots no money, so just let this girl go on back to school . . . so she can get out an be sumpin. . . . But Nigger B laughin, say, Shit, take this bitch home to her house and hit it one times, two times. . . . She aint gone be no nurse. She ain't gone be nuffin" (69–70). As a means of conveying self-knowledge, this is clumsy, but it reveals as much about its ("real") author as about the character. Monk Ellison too carries many selves within him, some listed on the first page of his journal and others he barely recognizes: hostile Monk, cynical Monk, sexist Monk, frightened and bereft Monk, Black Monk, greedy Monk, self-important Monk, self-hating Monk. While Van Go's two selves battle for sovereignty, his dreams—such as one in which his "dick ain't nuffin but a bump" and the woman ridiculing it turns into his mother, whom he stabs (82)—unearth Go's and Monk's insecurities and fears of emasculation. It is no accident that "stab" is Go's word for penetrating a woman.

Go's "Nigger A" seems to be in charge when he accepts a job (arranged by his mother) with a wealthy man named Dalton—the same surname borne by the rich folks in *Native Son,* except that this family is African American. Enlisted as the glamorous Penelope Dalton's driver for an evening, Go brings her and her boyfriend to his own neighborhood, where they stare "out the windows like we in Jungleland or some shit. Niggers on the street be lookin at me drivin this fine car and I feels cool til I remember that I'm in the front by myself and . . . I be lookin like some flunky-ass chaffeur [*sic*]" (103). Grasping that "Mr. Dalton got all the money in the world. And I ain't got shit" (104), Go accompanies the duo ("Richie Rich and Veronica") to Ernie's Chicken Shack (relocated from *Native Son*) (106). After they get drunk and high, Penelope toys with Go, whose feelings are "all tied up in knots. I want to be like her. I hate her. I hate her money. . . . I hate the way she look at me like I don't know shit bout the world. But, damn she fine" (107). Penelope seems willing to have sex; when Go hears an intruder, he puts his hand over her mouth and then "stabs" her—not with a knife (108).

The next day Van Go is asked to appear on the *Snookie Crane Show* (a fictional version of 1990s humiliation spectacles like Jerry Springer's show). The invitation makes him "feel[] big" (110), even after he is made up to look darker, "like a proper TV nigger" (112). His actual role, however, is that of scapegoat, for the appearance is a setup so that the mothers of his kids can vilify him for failing to pay child support. Audience members gang up too, one asserting that he "gots a problem . . . wif his manhood" (115). Although this charge is true, this trait is required for his role as an avatar of Stagolee, who always goes "stag"—he's a solo operator who will never settle down with one woman (Brown 102). Feeling the blood rise to his face, Go begins to shake. Then the other shoe drops: Penelope Dalton has accused him of rape. So Go goes.

We've now entered *Native Son* territory, with Go playing Even Bigger Thomas as he progresses from petty to capital crimes. (Brown notes that Stagolee is the "paradigm for such literary figures" as Bigger [14].)[17] Seeing himself on a bank of television screens, he vows to kill the "K'rean motherfucker" who once kicked him out of his store and called the police (122). When, during his robbery attempt, the owner brings out a shotgun, Go blasts him. "Shit," he says, "fuckin K'rean made me kill his ass" (123). On the lam, he encounters a wino named Willy, who claims to be his father. "I hates this man. I hates my mama. I hates myself," Go thinks. "I see Rexall, without a brain, growin up and axing, 'Why not me?' I see my daddy. I see myself. I shoot the muthafucka. Pop! In the gut" (124). Hiding in a basement, Go is taunted by Willy: "You say you aint shit. . . . You say I aint shit. Well, I is shit and so is you" (125). Increasingly desperate, Go takes a woman hostage in exchange for a sports car and money. But when he starts up the car that the police have provided, its air bag engages, stunning him and covering him in "powder shit." Go is done, but he barely cares: "The cameras is pointin at me. I be on the TV" (131).

Verse: I Mean You

> Satyr [satire] is a sort of Glass, wherein Beholders do generally discover every body's face but their Own.
>
> —Jonathan Swift, *The Battle of the Books*

Monk dismisses the novella as merely an "expression of [his] being sick" of the publishing industry (132), and it's no accident that Go bears Juanita Mae Jenkins's surname. In his heat, however, Monk neglects a salient fact: that, as Linda Hutcheon reminds us, "in imitating, even with critical difference, parody reinforces" (26). Most readers consume the stereotypes in *My Pafology* instead of questioning them. Astute readers of *erasure*, however, comprehend that the parody also contains "meanings that exceed or contradict Monk's intended critique" (Larkin 162). A superficial reading misses the irony that "the 'ghetto' tale featuring a black male 'other' who rapes women rolls off the tongue of the self-professed highly educated, thoughtful writer" (Johns 92). That is, Monk harbors many of Go's beliefs and traits. For example, Go's ambivalence about his mother expresses Monk's buried hostility toward his own. Likewise, Go's dream of emasculation (that "bump") represents Monk's own sex(less) life as a man who might as well have no genitals, a man in his late thirties who has never married, apparently never experienced sexual intimacy, and treats women warily or dismissively. Perhaps he too feels castrated by his mother. Monk's alter ego, then, embodies his rage, his mixed feelings about his family members, his insecurities regarding masculinity and race, along with "misogyny, (ethically) lazy ambition, and blinding narcissism" (Johns 92). He also shares with Go, Bigger, and Stagolee a "deep sense of exclusion" from the social mainstream (Brown 204). One might even postulate that Van Go is a wish fulfillment, for he is not paralyzed by rationality: unlike his creator, Go doesn't think, he goes. It is tempting to conclude that while Monk is an artist of the brain, Van Go is an artist of the body. But Go is far from stupid, shrewdly measuring others' weaknesses and assessing their assumptions, making jokes at his own expense, and displaying a self-awareness that often surpasses Monk Ellison's.

In *My Pafology* Monk transposes his sadness into violence, using a disguise to dramatize his feelings of inadequacy and alienation. Stagg Leigh has been conjured up by Monk's blues, a feeling described by Ralph Ellison as "an impulse to keep the painful details and episodes of a brutal experience alive in one's aching consciousness, to finger its jagged grain, and to transcend it . . . by squeezing from it a near-tragic, near-comic lyricism" (78). *My Pafology* captures this condition in its sometimes hilarious, sometimes shocking, sometimes ludicrous, sometimes pathetic narrative. Riffing on the blues, Monk, and by implication, Everett, transforms them into jazz by signifying on Wright, Ellison, and Sapphire in his intertextual pastiche.

But Monk now must decide whether to tell the truth about his authorship. Yul warns him that "everybody's going to be offended," but

Monk instructs him to submit the MS without commentary. "If they can't see it's a parody, fuck them" (132). To their immense surprise, Random House quickly offers a $600,000 advance—far more than Monk has earned from his other novels. The editor calls it "true to life . . . an important book, . . . magnificently raw and honest, . . . the kind of book that they will be reading in high schools thirty years from now" (136). No one recognizes the parody; instead, they praise its honesty. Readers of *erasure* have responded similarly. For many, as Russett notes, *My Pafology* is "the most compelling section of *Erasure*—fast, mean, and very funny" ("Race" 364). Everett himself acknowledges that "despite all my efforts to the contrary, it works in some weird way" (O'Hagan interview 33). He states that he intended to "mak[e] fun of satire" while also "satirizing social policies" (Shavers interview 65): *My Pafology* exposes the limits of satire. But is making satire Monk's only aim?[18] "Maybe," he confesses, "I felt a bit of vindication somewhere inside me. Certainly, I felt a great deal of hostility toward an industry so eager to seek out and sell such demeaning and soul-destroying drivel"—drivel he is nonetheless willing to market to the highest bidder (137). He assures himself, "It was not exactly the case that I had sold out" (139). What sells *My Pafology*, remarks Ridley, is the erasure of its parody (102). The text also erases Monk Ellison's career as it has existed until now, along with his name and his artistic principles. It is a kind of suicide. What is not erased is Van Go, who haunts Monk for the remainder of the novel and, in the person of Stagg Leigh, engulfs him. When does parody become prostitution? When Monk's "fuck them" ends up fucking him.

Solo: Pannonica

Thelonious Monk experienced the kind of racist humiliations that plagued every Black artist of his era. In October 1958, on their way to a gig in Baltimore, he, saxophonist Charlie Rouse, and Baroness Pannonica von Koenigswarter (a legendary jazz patron and close friend of Monk) were arrested for narcotics that belonged to her. Because Monk asked the officers why he had to exit the car, they beat the pianist's hands with a billy club, rendering him unable to play for several days. His cabaret card was suspended again. A few days later, he had a breakdown at Penn Station and was sent to Rivercrest Sanitarium in Long Island (Kelley 253–54).

Verse: Evidence

As his mother withdraws into dementia, Monk Ellison remembers moments from his youth that cemented his position outside his family, as when his father informed his siblings that Monk "will be an artist. He's not like us," leaving him feeling both "celebrated and ostracized" (143). The memories spur him to inspect the private papers his father left. Among them Monk finds love letters to a white nurse named Fiona, with whom his father carried on an affair while stationed in Korea and afterward. The letters let him hear the voice of a different father, a "tender voice, an open voice" (150): everything he thought he knew about his father is at once affirmed and abolished. On the one hand, he grasps that his father "told all of us any number of times that he was married to the wrong woman" (154). The hints were there; he didn't heed them. On the other hand, he learns that his father was not merely the reserved rationalist his family members knew; he was also a deceitful man who kept a shameful secret for decades and a passionate man capable of sustaining a lengthy love affair; most shockingly, he was the father of a daughter, Gretchen, whom he never met.

His sister is dead, his mother is disappearing, and his brother hates him. Fortunately, Monk meets a compatible woman, Marilyn, who tells him she liked *The Second Failure* (165). They hit it off, date, and prepare to have sex. The moment is ruined, however, when Monk spots a copy of *We's Lives in da Ghetto* in Marilyn's bedroom and she tells him she found it "pretty good" (188). Instead of swallowing his outrage and envy for a chance at intimacy, he barks, "I find that book an idiotic, exploitive piece of crap and I can't see how an intelligent person can take it seriously." So much for that relationship. After Monk rescues his mother when she tries to drive a boat by herself, she agrees to be admitted to an Alzheimer's facility (200–202). But instead of empathizing with her loneliness, he can think only of his own (203). Afterward, he argues with Bill, who shouts, "*I'm true to myself in spite of the detours and interruptions*"—far truer than Monk is. Upon departing, he leaves a note that sums up his feelings: "*FUCK YOU!*" (216). Monk is now a solo artist.

But not quite: he still has Stagg. Or rather, Stagg has him.

Bridge: Misterioso

> You know, people have tried to put me off as being crazy. Sometimes it's to your advantage for people to think you're crazy.
>
> —Thelonious Monk to Frank Brown

Monk directs Yul to warn editor Paula Baderman that Stagg Leigh is just out of "the joint" and hasn't adjusted to life outside. "Tell her he's afraid he might *go off*" (153, italics in original). She is primed to talk with a fascinating and mysterious figure, but Stagg still shocks her when she asks how long it took him to write *My Pafology,* and he replies, "Just a little over a week" (156). Although "Stagg" has vowed not to "put on an act for her," he is deceiving himself, for he is already a thespian. Indeed, Monk seems well versed in the lore of Stagolee, who, according to Brown, long ago metamorphosed from murderer to a "symbol of rebellion, oppositional, subversive, 'underground,' and largely invisible as part of the unofficial subculture" of criminality—an icon for defiance of white laws and norms and a "metaphor that structures the life of black males" (120, 2). One ballad, for example, recounts Stagolee's murder of Lyons, and then describes how

> . . . them deputies took their pistols
> And they laid them on the shelf.
> "If you want old Stackerlee,
> Go arrest him by your own damn self." (Brown 168)

Stagg's aura of violent unpredictability is one "whites found disreputable or downright threatening" (Brown 207)—and also titillating. Monk is hip to this fact, so when Baderman inquires why he was in prison, Stagg demurs, while acknowledging that "white people will get a big kick out of" the book. That sentence, he suspects, has sent "walking fingers up her spine" (*erasure* 156): his menacing mystery makes him sexually attractive. But Stagg is even more menacing for Monk. In "toasts" (ritual storytelling contests) about this antihero, the narrator often *becomes* Stagolee (Brown 178); the same fate awaits Monk Ellison.

He begins to comprehend his bind when he learns that the publisher has bought full-page ads for *My Pafology* in the *New York Times* and

Washington Post. The novel he submitted "for the very reason it was not good" is now "killing" him. "It was a parody, certainly, but so easy had it been to construct that I found it difficult to take it seriously even as that." Worse, it "inhabited no space artistically that I could find intelligible." Then he catches himself: "I was thinking myself into a funk about idiotic and pretentious bullshit to avoid the real accusation staring me in the face. I was a sell-out" (160). True. But that is not his most difficult challenge; once again he is invisible to himself. Monk's more vexing problem—because he does not acknowledge it—is that Van Go Jenkins and Stagolee embody a secret wish, painting a portrait of his own soul, of himself as a "real" Black man. Why was the novella "so easy to construct"? Because it bespeaks a part of Monk that he, like his father, has suppressed. In some ways, indeed, Monk's fake book is more authentic than any of his previous works, because it issues from emotions rather than intellect.

Walking along the beach one day, he spots the Frederick Douglass house and recalls that James Weldon Johnson wrote *The Autobiography of an Ex-Colored Man* from its lookout tower. This apparently random reference is meaningful, for Monk is, like Johnson's protagonist, passing—not as a white man, but as a Black(er) man. He wonders how far he should take the Stagg Leigh imposture. "I might in fact become a Rhinehart [*sic*], walking down the street and finding myself in store windows" (162). A mysterious figure in *Invisible Man* whom we never meet in person, Rinehart, "a metaphysical version of Stagolee" (Gysin n.p.), eventually subsumes the narrator. Dismissing this danger, Monk determines to "let Mr. Leigh continue his reclusive, just-out-of-the-big-house way. He would talk to the editor a few more times, then disappear, like down a hole"—as does the other invisible man (162). Again he dupes himself: once conjured, Stagolee cannot be so easily banished. Monk is the one who will disappear.

Here Everett interpolates a fable called "Appropos de Bottes," one of many such insertions. Some are excerpts from Monk's novel-in-progress that depict imaginary ethical and aesthetic discussions between artists. This one glosses the battle royal episode of *Invisible Man.* A person who calls himself Tom Wahzetepe is scheduled to appear on a television quiz show. Before he goes on, he is made up, like Van Go, to darken his skin (173); he endures it because the producer, Damien Blanc (!), predicts that this appearance may lead to a recording contract or sitcom offer (172). The quiz is rigged. The white contestant, Hal Dullard, is fed ridiculously easy questions such as who slew Goliath or what was the name of the first US president, while Tom is expected to answer outrageously arcane questions about science or to recognize obscure quotations. But the aptly named Dullard fails to answer a single question correctly while Tom aces his. He wins, but when he looks out at the all-white audience, he realizes that they are all dead (178). The show allegorically renders Monk's hoax: Tom is Monk in blackface as Stagg Leigh, forced to excel at "white" cultural achievements. When he succeeds, he finds that, as Everett points out in "Signing to the Blind," there is no audience: once blackened, Monk is blacked out, because his readers cannot plug his achievement into their racial pigeonholes.

Verse: Reflections

> I don't run, white folk, when I got my forty-one.
>
> —Untitled Stagolee ballad

Monk rationalizes his ethical transgressions by assuring himself that *My Pafology* is merely a "functional device," "a warning perhaps, a gravestone certainly" (*erasure* 209). This excuse enables him to accept the $3 million for movie rights. "Stagg" even agrees to meet with the producer, Wiley Morgenstein. In the meantime, in an apparently self-sabotaging move (or perhaps a further test of the market's willingness to bend over for bucks), he informs his editor that he is retitling it. The new title: *Fuck.* The new name is necessary, he tells Yul, because the "thing is a work of art for me. It has to do the work I want it to do" (221). The "thing" is not *Fuck*, however, but "fuck you": as in many forgeries and hoaxes, the real work of art is not the art object but the hoax itself (see thesis 14). Monk finds the irony "beautiful": "I was a victim of racism by virtue of my failing to acknowledge racial difference and by failing to have my art be defined as an exercise in racial self-expression. . . . And I would have to wear the mask of the person I was expected to be. . . . The game was becoming fun" (212; see thesis 11). But his "fun" is a form of minstrelsy. Nor can the quotation from Paul Laurence Dunbar's poem "We Wear the Mask" be accidental, for Monk is doing what Dunbar describes, wearing a disguise that "grins and lies." Perhaps Monk/Stagg should ask if he will eventually have to pay what Dunbar calls his "debt" to "human guile."

Monk's interview garb—khakis, a striped white shirt, weejuns, sunglasses—suggests uncertainty, but in person he plays mystery man to the hilt. Morgenstein immediately observes that Stagg is "not at all like [he] pictured" him; he thought he'd be "more street, more . . ." Stagg supplies the missing word—"black"—but his order, a gibson cocktail, soup, and a lightly seasoned plate of fettucini, is not "street," either (217). When Morgenstein presses him about why he was in prison, for the first time he lies baldly: "They say I killed a man with the leather awl of a Swiss army knife" (218). "They say" exactly this in Papa Hull's well-known song about "cruel Stack O' Lee," in which he is reported to have "bullied two, three coppers down / With a ten-cent pocket knife" (Brown 198; cf. Gysin n.p.). The answer pleases Morgenstein: "I was about to think you weren't the real thing." Living up to his name (he is a stag, after all), Leigh turns to Morgenstein's assistant, Cynthia, and remarks, "Cynthia knows I'm the real thing. Don't you, Cindy?" (218). When Morgenstein asks for his phone number, Stagg gives a "cool laugh" and walks out (219). Yul reports Morgenstein's telling him, "*That fuckin' guy is the real thing*" (italics in original). Monk: "He's right" (222). Although one is tempted to comment that Stagg is only a real fake because he does not exist, he can be whatever the audience or performer wants him to be. In that sense, he is realer than real.

By moving from forgery to impersonation, Monk expands the game from verbal improvisation to physical imposture, inscription to incarnation. Like Harriet Burden, who must enlist actual males as her stand-ins, Monk has to furnish a body to certify his hoax. In this regard these two hoaxes differ from the others discussed here: whereas a forgery begins from and relies on the false signature that connects the time of composition and the time of reading, with the pen serving as a synecdoche of the signer's bodily presence, impostures conjure from the signature a breathing corpus. They are not just bigger lies; they also require a more elaborate and calculated performance. The lines between physical and literary production, between literary and physical bodies, blur and blend, as they do when Bob McCorkle intervenes during Chubb's trial in *My Life as a Fake*. (McCorkle's creator does not *intentionally* bring him to life, unlike Stagg Leigh's.) As a "conjurer and trickster," Stagolee is an ideal presiding spirit for such frauds, since he already embodies "ambiguity and paradox"—like Thelonious Monk and his music (Brown 210; Gysin n.p.). And because he is always "the shadow" (Brown 225), Stagolee occupies a position in mainstream culture like the forger's: the abject one, the negative force that allows the economy to operate. The chief source of Stagolee's power is his ability to function both as "the viewing subject and the subject incapable of being viewed" (Brown 227). Monk is well aware of this power: directly after this meeting he quotes the other Ellison—"*Behold the invisible!*" (*erasure* 219). This line sums up the paradox of the forger, who must be beheld in the act of remaining unseen. Stagg the trickster must keep moving, improvising; in so doing, he "complexly extends" (as Gates writes [63]) his sources, like a jazz musician playing a solo. In Leigh, Monk's fake book becomes real. Yet Monk leaves the meeting feeling "confused, angry"; he "scratche[s] the dark glasses from his face and disappear[s]" (219).

Verse: We See

> You've got to know the importance of discrimination, also the value of what you *don't* play.
>
> —Thelonious Monk to Steve Lacy, 1960

Monk now realizes that he has become "an overly ironic, cynical, self-conscious and yet faithful copy of Juanita Mae Jenkins" (221). Guiltily, he begins a new novel he hopes will "redeem" his "lost literary soul" (223), excerpts of which appear throughout *erasure.* In one, artist Mark Rothko professes to filmmaker Alain Resnais that he is sick of *"painting these damn rectangles."* Resnais responds, *"But the idiots are buying it"* (222, italics are in the original for this and subsequent quotations). A few pages later, Robert Rauschenberg asks Willem de Kooning to draw a picture so that Rauschenberg can erase it. Four weeks later, Rauschenberg shows de Kooning the finished product—blank paper where the drawing once was. Informed that Rauschenberg has already sold it for "*ten grand,*" de Kooning replies, "'*You sold my picture?' Rauschenberg: 'No, I erased your picture. I sold my erasing*'" (228). Rauschenberg's work mirrors the final efforts of Gaddis's Wyatt Gwyon, who consummates his forgery career by scraping the paint from old oil paintings.[19] This work actually exists, but what matters more is that erasure is a part of many, if not all, creative acts, not only forgeries. This erasure's condition as art, however, depends on the viewer's awareness that another work was once present. In that respect Rauschenberg's erasure is parasitic. Yet one might say the same about works like Jean Rhys's *Wide Sargasso Sea,* which presents the previously untold story of *Jane Eyre*'s Bertha Mason: as I suggested in chapter 3, these are not parasites but epiphytes. What does *Fuck* erase? *Native Son? Push?* Not really: each text is partially reconstituted, perhaps rehabilitated, through parody, just as a "faked" version of a standard tune pays homage to the original. *Fuck* acts as a stencil permitting the outlines of another work, another author, to be detected. Similarly, Van Go and Stagg define by negation who Monk is and what, for him, art is.

Verse: Criss Cross

> You've been making the wrong mistakes.
>
> —Thelonious Monk to a fellow musician

"A lonely man, seemingly having shed all his friends. . . . Too mystified to actually be depressed" (*erasure* 225): this is Monk's self-description, presented alongside the bio-bibliographic sketches of the other judges for The Book Award (i.e., the National Book Award). His "widely unread" works make him just as alienated from this circle as he is from the splintered Ellison family. The entry of Monk's *Fuck* into the award competition engenders another ethical dilemma. "I refused to admit that I, Thelonious Ellison, was also Stagg R. Leigh, author of *Fuck*. I could not disqualify myself, because I would betray my secret" (233). He decides to say nothing because "who in his right mind would consider giving that novel an award?" (234). His decision is either naive or disingenuous, given how much attention *Fuck* has already received. Not only is he "unwilling to divest himself of a powerful position from which to censure it" (Ridley 108); his stance toward *Fuck* is more ambivalent than he claims. As with many forgers, self-erasure has won him (as Stagg) flattering exposure. In short, Monk wants it both ways. To his immense (apparent) chagrin, the other judges love *Fuck*. Monk complains that it "didn't capture me"—a telling phrase, for, as we have seen, the novella does capture parts of Monk. And in a different sense, he has already been captured by Stagg Leigh. Fittingly, in his hotel room that night, he watches *Imitation of Life*, a 1959 movie about racial passing.

Monk imagines how Stagg would conduct a public reading of *Fuck*. He would preface it by confessing that the novella is *"not true factually, but it is the true story of what it is like to be black in America. It ain't pretty*" (italics in original, here and below). He might profess that he intends to become "*rich by simply telling the truth*" (235). But when Kenya Dunston asks Stagg to appear on her show, although the prospect fills him with "fear and hate," he admits that "the money was more than significant, nearly doubling my advance" (236). How easily is his conscience assuaged by cash! Monk's fraud may not be as mercenary in its motives as Irving and Suskind's bogus Hughes biography, but the pelf nonetheless permits Monk to swallow his scruples without indigestion. On the flight to New York, Stagg and Monk occupy the same seat while he worries that he might "slip into an actual condition of dual personalities. . . . I was acting, pure and simple, and my pay was substantial and deserved. So, *we* were there dressed as myself" (238). But Monk isn't just passing; he's passing away. He has come to resemble Victor Frankenstein and Christopher Chubb, tormented and consumed by his creation. Indeed, Monk's plight may be worse, for Stagolee is immortal.

While in New York for the awards show, Monk hunts down his lost half-sister, who greets him with hostility and bitterness. Hoping her feelings will be as easily soothed as his own conscience, he writes her a check for $100,000. That is, Monk uses the proceeds from his bastard text to pay off his bastard sibling. His fantasy of reconciliation and reparation dashed, he is left more alone than ever.

Bridge: Ask Me Now

> I always had to be alert with Monk, because if you didn't . . . you'd suddenly feel as if you'd stepped into an empty elevator shaft.
>
> —John Coltrane

The final section of *erasure* is pervaded, Rachel Farebrother notes, by images of "burial, falling, and hiding" as Monk/Stagg rides elevators and takes the subway to the TV studio (128). He is dressed entirely in black, fittingly, since Stagg is Blackness personified. The camouflage is so good that another judge who shares the elevator (going down) fails to recognize him (*erasure* 245). Nor does Monk recognize himself: "Had I by annihilating my own presence actually asserted the individuality of Stagg Leigh? Or was it the book itself that had given him life? . . . What would happen if I tired of holding my breath, if I had to come up for air?

Would I have to kill Stagg to silence him? And what did it mean that I was even thinking of Stagg as having agency?" (248).

There's no time for answers, because the talkshow is about to begin. Stagg has stipulated that he must remain behind a curtain, for Stagolee must see but be unseen. Unfortunately, Dunston didn't expect nonanswers, which is what Stagg's monosyllabic responses afford: "Would you like to tell us how this story came to you?" "No." "Is Go Jenkins based on anyone in particular?" "No" (248–49).[20] Farebrother aptly observes that here Stagg is "at once visible and invisible, a subversive trickster and an insubstantial, two-dimensional 'silhouette'" whose identity rests on little more than "visual props" (127, 128).[21] After the commercial break, Stagg is no more compliant, and so Dunston reads a passage from *Fuck*—the "Nigger A" and "Nigger B" interior monologue, which fits the situation perfectly: Go's self-division mirrors that of Monk, torn between two identities, two versions of Blackness, two visions of masculinity. Then Stagg walks out.[22]

Verse: Monk's Dream

> I would not think of them,
> one way or the other,
> did not they so grotesquely
> block the view
> between me and my brother.
>
> —James Baldwin, "Staggerlee Wonders"

Feeling "as near suicide as [he] ha[s] ever felt" (253), Monk dreams that Nazi soldiers are pursuing him. He watches them burn a house from which a woman manages to save a painting—*Starry Night.* When the soldiers snatch the painting and lance it, the dreamed Monk senses a sharp pain in his stomach. They chase him; he fires at them. A wounded soldier crawls toward him, singing "The Stars Fell on Alabama," and asks, "Wie heissen Sie?" [What's your name?] He does not know the answer (255–56). The dream expresses Monk's anxiety about his hideous progeny, for the painting is, of course, by Van Go(gh)—a metonym for *Fuck*—and the stabbing represents the pain both of childbirth and of penetration. Monk has delivered a monster. Is the monster himself? If the painting represents his alter ego, then Monk is also the one being stabbed—fucked, in Go's idiom. Exacerbating these traumas is the converse wound, castration. "I had managed," Monk thinks, to "reconfigure myself, then disintegrate myself, leaving two bodies of work, two bodies, no boundaries yet walls everywhere. . . . Somehow I had whacked off my own *willy*" (257). Go's dream of the bump has come true.

Another turn of the screw follows when Monk learns that the other judges have "fallen in love with Stagg Leigh's *Fuck*" (254), deeming it a "true, raw, gritty work," one so "vivid, so life-like" in displaying the "energy and savagery of the common black" (254). These are the same terms in which *We's Lives in da Ghetto* is lionized: demeaning stereotypes are read as realistic. Not one reader grasps that it is a parody. When *Fuck* makes the final five, Monk's off-putting title comes back to bite him: having fucked them, Stagg is now fucking him. The situation mirrors the one Everett laments in his 1991 essay, where he pictures African American authors "standing in the dark, signing to the blind" (11). Like Thelonious Monk's version of "'Round Midnight," Monk Ellison's real books have been buried by the fake book. He resolves to "defeat myself to save my self, my own identity. I had to toss a spear through the mouth of my own creation, silence him forever, kill him, press him down a dark hole and have the world admit that he never existed" (259). This mission is made more challenging in the wake of laudatory reviews like the one in the *New York Times*, in which Wayne Waxen moons over *Fuck*, using words like "true" and "real" (260). Monk desperately tries to convince his fellow judges that *Fuck* is not merely a bastard but "a failed conception. . . . offensive, poorly written, racist and mindless. . . . It's not art." "I would think," snaps the judge who failed to recognize him in the elevator, "you'd be happy to see one of your own people get an award like this" (261). The novella, another judge contends, could "only have been written by someone who has done hard time. It's the real thing." The fake book, the *Fuck* book, wins.

Monk attends the award ceremony; when the winner is announced, he approaches the dais, his head spinning. Everett renders his disorientation cinematically, as Ellison seems to enter his namesake's novel. As the floor turns to sand, he beholds a small boy, perhaps himself, holding up a mirror. "I could see my face and it was the face of Stagg Leigh. 'Now you're free of illusion,' Stagg said. 'How does it feel to be free of one's illusions?'" (264). The words echo those of Jack, a white leader of the Brotherhood in *Invisible Man.*[23] "The answer is *Painful and empty,*" Monk replies (265, italics in original)—the same answer given there. What were Monk's illusions? One: that he is not Black. Two: that he could defeat stereotypes by using them, dispel myths about African Americans by reproducing them. Three: that *Fuck* is not his real voice. Four: that he is *not* Stagg Leigh. Five: that he can vanquish Stagg. Monk's hallucination, in which his "bastard novel [is] envisioned as a living child," identifies literary and physical production, with Monk as the father obliged to accept responsibility for his progeny (Ridley 108). Many of the Stagolee songs end with his descent into hell, "where he throws out the devil and takes charge himself" (Brown 168). But here it is Monk who strives to cast out the demon Stagg. Hence, his self-exposure must also be an erasure—of his disguise, but also of the liberating voice that disguise has produced. The boy remains in the mirror as Monk gazes up at a camera and says, "Egads, I'm on television." His final words echo Van Go's. A more fitting utterance might be Not Sidney Poitier's upon receiving his Oscar: "I AM NOT MYSELF TODAY" (234).

Solo: Let's Call This

Thelonious Monk is now revered as one of the most important innovators in jazz history, a genius and sage whose compositions are performed on bandstands around the world. His commercial difficulties, eccentricity, refusal to compromise, as well as his wit and humor, serve as models for his fictional namesake. But it seems unlikely that Monk Ellison will equal the jazz master's fame or artistic success. Nor does he qualify as a genius, according to his predecessor's definition, for Monk Ellison cannot be "most like himself" until he knows who that self is.

Coda: Bye-Ya

The novel ends before Monk divulges his authorship; the consequences are likely to be dire. *Fuck* will be discredited, and Monk's career as a literary novelist will be obliterated as readers resent that they've been duped. That is why, notes Ridley, Monk's efforts to reclaim his identity and integrity endure beyond the recalled events: the journal itself is an attempt to "control his bastard novel's public reception" (109). Everett, too, has sought to manage the reception of *erasure,* stating that it is about "how our culture seeks to interfere in the production of art" (Mulholland interview 31) and claiming that what interests him most about Monk is his "selfless examination of himself" (O'Hagan interview 32). But is that self-examination successful? Russett proposes that he is now "trapped in an even more reductive version of the stereotype he despises" ("Race" 365). Likewise, Farebrother sees Monk and his alter ego as equally "implicated in the cultural commodification of blackness" (131). I agree. Yet his imposture has enabled him not only to achieve financial success but to conjure a powerful creative spirit. Everett has lamented that *erasure* is the work for which he is best known and has noted the "terrible irony" that the novel has gained attention "for the very reason" that he wrote it: everyone is interested in "the race question . . . instead of the book itself. The parody within the parody" (George interview 11). Everett's downplaying of its racial theme seems disingenuous when one realizes that he composed most of it with a crow named Jim perched on his shoulder. "He wrote *erasure,*" Everett has declared (Ehrenreich interview 26). (Jim appears in Everett's author photo.)

Everett's novel brilliantly dramatizes several of my fifteen theses, but particularly thesis 7: that an author is always a fictional character, an impersonation, a mask. To write is always to pass as someone else, and Monk Ellison's sojourn into Stagolee's territory suggests that he has *always* been passing. In this sense, his previous novels are forgeries, too, because they issue from only one part of his imagination and identity—the rational part—and hence are less than fully authentic. The novel dramatizes once more how a forgery or hoax inevitably assumes a life of its own and eludes the control of its creator (thesis 12). And it demonstrates pithily the dialectic between self-erasure and self-exposure that characterizes every literary and fine art fraud. As for Chatterton, Meredith, Ireland, Phillips, McAuley, Stewart, and Chubb—and as for many real-life hoaxers and forgers—faking enables Monk to fashion a fresh authorial self (thesis 2). Alas, this self, as with McCorkle and Chubb, steals his soul. But if Monk's cultural critique (thesis 10) is coopted by the system, Everett's is not. His fiction of forgery manages to do what all successful forgeries accomplish: lay bare the "conceptual shoddiness and the expediencies" of the literary establishment (Ruthven 4).[24] By portraying a fraud, *erasure* divulges and denounces the "cultural practices that foster the so-called genuine article" we call literature (Ruthven 171). And through his sly deployment of the jazz aesthetic—intertextual signifying, satire, collage, improvisation—Everett's book of fake books embodies thesis 15 and earns the description Duke Ellington applied only to the greatest music: it is "beyond category."

PART II

FAKE ART

Masks

> Man is least himself when he talks in his own person. Give him a mask, and he will tell you the truth.
>
> —Oscar Wilde, "The Critic as Artist"

5

Original Sins

PAINTING THE PERFECT FAKE IN *THE RECOGNITIONS*

> The dragon bites and eats its tail,
> And feeds itself from a part of itself.
> Submit it to sword, hunger and imprisonment;
> So that it devours itself and vomits it up,
> So that it kills itself and is born again.
>
> —Epigramma XIV, from Michaël Maier's *Atalanta Fugiens* (1617)

Frame 1: Circles

"Cave cave Deus videt," reads the legend at the center of the circular painting: "Beware, beware, God is watching" (fig. 10). As we walk around it, we see in the bottom panel a man holding a chair and a blade as a second man prepares to slash him with a saber; one step to the right, a woman admires her new hat in a mirror held by a demon; five more steps bring us to a judge who listens to a plaintiff while accepting a bribe from the other party. These are wrath, pride, and avarice—three of the painting's seven sins. The four corners of the rectangle surrounding the circle show "the potential points of salvation or condemnation which would result from refraining from, or submitting to, these sins"; they represent Death, Judgment, Heaven, and Hell (Charney, "Seven"). Mind you, we are also being watched as we view these vignettes: the blue center of the table, portraying a stigmatic Christ rising from the dead, serves as the pupil of His eye. "It is you, the viewer, to whom this work is addressed. You are the subject of Christ's stare, as he watches your every move, should you fall into sin" (Charney, "Seven"). As one seventeenth-century critic commented, the painting is a "mirror in which the truth of Christianity is reflected so we might all see ourselves in it." In case we miss the point, the banderoles at top and bottom quote Deuteronomy 32:28–29: "For they are a nation void of counsel, neither is there any understanding in

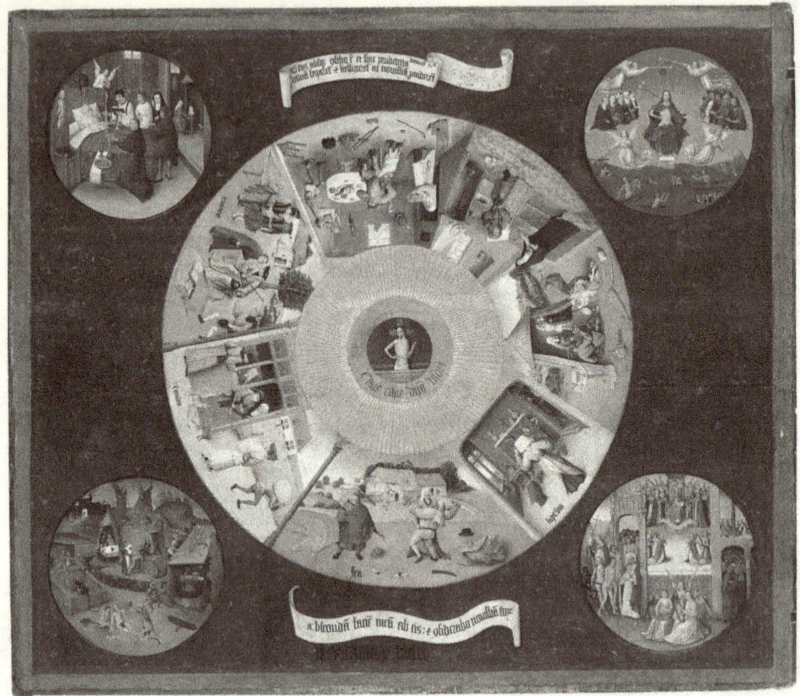

FIG. 10. "God is watching," reads the legend on Bosch's table painting, *The Seven Deadly Sins and the Four Last Things* (c. 1500). The painting represents both the structure and moral vision of Gaddis's novel. Oil on wood, 120 × 150 cm. (© *Museo Nacional del Prado*)

them"; and "O that they were wise, that they understood this, that they would consider their latter end!" (King James Version; Büttner 120–21). Patches of blue sky peep through behind Jesus, but otherwise the dominant colors are green and gold—representing envy and greed. A person eating at this table might well feel her digestion disturbed.

Hieronymus Bosch's early sixteenth-century tabletop painting *The Seven Deadly Sins and the Four Last Things* plays a central role in William Gaddis's novel, *The Recognitions* (1955).[1] The pastor father of the protagonist, painter/forger Wyatt Gwyon, purchases it in Spain soon after his wife dies and brings it to his parsonage in New England, where it becomes a household fixture.[2] The painting's circular design represents Wyatt's trajectory as well as the novel's structure, which is less a circle than an ouroboros. The novel's frontispiece—borrowed from Maier's alchemical tome *Atalanta Fugiens,* which features a drawing of a dragon eating its own tail—reinforces this trope of circularity (Eliade 77).

Young Wyatt copies the table and sells the original—one of his many sins against originality. Later he sits at the same table while he and his associates plan a forgery scheme. Is it the same table? And is Gwyon's table the original or a copy? We are never entirely sure; hence, Bosch's painting embodies Gaddis's primary theme.[3] The painting's murky provenance epitomizes how Gaddis unsettles the opposition between authenticity and forgery, the real and the fake, to develop his thematic questions (M. Taylor, *Rewiring* 12–13; Wilkens 605). These are, as Joseph Salemi articulates them, "*What is the nature of, and what are the conditions for, genuine art?*" (47, italics his). These questions both vex and vitalize Wyatt, who becomes a forger not to make money or to take revenge on experts but to pursue a queer form of aesthetic piety. He seeks to resurrect fifteenth-century Flemish masters and to reconstitute their world, one charged with the grandeur and gravity of an ever-vigilant deity. Inculcated with a puritanical brand of Calvinism, Wyatt eschews originality to seek the perfection possible only in imitation and thereby to transcend his own time, which he perceives as a wasteland of corruption, commodification, and counterfeits.[4] Only through imitation—which for him means not only studying and copying works, but re-cognizing their initial cognitions—can an artist conceive immaculately. Only forged works, for him, are truly genuine.

If, as Klaus Benesch proposes, Gaddis aims to rewrite the history of Western art as a "history of doubling and counterfeiting" (31), then Gaddis must engage in similar doubling and imitation. And so he does, recycling, repeating, and reframing images, phrases, themes, scenes, and dialogue throughout the novel, transforming it into a "literary echo chamber" (31) where, John Johnston observes, he "plays continuously on our 'recognitions' of their similarity and difference" (7). Beyond these intratextual repetitions, the novel quotes and recycles previous texts in a manner akin to Joyce's *Ulysses,* though less programmatically. For example, the title indicates that Gaddis's primary source is "the first Christian novel," *The Recognitions,* a first-century text mistakenly attributed to St. Clement. Gaddis knew that the pseudo-Clementine text is of questionable origin. As the crooked art connoisseur Basil Valentine remarks in Gaddis's novel, the Clementine *Recognitions* concerns a pilgrim's quest to learn magicians' secrets of immortality;

it is "the beginning of the whole Faust legend" (373). Gaddis's novel itself reenacts *Faust,* as Wyatt, in effect, sells his soul to Valentine and his associate, the shady dealer Recktall Brown. These are just two of the innumerable intertextual threads in this gargantuan novel, which cites texts ranging from early Christian writings and classical poetry to works of art history and the poetry of Robert Browning and T. S. Eliot. Gaddis's "extensive incorporation of imitated and disguised quotations . . . produces a tessellated surface on which every relationship between 'original' and imitation, copy and counterfeit . . . is ceaselessly played out" (Johnston 156).

Beneath this enormously complicated surface several stories intersect, as Wyatt's endeavors parallel and play off those of a group of young artists (and would-be artists) and their friends in post–World War II Greenwich Village. Entire chapters pass with little or no mention of Wyatt Gwyon while we follow the aspiring playwright Otto Pivner, the young composer Stanley, Wyatt's wife Esther, his model Esme, and their acquaintances and hangers-on. Here, however, I concentrate on the art forgery narrative to limn Wyatt's story, which, Kevin Attell observes, amounts to a broken bildungsroman or compromised *Künstlerroman* (267). Although key scenes are set on Christian Holy Days—the novel begins on All Saints' Day, lingers for hundreds of pages in the Christmas season, and ends on Easter Sunday (Taylor, *Rewiring* 20)—Gaddis remarked that *The Recognitions* is really about "being born again in *this* life" (Abádi-Nagy 6). To be reborn, however, one must first possess a self, and Wyatt's self is as shifting and shadowy as his artistic style. His identity is formed and then stripped away layer by layer over the course of the novel, as if he were a painting undergoing scraping and restoration. Each of my subtitles thus indicates a layer or ingredient of a painting. Ultimately, Wyatt embodies his own artistic goal: he becomes the perfect fake, a man with no identity, before arriving at an ambiguous resolution. The epigraph to the first chapter, drawn from Goethe's *Faust,* is *Es wird ein Mensch gemacht:* "A man is being made." He is also being unmade.

Inherent Vice

> Inherent vice, said Basil Valentine. . . . No one insures against inherent vice.
>
> —*The Recognitions*

Wyatt Gwyon's mother, Camilla, dies from appendicitis on the *Purdue Victory* during a voyage to Europe. The ship's surgeon who fails to treat her is not a physician but a counterfeiter named Frank Sinisterra (5). Camilla is buried in a cemetery in San Zwingli, Spain, near the Real Monasterio de Nuestra Senora de la Otra Vez. (Counterfeiter, town, and monastery reappear later.) Her corpse, however, is confused with that of a young girl who has been raped and murdered, which is later disinterred in its stead. Hence, Wyatt's father returns not with his wife's body but with only her prized earrings ("heavy Byzantine hoops of gold" [14]), the Bosch table, and a Barbary ape named Heracles. Among the reverend's many books are eyebrow-raising volumes such as *The Golden Bough, Malleus Maleficarum,* and *The Egyptian Books of the Dead.* Moreover, his copy of St. John of the Cross's *Dark Night of the Soul* has been hollowed out, the better to hide bottles of liquor—more comforting during his own dark nights than the saint's aching account of spiritual crisis. The reverend is not very reverent, and he becomes less Christian and more committed to Mithraism—an ancient sect of sun worshipers—as Wyatt grows up.

Camilla had wanted to name her son Stephen, after the first Christian martyr, but the reverend's dour, censorious Aunt May intervened and named him Wyatt. As his father withdraws into grief and pagan rituals, Aunt May becomes Wyatt's surrogate mother—not a nurturing one. Lucifer's sin, according to her dubious theology, was striving to become "original, to steal Our Lord's authority, to command his own destiny" (34).[5] Nonetheless, in addition to copying illustrations from Christian texts, Wyatt continues to compose original works, which he buries behind the barn. For Wyatt, originality is the original sin (Abádi-Nagy 4). Yet the sin of pride, represented by that woman admiring herself in a mirror, amounts to loving an image of oneself—a copy. Hence, Wyatt is trapped in a dilemma: if loving a copied image is a sin but making original works is equally wrong, what is one to do?

Although he is unable to finish any original drawing, his "copies continued to perfection, that perfection to which only counterfeit can attain, reproducing every aspect of inadequacy, every blemish on Perfection in the original" (55). He refuses to complete the portrait of his mother he has begun, because, he haltingly explains to his father, "There's something about a . . . an unfinished piece of work. [. . .] Where perfection is still possible? Because it's there, it's there all the time, all the time you work trying to uncover it" (57). Reverend Gwyon, who bequeaths to Wyatt those golden earrings, urges him to finish the portrait; otherwise "she will be with you always" (60). But, of course, that is the point: to keep her pure image before him. Wyatt's juvenile masterwork, however, is not his mother's portrait but a replica of the Bosch table, which he secretly paints sin by sin, "unbroken by any blemish of originality" (55). We later learn that he sells the original, his distracted father unaware that he is dining not merely on a representation of sins but on a product of the (less deadly) sin of fraud.[6]

"Inherent vice" refers to a condition in which the "seeds of the deterioration are the chemical components" of an artwork and their "interactions with environmental agencies" (Scott 84)—for example, the propensity of oil paint to crack with age. No insurance policy will cover it, just as, for Catholics, there is no remedy for original sin outside of the sacraments. Wyatt's inherent vice is his obsession with painting, which collides with the tenets of his great aunt's religion. The result is a crippling ambivalence about artmaking, which he paints over with aesthetic piety—a belief that through copying he can transcend human flaws. Wyatt may be right that only a forgery can be perfect. That is, an immaculately copied fake may achieve perfection, whereas an original work bears with it the inherent vices and limitations of its creator and thus (according to Wyatt) always fails to match the artist's inspiring vision. How do we know if a work is excellent and genuine? Experts tell us. But they carry their own inherent vices, as Wyatt learns when he moves to Paris.

La Macule

is a Paris art journal whose chief critic is stained by greed. In the French capital Wyatt finishes seven original paintings and restores several others but finds the city overrun by frauds and fashionistas. (These paintings are later destroyed when the warehouse where they are stored burns to the ground [90].) He tells a critic named Crémer that he has completed one work in the "manner of [Hans] Memling," a late fifteenth-century German who lived and worked in Flanders (70). Herr Koppel, Wyatt's teacher, had compared the painting to Gerhart David's *Flaying of the Unjust Judge.* As if to remind Wyatt that "pictures are bullion" (73), Crémer offers him a deal: a positive review in *La Macule* of his upcoming one-man show in exchange for 10 percent of the profits. Wyatt turns him down. So Crémer pans his work as "derivative [. . .] heartless, without sympathy, without vitality, full of the spirit of death without hope of the Resurrection" (74, my translation). At the same time, a German journal reports a newly discovered work by Memling that has been crudely overpainted; beneath it is a work resembling *Flaying* that experts attribute to Memling. It is actually Wyatt's painting. This misattribution and the German critic's jingoist opinion that Memling was a greater artist than Van Eyck, Bouts, and Van der Weyden (75) reinforce Wyatt's mistrust of experts, for Van Eyck's importance—and superiority to Memling—is beyond doubt.[7] What matters more for Wyatt is that the supposed cradle of artistic creativity produces only maculate conceptions.

Fished For

The unfinished portrait of Camilla accompanies Wyatt to New York, where he lives with his wife, Esther, while working as a draftsman and bridge designer. He seems to value that cracked, soiled painting more than Esther, whom he neglects.[8] Distraught over his aloofness, she insinuates that Wyatt (like her new friend Otto) is homosexual (106). He doesn't bother to rebut her, instead retreating to his studio where he "finishes the argument alone" (126). Their shaky marriage is one example of the novel's theme of separateness in relationships and in artistic practices. The narrator declares that we deny that we are "drawing away from one another, that we share only one thing, the fear of belonging to another, or to others, or to God; love or money, tender equated in advertising and the world, where only money is currency, and under dead trees and brittle ornaments prehensile hands exchange forgeries of what the heart dare not surrender" (103). Instead of love we exchange commodities or currency, counterfeits of real tenderness, angling for meaning and transcendence but failing to find them. Gaddis's vision of the mid-twentieth-century West is bleak: despite the novel's abundant parties and gatherings, it is almost entirely bereft of intimacy, love, or true community, and most of the art it depicts is fatally compromised by capitalism or corruption. Wyatt seeks to remedy this alienation through an art that will inspire recognitions of truth, transcendence, and shared humanity. When a recognition occurs for most people, he tells Esther, everything breaks into pieces, and one "can never put them back together quite the same way" (114). The artist tries to reassemble them until he or she renders "the whole thing in all its dimensions"—the "thing" being a re-cognition of the world and humans' shared place in it. As Gaddis wrote in a letter to J. Robert Oppenheimer, *The Recognitions* is about traditions as "'both bonds and barriers among us,' and our art which 'brings us together and sets us apart'" (qtd. in Alberts 19). But recognition is arduous: as Wyatt laments, "The discipline, the detail [. . .] is too much to bear" (114).

This discipline also narrows and isolates him. Even the "moments of exaltation" he experiences while he paints are entirely private. So consumed is he with personal aesthetic perceptions that he does not even notice Esther spying on him at the Metropolitan Museum, being too mesmerized by Picasso's *Night Fishing in Antibes,* its haunting blues, purples, and greens punctuated by circular designs that resemble eyes gazing back at us. As soon as he encountered it, he tells her, everything was "freed into one recognition, really freed into reality [. . .]. Most paintings, the instant you see them they become familiar, and then it's too late" (92). This is precisely the sort of epiphanic recognition—a wedding of reality and representation that renews our apprehension of both—that he will seek to incite with his forgeries. Wyatt speculates that we are "fished for" by supercelestial beings who catch us in those moments of re-cognition (87). Such auratic recognitions, he believes, are inhibited by the quest for originality, which Herr Koppel described as a "romantic disease." Two hundred years ago, Koppel opined, to be original was to admit "you could not do a thing the right way, so you could only do it your own way. When you paint you do not try to be original, [. . .] so you copy masters" (89). Beneath Wyatt's aesthetic credo lurk Aunt May's prohibitions: originality is humanity's inherent vice.

Everybody and Nobody

Wyatt barely notices when Esther begins an affair with Otto, using him as Wyatt's surrogate. Otto is happy to oblige, for most of his pronouncements about art are quoted (without attribution) from Wyatt, such as his opinion that Memling piled up "perfection layer by layer" (124). Gaddis once stated that Otto is a "two-dimensional imitation of Wyatt; he wants to be Wyatt but has none of the equipment" (Abádi-Nagy 6). Yet Wyatt too is unformed: "With his ability and your ambition," Esther tells Otto, he would have "quite a remarkable man" (136). Indeed, Wyatt is in many ways more a vector than a character. According to David Koenig, who worked from Gaddis's notes, the author intended many of the minor characters to "represent facets of Wyatt," who becomes the "symbol of what all the others had lost" (30–31). He also loses himself: after page 118, the name "Wyatt" never appears. Joseph Tabbi suggests that Gaddis endorsed a "disciplined self-effacement" (152), echoing Wyatt's remark that an artist is merely the "dregs of his work" (*Recognitions* 96). Self-effacement is necessary for a forger, who must vanish into the style and signature of his model(s). Not coincidentally, the erasure of Wyatt's name occurs just before the entrance of Recktall Brown, who lures him into his forgery scheme. In becoming a forger, Wyatt seeks to become other artists; to do that, he must erase himself.

But erasure is not the end. Wyatt ultimately becomes a sacrificial victim who is, writes Dominick LaCapra, "dismembered and disseminated into those around him," becoming a "blank space into which other characters project their desires for redemption" (38). Others also use him to make money, to augment their artistic credentials, or to atone for their misdeeds. Perhaps a better image of Wyatt, then, is that of a cracked magic mirror that reflects everyone else's transgressions and aspirations.[9] This image is fitting, since Wyatt uses mirrors to paint himself into his forgeries—to find himself in his work. The mirrors reflect how Wyatt is ensnared in the forger's dilemma, as outlined in thesis 4: he wants to be both elevated and eliminated.

Gold

> So you will see I am the suffering shadow
> of Capocchio, who, by practicing alchemy,
> falsified the metals, and you must know,
> unless my mortal recollection strays
> how good an ape I was of Nature's ways.
>
> —Dante, *Inferno,* Canto XXIX.136–40

God

To create perfect fakes, Wyatt must evade the "trace paradigm," according to which any work is said to be a "conglomerate of the traces of its own production process and of the many conditions that have contributed to shape it" (Lenain 235). Indeed, even the possibility of an undetectable fake threatens to topple the edifice of art history and connoisseurship; in this respect the subversive power of art forgeries mirrors the way counterfeit money erodes faith in the economic system and the way that literary forgeries "disturb the societies in which they are produced" (Ruthven 2). The bête noire of art connoisseurship and "the opposite of the unquestioned metaphysical idea of the authentic masterpiece" (Lenain 267), a perfect forgery is nonetheless a product of the same system: there would be no forgeries were there no masterpieces eliciting high praise and higher prices. Indeed, art history depends on the threat (if not the existence) of forgeries, for, as I note in thesis 1, an original has no meaning without the possibility of a copy, for the concept of originality requires the potential existence of something unoriginal. Wyatt's forgeries, then, are the dark doubles not just of the masterpieces he imitates but of art history itself. According to the trace paradigm, an artwork has the "nearly magical power of making its own origin authentically present and perceptible" (Lenain 235). Against this magic Wyatt plies a different brand of sorcery—alchemy.

With the emergence of the science of chemistry during the Enlightenment, alchemy was "turned out like a drunken parent, to stagger away, babbling phantasies" (*Recognitions* 132). But while writing *The Recognitions,* Gaddis came to perceive parallels among "perfection in painting, perfection in the godhead, finite attempts to create beauty and Christianity on earth, [and] alchemy as an expression of turning base metals into gold" (LeClair 22). As Wyatt explains to Otto (who explains it to Esther), alchemy was not just a process of "making gold" but a path toward "redemption" (129). Alchemists considered gold to be nature's completion and attempted to assist nature in fulfilling "her final goal, . . . which is the perfection of its progeny . . . to its supreme ripening, which is absolute immortality and liberty (gold being the symbol of sovereignty and autonomy)" (Eliade 52). An emblem of immortality, gold represents a perfect state of being (151).[10] The alchemist was Christ's minister and assistant, redeeming matter in order to redeem humanity—beginning with the alchemist. That is, in endeavoring to perfect nature, the alchemist was also "working to 'make' himself," so that at the end of this process he had forged a new personality (47, 160). The goal of alchemy, then, was "to become as good as gold . . . which is the most rarefied form of the *prima materia*" (Taylor, *Rewiring* 16). In short, alchemists strived to transform humans into gods. (This heretical aspiration is likely why Dante consigned alchemists and forgers to the same bolgia of the eighth circle of hell [Moore 20].) Wyatt, however, understands alchemy as a model for his artistic enterprise, which he envisions as a brand of sacred sorcery, the *telos* of which is to re-cognize the world and remake himself. No mere fakesmith, he conceives of himself as a soulsmith.

During the alchemists' era, gold signified the very possibility of exchange and transformation. It served as a transcendental signifier, the measure of all values and virtues. According to Jean-Joseph Goux, gold, as the foundation of economic exchange, "brought together the functions of *archetype*, of *token*, and of *treasure* into a single object" ("Cash" 115). That is, by anchoring monetary exchanges as a universal equivalent, gold functioned not only as store of wealth (the "real" function) but also as a circulating medium (its "symbolic" function) and a measure of value (the "imaginary" function) (*Symbolic* 47–48, 54). Just as gold "guarantees—even forms the basis of—a system of monetary exchange," writes Johnston," for Wyatt "the existence of the original guarantees the meaning and efficacy of an aesthetic economy" (10). In Goux's system gold is isomorphic with God (in the theological register) and with the phallic father (in the "psychic economy") through a "process whereby the established domination of the universal and normative equivalent (money, father, phallus, sword) centers or anchors all products of exchange in a single point" (*Symbolic* 44). In other words, just as gold once stabilized the economic system, God and the phallic father serve similar functions in other registers. Wyatt, having rejected his father and his father's religion, unconsciously seeks a replacement for both. Aiming to substitute art for religion, he understands gold as a symbol of perfection and transcendence.

But what if there is no gold? Theologically, a goldless world is a godless world; psychically, a world without gold is a realm with no moral center—the *Seven Deadly Sins* table sans its central judging, penetrating eye—and no prospect of heaven. What happens when gold no longer grounds monetary exchange? That is the world that we (and Wyatt) inhabit. Modern currency cannot be exchanged for gold; it is based on nothing more than a communal agreement to accept worthless tokens as circulating media and measures of value. A similar transformation in the aesthetic economy—as has occurred in postmodernism—would evacuate originality as a principle or goal. The result would be a realm where distinctions between the authentic and the inauthentic, originals and forgeries, have given way to what Jean Baudrillard describes as a "*precession of simulacra*"—copies without originals, signs exchanged for each other "in an uninterrupted circuit without reference" (or reverence) (166, 170, italics in original).[11] Wyatt's forgeries foster such a domain. Paradoxically, even as he subverts the cult of originality, he relies on originals, for without them he could forge no gold in his smithy. No gold would mean no magic, no redemption, and no value. This becomes Wyatt's bind.

Dog

Interrupting Wyatt's cogitations on alchemy is a poodle, harbinger of one of the novel's dual devils, Recktall Brown (140).[12] If gold symbolizes the possibility of transcending matter, Brown, as his name indicates, represents a soulless materialism in which money is excrement (see Wolfe 128). To Wyatt's lofty notion that a "work of art redeems time," Brown offers a pragmatic riposte: "Buying it redeems money. [. . .] That's why old art gets the prices," and why "they copy them right and left" (144–45). But suppose some old master's pictures "turned up here and there. They might turn up a little restored, like the kind of work you do." And if someone like Wyatt were to restore such a work, why he "might find an undiscovered picture there by Master whatever-he-was. [. . .] It might be worth fifty" thousand (145). Has Wyatt ever considered doing such a thing? Instead of recoiling in disgust, Wyatt merely remarks, "It would be a lot of work." A spark is lit in Wyatt's smithy: he will paint forgeries; Brown will sell them. As Valentine later points out, Wyatt becomes another of Brown's possessions, like his dog (235).

For Brown forgery is simply a shrewd way to take advantage of inflated prices and egos, and a forged painting is just a commodity like a "tube of toothpaste or a laxative which induces spastic colitis. You can't sell any of them without publicity" (244). For Wyatt, however, it is a means to fulfill his aesthetic credo, according to which "every work of art is a work of perfect necessity" and "every line you put down couldn't go any other place" (144). Whereas creating an original work involves countless decisions about color, composition, medium, and perspective, with no guarantee of success, imitations of old masterworks can be evaluated by simple yardsticks. Have I captured the style and spirit of the model? Does it fool the experts? Does it bring a high price? When success is determined by dollars, aesthetic values are subsumed by economics. Wyatt's pursuit of perfection will allow others to exploit his skill and to promulgate the antithesis of his ideals. His gold will inevitably fade to brown.

Layer by Layer

> In our art, the thing that is unjustly defiled by the one will be absolved, cleansed and delivered from that foulness by another that is contrary to it.
>
> —Raymond Lully, *Codicillus,* in *The Recognitions*

The alchemist Raymond Lully refers here to the philosopher's stone, the possession of which promotes the unification of opposites. Such a merger takes place when we reencounter Wyatt, in chapter 7, as he is introduced to Basil Valentine. This erudite, Jesuit-educated aesthete and critic acts as counterpart to the earthbound, paternal Brown. Although Valentine's manner of speaking and habits code him as gay, he is phobic about touching others (he constantly washes his hands) and likely celibate. Whereas Brown treats Wyatt as a wayward son, Valentine plays devil's advocate, spurring Wyatt to greater exertions. The trio function as an unholy trinity: father, son, and phony ghost. The alchemist Basil Valentine (the namesake of Gaddis's character) wrote, "Evil must become the same as good" (qtd. in Eliade 166). Likewise, by committing fraud, Wyatt believes he is doing good. His associates are not burdened with such delusions, and Gaddis cloaks them in infernal imagery—the smoke from Brown's cigars and Valentine's ubiquitous cigarettes.

Valentine admires Wyatt's remarkable ability to "move from the painstaking, meticulous strokes of [Dieric] Bouts to the boldness of Van der Goes" (229–30). But he notes that most "forgeries last only a few generations, because they're so carefully done in the taste of the period, a forged Rembrandt, for instance, confirms everything that that period sees in Rembrandt" (230). In this sense the loss of Wyatt's originals is fortunate, since a forger "can't suppress all of [him]self" (247).[13] Wyatt's stylistic studies and painstaking techniques are meant to sidestep this pitfall. He has succeeded so far: Valentine reads from an issue of *Collectors Quarterly* that praises a newly discovered Van der Goes *Descent from the Cross* for instantiating the "most characteristic expression of the genius of Flemish art." It is, Valentine remarks, "almost perfect" (239). It was painted by Wyatt Gwyon.[14]

Superbia

It is experts who decide whether a painting is genuine, and once an expert certifies a painting, it is likely to stay that way. Experts have validated Wyatt's Memling, Bouts, and Van der Goes forgeries, and Valentine knows how the process works. These authorities *want* to be deceived, and if "they want to be deceived, let them be deceived" (245). As we have seen with Chatterton and Ireland, even when a work is later found to be questionable, believers resist changing their minds, for they are now invested in their decision and dread seeing their reputations tarnished: "So long as people are afraid of being found out, you have them in the palm of your hand" (234). (This is thesis 13.) Having contracted the virus of belief, they don't want to be cured. Valentine hastens this process. Thus, after Wyatt finishes his first Van der Goes, it is overpainted so crudely that even customs officials detect it. Beneath lies a "genuine, duty-free, original work of art" that Valentine has verified as authentic (244). Thus do critics, dealers, and artists collude in sustaining the system, even if that means allowing forgeries into the canon.

Brown is aware of the most important secret of the forger's art, outlined in thesis 3: it's all about the story. The more convincing its tale of provenance and history, the more probable is a forgery's success. Wyatt, however, is supremely confident that he can dupe the experts through pure skill and describes the techniques and materials he has developed to do so: oil of lavender, egg tempera, a varnish glaze, and, for the Bouts painting, linen threads in the gesso that he bakes. For his latest Van der Goes, he has laid on the canvas a thin layer of gesso that cracks "of its own volition" (248). He controls this "damned world of shapes and smells" with glair—a liquid distilled from egg whites, which crackles without being heated or aged (248). The technique, Wyatt crows, is "foolproof" (249).

Another Blue Day

Wyatt's newest Van der Goes forgery began as an Annunciation but has evolved into a Death of the Virgin, with the mysterious Esme as the model. Brown has even bought an old farmhouse in Vermont where the painting will be "discovered." One problem: a *Death of the Virgin* by Van der Goes already exists (fig. 11).[15] Notable for its "intense representation of sorrow," the painting exemplifies his skill at individualization, as each of the apostles attending Mary's bedside engages the viewer's

FIG. 11. Wyatt Gwyon recasts this painting in one of his forgeries, then mutilates Mary's face to counterfeit aging. Hugo van der Goes, *Death of the Virgin* (c. 1480). Oil on wood, 147.8 × 122.5 cm. (© Scala, Art Resource, New York)

identification and sympathy through the artist's brilliantly expressive renderings of heads and hands (Borchert 161–62; Friedländer 39). To quote a phrase that recurs throughout the novel, the painting depicts "another blue day" for Mary and the apostles—blue, identified with the BVM, being its predominant hue. Wyatt's forgery will not be a copy but a recasting of the subject that the master could have painted late in his life. He must, however, damage the painting to create the illusion of inherent vice without "trying to preserve the parts" that he most loves. This is, he notes, where many forgeries fail: the artist cannot bear to kill his darling (242). The mutilated face of Wyatt's Virgin, which enhances its aura of authenticity, also reduces its price and later becomes a point of contention among the three conspirators.

Valentine remarks in passing that Van der Goes "died mad," and it is true that he spent the final years of his life in a monastery near Brussels as an alcoholic plagued by "fits of melancholy that sometimes mounted to delirium" and was subject to "the manic idea that he was doomed to perdition" (Friedländer 40). His days were blue. As several critics have pointed out, Wyatt's life mirrors this Flemish master's (Morrissey 7; Knight, *Hints* 56–58). His painting does as well: Valentine remarks on the "incredible" flesh tones in Wyatt's *Descent* and its "exquisite control of brilliant colors" (233). Friedländer names Van der Goes the "greatest pioneer in Netherlandish panel painting of the fifteenth century," second only to Jan van Eyck (35). It is clear, then, that Wyatt is more than a skillful copyist; in a queer way, he is a master.

Avaricia

It is both ironic and appropriate that the conspirators' conversation takes place around Bosch's *Seven Deadly Sins* table, which Brown purchased in Europe. Sometimes the references to the table are sly jokes, such as when Valentine leaves his cigarette case on the column separating Greed from Envy while he and Brown discuss how best to make money from fraud (227). Brown spills his drink on *Invidia* just after he has jealously mocked Valentine for his "smart-aleck sayings in foreign languages" (236). A few pages later, Brown drops his cigar ash on *Gula* (Gluttony), as if to remind us that nicotine addiction is a type of hunger (241). Throughout the scene, Wyatt stares at the table, his lips shaping the words "*Soberbia, Ira, Lujuria, Pereza*" (Pride, Wrath, Lust, Sloth [238]). As Valentine describes how the trade in holy relics gave birth to forgeries, his eyes settle on the table: "Intricate, cunning forgeries like this," he says, sweeping his hand over the table (245). Wyatt protests that it is not a forgery, and Brown agrees. Valentine then relates a story: when the Conte di Brescia died, his survivors tried to sell his paintings, only to learn that they were all forgeries. The old man had had them copied, sold the originals, and kept the replicas. After Brown assures Valentine that he purchased the table during the conte's sale of the originals, Wyatt half-reveals his own role in this nexus, describing an anonymous boy who copied his father's original, kept the replica, and sold the original for "just about nothing" (246). Wyatt *needs* this painting to be authentic, because for him it represents the gold that is the goal of and goad for his alchemical artistry.

Valentine has contrived a new project that will "really challenge [Wyatt's] genius" (229): a painting by Hubert, the mysterious brother of Jan van Eyck, that would constitute the "art discovery of the century," worth as much as "all the rest [of Wyatt's works] put together" (249). Valentine declares that Hubert van Eyck never existed; Wyatt believes he did, citing the famous Ghent Altarpiece, the inscription of which proclaims that it was begun by Hubert and finished by Jan (254).[16] If a genuine painting by Hubert van Eyck were to appear, Valentine states, the "experts and art historians who have been insisting" he was a real person "will pounce on this new picture. They won't question it for a moment, because it will prove their point. [. . .] The painting itself doesn't matter to them, their authority is all that's important" (255). Hubert van Eyck is an ideal model for Wyatt, who, like him, "has no definite identity" (Morrissey 7). To execute this new work, an *Annunciation* (256), he must *become* Hubert: he must efface himself, layer by layer. Can he do it? "Of course I can do it," Wyatt announces (249). A new *Annunciation* is conceived.

Invidia

The trio's plan to incorporate critics and experts into their scheme has real-life antecedents—at least one of which Gaddis studied. In the 1930s Han van Meegeren perpetrated a series of forgeries that fooled the art world for several years. He despised modern art and believed his own, old-fashioned work had been unjustly slighted: as thesis 6 holds, he was motivated by envy and a thirst for revenge against the experts. And so he became a Vermeer authority—the better to fake his paintings—and developed techniques that defeated the tests of the time (see Werness 25).[17] Critic Abraham Bredius was reputed to be a Vermeer authority who, fond of contravening other experts' opinions, often made snap judgments. Van Meegeren realized that he could exploit Bredius's "pet theories and style criteria to create forgeries that were almost tailor-made" for him (Werness 20). In 1932 Bredius praised a Van Meegeren Vermeer and accepted it as authentic. Postulating a gap between Vermeer's early paintings and his more Italianate mature work, he predicted that similar Vermeers would appear (Werness 25). With his pigeon primed, Van Meegeren accepted the invitation. He scraped off a seventeenth-century painting of the raising of Lazarus, damaged the canvas slightly, and on it painted *The Supper at Emmaus,* which depicts Jesus with his disciples after the Resurrection; he then asked an acquaintance to notify Bredius. The plan worked brilliantly. Bredius certified its authenticity and wrote a gushing article in the September 1937 issue of *Burlington Magazine.* Later viewers have been perplexed that these clumsy works, with their cramped compositions, banal lighting, and unconvincing anatomy, could have been accepted as Vermeeers (Werness 41). But critics wanted to believe and buyers wanted to believe the critics: the virus of credulity had already spread. The painting sold for the enormous sum of 520,000 guilders.

Van Meegeren continued to paint and sell his forgeries of Vermeer and other Dutch masters throughout the war years. Unfortunately, his *Christ with the Adulteress* fell into the hands of Hermann Göring. After the war, when Göring's collection was recovered from an Austrian salt mine, the painting was traced to Van Meegeren, who was arrested as a Nazi collaborator. To save his skin, he admitted having forged that painting and several others, including the *Supper at Emmaus.* Few believed him. Hence, he volunteered to paint another forgery—*Young Christ Teaching in the Temple*—while police officers watched. After two months the painting was complete, proving that Van Meegeren had forged the Vermeers. (A commission later judged all his Vermeers to be fakes [Werness 45].) During his trial in March 1947, Van Meegeren testified that he had found forging so compelling that he had become "powerless" to stop himself (Werness 48). He also insisted that he had fabricated the paintings simply "from a desire to paint" (Werness 48): he never mentions envy or monetary gain. We observe again thesis 3: forgeries foster fictions, and forgers' justifications are usually false. Cleared of treason, Van Meegeren was sentenced to two years in prison for forgery but died before his incarceration began. Bredius, "entangled in the wisteria of his own determination to be right," never recanted (Charney, *Art* 100).[18]

Gray Area

Gaddis likely modeled some of Wyatt's procedures on Van Meegeren's. But there is another artist whose work even more closely resembles Wyatt's and who has never been acknowledged: Josef "Jef" van der Veken. A restorer of old paintings who specialized in fifteenth-century Flemish masters, he mended Jan van Eyck's *Madonna with Canon van de Paele* and Rogier van der Weyden's *Madonna and Child.* But when the latter painting (restored in 1915) was tested with X-rays and infrared spectrometry, it was found to be 75 percent Van der Veken. The museum exhibited it as an original anyway (Charney, *Art* 51; Scott 87–88). Is it a restoration or a forgery? It occupies a gray area. Van der Veken was the favorite consultant of Emile Renders, who owned a large collection of fifteenth-century Flemish works, several of which were eventually determined to be the work of a different Low Countries master—Jef van der Veken. During World War II Göring bought the entire Renders collection. Among these was a Memling painting the Nazi loved so much that he tried to take it with him when he fled. This painting was also Van der Veken's work (Charney, *Art* 52). Perhaps these were not strictly forgeries, since he never claimed that they were genuine. They too fall into that gray area.

His masterwork was a legally made copy. In 1934 one panel of the Van Eycks' Ghent Altarpiece—the so-called Righteous Judges piece (on the extreme bottom left)—was stolen (fig. 12).[19] It was not recovered, and so in 1939 Van der Veken volunteered to make a copy, using a two-hundred-year-old cupboard door, photos, and an existing reproduction. He inserted three small alterations to distinguish his work from the original, and this copy—also located in the gray area between forgery and restoration—is displayed with the eleven original panels today (Charney, *Art* 56). In effect, Van der Veken became the third Van Eyck brother. A painting of the Man of Sorrows owned by the Metropolitan Museum of Art was relegated to the storage basement when, in 1974, experts from the Courtauld Institute deemed it a forgery. Tests conducted in 1992 revealed that it was based on an original painting to which the restorer had added deceptive new elements. The restorer was Jef van der Veken. Whoever executed the copy, according to Hubert von Sonnenburg, achieved a "very deceptive stylistic transformation . . . with astounding technical skill and art-historical knowledge" (18). A deceptive transformation, also known as a forgery. Or is it a restoration? Color it gray.

Wyatt is at least as skillful a fakesmith as Van der Veken, and he too (at first) resides in the gray zone between restoration and fabrication. But isn't restoration always a kind of forgery? After all, restorers add their own paint to an original without taking credit.[20] And although Wyatt collaborates in the scheme to defraud buyers, he conceives of his art not as a way to make money but as a mode of monkish piety, an alchemical experiment aimed at attaining perfection. If restoration is

Fig. 12. The missing bottom left panel of Van Eyck's Ghent Altarpiece at the Cathedral of St. Bavo was restored by Jef van der Veken. Oil on wood. (Photo: Erich Lessing/Art Resource, NY)

a type of forgery, so forgery, for him, is a type of restoration. Despite its brown origins, he believes this work can yield gold. What purifies the project for Wyatt are his principles, his piety, and his procedures. These are the layers he uses to mask his guilt and bake in his ideals of artistic discipline; in so doing, he strips further colors from his own self-portrait.

Lavender

> Seulement les plus beaux, ce sont le faux.
>
> —Paul Eudel, *Trucs et truqueurs*

Mansit Odor

Oil of spike lavender has long been employed as a nontoxic substitute for turpentine, and its smell permeates Wyatt's studio (83). Early in his marriage to Esther, the odor represents her loneliness and his devotion to art. As the novel proceeds, lavender oil becomes a symbol of alienation and bad faith, its aroma signaling Wyatt's lingering presence or connecting forgery to other forms of fraud. Thus Otto mentions its "funny smell" while discussing alchemy with Esther (129), and when Brown first meets Wyatt, he too comments on the "funny smell" (141); here it presages Wyatt's Faustian bargain, in which beauty is tainted with the stench of fraud. During the lengthy conversation among the three plotters in part 1, chapter 7, lavender is mentioned just after Brown tells Wyatt to "be God damn careful of that pansy" (i.e., Valentine). Wyatt quotes Ovid: "Mansit odor, posses scire fuisse deam" (An odor remained; one could tell that a goddess had appeared [254]). Most obviously, lavender represents Wyatt Gwyon—his thinned-out identity, his attraction to beauty (lavender boasts gorgeous purple flowers), and his obsessive dedication to his work. By the novel's end, the smell has migrated to Valentine, who has been touched by Wyatt's brush. More broadly, lavender indicates how aesthetic ideals are diluted or deformed into modes of deception, how loveliness can lie. The trope also hints at Gaddis's own method: he too adds layer upon layer of colorful motifs to paint a picture of forgery.

Disciplined Nostalgia

Although Wyatt scorns reproductions as a "calumny" on his own work, Valentine points out that every piece he completes is "calumny on the artist you forge" (250). Most art historians would agree with him. Recall Denis Dutton's argument (outlined in the prologue) that forgeries are wrong because they misrepresent the history of artistic achievement (181). Michael Wreen similarly holds that they erode "the mutual trust and understanding" that underpins art scholarship (204). But Wyatt vehemently denies the charge of calumny. "Do you think I do these the way all other forging has been done? Pulling the fragments of ten paintings together and making one," or switching around elements of existing paintings? No, "the recognitions go much deeper, much further back" (250). In Peter Wolfe's apt formulation, Wyatt believes that a forgery may "stir in the viewer a recognition, that comfort combined with excitement stemming from the discovery of a heretofore hidden dynamism" (104). Siri Hustvedt explains such recognitions as "vivid renewals of wild being . . . transmitted by the artist and apprehended by the viewer as an electrical emotional charge, and these shock variations are less personal than . . . part of a larger human story" ("Remembering" 463).

What Wyatt aims to elicit with his forgeries, then, is not nostalgia but a feeling of timeless discovery in which the artist, having recognized his or her own universality, transmits that recognition to the viewer. He insists that "the purity of his material—the gold he uses, his pigments, his exquisite colors"—delivers him from the "defilement of art" (Karl 179, 178). His efforts thus resemble an "act of devotion" (Wolfe 104): he fashions misrecognitions that foster recognitions. He might well echo Robert Browning's Fra Lippo Lippi who, responding to critics who urge him to paint only souls, replies that great art permits us to see anew people and objects we have passed a hundred times. "Art was given" to enable us to recognize ourselves and our world as lovely and good (l.304). Indeed, if, as the epigraph above (which is also the epigraph to chapter 2 of the novel) states, only the most beautiful works are forged, then Wyatt's paintings, far from calumnies, affirm and augment the value of his models.

In fifteenth-century Flanders, recognitions and regulations were made by the guilds, which limited the number of apprentices a master could employ, established training procedures, imposed standards for materials and techniques, monitored sales, and even provided social welfare for members (Porras 53). Wyatt imagines himself as "a master painter in the Guild [. . .] and if they come and find that I'm not using the . . . gold, they destroy the bad materials I'm using and fine me" (250). Actually, the methods of many painters of the period resembled those of forgers, in that they would assign sections or works to assistants or journeymen from their workshops and sign them with their own name (Lenain 268). A related principle is active here, as well: the need for study. In a later conversation with Valentine, Wyatt declares that "criticism is the art we need most today, [. . .] a disciplined nostalgia, disciplined recognitions" (335). "Disciplined nostalgia" accurately describes the procedures and principles he employs to create artworks that are also critical essays. The adjective is essential: the discipline—carefully wrought techniques, painstaking study of styles, meticulous attention to mixing and color—converts nostalgia from maudlin sentiment to metempsychosis. Bearing out thesis 9, Wyatt's art is a product of reverse connoisseurship. Kevin Attell writes that Wyatt "attempts to become an artist of the past" (273). But it is not that simple. He needs temporal distance (one cannot be nostalgic for a time or place in which one already lives) to provide the discipline that pushes him toward perfection: the gap of time is what turns cognition into re-cognition.

Perspective

Why, Wyatt wonders, does everything in those Flemish paintings have "its own form and density?" "Because they found God everywhere. [. . .] And so in the painting every detail reflects . . . God's concern with the most insignificant objects" (251). In other words, *"Cave cave deus videt."* These artists sought to link the individual and earthly to the universal and divine (Friedländer 38), while embodying a "model of devotion and compassion" that encouraged the viewer to emulate those emotional states (Porras 61). Such confirmations of God's presence could emerge only through careful attention to naturalistic details: light and shade, anatomically correct figures, realistic landscapes and interiors, and sophisticated renderings of everyday objects (Borchert 19). This naturalistic quality distinguished these painters' works from their predecessors' and divorced them from a purely medieval point of view (Knight, "Flemish" 62). They approached the celestial through the terrestrial to demonstrate, as Browning's Fra Lippo Lippi proclaims, that "this world's no blot for us, / Nor blank; it means intensely, and means good" (l.313–14).

Holding up a rumpled reproduction, Wyatt asks his collaborators, "Do you get the perspective in this?" The answer must be no because "there isn't any single perspective. [. . .] The Flemish painter took twenty perspectives if he wished" so that "you can't include it all in your single vision [. . .] like you can painting when it . . . when it degenerates, and becomes conscious of being looked at" (251).[21] Jan van Eyck's famous portrait of Giovanni Arnolfini and his wife, for example (fig. 13), employs multiple perspectives, or "zones of focus" (Borchert 25). Here the primary orthogonal lines of perspective meet not at the rear wall, as one would expect, but in the tiny space behind the figures, which shows a small mirror (fig. 14) in which we see the subjects' backsides and, in sky blue, the painter himself painting them (see Pächt 105). Hence, the

Fig. 13. Jan van Eyck's famous portrait of Arnolfini and his wife employs multiple zones of focus. *Portrait of Giovanni(?) Arnolfini and His Wife* (1434). Oil on oak, 82.2 × 60 cm. (© National Gallery, London/Art Resource, NY)

viewer takes in not merely the husband and wife but also the painter and, by extension, him or herself watching the painter watch and paint: the viewer assumes God's point of view. We even see "behind" the painting to the process of its creation. These are the sort of recognitions that Wyatt hopes to generate with his forgeries and with them to replicate a world more sanctified and more pure. Through those perfect paintings, he also seeks to mold a reborn self.

FIG. 14. Detail from the Arnolfini portrait. In the central background viewers find an infinite regress inside of which resides the painter himself.

PERFECTION

Why does a man forge? Gaddis asks in "First Notes for a Television Program on Forgery." Because "forgery reflects the finite state of man, and the eventual imperfectibility of his creations, an aspiring toward a (Platonic) ideal just beyond reach . . . : the creator knows when he fails, the forger obviates this possibility by setting 'perfected' limitations beforehand" (qtd. in Knight, *Hints* 262–63; cf. Abádi-Nagy 4). Forgeries, Gaddis states elsewhere, present their makers with a "context for accomplishment, a tradition of delimited and delineated perfection" (LeClair 21). As an alchemist Wyatt seeks this philosopher's stone of perfection by recognizing the Flemish masters' wedding of piety and artistic performance and relaying it in his imitations. Forging permits him to combine the roles of priest and painter. Nevertheless, Valentine accuses him of being "mightily concerned" with his own originality. But why bother? Originality, he sniffs, is merely "a device that untalented people use to impress other untalented people" (252). This dismissal may not be persuasive, but, as thesis 1 states, the concept of originality has no meaning without the presence, even if merely implied, of imitation. In this paradoxical way, forgeries ratify the value of genuine paintings. The perfect fake, however, severs this connection, for an undetected forgery cannot shore up an original; far from an epiphyte, it uproots the tree and supplants it.

What else verifies a painting's authenticity? The artist's signature. And here Wyatt's reasoning falters. As he haltingly acknowledges, "When I attach the signature [. . .] that changes everything." Valentine: "Then corruption enters, is that it?" (251). Without a signature, a work cannot be a forgery because it is not designed to mislead. The signature engenders fraud, which enables a sale, the proceeds of which, in part, go to Wyatt. Even though he pays no attention to his fees, the money accrues in an account Brown has established (261): the gold of his aspiration is painted brown by the fact of payment. Where is the guild now?

Reproach

At the end of part 1, Wyatt defaces the Virgin in his Van der Goes forgery, and though he employs not a brush but a blade, his ministrations are identical: he works "layer upon layer, [. . .] as necessity disposed" (275). In part 2 Valentine visits him as he finishes the painting, warning Wyatt that Brown won't approve of damaging the Virgin's face. He replies, "It isn't as though I'd done that. [. . .] The painting itself, the composition took its own form" (336). The ostensible reason for the damage is to imitate aging, but unconsciously Wyatt may be trying to undo his desecration and partially atone for his sin while blinding Mary so she cannot witness his crime. (The scene foreshadows Wyatt's later erasures.) In the same scene, just after Valentine asks Wyatt to copy a painting by Joachim Patinir, another fifteenth-century Flemish master, Wyatt shows him a study for his new Hubert van Eyck forgery: a woman wearing Camilla's Byzantine gold hoop earrings. Valentine finds in her face a "reproach, like the faces, the Virgin in other things you've done" (336). Perhaps the reproach issues less from Mary than from Wyatt's (imaginary) deceased, saintly mother. That is, his paintings of Mary enable him to "complete" his portrait of Camilla without putting her to rest. Her face also furnishes a surface on which his ambivalence plays out: in one work he lends her a look of reproach; in another he scrapes it away. Brown protests (seemingly unaware of the irony), "What you've done to this picture here, it's a crime"—not against art but against his bottom line, for the damage will reduce its price by ten thousand dollars (359).

Full of misgivings about the forgeries, Wyatt saws off the edges of the fakes and hides them in the Horatio Street apartment where Esther still lives; they will be "proof," if it is ever needed, that these are his own work (336). But his partners insist that exposing the forgeries would be fruitless. The buyers, Brown argues, "don't want to know. They want to be told" about a painting's authenticity, and the experts want credit for discoveries (363–64). If Wyatt were to divulge their investments' true origins, they'd "all be mad as hell at you. [. . .] You could get up there and paint these things all over again, and they wouldn't believe you. [. . .] My boy, you've fooled the experts. But once you've fooled an expert, he stays fooled," he says (364), rephrasing thesis 13. The real-life forgeries of van Meegeren and of Elmyr de Hory, as well as the stories of Ireland and Chatterton, verify Brown's claim. No one is immune to the virus of belief, even—especially—experts.

The most vexing challenge for Wyatt, however, revolves around the Bosch table. During a conversation with Brown and Valentine, he alludes to the "cunning field full of fraud separating us here, seven and deadly. It's not even a very good copy" (359), then commences to pick at the table with his penknife. Brown stops him, insisting that "real experts" examined it after Valentine claimed that it was a fake; they concluded that it was the "genuine original" (360). Unconvinced, Wyatt remains disgusted with himself for having copied a copy: "Invidia, I was brought up eating my meals off envy, until today. And it was false all the time! [. . .] A child could tell it's a copy" (381). Frantically he wonders, "Now, if there was no gold. [. . .] And if what I've been forging, does not exist?" (381). If the Seven Deadlies table has been a fake all along, the foundation of his ethos, indeed, his very identity, will turn to ashes.

Throughout the novel Gaddis refers to a mysterious entity called "the self who could do more," a phrase that many critics have discerned as its thematic and moral center. Every person, Valentine cynically asserts, has a secret self "who can do more," who mocks him or her at every turn and yet eludes capture (386). Wyatt sees his own worst self in the Seven Deadlies table and in his forgeries—a self who tells him "you know you'll do it again . . . and again" (380). And so, at the end of part 2, chapter 2, he flees New York to return to his hometown where resides the "one [he] left behind," the "one [he] lost" (385): not his father, but his own better self.

Green

> Eight million counterfeits [. . .] moved with the plumbing weight of lead coated with the frenzied hope of quicksilver, protecting at every pass the cherished falsity of their milled edges against the threat of hardness in their neighbors as they were rung together [. . .] tumbling there in all the desperate variety of which the counterfeit is capable.
>
> —*The Recognitions*

> . . . I learned,
> there in Romena, to stamp the Baptist's image
> on alloyed gold—till I was bound and burned.
>
> —Dante, *Inferno,* Canto XXX.73–75

Echo Chamber

In chapters 4 and 5 of part 2, Gaddis circulates among Otto and his associates. These episodes, which display Gaddis's broader vision of a society in thrall to fakes, seem to take place in a giant echo chamber where numerous voices reverberate and several characters, especially Otto and Stanley, repeat Wyatt's ideas about art (460, 461). These characters, Gaddis has stated, are less-complex versions of the protagonist: Max is a plagiarist and bad painter who is unplagued by guilt; Otto is a younger, less talented surrogate; Stanley is Wyatt narrowed to an even more singular focus as he works throughout the novel on a single organ sonata. Yet they disagree about art. Whereas Stanley holds that "art is the work of love," Max asserts that "art is a work of necessity" (465). Wyatt's new quest is to meld the two, to marry love and need.

These characters are not only faded reflections of the now nameless Wyatt. They, along with several others, populate a teeming city of frauds, counterfeits, and hucksters. One major source of fraud is advertising, particularly a company named Necrostyle, which markets a contraceptive device called "Cuff" (366). (Read it backwards.) These characters exemplify the stratum condemned by Thoreau (one of Gaddis's chief influences) as the "most terribly impoverished class of all, who have accumulated dross, . . . and thus have forged their own gold and silver fetters" (Thoreau 59). Early in part 2 we also meet the pitiful Mr. Pivner, a lonely diabetic who comes home from work each day, reads the paper, injects himself with insulin, and, in a diluted, pop-cultural version of Wyatt's crusade, listens intently to self-improvement ads. The perfect consumer, whose bible is Dale Carnegie's *How to Win Friends and Influence People,* Pivner is a product of the echo chamber of spurious needs and specious remedies engendered by capitalism and its handmaiden, advertising. He is also Otto's father, though the two have never met. Otto sets up a meeting; each will recognize the other by his green scarf, Mr. Pivner having given one to his son as a Christmas present two years earlier (309).

Bills

Gaddis now incorporates counterfeiting into his anatomy of fakery. We already know that Otto, although treated somewhat sympathetically by the narrator, is the kind of young man who wears his arm in a sling even though he has no injury. (It verifies his lie about being involved in a revolution, elicits sympathy, and makes him seem exotic.) [22] His terrible play is a tissue of unattributed quotations, and he repeats others' wise sayings to make himself appear erudite. Otto is a living counterfeit. It seems fitting, then, that in chapter 5 of part 2, he encounters a genuine counterfeiter, Frank Sinisterra, the "doctor" who failed to treat Camilla Gwyon on the *Purdue Victory.* A Catholic, Sinisterra feels guilty for allowing her to die and has tried to atone (492). Frank resembles Wyatt in many respects. He too considers himself more craftsman than criminal, taking pride in using actual currency paper and hand-engraved steel plates for his products (490). He has a similar respect for past masters, in his case counterfeiters like Pete McCartney, Big Bill the Queersman (493), and particularly Emmanuel Ninger, known as Jim the Penman, notorious for hand-inking his beautiful counterfeit bills: "He was an artist," Frank declares (489).[23] Like the forger (and the novelist), Frank's success depends on disguise, and he possesses an array of costumes—wigs, false moustaches, clothing, make-up (and a large mirror)—to facilitate his impersonations (488). Even so, like a painter, he leaves a "little of [him]self" in everything he does (491) and frets that his work hasn't appeared in the *National Counterfeit Detector* for many years. His dilemma mirrors the forger's (thesis 4): he craves recognition but must remain unrecognized to succeed. He and Wyatt also share that olfactory signature, the smell of lavender, which pervades his lab and trails him like a stray dog (492).

Counterfeits are not exactly the same as forgeries. For one thing, as I noted in the prologue, every counterfeit bill or coin must be a perfect copy of authentic currency. Originality is worse than a flaw; it is a clue that will get the counterfeiter jailed. Whereas Wyatt relies on (the idea of) gold to ground his imitations, Frank's fakes rely on the absence of gold: his works are simulacra with no material foundation. That is, with the removal of the gold standard, money, as Simmel points out, merely substantiates "the exchange function through a common relation of interested parties to an objective institution" (183)—the government that certifies it. And that exchange function relies entirely on a "supratheoretical belief" that others will honor it as well (179). Money is a fiction. In this regard counterfeits and genuine currency are identical, for if everyone agreed to accept counterfeit bills as a medium of exchange and symbol of value, they would no longer be counterfeit. Both types of money are narratives. But whereas genuine currency tells a true story—its origins appear on the bill or coin—counterfeits crystallize a lie.[24] As Marc Shell has noted, a counterfeit (like a forgery) is a text whose stated origin does not match its actual one (160). Sinisterra is, in this sense, a storyteller. And if all counterfeits are stories, it may also be true, Gaddis suggests, that all stories are counterfeits, and the novelist is ineluctably a counterfeiter. Just as Wyatt Gwyon (note the initials) is a modified self-portrait of novelist and (by implication) forger William Gaddis, so Frank Sinisterra is a left-handed silhouette of the author who similarly borrows from past masters and hides behind invented characters. Just as Gaddis depicts New York as the greatest modern center of fakery, so Sinisterra has helped to make New York the "greatest modern center of counterfeiting money of every currency in the world" (495). His bills are also Bill's bills.

According to Goux's formula, a counterfeit, by presenting itself as a universal equivalent and transcendental signifier, operates as a deceptive deity, a false father. Wyatt is missing a father; Frank Sinisterra desires a son to replace his offspring Chaby, a heroin addict who disdains his father's trade. Here, then, Gaddis presents three strained or estranged father-son duos—the Gwyons, the Sinisterras, and the Pivners—as Sinisterra's spurious bills embody Gaddis's diagnosis of the deadly sins of modern culture: the separation of humans from one another, the inability of cultural institutions to unite us, and the consequent commodification of humanity. "What was the shape of Mr. Pivner's soul?" the narrator asks; is it "worth five cents?" Will it draw a "good price in the market place, say [. . .] thirty pieces of silver?" (503).

Queer

Male homosexuals are omnipresent in Otto and Esme's circle and are designated by the word "queer," which in 1955 had not been recuperated as a badge of pride. The word has also long referred to counterfeit money, as in Big Bill the Queersman. Gaddis brings these definitions together in a comic scene of misrecognition when Otto goes to a hotel bar to meet his father. Having inadvertently left his green muffler in Esme's apartment, where it was pilfered by Chaby Sinisterra, Otto has since obtained a new one; unbeknownst to him, Frank is wearing Otto's old scarf while visiting the same bar, where he is supposed to meet the "passer" of his counterfeit bills. Alas, the elder Pivner does not appear. Having neglected his insulin shot, he collapses in hypoglycemic shock in the hotel doorway; believing he is a drunk or an addict, the doorman boots him out. At that moment Otto enters, wearing his new green muffler. He has lost his wallet, so he has neither money nor identification: he is now in the perfect condition to receive queer bills. After soliciting a prostitute, he espies a man wearing a green muffler. This man recognizes Otto's matching scarf and approaches.

Otto misidentifies Frank as his long-lost father; Frank misrecognizes Otto as his passer. Enveloping Frank is a "familiar fugitive aroma"—the smell of lavender (514)—which Otto cannot name. As Frank takes Otto's arm, a disinterested observer, noting their mysterious signals and clandestine touching, might read the meeting as a gay hookup. Frank is wearing a black wig and has applied eserine eyedrops to change the color of his irises; Otto thinks eserine is a disease. The point is that each is blind to the other's true identity, although Frank susses out Otto's phony injury. ("You haven't learned how to handle it yet. You act like you're keeping a live squirrel in it" [518].) As they talk, Otto nervously rubs his leg on what he thinks is the table leg. The counterfeiter hands over the packet of long green—$5,000 in phony twenties—calls the bills "beautiful," and notes that "it takes six different artists to make one of these" (519). His task completed, he departs, leaving "the delicious aroma of lavender" (520) in the air as Otto clutches the money against his genitals. Exiting, Frank encounters the actual passer, who asks if he has the "Five G's in queer." Frank responds: "That fairy. He took every bit of it. He sat there rubbing his ankle against my leg" (520). They march off to find Otto, who has retired to the room he can now pay for; he opens the packet and marvels at his windfall. What a generous Christmas present from his father! Though heterosexual, Otto is indeed queer—not only a counterfeit but also a counterfeit counterfeiter (Wolfe 68). Frank, man of many disguises, is equally fake. In a sense, then, their exchange is indeed a queer hookup.

Otto does not learn that his bills are counterfeit until much later, when he is forced to flee to Central America where (karma displaying a queer sense of humor) he injures his arm in a revolution (729–30) and is "treated" by Dr. Fell—the same inept practitioner who failed to heal young Wyatt of a serious childhood illness. And so we come full circle, as on Bosch's table: Otto pays for his pride, avarice, envy, sloth, and lust, and now identifies himself as "Gordon"—the name of his play's protagonist (732). Always a patchwork of quotations, imitations, and ill-formed aspirations, Otto has been erased. As for poor Mr. Pivner, he is arrested because the robe Otto gave him was purchased with counterfeit money (564, 734). Its color is not revealed.

Anonymous

Wyatt's return to his hometown results only in further misrecognitions, and he comes to realize that "*no one knows who I am*" (439, italics in original). Back in New York, he confronts a different form of erasure: most of the money in his bank account has vanished. (We later learn that Valentine took it.) He informs Valentine that he intends to expose their forgery scheme (545) and that he has burned everything in his studio. His expungement nearly complete, in subsequent scenes he lurks at the margin, a shadowy figure who speaks in riddles. In chapter 7 of part 2, for example, he crashes Esther's Christmas party, where his estranged wife berates him. "I watched you turn into no one right here in front of me, and just a . . . a pose became a life, until you were trying to make negative things do the work of positive ones" (590): through reverse alchemy, she insinuates, he has turned gold into shit. Departing, Wyatt leaves behind the scent of lavender (638).

Brown

> So shalt thou see I am Capocchio's ghost,
> Who forged transmuted metals by the power
> Of alchemy; and if I scan thee right,
> Thou needs must well remember how I aped
> Creative nature by my subtle art.
>
> —*Dante,* Inferno, *Canto XXIX.134–38*

Ira

The climax of part 2—and the collapse of the forgery scheme—occurs in chapter 8, during a party for collectors and connoisseurs hosted by

Brown. When Valentine rejoins the party, after a meeting with a Hungarian assassin named Mr. Inononu (they are coconspirators in an espionage plot), he discovers that Wyatt has already been there, manically trying to prove that the works are fake. Nobody believed him (662). Indeed, the party is another scene of colliding misrecognitions. For example, Wyatt's old enemy Crémer puts out feelers to buy the "Memlinc" (Wyatt's early forgery [656, 659]): this "expert" cannot distinguish Wyatt's work from a genuine Memling. Forget créme; he should be wearing green. When another patron quotes to him Wyatt's remarks about the painting's sky—hued in Prussian blue, a shade that didn't exist in the fifteenth century—Crémer only shrugs (660). The BVM's face in another painting presents a different problem for a patron who notices that the highlights around her eyes use zinc white—an eighteenth-century color (670–71).

Brown, still annoyed by Wyatt's profit-reducing defacement of the Virgin, argues vehemently with Valentine. The former wants to show other (forged) paintings; Valentine believes this is a "stupid moment" for such a ploy. Then, for no apparent reason, Brown squeezes himself into the fifteenth-century armor (probably fake) he keeps as an *objet d'art* (672). Just as Wyatt reenters, Brown tumbles down the stairs to his death in his ill-fitting armor, the beaver falling over his face (679). Wyatt waves the charred fragments he has saved as evidence of fraud, but the rapidly departing buyers pay no heed. Astoundingly, Crémer is still interested in the "Memlinc," and another man still wants to buy the Van der Goes Virgin with the ruined face (680). Brown was right: once fooled, an expert stays fooled, credulity being as constricting as Brown's armor. But why is the wood from the paintings charred? Because Valentine burned Wyatt's evidence. Wyatt's work, perhaps fittingly for a painter who conceives of his art as alchemy, has been subjected to three fires: the warehouse fire that burned his originals; the above-mentioned fire that destroyed his evidentiary fragments; and now a third, which Wyatt has just learned of, which destroyed the building where he once lived. The last was ignited by . . . oil of lavender (686).

Valentine and Wyatt face off over the Bosch table. Wyatt asks, "Do you know what it was like, coming in here years later with him, and seeing it here? [. . .] A child could tell [it is a copy], even in this light" (688). Valentine explains that although the table Wyatt first saw in New York was the original, this one is a copy that Valentine picked up in Rome. He had told Wyatt that the original was a copy "simply to hear you defend it. I knew Brown would trust your judgment" and would have it tested again, so "that once I'd exchanged the two, no matter who called this a copy, he'd simply laugh at them. [. . .] And the original? It's on its way back to Europe where it belongs" (688–89). A relieved Wyatt expostulates, "Thank God there was the gold to forge!" (689). He believes Valentine. Should we? After all, he is a liar, thief, and con man who could be feeding Wyatt a fib to get himself off the hook. As always, forgeries breed stories, usually fictional ones (thesis 3). It is impossible to discern the truth here.

Valentine then explodes into a lengthy tirade in which he derides Wyatt's beliefs. The fifteenth-century world that Wyatt idealizes was a cesspool of "vulgarity, cupidity and power."

> And your precious van Eyck, do you think he didn't live up to his neck in a loud vulgar court? [. . .] Do you think any painter did anything but hire himself out? These fine altarpieces, do you think they glorified anyone but the vulgar men who commissioned them? Do you think a van Eyck didn't curse having to whore away his genius? (689–90)

Valentine cynically repaints Wyatt's golden ideals in dark tones, tarnishing his rosy picture of the painters' piety and recasting Wyatt's quest for perfection as a dupe's pilgrimage.

> Fear, fear, pessimism and fear and depression everywhere, the way it is today, that's why your pictures are so cluttered with detail, this terror of emptiness, this absolute terror of space. Because maybe God isn't watching. [. . .] Is there a moment of faith in any of their work [. . .] or is it vanity and fear, the same decadence that surrounds us now. (690)

In a whisper Valentine laments that all is "cluttered with separation, everything in its own vain shell, everything separate, withdrawn from everything else." There is truth in Valentine's claims—although, as Porras observes, the courts and patrons weren't entirely venial, and the "performance of faith and of civic pride were often inexorably linked" (70)—and it is typical of Gaddis to place his own ideas about alienation and art's unifying potential in the mouth of a villain. But even if earlier artists had to pander to their patrons, that fact need not invalidate their works' spiritual impact. Nevertheless, Valentine shows Wyatt the "fallacy of locating divinity so entirely in the past" (Knight, *Hints* 63). His obsession with painting the late medieval world in unblemished white and his own world in dark brown fails to recognize that the truth lies in a gray area where ambiguity and flexibility prevail.

As the two stare at Brown's dead eyes, Valentine says, "This man is your father" (691)—a partial truth—then, in true Mephistophelean fashion, vaguely promises a new partnership, admitting that "you're . . . part of me . . . damn you, damn you, damn you" (692).[25] His plea fails. An enraged Wyatt, having picked up Brown's wayward knife, stabs Valentine repeatedly in the chest (692).[26] But Valentine is indeed a part of Wyatt: he may as well have been conjured from the artist's tortured unconscious to exaggerate his own worst features—his aloofness, his arrogance and pride, his tortured Christianity and attraction to evil, his snobbery. In stabbing him, Wyatt aims to destroy those aspects of himself along with the evidence of his crimes—wipe out the lavender, whiten the brown. But Valentine's diatribe echoes Wyatt's own thoughts: he would not have needed to recreate these masters' works if he weren't afraid of himself.

Exultant, Wyatt shouts that he is now "as free as the day I was born" (692). But he has one more task to complete. Turning to the Bosch table, he slides off the glass top, smashes a foot through the surface, and, in an orgasmic frenzy, tears it apart piece by piece, shouting "Cave, caveat emptor, Dominus videt, Christ! the original! . . . a whisper broken by laughter,—yes, thank God there was the gold to forge!" (693). Having committed most of the sins pictured on it, Wyatt believes that shattering the table will obviate the separations his crimes have wrought.

Titian

In a letter written in 1972, Gaddis says that Wyatt's cry about gold is "the key to book if there is such" (qtd. in Eckley 132; cf. Abádi-Nagy 6). Yet Mark Taylor contends that Wyatt's sentence "settles nothing. With copies proliferating and the original increasingly obscure, it is not clear how to read this line" (*Rewiring* 36). I can clarify it. Remember that Wyatt conceives of himself as an alchemist and his studio as an alchemist's crucible. Alchemists aimed to transform base metals into gold, which symbolized God and redemption and served as the measure of all values and virtues. If there was no gold, then Wyatt's mission to attain perfection through art has been fatally misconceived. In monetary terms, if there is no gold, there is no anchor for exchange, nothing but belief, and no belief is better than any other. The idea of authenticity would be not only impossible but absurd. The Bosch table thus symbolizes these dual possibilities: if it has been a fake all along, it exemplifies a regime of infinite transformation in which perfection (not to mention sin and atonement) has no meaning. If there is gold—if, despite the ubiquity of fakes, authenticity and perfection subsist as recognizable ideals—then there remains some path to redemption and reinvention. If there is no gold, Wyatt will never remake or re-cognize himself, and any self-portrait, no matter its hues, would be a pretty picture covering a dark void. Conversely, if the table is genuine, he can expiate his sins and purify his brown soul. Wyatt's belief in gold is thus essential as both foundation and *telos;* without it not only his artistic endeavors but his entire existence becomes null.

Earlier, Otto related a story about a forged painting attributed to the sixteenth-century Venetian painter Tiziano Vecelli, better known as Titian, which, after its paint was scraped away, exposed a worthless painting beneath. When that painting was in turn stripped off, a real Titian was revealed. "It was as though when the forger was working, and he didn't know the original was underneath, [. . .] it knew, I mean something knew. [. . .] That underneath that the original is there" (450–51). The forger—or, as Otto frames it, the painting itself—needed to know that an original lay beneath the imitation, because without originals, forgeries are impossible (thesis 1). Like the forger of the Titian, Wyatt must know that "gold"—perfection, redemption, authenticity—exists both "beneath" his forgeries and "above" them, as their goal, so that he can fashion works that are "fixed in intimate detail upon the established forms [. . .] layer upon layer, constructed from within as necessity dispose[s]" (275). (This is the narrator's description of Wyatt's method.) The Titian story again suggests that "originals" build upon what already exists, layering themselves over previous paintings. Hence, not only do forgeries need originals and vice versa; they are in many respects the same. We leave Wyatt in purgatory, his artistic prospects annihilated, his marriage a memory, his partners dead or moribund, his identity voided, his paintings charred embers. But perhaps, like that scraped-off Titian, another painting, another Wyatt, will rise from the ruins.

Ash

> In my beginning is my end. . . .
> Old fires to ashes, and ashes to the earth
> Which is already flesh, fur, and faeces.
>
> —T. S. Eliot, "East Coker," 1, 6–7

Before we reencounter Wyatt, who has fled to Spain, a montage chapter crosscuts among several characters, including Stanley and Esme, who have embarked on a ship to Europe. One passenger is a mysterious character called "the cold man," whose finger flashes a "glint of gold": it is Valentine, very much alive, if not exactly well (767), en route to execute his espionage (and assassination) plan. Chapter 3 of part 3, which unites Wyatt and Frank Sinisterra, is one of only two chapters with a title. The novel's first chapter is entitled "The First Turn of the Screw"; this one, "The Final Turn of the Screw," is the point at which the novel begins to eat itself, like that dragon with its tail in its mouth.

Mummy

Now going by the alias Mr. Yák, Sinisterra has come to Spain after altering his passport in "lavender stamp-ink" (773) and his appearance with a new wig and mustache. He is hiding in San Zwingli, where Camilla was interred and where Wyatt has taken refuge. The forger and the counterfeiter meet, the latter aware that Wyatt is the son of the woman whose death he caused decades earlier. Wyatt has lapsed into alcoholism and lacks the will to do much of anything but drink and fornicate. It just so happens that Frank has a passport ready that will enable Wyatt to "put on the new man, like it says in the Bible" (785). The name it bears is "Stephan Asche" (795). Preemptively calling his new friend "Stephan," Yák persuades him to collaborate on a scheme to create a fake mummy, using the corpse of the same raped and murdered girl whose beatification ceremony will be attended by passengers on Stanley and Esme's ship (remember: the bodies of the girl and Camilla have been switched). Wyatt knows how to do this job (take out the organs, fill the cavity with linen and resin [787]), and so the two become partners, thereby marrying the novel's two forms of fakery and its two master fakesmiths. Perhaps the mummy will atone for the death of Wyatt's mommy.

Indeed, the two are doubles—men who, conceiving of themselves as artists, have betrayed and defrauded others. In a deeper sense, their relationship is familial, as Wyatt acquires a father and Frank gains a new son whom he constantly warns (ineffectively) about drinking and whoring. Gaddis's narrator states that they are at once "mutually dependent and at constant cross purposes": Frank attends to Wyatt's actions mostly to disapprove of them, while Wyatt's "total lack of interest in the elder's activity only spurred that one on to redouble it" (800). Yet each relies on the other, fostering "an arrangement similar to that magic formula of modern marriage" (801)—a queer, incestuous one, to be sure. More importantly, perhaps, Wyatt reassumes his "real" name, Stephen (adapted from "Stephan"), the one Camilla intended to give him before Aunt May's intervention. The name of the first Christian martyr, it also echoes that of Joyce's artist-hero, who vowed to "forge in the smithy of [his] soul the uncreated conscience of [his] race" (*Portrait* 224). This Stephen's aims are more modest: to reforge his own soul, to rise like a phoenix from the "asche" and beget a newly created conscience.

The pair fabricate a plausible mummy and, in a comic episode, transport the corpse via train, pretending it is "somebody's mother" who is "real stiff in the joints" (811). In fact, this is the body of the young girl whose corpse was switched with Camilla's thirty years earlier; the mummy is not really a mommy, and her face, like that of the Virgin in Wyatt's forged painting, has decayed (815). During the trip Yák confesses that crime no longer gratifies him and that he must "look up, and look for something bigger" (814), even make amends. Stephen avers that atonement is impossible, but Yák argues that one can compensate for crimes against one person by treating someone else well, as he is doing here. One need only work so that "all the love you've hoarded all your life" is spent (817). We don't know if Stephen accedes to this, for when Yák arrives in Madrid, he learns that police are searching for a North American "falsificador" and that Stephen, having heard this news, has absconded (leaving behind his new passport). Their partnership—Frank's quest for atonement through fraud, a mirror of Wyatt's forgery scheme—is as dead as the mummy. Yák is left wondering if there may be a time, a place, where "love and necessity become the same thing" (821).

Blade

> The only hope, or else despair
> Lies in the choice of pyre or pyre—
> To be redeemed from fire by fire.
>
> —T. S. Eliot, "Little Gidding," 204–6

Stephen, though beset by feelings of emptiness and despair, continues to seek the wedding of love and need.[27] Meanwhile, on Esme and Stanley's ship there is much talk of the martyred girl, and Valentine, who now wears his left arm in a sling (as if reincarnating Otto [833]), has beguiled Esme. A Spanish sailor whose ship has capsized is brought aboard. The ship is the *Purdue Victory,* the same vessel on which Camilla Gwyon met her demise: here, too, the novel comes full circle. Esme, however, believes the sailor to be Wyatt and demands to see him; at the same time that Wyatt is fabricating a corpse, Esme believes he *is* a corpse. She is metaphorically right, since Wyatt has turned into "asche." At the end of the chapter Stanley spies Esme walking away with Valentine as the ship docks at Naples (854).

Before that transpires, we meet a passenger named Ludy, a popular novelist who is on his way to San Zwingli to write an article. In part 3, chapter 5, we accompany him as he wears an expression of "intent vacancy," that of a man "having, or about to have, or at the very least sincerely trying to provoke, a religious experience" (857). Whether he is capable of such an experience seems doubtful, for Gaddis furnishes enough of Ludy's work to verify that he is a shallow and pretentious writer whose insights, if he were to have any, would be couched in clichés. In short, he is a fraud. In the San Zwingli chapel, Ludy beholds someone scraping a painting of a man "in religious habit kneeling before a crucifix suspended in midair" (867). The painting, supposedly of St. Dominic, is by the sixteenth-century Spaniard Juan Fernández Navarrete, called "El Mudo" because he was deaf and mute, who studied with Titian and was later employed by Philip II of Spain as a court painter. The man with the blade is Wyatt Gwyon; when asked his name, he answers, "People I've never seen before in my life call me Stephen" (867). Having accepted his new name, Stephen seems to have achieved his alchemical quest to (re)make himself. But where is the gold? And where is the redeemer? Rather than becoming Christ-like, Wyatt more closely resembles the thief crucified next to Jesus; he even states, "All my life is lived as a thief" (868).

Is Stephen restoring this painting? Ludy asks. Stephen responds that the Mona Lisa's ambiguous smile was a result of Leonardo's eye disease, then insinuates that other disabled artists—Milton, Beethoven—created their greatest works *because* of, rather than despite, their disabilities. Perhaps he has accepted his own imperfections. Yet his utterances remain enigmatic: "Get things nice and separated. Then you can be reasonable" (871). Ludy mentions an El Greco he viewed in the monastery; Stephen replies that El Greco studied with Titian, who taught him to "simplify," "not to be afraid of spaces, not to get lost in details and clutter, and separate everything" (872). Stephen aims to emulate El Greco, reversing his earlier penchant for filling every space, while muttering, "Separateness, that's what went wrong [. . .]. Everything withholding itself from everything else" (874). Earlier, Gaddis's narrator had proclaimed that separateness, and art's inability to end it, was the sickness unto death of modern culture. Stephen's artistic ethos now seems to be moving toward his creator's, as he seeks to avoid separating elements and to eschew the clutter that designates fear.

Has he given up his goal of perfection and unification in favor of a modest career as a restorer? Not exactly, for his restorations take an unorthodox form. Ludy notices that Stephen is scraping away an undamaged section of the Navarrete. Stephen says he will restore the El Greco next. But Stephen's "restorations" consist of scraping the paint away to expose the blank canvas. He holds the blade "before him as though it were a brush, and he [is] sighting some line along its tip before adding another touch to the canvas" (871). Critics have struggled to come to grips with Stephen's intentions and Gaddis's meaning here.[28] But what if we regard his blade as completing the work of his brush and Stephen/Wyatt's erasures as merely an extension of his previous endeavors? That is, what if Stephen's work of destruction imitates—or is identical with—the work of restoration?

His actions suggest that restoration is always a type of destruction insofar as it interferes with the original artist's work. Restoration, in this sense, is worse than forgery because it pretends to be saving a painting while actually desecrating it. Yet Stephen's restorations imply that making art always involves scraping away the accumulated conventions that have been encrusted over the centuries and replacing them with something fresh or less flawed. As we have seen, all forgeries involve erasures—of the name and presence of both the original artist and those of the forger. Stephen's blade, however, is not merely erasing the paintings; it is restoring them to a previous condition. I have already discussed how Van der Veken exposed the gray area where restoration and forgery become indistinguishable. This area grows denser when we consider the following definition of restoration, offered by a distinguished art historian, as that which "seeks to alter the current state of a work in the name of an aesthetic realization of an earlier desired condition" (Scott 85). According to this denotation, Stephen *is* restoring these paintings, because he seeks an "aesthetic realization"—call it a recognition—by returning them to their earlier state of blankness.[29] Scraping off the paint restores the canvas to its condition before it was stained by the inevitably maculate painter.

Real-world parallels to Wyatt's work suggest further implications. René Magritte's painting *L'Eclair* (1948) depicts a colorful bouquet that has been erased and replaced with a gray blur of the same shape.[30] Likewise, Robert Rauschenberg's famous *Erased de Kooning Drawing,* discussed in chapter 4, is just what it says. However, when digitally enhanced, the "image reveals a field of marks" where we see "de Kooning at work, in process, thinking with his pencil and charcoal." The catalog asks, "Was it an act of homage, provocation, humor, patricide, destruction, or, as Rauschenberg once suggested, celebration?" ("Robert Rauschenberg").[31] We may ask the same questions of Stephen's restorations. These works, contemporary with Stephen's, suggest not only that erasures can be art but that his work is modern, even avant-garde. Stephen's restorative destructions constitute an even more radical means of seeking perfection, of bringing about an immaculate aesthetic conception that triggers self-recognition.

He explains his motives by alluding to a story Otto told Esther (probably after hearing it from Wyatt) more than seven hundred pages earlier (875). In a passage in the *Paradoxa,* "Cicero gives Praxiteles no credit for anything of his own in his work, but just for removing the excess marble until he reached the real form that was there all the time" (124). Otto presents artmaking as a process of discovery—a recognition—in which the artist's task is to free beauty from its impediments and permit it to shine forth. An artist does not invent; she or he "knows" what the artwork "wants," as Otto described the overpainted Titian forgery. Young

Wyatt similarly explained why he left his works unfinished: "Because it's there, it's there all the time, all the time you work trying to uncover it" (57). His scraped canvases are, in this sense, merely incomplete. In other words, Stephen's new project not only confirms his earliest aesthetic principles; it also lays bare these truths: that restoration is destruction and vice versa; that true creativity involves stripping off, as much as building upon, what has been previously laid down; that the modern is always a version of the ancient (and the ancient a form of modernity); that a work of art is never finished, and must always respond to its audience's remaking; and that all creative productions, including forgeries, involve erasures as well as exaltations.

Hoc est enim corpus meum

Ludy agrees to share some of the bread Stephen has been eating throughout the scene. This is not just any bread. Reverend Gwyon had been sending packages of food and flour to the monastery ever since his wife died. This time, however, there is "some kind of powdery stuff in a tin box they mixed with the flour when they made this bread, and it came out funny" (884). The bread has a "crumbled fine gray texture flecked with spots 'like blood.'" The powdery stuff is Reverend Gwyon's ashes, which his replacement, Reverend "Dick" (always in quotation marks), mistakenly sent to the monastery (717–18). They have been baked into the bread; Stephen has eaten them. This convergence seems to be an ironic, even grotesque conclusion to Wyatt's lifelong quest for the gold of fatherhood and perfection. It may appear shocking that Wyatt/Stephen cannibalizes his father, but he has already (metaphorically) ingested his artistic fathers, as all artists do. And what is forgery but a method of devouring one's precursors? Wyatt has also consumed his father's ideas and behavior: the reverend's apostate piety is everywhere in Wyatt's work—in his choice of subjects and masters, in his philosophy, in his pursuit of transcendence. Like that dragon in the alchemical manual, Wyatt is eating his own tail. This bizarre development implies that Gwyon has become his son and Stephen has become his father—someone who, disenchanted with his original creed (Christianity, or aesthetic perfection via forgery), has chosen a different one (Mithraism [father]; restoration [son]).[32] This new creed, seemingly the opposite of the first, in fact forms its basis. Just as Christianity adapted the holidays and practices of pagan religions, so Wyatt's pursuit of perfection through imitation has metamorphosed into a radical brand of restoration. Fittingly, this scene takes place during Easter weekend: through the crucible of his forge, Wyatt has been sacrificed so that Stephen may live.

Dilige et quod vis fac

An old man lurks in the corner of the room where Ludy and Stephen converse: the man who raped the cross-eyed (soon-to-be-beatified) girl, now atoning by working as a porter at the monastery. How does one atone? Stephen asks Ludy. "By locking yourself up in remorse with what you know you have done? Or by going back and living it through? By locking yourself up with your work, until it becomes a gessoed surface, all prepared, clean and smooth as ivory? Or by living it through?" (896). In other words, his restorative destructions are a metaphor or preparation for his most important restoration—that of himself. Whereas Wyatt earlier seemed to flow out into other characters, he has now become a "blank space" (LaCapra 38). Stephen announces that he has learned to live "deliberately"; "There's no more you and I," he tells Ludy; "we'll simplify" (900). These words of wisdom are, of course, borrowed from *Walden* (Moore, *Guide* 285; Thoreau 135). Thus, Benesch comments, "simplification becomes erasure" (42). Stephen's quest is the same as Thoreau's: to determine what, finally, has value.

There comes, says Stephen, a moment when "love and necessity become the same thing. And now, if the gods themselves cannot recall their gifts, we must live them through, and redeem them" (898). The wedding of love and necessity has been Wyatt's goal all along, but it remains unclear how his current condition embodies this marriage. Perhaps his final words of advice, a quotation from St. Augustine's *On the First Letter of John*, help to explain. "*Dilige, et quod vis fac*" (Love, and do what you want to [899]). John Leverence writes that these words conclude Wyatt's "long and perilous journey from a childhood of religious terror to a maturity of spiritual recognition" (45). Knight, in contrast, argues that Wyatt has learned that neither art nor any other discipline can "sufficiently elucidate the profounder questions concerning Being" (*Hints* 69). But if so, why does he continue to scrape? These readings impose a terminus where none exists. In fact, even in his new guise Wyatt has not completed his alchemical project of forging a new self out of the ashes; he has not attained what Jung, referring to alchemy's aims, calls "individuation," the "integration of the Self" (Eliade 225). The process has been painful, as the recurrent fire imagery implies, and Wyatt has been burned badly; to become Stephen (a martyr), he has been forced to pass through a crucible and to become someone else—but not entirely, for his restorative destructions are partly congruent with his previous ideals and practices. His new self is inchoate. And yet, as Gaddis once stated, Wyatt has learned to "live without Absolutes . . . [which are] essentially childish, born out of a fear of a purposeless existence" (Abádi-Nagy 12). Beholding one of his scraped canvases, Stephen might well say, "This is my body." The outcome is not gold, but neither is it merely ash. It is, rather, a gray area like the one in Magritte's painting, a (nearly) blank canvas where the erasure remains visible. Stephen has found necessity. Now all he needs is love.

We have painted the perfect fake, which turns out to be a portrait of Wyatt/Stephen. By adding layer after layer to this picture, Gaddis discloses how inherent vice—humanity's built-in flaw—causes us to crack and mar. No mere protagonist, Wyatt Gwyon is a vector for the traits of his society, an embodiments of its shades and sins: green for greed and envy; lavender for betrayal and fraud; brown for cynical materialism, which Gaddis renders as a form of gluttony; gray for the moral ambiguities involved in restoration and forgery; blue for the sadness that pervades his characters' lives; scarlet for the rage that drives them to violence; and, of course, the gold of self-transformation and potential redemption. The perfect fake is every human who seeks godlike status and, inevitably, fails to attain it.

Does Gaddis endorse authenticity and originality and deem forgery a calumny? Or does he espouse the radical view that, as I suggest in the next chapter, Orson Welles champions in *F for Fake,* according to which art experts are frauds and forgery is not only legitimate but essential because it forces us to question our conventions and premises? Johnston argues that the novel oscillates between these two positions without synthesis (21). I would argue instead that, like Wyatt, Gaddis believes that there *is* "gold to forge," that original art must be valued as an ideal but elevating it into a fetish encourages fraud and enables the collapse of aesthetic value into economic value. He also shows that all artists copy, repeat, steal, borrow, even forge, and that such actions are the best means of evoking the kind of recognitions—or call them "creative misrecognitions" (Johnston 21)—that both prompt the joy that great art elicits and sustain the possibility of uniting us in wonder and appreciation. Siri Hustvedt articulates this synthesis beautifully, writing that "when we love a work of art, there is always a form of recognition that occurs. The object reflects us [and] . . . the vision of the other, of the artist, that we have made our own because it answers something within us that we understand is true. This truth may be only a feeling . . . or it may become a vast discursive statement, but it must be there for the enchantment to happen—that excursion into you that is also I" ("Embodied" 354). Any artwork that inspires such recognitions is a masterpiece. By making his perilous excursion into the "you that is also I," Wyatt/Stephen and Gaddis force us to recognize ourselves in the mirror. Such recognitions, whether deriving from "forged" or "original" art, occur only when love and need are one.

Frame 2: Insomnia

> I had not thought death had undone so many.
>
> —Dante, *Inferno,* Canto III.53

With Wyatt/Stephen having passed through the orbit of the Seven Deadly Sins and begun again, we have almost finished our circuit around the table. But what of those last things occupying the corners? In the epilogue Gaddis completes the other characters' stories, subjecting them to death, judgement, hell, and heaven. Otto, free of the stain of counterfeit green, may finally escape his purgatory. His father, however, is less fortunate: "science," having determined that there was "something wrong somewhere," has lobotomized him (934). A nameless counterfeiter (whom we recognize as Sinisterra) has been apprehended in a Spanish hotel, where he commits suicide. Stanley finally performs his finished organ sonata in an ancient chapel in Fenestrula, but the chapel collapses, crushing him to death. The enigmatic Esme comes under Valentine's influence and dies from a staph infection (953).

And what of Basil Valentine? As The Cold Man, he is overheard by Stanley elucidating the motives behind his crimes: "To control people, . . . to give them something . . . anything cheap that will satisfy them at the moment, [. . .] to keep them where their hands can't touch beautiful things, their hands that . . . touch and defile and . . . break beautiful things" (924). No mere cynic or crook, like many art forgers he sees himself as a sentinel protecting the canon from philistines' grubby paws (see thesis 5). But he cannot protect himself: the sore lip that plagued him throughout the final scene at Brown's has left a permanent scar, and his left arm (the sinister side) has been amputated. We find him in a hospital room in Budapest being treated for terminal insomnia. The man who sneered at others' dreams now cannot dream, though dream-like figures intrude upon his waking vision. His final words are addressed to these hallucinated figures, particularly Wyatt. "Eh, my dear fellow? [. . .] [R]emember saying 'Thank God there was the gold to forge'?" As a priest administers last rites, Valentine asks, "What is that smell, oil? oil?" (949). Wyatt's ghost stands before him, exuding his signature aroma. It signifies inherent vice. And there is no insurance against that.

6

But Is It Art?

ORSON WELLES'S CUBIST PORTRAIT OF THE FORGER IN *F FOR FAKE*

> We have learned to whittle the Eden Tree to the shape of a
> surplice-peg,
> We have learned to bottle our parents twain in the yolk of an
> addled egg,
> We know that the tail must wag the dog, as the horse is drawn by
> the cart;
> But the Devil whoops, as he whooped of old: "It's clever, but is
> it Art?"
>
> —Rudyard Kipling, "The Conundrum of the Workshops"

ORSON WELLES loved looking-glasses, and not just because of his monumental ego. He used a motif of multiple mirrors several times, most famously in the dazzling sequence that climaxes *The Lady from Shanghai* (1947), when femme fatale Elsa Bannister (Rita Hayworth) is shot by her husband in a carnival funhouse, and the overlapping images of Elsa, Bannister (Everett Sloane), and O'Hara (Welles) make it nearly impossible to determine which bodies are bone and which are glass (fig. 15).[1] This image serves as a suitable trope for Welles's experimental documentary *F for Fake* (1974). The repetition of these same faces in mirrors indicates the film's self-reflexivity as well as its themes: the recognition that viewers—both experts and amateurs—see themselves in what they perceive; that the membrane between the real and the representation, truth and lies, genuine and fake art is not solid but permeable; that the film's subjects are not single but multiple selves. In this film Welles advertises and elaborates on his own multiple personae as he meditates on the careers of two infamous fakesmiths, art forger Elmyr de Hory and writer Clifford Irving, coauthor of the notorious fraudulent autobiography of Howard Hughes.

FIG. 15. A glimpse of the famous hall of mirrors conclusion to *The Lady from Shanghai* (1947). The overlapping images make it nearly impossible to determine which bodies are bone and which are glass.

Watching this disorienting film, the viewer may feel that she has entered another one of Welles's "centerless labyrinths" (Combs 223). But this one has a center: Welles himself. The "metamorphic" director was, notes Peter Conrad, a "myriad-minded man" (75, 3). He would begin his one-man shows by introducing himself as "author, composer, actor, designer, producer, director, scholar, financier, gourmet, ventriloquist, poet" (5). *F for Fake* adds to this list charlatan, child, con artist, educator, imp, impresario, magician, and, above all, auteur. It presents a gallery of Welleses, an alphabet of avatars, a prism of personalities. Using de Hory, Irving, Hughes, and Pablo Picasso as mirrors, Welles paints a cubist portrait of himself, and, by implication, of every artist, as an inveterate fraud.[2] This "fractal method of inquiry" (Keller 34) is necessary to encompass fakery's many facets. Deploying the full palette of cinematic tools—freeze-frames, stills, dissolves, nonsequential editing, voiceover, found footage, nondiegetic inserts, flashbacks—Welles demonstrates his mastery as well as his trickery. Such ingenious methods of deception, he suggests, are precisely what makes fakers true artists. Claudia Thieme has noted that eyes are everywhere in the film (55), from the leering pupils of its male voyeurs to the piercing orbs of Welles and Picasso. These eyes gaze back at us as we seek a narrative thread among the film's panoply of devices, exposing our desire to believe the stories we are told, much like de Hory's art-world dupes and Irving's book-buying gulls. Ultimately, the film's self-reflexivity bends back on itself in such a way that *F for Fake* is not only, as Thieme declares, "a film about the making of *F for Fake*" (49) but a film about the viewing of it.

S for Sorcerer

Some might argue that *F for Fake* is itself a fake, since Welles borrowed much of its footage from François Reichenbach's television documentary about de Hory. Like a forger, Welles appropriated and repurposed someone else's work. Such sleight of hand fits his initial persona in the film, that of magus. At the opening, he stands before us in an immense cape and performs tricks for a young boy. He tells us that a magician is "just an actor" playing a magician; likewise, "I'm a charlatan," he declares, as he transforms a key into a coin and back into a key. "This is a film about trickery, fraud, about lies," but that is not remarkable, since "almost any story's almost certainly some kind of lie." Welles was, James Naremore reminds us, both magician and pedagogue (13), and he combines these roles by bringing us into his workshop to show how his artifices are executed. Taking to heart Irving's later comment that what matters is not whether a work is real or bogus but whether it's a "good fake or a bad fake," Welles shows us what a good fake looks like and how it is made.

The credits proclaim that this a "film by Orson Welles, with the collaboration of certain expert practioners [*sic*], and Introducing Oja Kodar." Right away we see plenty of Ms. Kodar (Welles's romantic partner at the time) as she walks through traffic in a tight miniskirt. Beginning at about five minutes and fifteen seconds, shots of her shapely derrière are intercut with shots of men ogling her. An attentive viewer might notice that Kodar and the men never appear in the frame together, and soon Welles intimates that the shots of leering men were taken from an entirely different movie: they weren't looking at her at all! Thus does the sorcerer lay bare "the essential 'lie' upon which cinema is built: the editing process" (Naremore 273).[3] The lie was a laborious one to create, too, for editing the film took Welles a solid year, working seven days a week in three different editing rooms. Here, as elsewhere, Welles both critiques conventional notions of authorship and displays his own authorial skill, at once celebrating and deconstructing cinematic grammar (Hoyle 152).

C for Conglomerate

Through editing, Kodar is cut into pieces and reassembled. This sequence typifies how Welles's film consists of "a pattern of fragments . . . put together in the . . . persuasive rhythms of fabrication" (Thomson 407).

David Thomson's words could also describe cubist art, similarly characterized by "aggressive . . . disjunctiveness . . . [and] explicitly unharmonized conglomeratic unity" (Staller 80), as embodied, for example, in Picasso's *Ambroise Vollard* (1910),[4] in which the head and body of the subject, an art dealer (who resembles Welles slightly), seem to be moving or ready to explode; the lines become arrows pointing in several

FIG. 16. In Picasso's *Portrait of Ambroise Vollard* (1910) his head and body seem ready to explode. Welles's cinematic techniques imitate the unharmonized disjunctiveness of such cubist paintings. Oil on canvas, 93 × 66 cm. (Pushkin Museum of Fine Arts; photo: Erich Lessing/Art Resource, NY)

directions, perhaps to represent the income and outgo of money and art (fig. 16). Welles had long been fascinated by cubism, and movies such as *The Lady from Shanghai* and *Touch of Evil* (1958) display its influence: abrupt cuts from medium shots to extreme close-ups; "wrong" camera placements; arrhythmic juxtapositions of long takes and rapid montage sequences.[5] In pitting physical elements against each other, his films also recall Picasso's collages, which brought unlike components into novel configurations and mashed together materials from disparate sources to generate a disorienting effect (Staller 1, 236). In *F for Fake* Welles's cubism forges a kaleidoscopic—or to adapt a Joycean coinage, a collideorscopic—experience (*Finnegans Wake* 143).

F for Fake follows the cubist principle—and the forger's credo—that artmaking should be playful (as described in thesis 11). Welles plays many games in the film, his trick with Kodar being one of them. He also challenges us directly, promising (at 9:20) that, for the next hour, everything in this film will be "strictly based on the available facts." Initially, he follows through on this promise (though he later tricks us), thereby differing from de Hory and Irving, both of whom turned prevarication into a vocation. Motivated by greed and resentment over his lack of recognition, de Hory made and sold forged artworks all over the United States and Europe for more than twenty years. Inspired by the forger's career, Irving (and his partner) fabricated the infamous hoax autobiography of Howard Hughes. Irving's 1969 book, entitled *Fake!,* recounts de Hory's career in fascinating detail; yet, Irving shows, de Hory always insisted that he had done nothing wrong (*Fake!* 82). Which again raises a question addressed in Welles's film and throughout this book: What is wrong with a well-made forgery? Or, as Kipling wonders, "It's clever, but is it Art?"

Q for ?

During production the film went by many titles, including *Hoax, Nothing but the Truth,* and *Lies* (Naremore 272). As late as September 1974 Welles was calling it *QUESTION MARK,* and the opening credits imply that this is still its title.[6] These metamorphoses suggest the power of forgeries to vex connoisseurs and scholars with the problem of what to call them. One reason is that successful forgers are extremely skillful. Hence, as Alfred Lessing states, any attempt to define (and deprecate) forgery fails if it assumes that a forged work is automatically inferior to a genuine work (66). And if, upon examining a forgery, even an expert cannot distinguish it from an authentic work, on what principles is the fake objectionable (Lenain 23)? These principles cannot be purely aesthetic; they must be moral or philosophical. One such principle is a belief about freedom; recall Leonard Meyer's pithy pronouncement (as noted in the prologue) that "Creation is possible only if there is choice. And choice is possible only if there is freedom" (83). But if the ideal of perfect originality is our standard, why do we not condemn pastiches or parodies? And don't all artists imitate other artists? This standard is too restrictive, ignoring the intertextuality that informs all artworks and particularly forgeries. Meyer further holds that genuine art must make a discovery or teach us something new; such discoveries can be made only once (82). It follows that original works have value because they "risk[ ] failure" (Meyer 83). But clearly forgers risk failure, too (albeit of a different kind)—and their failures bring dire consequences. Moreover, as Sándor Radnóti has shown, a copy can solve problems that the original could not, and in that sense may be *better* than the original (80). Further, not all forgeries are copies: de Hory did not merely replicate a specific work but rather imitated a given artist's style and signature; Wyatt Gwyon's (fictional) forgeries are not copies, nor were the Ern Malley poems. Ultimately, as I argued in the prologue, we must invoke not invention but intention. To repeat my definition: *a forgery is an artwork, artefact, or document designed to dupe someone.*

Malicious motives notwithstanding, forgeries have positive effects on nonforged art. They arise from and promote a symbiotic relationship with collecting: collecting creates demand, which raises prices, which encourages fakes (Radnóti 6). As I note in thesis 1, genuine works and forgeries engage in a mutually enhancing dialectic whereby a genuine work gains greater value from the threat of being copied (which creates incentives for forgeries); indeed, the mere fact that an artist's work has been forged is a backhanded acknowledgment of that artist's importance. Forgeries fascinate because they rock the boat, critiquing, like Gwyon's work, the entire system of art connoisseurship by exposing its shaky foundation on the trace paradigm—the idea that any artwork has the "nearly magical power" to reveal its origin by leaving traces of its production and shaping conditions (Lenain 235). Against such magic, forgers conjure dark arts. What Lenain calls the "sorcerer's aura" surrounding forgers thus derives from the fact that they use the same skills as authentic artists (38). Hence, the perfect fake, that bête noire of the art world, is the mirror image, the dark double, of the masterpiece (Lenain 267). Welles suggests as much by quoting, throughout *F for Fake,* Kipling's "The Conundrum of the Workshops," particularly its variations on the repeated question, "Is it art?" Kipling suggests that critics—the Devil's mouthpieces—have asked this question since Adam first "scratched with a stick in the mold." Forgers play a diabolical role, prodding artists to define aesthetic value as something beyond beauty ("it's pretty": line 4), dynamism ("it's striking": line 10), and ingenuity ("it's clever": line 24). Forgeries, as we witnessed in *The Recognitions,* expose the art industry's reliance on experts, who inflate the value of certain names and conflate aesthetic value and economic value. In contrast, Welles seems to advocate the "anarchistic solution": the view that there is no such thing as a genuine artwork—that, as Picasso once stated, "there are no fakes because there are only fakes" (qtd. in Lenain 30).

De Hory and his partners learned that the success of a forgery finally depends less upon the work itself than upon its certificate of authenticity. The certificate, in turn, is verified by stories, both the mythos of the maestro and the tale of provenance told by the forger(s) and rendered credible by written documents. As I have insisted (see thesis 3), any forgery is only as good as the story behind it. And, like all successful forgers, Elmyr de Hory was a master storyteller.

Freeze-Frame: Elf

"Who is Elmyr?" Welles asks early in *F for Fake.* Elmyr seems to answer, "I'm not a professional actor." Not true. Much of his stunning success stemmed from his charming demeanor—that of "a slightly wicked forest elf" (Irving, *Fake!* 3), a sprite with magical powers of transformation (fig. 17). Elmyr is Ariel to Welles's Prospero (Conrad 354), or, perhaps better, Puck to his Oberon. As metamorphic as the director, de Hory used numerous pseudonyms as he traveled, like a picaresque hero, across North America with his art and quiver of tales.[7] He would say he had known the artist (whose work he had forged) and regale his auditor with gossip; he would claim that he wanted to dispose of a Matisse he had inherited; or he would lament that these few works were "all he had managed to save from his family estate in Hungary" (*Fake!* 49, 66, 37). Was he Baron de Hory? Or was he L. E. Raynal, Louis Casso,

FIG. 17. Art forger Elmyr de Hory smiles in self-satisfaction in Welles's *F for Fake.*

Baron Herzog, or Josef du Pont? He was all of them—a cubist portrait in mendacity. What a coincidence, Welles remarks, that "two world leaders in fakery," de Hory and Irving, ended up on Ibiza. Yet Irving's attitude toward de Hory is "very mixed" (*F for Fake* 13m); he describes him as dwelling in a castle of delusion, one turret of which is the fantasy that he "has not broken any laws." Cut to Elmyr shrugging: "As long as people enjoy it." Irving continues: de Hory "would be horrified" if told that he had cheated people. Cut to Elmyr, whose reaction shot actually comes from an unrelated scene in Reichenbach's documentary (fig. 17). Thus does Welles use cinemagic—his own brand of faking—to create a contretemps that never occurred.

Irving describes de Hory as "the greatest art forger in the world." Welles too praises him as a "Paganini of the palette," and as we witness him nonchalantly draw a Matisse, Elmyr indeed resembles a wizard with a wand. Because Irving has yet to "transform himself before our very eyes into a superstar," Elmyr is the "emperor of the hoax," Irving merely "the pretender." Basking in this notoriety, de Hory proudly shows his party guests an article spotlighting him as the man "who holds the art world to ransom." Irving's book is, Welles tells us, about a man "taking the micky" out of art experts, exploiting their shallowness, complacency, and avarice, translating "disappointments"—de Hory's inability to sell his own works—into a "gigantic joke." But the joke was eventually on Elmyr.

Flashback: Emperor

Supposedly the only child of wealthy Hungarian parents, Elemér Hoffmann (born 1906) studied art in Munich between the wars, continuing in Paris under Fernand Léger.[8] After World War II he faced a financial crisis that was resolved in 1946 when Lady Malcolm Campbell mistook one of his paintings for a Picasso. Elmyr sold it to her as such for £40 (*Fake!* 22). (De Hory recounts this story thirty-nine minutes into the film.) He then went about drawing more Picassos, claiming they were a gift from the Spanish master. He didn't mean to "harm anyone or even [have] the idea of making a fortune. It was a matter of survival," he insisted (*Fake!* 24). De Hory repeated this justification throughout his career, though he made no attempt to get a real job. Before long he and his friends were selling "Picassos" all over Europe and living the high life (27). (He made $6,000 on five drawings.) As soon as Elmyr obtained money, he spent it, which meant that he was "forced" to keep forging. In 1948 he traveled to New York, where he tried to make it as a legitimate artist, abandoning the effort after selling only one portrait from a one-man show (34). Then he lit out for California, where he passed off numerous paintings and drawings under an array of pseudonyms. Bigger pigeons roosted in Dallas, so he flew there for a short stay, then returned to Los Angeles where Frank Perls, noticing that the Baron's Matisses, Renoirs, and Picassos all seemed to have been made by the same hand, kicked him out of his gallery (45). After assiduously studying Modigliani's works, Elmyr adopted him as a favorite alter ego (47). Indeed, Elmyr's success derived from this method of reverse connoisseurship whereby he studied and imitated an artist's signature styles (and signature). That is, he rarely copied a particular work but mimicked gestures and techniques. He was equally talented as a salesman, conning countless experts and dealers who, charmed by his European manners and aristocratic airs, failed to examine his wares closely. Indeed, Elmyr was "acting" in two different senses: while creating the works he reenacted the performance of the original artist; while selling them, he pretended to be someone he was not. He was both an impressionist and a postimpressionist.

By 1952 he had sold a hundred drawings and several other works, but the spoils of his shady labors amounted only to a few rings and $1,500. Feeling that he had betrayed his talent (*Fake!* 54), he tried to sell his own art again but was told he looked too affluent to be a painter. Soon he was back to faking, expanding his repertoire to include Braque, Renoir, Derain, Degas, and Vlaminck—and especially Matisse, although he considered him "overrated" (67). During this golden age de Hory completed about seventy works and earned around $160,000. We can almost hear him exclaim, "Lord, what fools these mortals be!"

Puck's American career collapsed when Chicago art dealer Joseph Faulkner realized that a Renoir that "Raynal" had sent him was already in a Budapest museum (*Fake!* 77). Breaking from his usual practice, de Hory had copied a reproduction from a portfolio and replaced it with his own work, then passed off the reproduction as the original. When Faulkner asked for a certificate of authenticity, de Hory, realizing the jig was likely up, fled back to California. He then moved to Mexico, assumed the sobriquet Josef du Pont, and began working with a Mexican dealer who pretended not to know he was a forger, until one day he said, "Don't you think you ought to put the *e* in Matisse's signature?" (90). Almost everyone else was bamboozled: one dealer even attested that "De Hory had some talent, but the outstanding forger of our time was Raynal" (117)! With the FBI in pursuit, Elmyr lammed it to Canada, then to Detroit, where during a museum visit he came face to face with one of his own Matisses (93). Though gratified by such successes, he felt the world closing in on him. In *F for Fake* de Hory declares that his goal was to "explode the myth of the infallibility of art dealers and museum directors. To expose their crookedness, their evilness and their viciousness." But who even knew about this mission? Thus did he grapple with the forger's paradox (thesis 4): success requires anonymity, but to be appreciated one must be exposed. "My so-called crusade against art museums, art dealers and art galleries was finished; I had proved my point. What had it got me?" (101). Penniless and without prospects, in 1959 the erstwhile emperor took an overdose of sleeping pills. He survived.

E for Experts

"We hanky-panky men have always been with you," Welles observes, twenty-one minutes into the film; "What's new are the experts." Though they "speak to us with the absolute authority of the computer," they are "God's own gift to the faker," as de Hory's (and Wyatt Gwyon's) career proves. Irving explains, "The great faker of the twentieth century becomes a modern folk hero for the rest of us, who have a bit of larceny in ourselves but simply don't have the courage or the opportunity to . . . express it." (Irving had more than a bit of larceny in him.) He shows us a de Hory Modigliani that he brought to a gallery owner.[9] Once he told the owner it was a fake, the expert immediately found reasons to condemn it. At the next gallery, however, Irving called the same work authentic, and the expert praised it as one of Modigliani's finest. "After that," he admits, "I lost my faith in the concept of expertise." Elmyr insouciantly adds, "I don't feel bad for Modigliani. I feel good for me." He then paints a Matisse, boasting that his own line is "more flowing" than the master's. A few minutes later he avers that he *never* offered a painting to a museum that was refused (untrue, as we have seen).[10] Welles notes that one nod from an expert would make the forged canvas "worth maybe a couple of hundred thousand dollars." But is it art? "What's the value? The value depends on opinion, opinion depends on the experts. . . . Elmyr makes fools of the experts, so who's the expert? Who's the faker?"

Flashback: Hanky-Panky

Can a faker be faked? Elmyr's ensuing career proves that the answer is yes. The fakers who faked the faker were Fernand Legros and Réal Lessard—Mr. Hanky and Mr. Panky—who entered his life in late 1959. Part Greek, part French, and a naturalized American citizen, Legros was, according to Irving, a "born con man" (*Fake!* 107), and he would know. The French Canadian Lessard joined them at the age of nineteen, at first serving subsidiary roles but eventually matching Legros as a businessman and later becoming a painter. Elmyr started creating works for them in New York before deciding to return to Europe. To make that happen, Hanky and Panky forged the Canadian passport of an actual insurance clerk named Joseph Boutin, who was unlikely to leave Canada (115). As years passed, Legros and Lessard metamorphosed from Elmyr's partners to his predators after Elmyr agreed to give them sole rights to sell his forgeries. They pocketed most of the proceeds and lived jet-set lifestyles while limiting Elmyr to a $400 per month salary and, starting in 1964, maintaining him in an Ibiza villa owned by Legros. Like Elmyr, both were gay, and Legros pitched jealous tantrums over any sign of infidelity from Lessard and employed both flattery and threats to keep Elmyr in line. Truth be told, Elmyr was easy to exploit: he didn't question the arrangement until it was too late, kept no records (because doing so would be an admission that forgery was his vocation), never saved money or planned for the future. And so he became their indentured servant. "It all happened so fast," he recalls. Bewildered and frightened, but also relieved, he (recalling Wyatt Gwyon's plight) "felt like Faust must have felt after he'd sold his soul to the Devil" (*Fake!* 137).[11]

The twin Mephistos pressured Elmyr to churn out forgeries and furnished materials so he could study styles (*Fake!* 141). The results were so plausible that an elderly Kees van Dongen "recognized" one of Elmyr's fakes as his own work (146). The shrewd Legros also devised a shortcut: increase the fees for the experts who would authenticate the forgeries. Between 1962 and 1965 he and Lessard sold forty-five paintings to New York's Parke-Bernet Galleries, each one spurious (147). They also created false customs stamps, which enabled them to sell several works in Japan, which brought in $250,000. Elmyr's reward? A small black-and-white television. "We had to keep him poor," Lessard sardonically commented, "or he'd have quit. . . . He was like a child" (158–59). The sorcerer had been reduced to an apprentice. Their scheme was threatened when the real Joseph Boutin was indicted for possessing stolen property in Canada, but Elmyr then received legal residency in Spain as Joseph Elmyr Dory-Boutin (169).

Now specializing in the Fauvists, de Hory succeeded grandly. Meanwhile Hanky and Panky's quarrels became more frequent and intense. Once Lessard collected $92,000 in unpaid promissory notes from Legros, which enabled him to get a writ of seizure for the latter's Paris apartment (*Fake!* 192). Legros then stole Lessard's briefcase filled with business documents; Lessard had his partner arrested—only to drop the charges (194). Under such stress, Elmyr's work suffered. One of his Dufys was so bad that they changed the signature from Raoul's to that of his less talented brother, Jean, but the dealer detected the forgery. Yet these mistakes didn't matter as long as they kept their prime pigeon cooing. That bird was a Texas oilman—not Howard Hughes but a more gullible mirror image named Algur Hurtle Meadows, who between 1964 and 1966 bought from Legros forty-six paintings attributed to Vlaminck, Modigliani, Matisse, Picasso, and others (170). After getting wind of the briefcase affair, Meadows had his collection examined by Klaus and Frank Perls and Daniel Saidenberg. All forty-six works were phonies. Yet so different were the styles and quality that Klaus Perls couldn't believe that they had all been made by the same person (196).

Legros offered to buy them all back for $350,000; Meadows turned him down.

Our puckish chameleon was broke again. De Hory stayed on Ibiza because he had nowhere else to go: since he had not sold any fakes in Spain or forged any Spanish artists' works while there, he could not be extradited to France, where he would be arrested (*Fake!* 216). But he was incapable of keeping a low profile and blithely drove his red Corvette around the island until he was finally arrested for being "socially undesirable"; he spent two months in Ibiza's very comfortable jail (belying his claim in *F for Fake* that "a jail's a jail"). In May 1968 de Hory received a three-month suspended sentence for using a forged passport to enter Switzerland and in October tried again—and failed again—to commit suicide. Meadows pressed charges against Legros (222), but without witnesses who had seen Elmyr creating the fakes, signing them, and giving them to Legros and Lessard, a conviction was unlikely (223). Legros was finally indicted and convicted for forgery and passing bad checks in France in 1973 ("Fernand Legros").

A for Alchemist

The Legros-Lessard-de Hory trio created an "alternate world," writes Jonathon Keats, "conjured by their coordinated effort" (123). Art dealers and experts dwelled there with them.[12] One would think that a scandal so massive would trigger major changes to the industry, but most dealers and galleries merely pretended that Hanky, Panky, and Puck had never existed. Elmyr complained, "It's just incredible that someone like a Picasso . . . makes a little drawing and that is transferred immediately into gold" (*Fake!* 227). For de Hory as for Gwyon, artists are alchemists—or at least their dealers are. If de Hory's forgeries "mock a society that converts originality into capital" (Naremore 276), they also sabotage the trace paradigm. Elmyr's decades-long adoption of others' styles squashed whatever artistic originality he may have possessed, but clearly his real talent *was* for imitation. Again he confronts the forger's dilemma: "In spite of having absolutely no personal recognition for myself," he proclaims, "I obviously was an artist of consequence" (*Fake!* 235). Others agreed: upon learning that his Modigliani was a forgery, one of Faulkner's clients asked him for a certificate reading "I, Joseph Faulkner, certify that this is an original and genuine Modigliani fake by Elmyr de Hory" (232). Elmyr transformed paint into gold—but not for himself. The dealers "made themselves fortunes on the paintings of Elmyr," Welles reminds us, but left de Hory with not "a dime to [his] name."

Legros and Lessard later published self-justifying memoirs. The former disputed Elmyr's version of events and called him a "*faux faussaire*" (a fake faker); Lessard stated that he himself had painted the forgeries, Elmyr adding only the signatures (Keats 131).[13] As always, forgeries are fertile sources for fictions—not only the lies used to authenticate them but also the false stories aimed at explaining them. They also give birth to multiple ironies. For example, in 2010 a retrospective of original de Hory paintings was installed at the Hillstrom Museum of Art in Minnesota—too late for Elmyr to profit. In his book *Enigma!* (1991), Ken Talbot presents several de Hory reproductions—which were later determined to be forgeries *of* de Hory's works. To top it off, Talbot's book was plagiarized from Irving's *Fake!*[14] Thus were the fakers faked. With forgeries, the fictions never finish.

Elmyr also had a powerful effect on Irving. Although he punctures the fakesmith's delusions and points out in Welles's film that de Hory has "no personal vision," his career likely inspired Irving's titanic scam of penning an invented biography of Howard Hughes. As Welles notes, "The author of a book about fakes was himself a faker, the author of a fake to end all fakes that he must have been cooking up when we were filming him." In his tell-all book about his Hughes fraud, *The Hoax* (1981), Irving barely mentions de Hory, but there seems little doubt that, as Welles asserts, Irving learned at least one valuable lesson from the forger: "Don't be spooked by the experts." In truth, Irving needed few lessons, for his skill as an actor and prevaricator is amply exhibited throughout *The Hoax* and in the account of the scheme written by journalist Stephen Fay and two coauthors.[15] To perpetrate this immense con job about the ultra-mysterious Hughes, Irving drew on a deep well of duplicity he had developed throughout his life as a second-rate novelist and serial philanderer. He and his partners—writer/researcher Richard Suskind and Irving's fourth wife, Edith—almost pulled it off due to an extraordinary combination of luck, chutzpah, skillful improvisation, monumental stupidity, and enormous cupidity. Another reason that Project Octavio—the secret name that Irving's publisher McGraw-Hill gave to the Hughes autobiography—nearly succeeded was the nature of the subject himself.

Freeze-Frame: Octavio

At around thirty minutes into *F for Fake,* Welles shows us stock footage of Howard Hughes's "hermitage" at the Desert Inn in Las Vegas and wonders, "What were they doing to him? . . . Was it a cry for help?"[16] The director sympathizes with the eccentric billionaire; indeed, his fascination with Hughes dated back to the 1930s. According to Joseph Cotten, who addresses us in *F for Fake,* the original subject of Welles's film about "a certain tycoon" was to be Hughes, not William Randolph Hearst, and Charles Foster Kane's life eerily presages Hughes's descent from adventurous aviator to movie studio head to reclusive oddball. Fifty-one minutes into *F for Fake* Welles presents a *News on the March* segment that echoes the opening of *Kane,* except that the subject is Hughes (fig. 18). It's a parody of a pastiche! Like Kane, Hughes was a man "with a dozen personalities rolled into one"; he even used doubles to avoid being seen (Fay et al. 3). The metamorphic Welles identified with the mogul, once telling a friend that he had become "the Howard Hughes of the cinema" (Conrad 129).

Hughes's father made his fortune by inventing a bit for oil drills, and his son (born in Humble, Texas, in 1905) inherited his engineering mind. In the 1930s the handsome young magnate circumnavigated the globe in record time and went to Hollywood, where he produced movies, dated actresses, and designed a bra for Jane Russell to wear in the film *The Outlaw* (1943) (which was, Welles's narrator tells us, "the cause

FIG. 18. Drawing of Howard Hughes from *F for Fake.*

of a great uplift"). Hughes's aviation obsession led to four plane crashes, one of which nearly killed him, and yielded his great folly, the so-called Spruce Goose (actually built of birch), a wooden behemoth designed to transport cargo that was so huge and unwieldy it could barely get airborne. In the late 1940s the Hughes Tool Company obtained a controlling interest in RKO studios, where the right-wing mogul produced anti-Communist pictures and purged "subversive" employees before selling the company in 1955. Increasingly secretive, he formed a subsidiary, Rosemont Enterprises, solely to prevent anyone from writing about him. So reclusive was he that even the most trusted members of his "Mormon Mafia" (he preferred to employ Latter-day Saints because they seemed incorruptible) never met him in person. This mania for privacy only fueled the public's fascination while rendering him a ripe target for the hoax autobiography. As Irving knew, the lack of information about Hughes made it nearly impossible to fact-check, and a disavowal could be viewed as just one more eccentricity.

Flashback: Mercury

The mercurial founder of Mercury Theatre could have passed the title to Irving, for the latter resembles the Roman god of thieves (fig. 19). Born in 1930 (he died in late 2017), Irving resented his lack of success as a writer and craved recognition (Fay et al. 20)—emotions, that, as we have seen repeatedly, impel many fakesmiths (see thesis 6). By the time of his fourth marriage, to Edith Sommer, in 1967, he had published four novels, one of which may have been plagiarized.[17] Richard Suskind, a "writer of speedily produced nonfiction" (31), was working on a children's book about Richard the Lion-hearted when Irving, who had read a *Newsweek* story about Hughes, proposed a "wild idea": to write a biography of Hughes based on fake interviews. It would be a "hoax, a gorgeous literary caper, in which publisher and author would collaborate" (Irving, *Hoax* 5). Why try such a thing? Irving was not destitute, as Lasse Hallström's film adaptation of *The Hoax* (2006) contends: he was three books into a $150,000 four-book deal with McGraw-Hill, though none of them had sold well. Nor, claims Irving, did he care about the money he might make on the hoax. He asserts that he planned to divulge the fraud and give the money back once the book was finished. Or maybe

FIG. 19. Clifford Irving, caught midconversation in *F for Fake*. Given his skills as thief and actor, he could be a member of Welles's Mercury Players.

not: he hedges. The scheme was mostly a self-dare, a game, and a prank (as noted in thesis 11) perpetrated by a man who (as his eventual six marriages testify) was pathologically restless: "I had formulated my own challenge, and that was motive enough. The rest was peripheral" (*Hoax* 34). The peripheral stuff included Edith, his two small sons, as well as the publishers, friends, and lawyers whom he defrauded. Whatever else he may have been, Clifford Irving was a first-class narcissist.

Suskind was at first skeptical. ("Forgery is a *profession*," qtd. in Irving, *Hoax* 22, italics his.) But the conspirators eventually settled on a 75/25 Irving/Suskind split (Fay et al. 66). (I focus on Irving because Suskind does not appear in Welles's film and stayed in the background during the hoax.) The mercuric Irving also had a model: a "letter from Hughes" published in *Newsweek*. He laboriously crafted a letter by Hughes (*Hoax* 29) and called Beverly Loo, an editor at McGraw-Hill, with a blockbuster: he had permission to write Hughes's biography. She brought the forged letter to her boss, Albert Leventhal, who took the bait. The plan received a boost in January 1971, when *Life* published Hughes's handwritten letter to Bill Gay, a Hughes company executive, and Chester Davis, the billionaire's long-time lawyer, about a lawsuit (Fay et al. 66). Irving used that item to refine his rendering of Hughes's hand for future correspondence. In February, after Irving showed his publisher "excerpts from interviews" with Hughes in Oaxaca and New Orleans, the company offered an advance of $100,000, with another $100,000 upon completion of the research and $300,000 upon delivery of the manuscript (Fay et al. 74). *Life* pledged another $250,000 to publish excerpts, and Dell purchased paperback rights for a cool $400,000. The contract did contain one strange clause: Hughes's $500,000 fee would be distributed in checks made out to "H. R. Hughes."

Freeze-Frame: Helga

Enter Edith (fig. 20). Or rather Helga, for that is the alias she adopted to impersonate H. R. Hughes. Her husband's literary forgery required other forgeries, including Helga R. Hughes's signature on a fake passport used to open an account at Credit Suisse and her endorsements of McGraw-Hill's checks. Though aware that what she was doing was "*foolish and crazy,*" Edith hoped it would keep her husband out of the clutches of "*Baroness von Slut*"—singer Nina van Pallandt, with whom Irving had been carrying on an affair (*Hoax* 83, italics in original). Disguised as Helga, Edith opened an account, then disguised herself as her ex-husband's new wife, Hanne Rosenkranz, to cross the border into West Germany. At one point she owned three different identity documents: her own passport, Helga's passport, and Hanne's national ID card. She was a living cubist portrait. How did Irving justify bringing his wife into the scheme? By assuring her that they would give the money back, that "it was a hoax, not a crime" (53). "We haven't stolen anything," he reminded both her and Suskind. "I've lied, that's all" (60). Astonishingly, he also echoed the very excuses for which he criticizes de Hory: "No one would be hurt. . . . For whatever we received, we would be giving fair value" by producing "an important book" (61). Con-man Cliff and tricky Dick had another, less tangible partner: the credulity and avarice of their victims. The McGraw-Hill executives had caught the virus and "wanted to believe" (58). Blinded by dollar signs, they couldn't see what they didn't want to see.

FIG. 20. Edith Irving, also known as Helga Hughes.

Flashback: Bonanza

Not that the fakesmiths weren't diligent. Over the next year Irving pretended to conduct clandestine interviews with Hughes in Florida, Mexico, and the Bahamas. He and Suskind invented mysterious figures such as a pilot named Pedro and a liaison called George Gordon Holmes. They traveled to the locations of the imaginary meetings to generate receipts; they flew back and forth to Ibiza. They imagined themselves as picaresque heroes, rogues tweaking bourgeois noses. All along, of course, the monarchical "Octavio" was actually living in seclusion in the Britannia Beach Hotel in Nassau; rather than interviewing him in Oaxaca, Irving had enjoyed a romantic rendezvous there with Van Pallandt. Irving and Suskind also trekked to Texas to study Hughes's early life; to Los Angeles, where they perused documents related to his movie career; and to the Library of Congress to read transcripts of Hughes's 1947 Senate hearing (*Hoax* 70). In one of his book's most thrilling scenes, Irving describes stealing the transcripts from the library by secreting them in his trousers (70–73). Afterward he told Edith that this escapade was "the beginning and the end of my criminal career" (74). Not quite. Soon the pair stumbled onto a true bonanza. While visiting Irving's aunt in Palm Springs, they ran into a Hollywood producer and hanger-on named Stanley Meyer who, through a complicated web of connections, possessed a copy of the unpublished memoirs of Noah Dietrich, Hughes's long-time accountant. Ghostwritten by a journalist named James Phelan, the manuscript had not found a publisher; Meyer asked the pair to read it. (See *Hoax* 103–7 and Fay et al. 246–66 for details.) The elated duo photocopied the manuscript, returned it, and told Meyer it was unpublishable. They now had material few others knew even existed. "We were on the road to a unique creation," writes Irving. "A remarkable man telling a remarkable life story, all the more remarkable because it was based on fact and yet we had the freedom and power to infuse fact with the drama of fiction. . . . Our Howard Hughes would blossom like a plant beamed on by twin suns" (*Hoax* 117).

The twin suns took turns impersonating him as they staged mock interviews with each other over the next few months. To flesh out their sketchy material about Hughes's early life, Irving supplied tales from his own childhood. They also fabricated several far-fetched incidents and relationships, including an entirely fictitious friendship between

Hughes and Ernest Hemingway and a ludicrous anecdote about shoplifting Oreos from a supermarket. They stitched together stories "from the multicolored fabric of our imagination, our own views, . . . and our vision of what Howard Hughes might have been had we lived in his skin" (133). In other words, they *became* Hughes, painting a cubist portrait of a composite figure whom we might call Howcliff Hugheskind. The twin suns had become Howard's twin sons. It was clever, but was it art? Perhaps so: they begot a better Hughes than the real one, imitating and improving his voice in a performance that was, despite its chicanery and bad faith, riveting.

A snag in the fabric appeared when a different publisher announced a forthcoming Hughes biography by Robert Eaton. In a stroke of flim-flam genius, Irving manipulated this threat to finagle more money out of McGraw-Hill. Writing more letters in Hughes's name, he specified that he (Hughes) would publish his book with them only if they paid Irving the full amount on the same day they announced publication. He also asked them to scotch the other book, authorized Irving to write his account as an autobiography, and raised his fee (payable to Irving's "Hughes" account) to a million dollars (Fay et al. 98–99). Under his own name, Irving also penned a missive explaining that it would be "totally and nakedly unethical" for him to write an unauthorized biography of Hughes (*Hoax* 163). He faked indignation convincingly. He then pretended to "talk Hughes down" to $850,000; McGraw-Hill bought it. Presto! Mercury transformed a bone of contention into another bonanza. This incident also turned the tide on the hoax: the McGraw-Hill mavens were now convinced that Irving had some magical power over Howard Hughes (183). There was indeed shrewd sorcery in his exploitation of their credulity. As he reminded Suskind that December, their dupes *wanted* to believe because the book put them "in cahoots with [Hughes]. . . . That's the way *they'd* like to live. . . . The secrecy part . . . is what they love the most. That takes them out of the humdrum into another world. . . . I'm their buffer between reality and fantasy" (213). But the buffer was blurring. Others were living their own truth, and, as Irving writes "[I was] living mine. If mine is founded on a grand deceit, it's no less true. . . . I felt no shame" (200). As so often happens in forgeries and mystifications, the faker comes to believe his own fibs: "It was almost no longer possible to distinguish between illusion and reality" (214). Though proud of his achievement, he was bitter that the world was so easily mocked—and, though he didn't admit it, dismayed that nobody would appreciate his brilliance. As I note in thesis 4, a part of Irving *wanted* to be exposed.

Flashback: Voice

He got his wish once Hughes learned of the biography. After Chester Davis announced that the biography was a fraud, Hughes called Frank McCulloch, former Los Angeles bureau chief of *Time* (and the man who had conducted the last real interview with him in 1958) to insist that he didn't know Clifford Irving. Then McCulloch read the now-completed manuscript: the voice of Howcliff Hugheskind convinced him of its authenticity (*Hoax* 225). A group of handwriting analysts had already certified Irving's forged letters as genuine, but McGraw-Hill commissioned another test to be safe. Osborn, Osborn, and Osborn's affidavit assured them that it was "impossible" for anyone but Hughes to have written them (Fay et al. 133). Meanwhile, Edith's hand had endorsed and deposited the final McGraw-Hill check.

The polygraph Irving sweatily endured was inconclusive, but another technological intervention proved definitive. On January 7, 1972, Hughes held a phone conference with seven journalists (they "interviewed his voice," Welles notes). His Texas twang still audible, Octavio's voice rang true: "I only wish I was still in the movie business," he said, "because I don't remember any script as wild or as stretching of the imagination as this yarn has turned out to be." He swore that he had never met Irving, had never even heard of him until the biography was publicized. Our Mercury claimed that it was not Hughes on the phone but merely a "damn good imitation" (*Hoax* 256) and went ahead with his own scheduled interview on *60 Minutes*. Watching it afterward, Irving was appalled at his own naked insincerity, but the publishers thought he'd done a fine job. They *wanted* to believe. But let us give credit where it's due: Irving had become a talented thespian—an honorary member of Welles's Mercury Players. The pretender had become the new emperor of the hoax.

Flashback: Con

But the emperor's kingdom was about to crumble. Swiss officials had investigated the mysterious H. R. Hughes, whom a teller identified as

Edith Irving (Fay et al. 176), and hotel records proved she had been in Zurich when the deposits were made (*Hoax* 272). During a grilling at McGraw-Hill's offices, Irving provided some frankly ridiculous details about his meetings with Hughes, yet his listeners credited his story; McCulloch and his associates concurred that if Irving was a con man, he was "the best they had ever met" (Fay et al. 180). US Postal Service inspectors were less impressed, having unearthed evidence proving that the fictional George Gordon Holmes had never picked up the letter Irving had written to him to give to Hughes. They also tracked Irving's route in Miami for a meeting with Hughes and found it impossible (189). Cornered at the home of his attorney, Martin Ackerman, Irving admitted that Helga was Edith (194). Ackerman advised him to hire criminal attorney Maurice Nessen. Irving finally spilled the beans to Nessen's associate, and the "relief of confession was sweet beyond almost anything [he] had ever known" (*Hoax* 284). The coup de grâce was delivered on February 2, 1972, when van Pallandt admitted that Irving had been with her in Oaxaca the previous February 11 instead of with Octavio (Fay et al. 197). The Osborn experts then retracted their endorsement, calling the letters "clever forgeries" (Fay et al. 219), and on February 11, 1972, McGraw-Hill acknowledged that they had been hoodwinked (224). The February 21, 1972, cover of *Time* pictured the "Con Man of the Year," featuring a portrait of Irving painted by . . . Elmyr de Hory (267).

By March 3, Irving, his wife, and Suskind had confessed. Irving offered to take all the blame in exchange for immunity for Suskind and Edith but was denied. The federal charges included forgery, perjury, conspiracy to defraud, the use of forged instruments, using the mail to defraud; added to these was a New York state indictment for grand larceny (Fay et al. 276–78; *Hoax* 309). The trio also owed $1.5 million to McGraw-Hill, the IRS, and their lawyers (*Hoax* 312). Mercury would not be using his wings anytime soon: he was sentenced to two and a half years in prison and served seventeen months. Suskind was sentenced to six months in the New York penitentiary and served five; Edith, who received a two-year sentence with all but two months suspended, had been convicted of forgery in Switzerland, where she was sentenced to two years in jail and ultimately served fourteen months (313).

In *Hoax* Irving ruefully acknowledges that he betrayed Edith and recognizes that he and Suskind had "conned [them]selves again and again" (305, 284). But these mea culpas carry little conviction. "Were we heroes?" he wonders. "Anti-heroes? It puzzled me. Had we been truly *successful,* we might have felt like heroes—although the world would never have known" (304). Ah, there's the rub: in the classic forger's dilemma, Irving *needed* the scam to be exposed so the public could appreciate its "grandeur," its "reckless and artistic splendor" (284). Had it never been disclosed, no one would have appreciated how their "act of anarchy" had shown up "the Establishment . . . in all its corporate myopia, in all its craven worship of the golden calf" (284). These transparently self-serving statements do carry a kernel of truth. Like de Hory's forgeries, the hoax brought to light the fraudulence of experts and illuminated the dark side of an art industry that hides its naked pursuit of wealth behind fine words about aesthetic quality. Insofar as the authors sold the book under false pretenses, Project Octavio was a fraud, but as a cultural critique and a pop cultural phenomenon (see thesis 14), it was a spectacular success. Moreover, not only is Irving far better known for the Hughes hoax than for any of his other books; with his tell-all story, he managed to turn a scandal into another way to earn money. No wonder Welles calls him a "superstar."

W for Wells

At the end of *The Hoax,* Irving writes: "Men wear masks on which they carve portraits of what they would like to be or think they ought to be. Opportunity, like fortune, does not change a man—it unmasks him" (304). This maxim could serve as an epigraph for *F for Fake* and its subjects, including Orson Welles himself, except that their masks only reveal more masks. Early in the film Elmyr paints a portrait of Michelangelo, whom he calls "a great forger." With a flourish, he signs it "Orson Wells" [*sic*]; "Wells" replies that he is "honored." He later calls de Hory "our hero" and compares him to the bullfighter in Hemingway's "The Undefeated." Welles empathized with de Hory's poverty and beleaguered exile and reportedly became depressed when, in 1976, he learned that Elmyr had finally succeeded in killing himself (McBride 7). Welles similarly lauds Irving as holder of the "championship title" in fakery. Yet his praise is tempered by the cold eye he trains on their lies and self-delusions.

Nor does he spare himself: in the middle of the film he recounts his own career in fraud. Welles too was once a hungry painter: at sixteen he drove a donkey cart full of his paintings around Ireland until he sold them all to buy food. Desperate, in Dublin he landed an acting role by pretending he was a "famous star" on Broadway (thereby displaying the necessary qualifications). If that was a "fine case of art forgery," his next "flight into fakery was by flying saucer." Clips from the movie *Earth vs. the Flying Saucers* (1956) provide the visuals as Welles recalls his infamous radio adaptation of H. G. Wells's *The War of the Worlds*, which sent listeners across America into a panic. One unfortunate man who imitated the broadcast in South America even "ended up in prison, so I shouldn't complain, I guess. I didn't go to jail; I went to Hollywood." The dream factory *was* a prison for the former boy genius, a purgatory where producers and studio heads reedited his films, denied funding for others, and eventually drove him into exile.

Welles's most definitive evidence of his own fakery, however, is the film we are watching. For example, at sixty-four minutes Elmyr implausibly denies signing any of his forgeries. Welles cuts to Irving's skeptical face, then back to Elmyr, who looks defiant, then back Irving, wearing a sidelong smirk. He cuts back and forth repeatedly, interspersing freeze-frames and jump cuts, until Irving finally declares, "Of course they were signed." This conversation never happened: Welles edited together shots from different scenes in Reichenbach's documentary to create an imaginary conversation. Yet the sequence doesn't trick us just for trickery's sake: the cutting elicits nuances that "remained undeveloped until he applied his sensibility to the footage" (McBride 12), such as Elmyr's self-delusion and bald-faced lies and Irving's grudging admiration. "I'm a charlatan," Welles told us at the beginning of the film, but this sequence evinces not a charlatan but a sorcerer, a cinematic alchemist who, through cubist montage, spins movie gold "virtually out of nothing" (12).[18]

P for Pablo

"Now at last we come to Oja," Welles proclaims, along with a "reenactment of recent history" in which Kodar, her friend Olaf playing the trombone nearby, repeatedly saunters past Picasso's studio in Toussaint to sunbathe (fig. 21). Numerous shots of Kodar (overcranked to accent her pulchritude) walking in bathing suits are intercut or superimposed over still photos of Picasso, whose piercing eyes stare through blinds (fig. 22). "Was he tempted?" Welles asks, as Picasso's eyes become eyes in

FIG. 21. Oja Kodar, Welles's partner, walking to sunbathe.

FIG. 22. Pablo Picasso peering through the blinds, allegedly gazing at Kodar.

cubist paintings. At last Picasso draws her into his studio. To show that he was a "fast worker" and the collaboration "extremely fruitful," Welles intercuts or dissolves closeups of Kodar's body parts with body parts from cubist paintings, thus demonstrating his own cubism. Twenty-two portraits were "born under that virile brush," all of which the artist gave to Kodar. But when Picasso read that she was exhibiting these works in Paris, he flew there in a rage (Hurricane Pablo is represented through stock shots of tropical storms), only to learn that they were all forgeries.

We're now introduced to Kodar's Hungarian grandfather (who appears as an elderly man in an ascot), an art forger and the world's "least-known genius," who faces off with the world's best-known genius. The Spanish master charges, "She has stolen my pictures"; Grandfather counters, "She has given you a gift." Now Welles assumes the grandfather's part, complete with Hungarian accent, while Kodar speaks Picasso's lines. That is, Welles plays forger while his partner in crime impersonates the famous artist. The duo wear identical black hats throughout the sequence to emphasize that the forger and the master are doubles. Identities proliferate, reflect, and collide, as Welles—actor, forger, and director—confronts Kodar, who not only cocreated this sequence but performs as both Picasso and as his model. "I am not one of anything," says the forger grandpa; "Like you, I am unique." His uniqueness, like Elmyr's, paradoxically derives from his ability to imitate others: his fake Goyas, Manets, Monets, and Picassos hang in museums around the world. But is it art? Apparently so: Grandpa Welles echoes Elmyr by asking rhetorically, "Am I not one of the great painters?" If forging makes him a great artist, then it follows that Picasso, the greatest beneficiary of the corrupt art market, must be a forger. "Do you think I should confess?" asks forger Orson/Grandpa. "For what? Committing masterpieces?" Although Grandfather has burned the fake Picassos, he concludes, "I must believe that art itself is real." Indeed, forgers, like "real" artists, are magicians, alchemists who bring beauty and value to the world.

T for Truth

When this sequence concludes, it is "time for a confession." Our emcee had promised to tell the truth for an hour and that hour is over. "For the past seventeen minutes, I've been lying my head off," he admits. "We've been forging an art story." Of course, that is his job "as a charlatan"—to make the unreal seem real. We are assured that this confession is the truth and that "'Oja Kodar' is her 'real name.'" Except that it is not: her real name was Olga Palinkas. If even this clean breast is smudged, what can we believe? Ah, asks Welles, who wants reality anyway? Reality is "the toothbrush waiting at home for you in its glass, a bus ticket, a paycheck, and the grave." Orson the Magnificent then levitates a man covered by a sheet (allegedly the grandfather) and quotes Picasso: "Art is a lie. A lie that makes us realize the truth." But what is the truth? With Picasso's giant head superimposed over his own tiny silhouette, Welles informs us that Kodar's grandfather never existed. Then he replaces Picasso's head with that of the boy with the key from the beginning of the film. This child delighting in magic tricks is Welles, just as he is the cubist master (and lecher) Picasso, just as he is both Hungarian forgers, the American tycoon, and the tycoon's ventriloquist. The director folds them all into his cubist self-portrait.

Earlier in the film Welles sits before the cathedral at Chartres and contemplates the brevity of human lives. His voice growing quiet and pensive, he intones, "It might be this one anonymous glory, of all things—this rich stone forest, this epic chant, . . . this grand choiring shout of affirmation—which we choose . . . to stand intact, to mark where we have been, to testify to what we had . . . in us to accomplish. . . . Everything must finally fall into the ultimate universal ash. The triumphs and the frauds. The treasures and the fakes. . . . Maybe a man's name doesn't matter all that much." This anthem to anonymity may be touching, but it too is half a feint, one more facet of the director's fractal self-portrait. For it is impossible to watch this film and ignore Welles's physical presence—his bulk, his booming voice, his penetrating gaze—and his dazzling mastery of cinematic techniques. Although Welles deconstructs the distinction between originality and imitation and critiques the cult of artistic brand names, the film advertises its auteur's prowess in every frame. It leaves us "curious about the mystery of Welles's own personality—a personality that has become a work of art in its own right" (Naremore 279). *F for Fake,* in sum, constitutes what Jackson Ayres calls a "complicitous critique" that folds "back upon itself so that it . . . *ironically* reproduces that which it criticizes" (16, italics his). The film's mirrors reflect our eyes as we witness Welles at work, manipulating us through his mastery of cinema's tools of deception while we grapple with the paradoxes of its critique and counter-critique. We cannot help but grasp that this film, itself half a fake, has been definitively authored by Orson Welles (or Wells) as he rotates through his many guises—actor, editor, magician, journalist, raconteur, gourmand (we see him eating several courses at a restaurant), philosopher, bon vivant, fraud—and conglomerates them into a cubist self-portrait. And we cannot help but conclude that although this cubist may be a con artist, he is, above all, an artist.

7

Misrecognizing Harry

THE BLAZING WORLD'S HERMAPHRODITIC POLYPHONY

> Just like unto a *Nest* of *Boxes* around,
> *Degrees* of *sizes* within each *Boxe* are found.
> So in this *World*, may many *Worlds* more be,
> Thinner, and lesse, and lesse by still degree.
>
> —Margaret Cavendish, "Of *Many* Worlds in *This* World"

"ALL INTELLECTUAL and artistic endeavors, even jokes, ironies, and parodies, fare better in the mind of the crowd when the crowd knows that somewhere behind the great work or the great spoof it can locate a cock and a pair of balls" (*BW* 1). This first sentence in Siri Hustvedt's novel *The Blazing World* (2014) conveys the outrage of its protagonist, Harriet ("Harry") Burden. As we have seen in many of the frauds discussed in previous chapters, and as I posit in thesis 6, resentment and indignation are frequently the forger's spurs: unjustly treated, snubbed by a literary or art community consumed by fads and contaminated by money, the fakesmith exacts revenge by proving the experts' fallibility. Harriet Burden's ire impels her to respond to the sexism that has prevented her work from its due acclaim and to escape from the oppressive shadow of her recently deceased husband, the famous art dealer Felix Lord. Her original sin being her gender, Burden conceives *Maskings,* in which she presents three new works under the names of three males.

The first work, *The History of Western Art,* appears as a production of Anton Tish, who is, at twenty-four, an apparent prodigy, but Tish plays little role in the conception or execution of the work. The endeavor drains him dry, after which Burden shucks him off like an old coat. *The Suffocation Rooms,* the second *Maskings* work, is attributed to Phineas Q. Eldridge, a mixed-race drag performer who enthusiastically embraces the trap-hoax and contributes his own dash and panache. So far so good: the project is succeeding in its goal which is, in the words of the novel's purported editor, I. V. Hess, "not only to expose the anti-female bias of the art world, but to uncover the complex workings of human perception and how unconscious ideas about gender, race, and celebrity influence a viewer's understanding of a given work of art" (*BW* 1–2). Burden's diagnosis turns out to be more accurate than she expects: when she claims credit for the project, those same sexist critics and connoisseurs dismiss her. Worse, her third mask, an artist named Rune, declares that Burden is unhinged and that their work, *Beneath,* belongs to him. Both artists die before the truth emerges. Consequently, Harriet is forever snarled in the forger's dilemma: her fakes go undetected, which means that she is denied recognition for her most brilliant contrivance. Harriet dons male identities, paradoxically, in an attempt to enhance her own fame, emerge from her boxed-in history as Lord's widow, and empower herself as a female artist. Given the sexism that she deplores, she should have known that her genitals might doom her experiment. Her uncertain grip on her own identity, however, enables others to subsume it.

Like Burden, Siri Hustvedt conceals her artistry behind other personae—in her case, multiple narrators and texts—literary versions of the boxes, rooms, and dolls that make up *Maskings. The Blazing World* presents itself as an "anthology of voices" (10) that includes selections from Burden's twenty-six notebooks; essays by fictional critics; biographical statements by her lifelong friend, Rachel Briefman, by her children, Maisie and Ethan, and by her lover, Bruno Kleinfeld; recollections from a New Age hanger-on, Sweet Autumn Pinkney; and a letter by one Richard Brickman—actually Harriet's, since Brickman is another Burden mask—all arranged by Hess, an academic of indeterminate gender. Different facets of Harriet shine forth depending on the witness, which suggests that her identity is manifold, multiply gendered, and inextricably social. Like Welles in *F for Fake,* Hustvedt fashions a cubist portrait of the artist; as in Welles's work, behind this multiplicity lies the shaping intelligence of the author, whose identity as such becomes a function of that multiplicity. Harriet's creator, like Harriet, is at once singular and manifold. Thus, like Chatterton, Ireland, Arthur Phillips, and Thelonious Ellison, Hustvedt and Burden find in forgery a means to fashion fresh artistic identities (thesis 2).

Astrid Böger notes that the "problem of (mis)recognition haunts" Hustvedt's oeuvre (282–83) partly because, as Hustvedt has argued in her own essays about art, a work's "meanings are made in the encounter between the viewer and the art object, an experience that is sensual, emotional, intellectual, and dependent on both the attention and expectations of the person doing the looking" ("Louise" 247). A dialectical process transpires through which a viewer or reader ascribes meanings that activate a dormant work; yet each viewer activates different elements and hence views a different work. A viewer or critic inevitably understands a given artefact as issuing from a particular artist and frames it in terms of that artist's previous achievements as well as through the history of the form or genre. What happens when a work is misattributed? Answer: those intertextual and biographical considerations prompt misrecognitions. Though Burden *intends* her works to be misrecognized, she is surprised when the misrecognitions take hold. Whereas Burden seeks recognition incognito, pretending to be a male even as she laments male domination, Hustvedt's invisible narration enables the reader both to realize the truth of Harriet's claims and to recognize her entrapment by them. Hustvedt evades that trap by dramatizing how Harry misrecognizes herself and how her misrecognitions ultimately give way to a truer realization of her artistic aims and allegiances. Harriet's experiment becomes Hustvedt's, as her readers shuffle through these narrative cards in search of a queen who hides her authorship behind other faces. Each iris sees a different Siri.

Dolls

> I'm the gap between what I'd like to be and what others have made me.
>
> —Álvaro de Campos (Fernando Pessoa)

As we have seen in previous chapters, and as I suggest in thesis 9, intertextuality is an indispensable feature of forgeries and their fictions. Both *Maskings* and *The Blazing World* borrow from and build on earlier creations. Some of these are Hustvedt's own novels, which are "centrally concerned with questions of seeing and visual representation" (Däwes 295); like *The Blazing World,* her earlier novels stage the theories of art and perception that she propounds in her nonfiction. If, as Jason Tougaw proposes, those novels focus on "how the artist's tools . . . make new objects from selves" (117), they also reveal how artists make new selves from objects. Hustvedt's fictional artists create portraits of others that are also self-portraits and explore their manifold identities by making subjects, then objects, of themselves. Thus in *The Enchantment of Lily Dahl* (1996) the eponymous protagonist becomes involved with a man named Edward Shapiro, who paints portraits of Lily's townspeople that incorporate small boxes containing biographical vignettes.[1] As the title indicates, dolls play a prominent role in this novel, such as when the character Martin Petersen embodies his confused feelings for Lily by making a life-size doll of her (232). These dolls, portraits, and boxes anticipate Burden's *Maskings,* as do the works of another of Hustvedt's fictional artists, Bill Wechsler, in *What I Loved* (2004).

At the beginning of that novel, we read of Wechsler's *Self-Portrait,* which depicts not him but a beautiful woman (Violet Blom, whom he later marries) being gazed at by someone perceptible only as a shadow (*What* 4). Narrator Leo Hertzberg (an art historian and Wechsler's best friend) has written an essay on Wechsler entitled "Multiple Selves"—aptly, for Wechsler's works presume the sociality of identity, present the artist as multiply gendered, and press the viewer into that gallery of selves. Wechsler's other works, such as *Hansel and Gretel,* which is filled with little rooms (81–83), and *O's Journey,* comprising twenty-six boxes (125), presage Burden's productions. The piece called *The Changeling* offers a "play on identities, replicas, and pastiche" (114), in which a boy is replaced by an identical copy, as part of Wechsler's fascination with "the fake self" (116). The work foreshadows the devolution of Wechsler's son, Mark, who falls under the spell of a shallow shock artist named Teddy Giles, who may have killed a young acolyte and even murdered his own mother by pushing her down the stairs (273). Giles is Rune's forerunner, each one a cynical sensationalist who stands as the central artists' dark double. In one work, Giles destroys Wechsler's portrait of his son by penetrating it with the image of a dismembered woman (*What* 299). Admiring critic Henry Hasseborg writes that Giles embodies a "spectacle of shifting identities that includes the psychopathic killer" (338). But Giles exaggerates and distorts Wechsler's serious efforts to depict multiple and evolving selves: while claiming to comment on violence and commodification, he actually exploits these phenomena for cheap thrills. Whereas

Box 1: Pain

Hustvedt has acknowledged that her "obsessions with rooms, dolls, missing limbs, mirrors, violence, [and] nameless threats" owe much to Bourgeois's work, and each of these features is also evident in Burden's art ("Louise" 247). Hustvedt's Bourgeois is, like Burden, "complex, brilliant, contradictory, fiercely direct at times, but also discreet. . . . Sometimes she wears a mask" ("My Louise" 29). And sometimes she is a doll. For example, Bourgeois's *Structures of Existence: The Cells* series, an obvious model for *Maskings*, consists of twenty-eight separate spaces designed as rooms; some have closets and beds; one is a cage over which looms a giant spider; at least two feature mannequins. Hustvedt writes that this work displays "dolls of loss and mortality. I am looking at myself. I am looking at all of us" ("Louise" 252). If so, then all of us are immured, inchoate, disabled, disfigured. And suffering: Bourgeois states, "The subject of pain is the business I am in. To give meaning and shape to frustration and suffering. . . . *The Cells* represent different types of pain: the physical, the emotional and psychological, and the mental and intellectual" ("Louise Bourgeois" Tate.org). The headless figure in *In and Out* (1995: Figure 23) seems to be writhing in ecstasy or agony; the surrounding mirrors and silver globes multiply the sensation and mystery while injecting a quaint, quasi-Victorian steampunk aura. *Cell XXVI* (2003; see fig. 24), which displays a large cloth mannequin with human legs, is headless in a different way: beginning at the waist, the torso winds around itself like a thick snake or intestine or massive turd—or perhaps ice cream at the crown of a cone. A diaphanous white skirt or slip hangs next to the dangling figure. The writer for Artsy.net points out the "tension between quintessentially male and female forms" and Bourgeois's "recurrent interrogation of the male/female dialectic." That tension pervades *Maskings:* Bourgeois's sexless mannequins anticipate the genderless doll in Burden's *The Suffocation Rooms,* in turn lending Bourgeois's doll additional meanings.

Wechsler uses dolls to delve into the mysteries of human character, Giles merely treats humans as dolls.

The Blazing World also borrows from other artists, because like all forgeries, *Maskings* (and the novel in which it resides) is both an act of creation and an act of criticism. Elements of *Maskings* are adapted from the artwork of Annette Messager and Kiki Smith (Hustvedt has written about both), but the most important female precursor in the visual arts is Louise Bourgeois.[2] To capture Hustvedt's intertextual methods and to honor the spirit of these artists' work, I present brief profiles of these predecessors in text boxes.

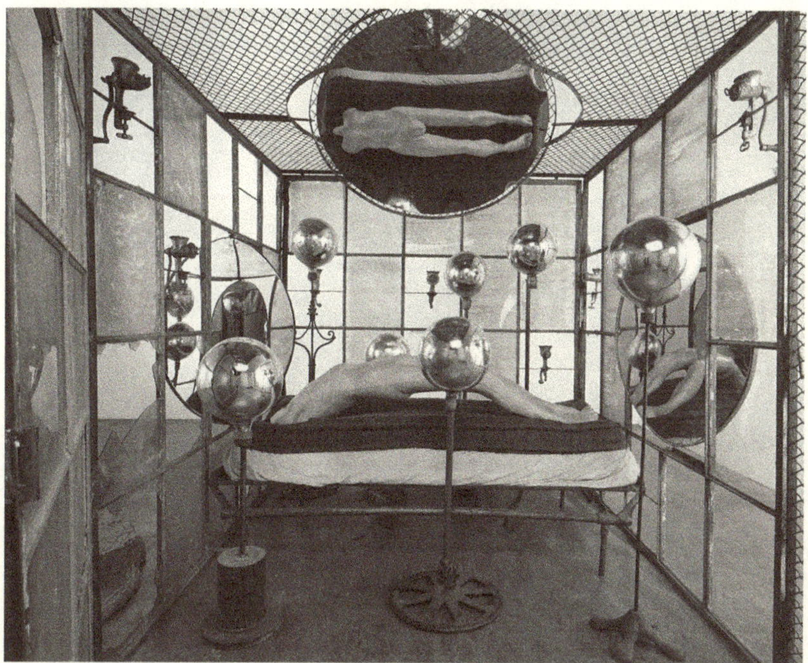

FIG. 23. The headless figure in Louise Bourgeois's *In and Out* (1995) seems to be writhing in ecstasy or agony; the surrounding mirrors and silver globes multiply the sensation and mystery. Metal, glass, plaster, fabric, and plastic. Cell 205.7 × 210.8 × 210.8 cm; plastic 195 × 170 × 290 cm. (© The Easton Foundation/Licensed by VAGA at Artists Rights Society, NY; photo: Christopher Burke)

Hustvedt explains her understanding of Bourgeois's work thus: "We consume other artists, and they become part of us . . . only to be spewed out again in our own works. When mingled with Søren Kierkegaard, the seventeenth-century natural philosopher Margaret Cavendish, Mary Shelley's monster in *Frankenstein,* Milton's Satan, and heaven knows whom else, my chewed-up and digested Louise Bourgeois returned" as Harriet Burden ("My Louise" 30). Shelley and Cavendish, Hustvedt's literary mothers, were pioneers—Shelley among the first English women to make a living by the pen, Cavendish the first important English female scientist and fantasy writer. Shelley's novel is also, according to Burden's friend Rachel, Harriet's "archetypal text, a fable of the self, a scripture for the reality of Harry Burden" (*BW* 51), and Harriet remains "preoccupied by monsters" throughout *The Blazing World* (5). After all, what

FIG. 24. This genderless figure appears to be in pain. Louise Bourgeois, *Cell XXVI* (2003). Steel, fabric, aluminum, stainless steel, and wood, 252.7 × 434.3 × 304.8 cm. (© The Easton Foundation/Licensed by VAGA at Artists Rights Society, NY; photo: Christopher Burke)

is Frankenstein's creature but a colossal animated doll? Hustvedt points out that "Harry is a monster because she does not fit any category, and like Frankenstein's monster, she is always outside looking in" (Becker interview 414). In that regard she herself resembles a forged artwork (see thesis 15)—as with *erasure* and Stagg Leigh. One hears echoes of Thelonious Ellison in this description as well. Nevertheless, if Harriet had reviewed her models' lives and works more closely, she would have anticipated that, as *Frankenstein* dramatizes and as thesis 12 proposes, once a creation is set free upon the world, it escapes its creator's control.

If we read Harriet as Victor Frankenstein (or Shelley) and Rune as her hideous progeny (whether we mean the monster or the novel), we grasp that *Frankenstein* predicts Harriet's plight.

Cavendish, the polymathic, cross-dressing Duchess of Newcastle, wrote, in addition to numerous plays, poems, biographies, and works of natural philosophy, a fantasy entitled *The Description of a New World, Called the Blazing World* (1666), in which a woman becomes empress of a utopian realm. The author's vision of female power starkly contrasts with her real-life reputation as an eccentric attention-seeker known as Mad Madge. Cavendish's work went virtually unread for centuries, due in part to the same sexism that enrages Burden. (I analyze her influence on Burden in Box 5.) By invoking these artistic mothers, Hustvedt both exposes Harriet's incomplete understanding of their achievements and reception and proves herself the superior critic. Yet despite Harriet's mistakes, *Maskings* represents the pinnacle of her career so far. Like the other forgers and fakers discussed in this study, she uses trickery to discover a truer artistic identity. In the aftermath of *Maskings,* nearing death, Harriet embraces Cavendish as an empowering muse, constructing a Brobdingnagian doll who bears within her a city, indeed a world, of human figures. This enormous, pregnant "Blazing World Mother creature" (*BW* 295) signals Burden's movement past *Maskings*' misdirections. The doll obliterates the binaries that have caged Harriet and embodies her endorsement of a more expansively gendered creative identity. This doll does not wear a mask.

Burden and Hustvedt follow the fakesmiths' tradition of fashioning their work intertextually, using real or imaginary predecessors to lend them voices and styles. Thus Chatterton created Rowley, who, in turn, created Chatterton as an author; thus Ireland used Fakespeare to forge his way into a literary career; thus Carey stitches together *Frankenstein* and Ern Malley to craft a fictional hoax; thus Everett depicts his fictional novelist's erasure and empowerment through impersonation; thus Wyatt Gwyon seeks to resurrect Flemish painters, and so on. The fakesmith is not only a fraud; she or he is also a critic, a canonizer, a recreator, and, perhaps most of all, a self-creator. These texts reveal a reciprocal interaction between the forged works and the works inspired by them. The same is true here: Hustvedt mirrors Burden by exploiting her text's multiplicity. The novel's inclusion of (mock) critical essays exhibits how a work's reception eventually becomes inextricable from the work. But Hustvedt is more clever than her character: by incorporating the reception of *Maskings* into the text, she both alerts us to how artworks become social and historical phenomena and anticipates her own novel's reception. Just as the responses to *Maskings* are an essential part of the hoax, so the critical essays about *The Blazing World* (including this one) will add more voices to its choir and become further elements of the work called *Maskings.* In creating her own *Blazing World* and using previous texts as sources of inspiration, Hustvedt calls down a chorus of voices—male and female, queer and cisgender—to compose a symphony of hermaphroditic polyphony that echoes Cavendish's and Shelley's masterworks. By forging her own tribute to Cavendish through Burden, Hustvedt ensures that the blazing world will never stop turning nor its fire die.

Balls

> And yet these fine collapses are not lies
> More than the pirouettes of any pliant cane;
> Our obsequies are, in a way, no enterprise.
> We can evade you, and all else but the heart.
>
> —Hart Crane, "Chaplinesque"

Hustvedt has stated that "*Maskings* is a game, a form of playing and competition" (Becker interview 411), a quality it shares with all forgeries and hoaxes (thesis 11). I would add that *Maskings* is a game of a peculiar sort—a ball game. Burden definitely has balls, in the colloquial sense of courage: she shows enormous bravery in mounting her elaborate hoax at the expense of the art industry. In another sense *Maskings* executes a kind of gender reassignment surgery in which Harriet acquires, by proxy, a cock and balls. A woman who has long been uncomfortable with her assigned gender, Harriet can, through *Maskings,* explore her "masculinity in ways she has never done before" (Becker interview 411). And why not? "I was over the hill and had never had a penis. It was too late for me to go as myself" (*BW* 31). She imagines what people will say behind her back: "That's Felix Lord's wife. She makes dollhouses. Titters." To her face, snark: "I heard that Jonathan took your work because he's a friend of Felix. Plus they needed a woman in the stable" (31). After Felix dies (as the novel begins), she tries to extricate herself from his patriarchal shadow by creating "husband dolls" that might make her the "ruler of [her] own little Brooklyn fiefdom" (26, 27)—a miniature version of Cavendish's empire. One of those dolls—she calls them "metamorphs" (30)—is a life-sized effigy of Felix, a "transitional object" that enables her to emulate Frankenstein (and Shelley) by creating hideous (but in this case) unthreatening progeny (29). Adding edge to her resentment is her awareness that her husband had lovers, male and female, that he barely bothered to hide. "It has nothing to do with you, my love," he once told her. Harriet's response: "I am erased" (140). Felix is one of the unnamed "them" she aims to render impotent.

An earlier, primal source of resentment is her father. In Notebook B she remembers the burdens he imposed upon her. Her friend Rachel recalls that Harriet's father, a professor with a "rigid moral imperative" (48), called her "Harry" because he wanted a son; the name stuck. Harriet understands that although, like millions of men, her father may not have initially wanted a child (or not a daughter), he ultimately came to love her (144). Even so, she cannot shake her original sin and believes something is amiss with her gender. It doesn't help that she grows up to be a tall, strong woman. "Your order is my wilderness, Father. . . . Stifled. I am trying to breathe, but cannot," she writes (145). The title and design of *The Suffocation Rooms* allude to this personal history. Indeed, as (real critic) Susanne Rohr remarks, the entire trilogy is "a reenactment of the original narcissistic wound: You should not be here—and Harry obeys and is not" (253). In seeking to exorcise these patriarchal specters, she expunges herself all over again.

While planning the hoax, Harriet ponders the experiences of real-life gender pioneers such as Dr. James Barry, a nineteenth-century English surgeon who, upon his death, was discovered to have been a woman, and Billy Tipton, a married and apparently male jazz pianist who was also found, after death, to possess female genitalia (*BW* 32–33). What fascinates her about these figures are "perceptions and their mutability, the fact that we mostly see what we expect to see" (33). This principle, as I have observed, applies to all forgeries and fakes. But for Harriet, what matters is not just their gender but others' acceptance of the purported gender. Closer models for Burden's male appendages seem to appear in artists such as George Eliot (Mary Anne Evans) and Currer Bell (Charlotte Brontë)—female novelists who camouflaged their gender (and preempted sexist prejudices) by adopting male pen names. An even closer

Box 2: Tip

Beginning in 1967 James Tiptree Jr. emerged from nowhere to publish strikingly original stories in science-fiction magazines, quickly winning the genre's two most prestigious prizes, the Hugo and Nebula.[3] Tiptree's tales were stereotypically masculine, packed with action and sex, and arrestingly violent and uncompromising; they read like "urgent messages from some haunted house on the corner of Eros and Mortality," according to biographer Julie Phillips (2). Although Tiptree never appeared in public, "Tip" sustained friendly, even intimate, correspondences with several peers, including Robert Silverberg, Harlan Ellison, and Ursula K. Le Guin, as well as with emerging female writers Vonda N. McIntyre and Joanna Russ. In 1972 Tip introduced a female protegee named Raccoona Sheldon, whose work was rejected by the same editors who had published Tiptree. Silverberg wrote an introduction to a 1975 anthology arguing that the stories' "lean, muscular, supple" prose displayed a "prevailing masculinity" and hence must have come from a male (qtd. in J. Phillips 3). In fact, several important Tiptree stories, such as the award-winning novella "Houston, Houston, Do You Read?" and the story "The Women Men Don't See," present provocative feminist themes.[4] Biographical hints Tiptree let slip to an enterprising editor led to the unmasking in late 1976. It turned out that Tip and Raccoona were aliases of Alice Bradley Sheldon, a woman in her fifties, a major in the US Army who had been a painter and a CIA agent and had recently earned a PhD in psychology. Sheldon, known as Alli, borrowed the "flamboyantly anonymous" Tiptree moniker from a brand of jam (J. Phillips 245) and thought of the entire charade, including the stories, as a "goof" (244; see thesis 11). No one was more surprised than she when they sold immediately and garnered enthusiastic praise. Sheldon, who had struggled to write conventional literary fiction in her earlier years (in 1946 she published a story under her own name in the *New Yorker*), found the male guise liberating: unlike Alli, Tip was not a writer who "struggled and bared his soul, but a guy who tossed off low-grade work without thinking about it too hard." Tiptree's fiction possesses not only the authority that Sheldon's lacked; it also displays "the courage to play games . . . to stop trying to be polished and perfect" (J. Phillips 247). Tiptree's shade cooled Sheldon down.

Upon learning her real identity, a delighted Le Guin referred to Sheldon as "my Gethenian Friend," alluding to the dual gendered natives of Gethen, in her classic *The Left Hand of Darkness* (qtd. in J. Phillips 417). But Tip's exposure altered the dynamics of her other literary relationships, alienating some correspondents, attracting others (Russ wrote her a love letter), and angering those who felt she had "robbed them of relative status" (qtd. in Ciuraru 263). Paradoxically, the Tiptree persona had licensed Sheldon to be herself: being Tip was "the first time I could be *really* real," she wrote to Le Guin (qtd. in J. Phillips 426). Tiptree was the "lie who helped Alli to speak the truth" (262). Strikingly presaging Harriet Burden, Sheldon understood that Tiptree had unleashed a "fount of hot lava: fury, red revenge" and wrote in her journal that "Tiptree was 'magical' manhood, his pen my prick. I had through him all the power and prestige of masculinity." He allowed her to "storm naked with hard-on waving thru the world spouting whatever comes" (qtd. in J. Phillips 258, 422, 6). The unveiling also laid bare her lifelong ambivalence about gender and sexuality: Sheldon had nursed unconsummated crushes on women, commented that her biography was "ambisexual" (*BW* 188), and confessed that she lived "in [her] body as in an alien artifact" (J. Phillips 422). With Tiptree unmasked, her work suffered: critics found the new stories vague and slack, lacking their former confidence and authority. Did the exposure of Sheldon's secret render her self-conscious? Or did the absence of that cock and those balls alter editors' and readers' expectations? Did her drug addictions (Benzedrine and Valium) and bipolar condition finally catch up with her (Ciuraru 260)? Phillips concludes, "Tiptree's performance reminds us that if writing must be a mirror of the writer's experience, then it is a funhouse mirror of a madhouse experience" (435). The madhouse didn't close until 1987, when Sheldon shot her ailing husband and then killed herself.

parallel, adduced by Maisie Lord, is that of acclaimed science-fiction author James Tiptree Jr. While preparing a documentary about her mother, Maisie learns Tiptree's fascinating story (*BW* 187).

According to Harriet, Ursula Le Guin realized an important fact when she learned Tiptree's identity: that "when you take on a male persona, something happens." What? "You get to be the father" (*BW* 187). Harry yearns to replace her father by becoming him, impregnating herself, as it were, with an imaginary cock and balls. Thus she protests that she wants "more than a 'George Eliot' as cover. I wanted my own indirect communications à la Kierkegaard" (34). A long-term fascination for Hustvedt, Kierkegaard is another pseudonymous ancestor, though his guises were all male.[5] Upon first reading read *Fear and Trembling* at the age of fifteen, Hustvedt recalls feeling as if she were "possessed by some demon (or angel)" (Becker interview 414), but she didn't register that the putative author was one Johannes de Silentio. Hustvedt describes Harry as a "Kierkegaardian figure. Like S. K. she is too clever, too ironic, too brilliant for her own good and suffers because others cannot understand what she is up to" (Becker interview 414). Indeed, S. K. was less an author than a "family of voices" (Hustvedt, "Kierkegaard" 492). In an appendix to "Concluding Unscientific Postscript," he writes that "in the pseudonymous books there is not a single word by me. I have no opinion about them except as a third party, no knowledge of their meaning except as a reader" (*Essential* 243). In this sly, ambiguous acknowledgment, he asks that critics cite his works by their purported authors and avers that he has merely "cooperated so that the pseudonyms could become authors" (*Essential* 245). Far from their proud artistic sire, he is an "indifferent foster father" (243). And yet his masks—including Johannes Climacus (*Concluding*), Victor Eremita (*Either/Or*), Vigilius Haufniensis (*The Concept of Anxiety*), and (my favorite) Hilarius Bookbinder (*Stages on Life's Way*)—are, writes Mark Taylor, "profoundly, if indirectly, autobiographical . . . , multiple masks that simultaneously conceal and reveal an interiority that sets writing in motion" ("Wounding" 159). His aims mirror Harriet's: to deceive the world "into an understanding of the truth" (Kierkegaard, "Point of View" 472). Hess, the ostensible editor of *The Blazing World,* is Hustvedt's Eremita; just as Kierkegaard dons masks to "probe the truth of subjectivity," so Hustvedt uses heterogeneous voices to explore the "multiple selves she and her readers knowingly and unknowingly harbor" (M. Taylor, "Wounding" 163).[6]

Maisie remembers her mother's kissing the statue of Portuguese writer Fernando Pessoa during a visit to Lisbon (*BW* 23). Since Hustvedt has acknowledged his influence on her thinking ("Kierkegaard's Pseudonyms" 497), it may be illuminating to examine his career briefly (see box 3).

According to Fernando Pessoa's definition of incognito authorship, the first *Maskings* work is pseudonymous, for Anton Tish plays almost no part in its design; after that, the project evolves into something closer to a collaboration with Eldridge before arriving at *Beneath,* a work attributed to Rune that, while deriving mostly from Harriet's ideas, appropriates his practices and exploits his celebrity. *Beneath,* in Pessoa's terms, is heteronymic. Just as *Maskings* borrows from other artists and from the personae of its ostensible creators, so *The Blazing World* harmonizes disparate materials and voices to compose a heteronymic, polyphonic chorus in which Hustvedt—hiding behind Hess and the others, motivated not by rage and resentment but by aesthetic allegiances and axioms—imitates her fictional artist and does her one better.

Writing about the first *Maskings* installation, one of Hustvedt's fictional critics—a "self-important little man" (*BW* 57) named Oswald P.

Box 3: Person(s)

Like Harriet an "artist of multifarious shapes" (*BW* 31), Pessoa (1888–1935) left at his death a vast trove of writings in which he had used more than seventy of what he called "heteronyms."[7] These were not ordinary noms de plume. Rather, Pessoa (whose name means "person" in Portuguese) endowed each heteronymic identity with a "biography, psychology, politics, aesthetics, religion, and physique" ("Fernando Pessoa"), as well as a distinct style. His first heteronym, Charles Robert Anon, was an atheist who wrote in English about philosophical questions (Zenith, "Table" 505). Alberto Caeiro lived most of his life in the country with an elderly aunt; he wrote Imagistic and cubist-inspired poems that were later attributed to a person named Pessoa (Zenith, "Table" 506–7). Ricardo Reis was a doctor and classicist who wrote Horatian odes. Pessoa's most prolific heteronym, Álvaro de Campos, was "a naval engineer, . . . a bisexual dandy who studied in Glasgow, traveled to [Asia] and lived outrageusly in London" ("Fernando Pessoa").[8] In him, Pessoa wrote, he invested "all the emotion that I give neither to myself nor to life" (qtd. in Sadlier 101). Some heteronyms wrote essays on other heteronyms; Caeiro cultivated acolytes, including Campos. Pessoa also published poems and other writings under his "own" name (which were given a negative review by Campos [Sadlier 103]), but the heteronymous poems are, "in terms of feelings and ideas, . . . not like those that [he] would write" (qtd. in Sadlier 74). "A pseudonymic work," he explains, "is, except for the name with which it is signed, the work of an author writing as himself; a heteronymic work is by an author writing outside his own personality: it is the work of a complete individuality made up by him, just as the utterances of some character in a drama would be" ("Fernando Pessoa"). His authority was achieved, paradoxically, by a "subordination of romantic authorship to a kind of ever-changing mimicry or textual performance" (Sadlier 8). If, as Foucault famously argues, an author is the name we give to "the principle of unity" (128), Pessoa was perhaps the most disunited author in the history of literature. As Darlene Sadlier comments, by blurring the boundaries separating influence, imitation, pastiche, and forgery, he "requires his readers to rethink the nature of authorship" (10). If, as I have argued in this book, forgeries challenge conventional notions of creative ownership, Pessoa rendered them meaningless.

Case—displays precisely the sort of dismissive sexism she excoriates. While praising *Beneath,* he deems Harriet's own work "fussy, pretentious" (44). And though he admits to being "as tickled by a great hoax as the next person, an Ern Malley, for instance, or David Bowie and William Boyd's Nat Tate," he dismisses Harriet as the "Queen of Deception."

Box 4: "None Has Survived"

Named after two prominent London museums, Nat Tate is presented as a real but neglected artist in Boyd's eponymous novella-disguised-as-a-biography (1998). The illegitimate son of a New Jersey maid and a seaman, Tate is brought up, after his mother's death, by a wealthy businessman and tutored by a disciple of modernism, Hans Hoffman, who was exhibited by Janet Felzer of the Aperto Gallery. (These persons and places are all fictional.) Adoring the poetry of Hart Crane, Tate creates a series of two hundred drawings based on Crane's magnum opus, *The Bridge,* as well as several triptychs and a series called *White Buildings.* But after visiting the cubist Georges Braque in France, Tate returns to New York disgusted, takes back every picture he has given away or sold and (like Wyatt Gwyon) burns them. Then, imitating Crane, he drowns himself (in Tate's case, by jumping off the Staten Island ferry [Boyd 58]). Of the works in the *White Buildings* series, "none has survived" (Boyd 35).

Tate represents the New York art world of the 1950s (another feature shared with Gwyon). Alas, Boyd writes (tongue firmly in cheek), his drawings are "now almost entirely forgotten" (9). Boyd never gives away the game, even enlisting real artists such as Gore Vidal (who remembers Tate's drunken debauches) and that maestro of masking, David Bowie, to furnish blurbs. The text is interspersed with photos of real artists such as Frank O'Hara and Franz Kline alongside fictional personages, including Tate, most of whose photos are blurry. There is even an acknowledgment to a fictional gallery. Why write such a book? Boyd calls it "a little fable" that is "particularly relevant" to the late 1990s, when "almost overnight, people are becoming art celebrities. . . . My hunch is that lots of these new artists have a talent that's too fragile to sustain the expectations" (Walsh). This is the case with Anton Tish, and the desire to deglamorize such artists is part of what Hustvedt has called Boyd's "sociological experiment" (Becker interview 411). She asserts that the Tate hoax lacked a "philosophical purpose," but here she is mistaken: like the Ern Malley poems, it was designed to discredit a specific genre of modernist art and the aesthetic assumptions that underlie it (qualifying as a trap-hoax [McHale 236]). As John Walsh observes, the hoax was a "blast at callow modernism and conceptualism, and the airs that their practitioners give themselves, . . . an old-fashioned attack on the Nat Tates . . . who throw themselves into avantgardisme without learning basic skills." Boyd states, "There's something lacking in the purely formal. You can analyze what you like about it, but it doesn't amount to very much" (qtd. in Walsh). Boyd's explanation echoes McAuley and Stewart's aims for the Malley forgeries: to dupe critics and prove their inability to distinguish the fabulous from the fraudulent. Harriet Burden's aesthetics are less retrograde, her motives more personal than Boyd's, and her animus against critics and conventions raises the stakes of *Maskings* considerably higher those in the Tate jest.

His double standard notwithstanding, Case is correct that the Nat Tate hoax offers another source and parallel.

Shit

> I'm half a woman, the other half a human being.
>
> —Maj. Alice Hastings Bradley Davey Sheldon, PhD (James Tiptree Jr.)

What *are* the stakes in Harriet's savage jest? And what are her motives? She states them baldly, early in the novel, in a paraphrase of my theses 5 and 6: "A general desire for revenge against twits, dunderheads and fools," emerging from "an ongoing, wrenching intellectual isolation" and a "growing sense that I had always been misunderstood and was madly begging to be seen" (*BW* 35). Burden's later claim that she wanted to test the powers of perception and suggestion is not listed. Of course, the goal of revenge will come to nothing unless she ultimately reveals the truth. Hence, *Maskings* exemplifies a trap-hoax contrived to humiliate its victims (McHale 236). Thierry Lenain would describe it as a "mystification" (41) that, like all hoaxes and forgeries, relies on misrecognition. Whatever we call it, Harriet's fierce obsession leaves little room for twenty-four-year-old Anton Tish's ideas or practices, nor does she bother to foresee how the project might affect him. She selects him mostly because his "distracted air" could be mistaken for sagacity and because he is "stupendously, heartbreakingly ignorant" and therefore exploitable (*BW* 37, 38). But anyone who knows anything about Harriet Burden would see through the lie immediately, for the first *Maskings* installation, *The History of Western Art*, displays an unmistakable feminist agenda.

Case describes its main feature as a "gigantic sculpture of a woman" that alludes to "Giorgione's painting of Venus, finished by Titian" (*Sleeping Venus*, fig. 25), whose "creamy body" is covered with "hundreds of minute reproductions, photographs and texts" drawn from sources as diverse as Diderot, Giorgio Vasari, and the letters of Van Gogh. "RESTRICTED" is etched on her thumb, "PRIMITIVE" scrawled on her forehead (41–42). The work's kinship with the art of Bourgeois and Messager is blatant. For example, Messager's *Désir, désir* displays a drawing of a woman on whose arms are written messages such as "a me désir."[9] Bourgeois's *Femme Maison* (1994, a reworking of a 1947 piece) depicts a nude female figure of white marble whose head has been replaced by a

FIG. 25. The primary feature of Harriet Burden's *The History of Western Art* is a sculpture based on this painting, *Sleeping Venus*, by Giorgione da Castelfranco (Titian), (1508/10). Oil on canvas, 108.5 × 75 cm. (© Gemaeldegalerie Alte Meister/Art Resource, New York; photo: Hans-Peter Klut)

house (fig. 26). Case sneers at the "all-too-predictable feminist critics" (*BW* 42) who notice a reproduction of a self-portrait by female Renaissance painter Sofonisba Anguissola in the sculpture's armpit (fig. 27). And there is another "person" in the room, a "male mannequin dressed in a navy two-piece suit and red tie with his hands behind his back" eyeing the Venus (42). This may be a Felix doll or perhaps a generic male observer of the type who pretends to be an art connoisseur so that he can ogle pictures of naked women.

Scattered around the female figure are seven hefty wooden boxes, each containing a story told via dolls in discrete rooms or cells. Story 3, which presents a large woman whose head touches the ceiling, alludes to *Alice in Wonderland,* as does Story 4 with its "disturbing fuzzy animal" (43)—the white rabbit? Perhaps the woman is Alice Sheldon, who underwent a transformation at least as profound as any that Carroll's plucky heroine endures. Story 5 presents a bathroom, its tub full of filthy brown water; the female metamorph from Story 3 hunkers on the floor, clutching the portrait of the child seen in Story 2. In Story 6, the same tub (dark ring lingering) rests on a floor piled with tiny books, one of which is marked

Fig. 26. Harriet Burden's *History of Western Art* is indebted to works such as this one. Louise Bourgeois, *Femme Maison* (1994). Marble, 12.1 × 24.2 × 7.6 cm. (© The Easton Foundation/Licensed by VAGA at Artists Rights Society, NY; photo: Christopher Burke)

"M.S. 1818" and which leaks a "embryonic gelatinous something": Mary Shelley and her hideous progeny (43). Story 7 seems to summarize the origins of this work and even hints to the savvy viewer its real provenance. Two-dimensional figures of a man and woman lie next to each other on a rug; a boy in an open doorway observes them, while holding a portrait of a girl over his head. Is this girl the boy's mask? Something like that: etched inside the large female metamorph is a quotation from Djuna Barnes's novel *Nightwood* (which has a major cross-dressing or transgender character): "*The last doll, given to age, is the girl who should have been a boy, and the boy who should have been a girl!*" (70, italics in original). The work is provocative, complex, and enigmatic, yet most viewers would discern themes of confinement, contamination, creativity, and queerness as well as its overt feminist message. Would a twenty-four-year-old straight male create such a work? Unlikely.

FIG. 27. In the armpit of the sculpture of *Sleeping Venus* is a reproduction of a self-portrait by Anguissola, perhaps this one. Sofonisba Anguissola, *Self-Portrait, Painting the Madonna* (1556). Oil on canvas, 66 × 57 cm. (Muzeum Zamek w Lancucie; photo: Erich Lessing/Art Resource, NY)

Writing years later, Case asserts that Harriet "bought and paid for" Tish and his successor, Eldridge, and that without her "bags of money" neither one would have agreed to participate (44). That is definitely not true of Eldridge, and probably not of Tish. In fact, Tish signs on eagerly when he realizes he will receive all the proceeds from sales and enthusiastically embraces her aim to investigate why "people see what they see" and to expose how expectations determine that vision (57–58). According to Rachel, the work prompts one to ask, "Without the imprimatur of high culture, hipness, or celebrity, what remained? . . . Had there ever been a work of art that wasn't laden with the expectations and prejudices of the viewer or reader or listener?" (104). Welles poses the same questions in *F for Fake* and arrives at the same answer: of course not. Tish tells Sweet Autumn Pinkney, one of the young strays whom Harriet picks up and houses, that Harriet is "like another mother" to him, parroting her contention that art "shouldn't be about names or about selling; it should lead you somewhere better on your path to higher understanding" (96). Is humiliating critics a path to higher understanding? It seems more like the low road. Still, Harriet's prediction comes true: "When presented as the work of a man, their art suddenly found an enthusiastic audience" (69). Because of Anton's youth, gender, and terse responses to interviewers' questions, the art world swallows "the Tish shit whole" (57). (She persuaded him to change the spelling of "Tisch" to create the anagram.)

Is Tish merely a "puppet," as (fictional) critic Rosemary Lerner opines (69)? If so, what does Pinocchio think about the project? At first he does resemble a marionette and seems mostly grateful to receive a "crash course in Western art" (105). But then, as so often happens with forgers and hoaxers, he starts to believe the lies and presumes that he "richly deserve[s] . . . praise" (105). As Sweet Autumn notices, his "vibes [go] completely weird": initially puffed up with self-importance, he undergoes a crisis of confidence and identity, complaining to her that he feels like a "reflection in one of those fun-house mirrors" (98, 99). Tish plays "a vital role in the theater [Harriet] had staged for a single viewer: herself," but once the play concludes, the actor finds himself voided (106). No longer able to believe in his own talent and incapable of making his own art, Tish begins to fray: when he looks in the mirror he sees Harry (108). Tish angrily cries, "Without me, none of this would have happened" and denounces her "learning, [her] esoteric crap; it's worth nothing out there" (107, 108). Instead of making his name, *The History of Western Art* unmakes him. But Harry sees that success has transformed this ingenuous youth into a "smug, deluded, pompous creep"—a shit. "I created a monster," she sighs (109, 108), never acknowledging that she has stolen his soul. Burden has emulated not Mary Shelley but Victor Frankenstein, who abandons his artificial offspring. As Rachel astutely points out, Harriet wanted an "empty male vessel," but "Anton was not hollow" (111): unlike Pinocchio, he was already a real boy. Ironically, Harriet even becomes envious of her cock-and-balled doll (111). In many ways she merits the anagram on his name more than he does.

Breath

> What I need is a voice as piercing as the glance of Lynceus, as terrifying as the groan of the giants, as sustained as a sound of nature, as mocking as an icy gust of wind, as malicious as an echo's heartless taunting, extending in range from the deepest bass to the most melting high notes, and modulated from a solemn-silent whisper to the energy of rage. That is what I need in order to breathe.
>
> —"Tested Advice for Authors," by A, edited by Victor Eremita, *Either/Or, Essential Kierkegaard*

Queer and racially mixed (black mother, white father), John Whittier has adopted the name Phineas Q. Eldridge to perform in drag. Or rather, in "'half drag,' half man, half woman, half white, half black, cut straight down the middle, and the two parts of him have conversations onstage" (*BW* 60). Arguments between the halves—Hester and Lester, modeled on his parents—engender much of his shows' entertainment. His act also seems to embody Harriet, who carries on arguments among her various selves in her notebooks and whose gender orientation has always been fluid. As someone who is "pretty much all hyphen" (128), Eldridge is an ideal partner for her next project, *The Suffocation Rooms:* as he asks rhetorically, "Hadn't I known what it felt like to be smothered?" (122). Harriet too has experienced firsthand how "fathers, teachers, and lovers *suffocate* women's reputations" (132, italics in original). A much happier couple than Burden and Tish, they form a "comedy team" that sometimes appears in costume as two men, sometimes as two women, and sometimes as a man and woman. Harriet exults that she has found "the real playmate [she] wanted" as a kid (124). Phineas's gender games also afford her a chance to experiment further with her Harry-ness, while she permits Phineas to fashion an "altogether butchier" identity: he borrows some of Harriet's conventionally masculine expressions and gestures when the work is exhibited (126).

The installation consists of seven small, nearly identical rooms, each housing a male and a female metamorph, a table, chairs, cups, and dishes. It is an ordinary kitchen—except that each room grows a little hotter as one proceeds, and the single "window" is actually a mirror ("more claustrophobic that way"). As the temperature increases (the final room feels like a "Finnish sauna"), so does the size of the objects, such that when the viewer reaches the seventh room "the scale of the furniture had turned you into a toddler" (123). Meanwhile, the metamorphs grow larger and darker, and each room becomes shabbier and more worn. (This is one of Phineas's contributions.) Visitors undergo an unsettling process of shrinking and aging simultaneously, as if growing older and younger at the same time. (The allusion to *Alice in Wonderland* is palpable.) *The Suffocation Rooms* seems to exemplify Hustvedt's thesis about Louise Bourgeois: that aggression and a desire for vengeance can be "refashioned and made into art, into cells, into rooms that summon in the viewer both prisons and biological bodies, bodies that love and age, but that escape the actual, mortal body of the artist herself" ("My Louise" 32). The installation also contains a box—a large, beaten-up trunk that stays the same size in each room but gradually opens as one moves through the exhibit. Emerging from it is a "hungry child" or "demon"—a skinny, transparent, "hermaphroditic" (tiny breastlets and wee penis) life-size doll with frizzy red hair (125). By room seven, the demon has exited the box to sit by the window/mirror; the soft and now immense metamorphs have turned to gaze at the being, who recalls Wechsler's *The Changeling* (*BW* 131). (Harriet is said to love Wechsler's work.) What does it mean? Phineas cagily asserts that "it means what you think it means" (125), but most critics think it means something about Phineas. Its reception proves Harriet's argument that people see what they expect to see and miss what they don't expect: not one viewer notices that on the wallpaper is written "*Phineas Q. Eldridge is really Harriet Burden*" (129, italics in original). Such "inattentional blindness," as Harriet calls it, renders her invisible. Yet according to Phineas, *The Suffocation Rooms* is a "self-portrait" of "Harry crawling out of that box—thin-skinned, part girl/part boy little Harriet-Harry" (130).

"Phinny and I: PH," Harriet writes, "make an *F* sound together, as in *phuck you*" (141, italics in original). This is, indeed, the underlying message conveyed by all three *Maskings* works. Alas, nobody gets the message. Harriet's son Ethan writes a cryptic sketch that predicts how *The Suffocation Rooms* will be interpreted. "When C [the viewer] looks at B [the artwork], C does not view A [the artist]. A is not present as body, but as an idea that is part of the body of C. . . . A has become one of the signs to designate B." What happens when A vanishes as both body and sign and is replaced by D (a different artist)? The artwork changes because "the idea in the body of C when observing B is now D rather than A. . . . C now understands B through the sign D" (135–36). The sign D also makes B much more valuable because B's presence enhances the self-image of the owner, who appropriates it to enrich her own symbolic capital. To put it more succinctly: the viewer's knowledge of, or beliefs about, the artist are inextricable from the viewer's response to the work. As we have seen, a forgery or fake is only as good as the story of origins that accompanies it, and Phineas embodies a powerful narrative. He is, after all, a performer, and even more obviously than other forgeries, *The Suffocation Rooms* is a performance. As Lenain notes, a fake is a "mirror-image of an expectation" (314), and those expectations dictate its reception. Thus, in his review in *Art Beats,* the fictional critic Patrick Dornan opines that the "eerie intersex person rising out of the seven chests speaks directly to the LGBT community" (*BW* 197). Blinded by theory (Guattari) and by his fixation on "Eldridge's life as a queering performer," imaginary critic Zachary Dortmund seems not even to have looked at the work itself (199). The reviews perfectly bear out Harriet's views; they also dramatize how the trace paradigm dominates, and perhaps disables, art criticism. As was obvious in *The Recognitions* and *F for Fake,* forgeries imperil the founding principles of the art industry.

As Harriet's comrade in arms, Phineas believes in the project and in its "eventual revelation, in payback day, in vindication" (191). Bruno, however, argues that Harriet's "philosophical game about perception is just a cover for [her] insecurity" (148). As with Ireland, Chatterton, and Bob McCorkle, a fake helps Harriet fabricate a new foster father; in her case, the father is Harriet Burden. She bets everything on the impact of her ultimate revelation, for without it, the entire experiment seems an exercise in self-sabotage: How will erasing herself earn her greater recognition? Is her exploitation of Tish a form of feminist payback or merely a reversal of the power play, with herself as oppressor? And if such exploitation is unfair to women, why is it fair when the valences change? Ironically, the woman protesting against patriarchy has imbibed its procedures and assumptions so completely that she fails to grasp the insight her own work yields: that great art evolves out of a larger system of intertextuality, collaboration, and interdependence. Harriet cannot admit that, like *The Blazing World* itself, *Maskings* is multiply authored, multiply gendered—or nongendered, like the metamorph emerging from the box. This is the new self that Harriet cannot adopt. Instead, her sardonic curse bounces back: she inadvertently "phucks" herself over.

Walls

> I'm the empty stage where various actors act out various plays.
>
> —Bernardo Soares (Fernando Pessoa), *The Book of Disquiet,* Text 299

"Rune had *it,*" writes Phineas (*BW* 130). He arrives with a "ready-made aura" and a reputation as a sensational subversive. His latest work, *A New Me,* presents multiple before-and-after ads, along with some "during" images displaying flayed skin, blood-soaked gauze, and physicians bent over cadavers (133). Ethan calls it "a pandering piece of shit for the stupid class" and asserts that his father "would have hated it" (133)—thereby inadvertently giving his mother another reason to enlist Rune. Harriet is attracted to Rune's "talent for manipulation, his persona," and for what he has accomplished with "bluster and swagger and drive" (161)—qualities she lacks, along with those male genitals. Harriet wants a mirror, and Rune does at first seem to be little more than a reflecting surface for whatever meanings his audiences want to impose. For example, he shares her opinion of the art world as a "stink hole of vain poseurs who bought names to launder their money" (164). By harnessing his star power, she aims to "prove how the machinery work[s], how ideas of greatness make greatness" (162). She even delights in his "name made of stone" (200). But that stone turns out to be very hard: Rune hides his real intentions and core self (if he has one) behind impenetrable walls. Harriet fails to realize that those involved in the star-making machinery don't want to bare its workings, lest they be exposed as frauds. She is convinced she can manipulate Rune to enhance her own symbolic capital and sate her "greed for recognition" but neglects to take into account Rune's insatiable appetite for celebrity (151).

Almost entirely a creature of surfaces, Rune proudly asserts that he fights "against every trace of originality" in his work (169). He spouts apothegms from various philosophies without understanding them and reads J. G. Ballard and Philip K. Dick without grasping the ideas behind their works; as with Andy Warhol, it is unclear whether Rune is satirizing celebrity culture or simply exploiting it. One of his earlier works, *The Banality of Glamour* (he has not read Hannah Arendt), used facial morphing technologies to alter his features in a series of videos showing him doing ordinary tasks. According to Case, who writes a hagiography of Rune after the artist's death, he was "a fabulist" who "reinvented himself again and again" and was thus a "man of our time, creature of the media and of virtual realities, an avatar walking the earth, a digitized being. No one knew him" (177). That is deliberate: Rune shares different versions of his biography with each interviewer so as to remain as mysterious as the letters that give him his name. Thus we hear three different iterations of a childhood incident in which someone murdered a litter of kittens. In the version Rune recounts to Case, Rune's father killed them, much to his and his sister Kirsten's dismay (181). Later Rune tells Harriet that his mother killed the cats, but Kirsten insists that Rune did it (311). Rune recalls (in Case's version) that he decided right then that "I wasn't going to be me anymore," that his family members would see "Rune Two, Rune Three, or Rune Four, but never Rune One" (182). He is a castle made of stone; the walls around his inner being are thick and unbreachable, perhaps even by himself. Given the tortuous nature of the path to his core, it makes sense that his collaboration with Harriet produces a labyrinth.

Most people would not try to grip such a slippery eel, but Harriet quixotically schemes to borrow Rune's "trickster self," crowing, "Look at me, a Prometheus" (203). Like that other modern Prometheus, Harriet is blinded by overconfidence and unprepared when Rune, like Frankenstein's creature, turns on her. She believes Rune will be her Kierkegaardian "Johannes the Seducer: terrible, sly, brilliant mask" (201). He is a seducer, all right, but not in the way she hopes, and his sociopathic qualities are amply displayed in these seductions. He flirts with Maisie before cruelly showing her a key that, he insinuates, proves that he and Felix were lovers (194). Rune claims to find Harriet's ideas "outdated" in this "postfeminist age of gender freedom" (219) but participates avidly with her in a disturbing gender-inverting game. Donning masks, she becomes Richard Brickman—as in "hard" and "dick"—while he plays Ruina, a "shrinking pinky of a girl," to act out stereotypical gender roles (222). Richard says, "You disgust me. You sound like a kicked dog"; Ruina whines and cringes. Richard grabs Ruina by the shoulders, shakes her like a rag doll and smacks her face; Ruina laughs (223–24). Play over. Afterward, Harriet is ashamed of her performance, and more so when she watches a soundless video of the performance. Muted, the game resembles an erotic dance—as indeed it was.

The masquerade also dramatizes some important ideas about Harriet and about art frauds. First, as we have seen, forgeries are performances in which the forger/actor unearths hidden elements of his/her identity (see thesis 11). It excites Harry that Rune elicits what has "been in her for a long time but had never been let out" (237)—the "dark thing" that "is in [her] as Richard Brickman. And Rune knows this" (232). Second, a mask—as Wilde famously observed and as we have witnessed in Chatterton, Chubb, Pessoa, Ellison, and Tiptree—enables its wearer to say or embody truths otherwise inexpressible. Their game allows Harriet to confront "*ruthless, cocky, loud, cold, superior, cruel, dismissive, and untouchable*" parts of herself (238, italics in original). These parts she has coded as male, indicating her ultimately conventional, binaristic understanding of gender. Their masque, however, demonstrates that gender is always a mask. More troubling is its revelation that such role-playing is risky because the role may consume the person playing it—as with Chubb and Monk Ellison. Lastly, the game reminds us that any creative work—be it novel, art installation, or play—produces a dialogue among creator(s) and audience that gradually alters the unfolding work while reshaping the creator as well as the viewer or reader. Harriet says to Rune, "We are all a ménage" (230), but (unlike Hustvedt) she underestimates the repercussions of this principle. As Tougaw aptly puts it, for Hustvedt "identity is relational, but its relations can be dangerous" (131).

If Richard and Ruina's dance is a game, so is *Beneath,* the work their collaboration yields. The viewer enters a labyrinth with high, milky-colored walls and passages that grow narrower and narrower. The windows are landmarks; slight changes from one window to the next mark the observer's progress. As Phineas comments, "Harry had cleverly designed an art object that forced people to pay attention to it because if they didn't, they'd never get out of the blasted thing" (246). One window shows "two full-face caramel-colored masks with big empty eyes," gauze, a black crayon, and a piece of lined white paper (246); sometimes the masks metamorphose minutely from room to room. Inset in the walls are "window films." In the first, Rune sits motionless with a cup of coffee. A camera moves slowly past charred cars in the second, and in the third, it pans over a shoe-store window, its wares covered with the "pale dust of 9/11." The fourth features "large snowflakes [that] fall slowly onto a wet sidewalk" (247). As we proceed through the exhibit, cracks in the walls appear, becoming more plentiful as we near the exit. Peepholes are drilled into the walls of the dead ends. One contains a small TV screen in which two black-masked figures stand face to face.

They dance, moving faster and faster until they trip and fall. The male pulls the woman up, but she fights him (replaying the Richard/Ruina masque). In the other peepholes the same scene is recapitulated and extended: after the woman collapses, the man continues his "lunatic waltz, but his once-solid human partner has been replaced by a spineless rag doll" (248). The man shakes the doll, throwing off its mask and cap to reveal a "Ms. Nobody." The third screen repeats this scenario, but after the man leaves, the doll reconstitutes herself and levitates, fashioning a "fairy tale ending."

Mark Taylor notes that, "staged as an elaborate con game, *Beneath* lies," for it is "'about' nothing, 'about' a void whose opening is simultaneously the impossibility and possibility of wounding words" ("Wounding" 174). But is it really about nothing? The window films comment on the complacency about others' suffering that prompted the 9/11 attacks. The black-masked dancers enact a scene of misogynistic violence that engenders transfiguration when the female doll rises above her box. Or does it depict her death? The title—which seems ironic, given Rune's fixation on surfaces—first elicits and then critiques the viewer's voyeuristic peeping into these private worlds. Beneath *Beneath,* then, as in Bourgeois's work, are more layers. Those layers lie within Harriet as well, for she has built walls between her life as Mrs. Lord and her burgeoning artist selves; between her longing for respect as a genuine artist and the questionable means with which she pursues it; between her male and female avatars. Like *The Suffocation Rooms, Beneath* also offers an allegory of its own creation, the dance cluing in the perceptive viewer to the collaborative nature of the work. Indeed, it reveals how Harriet-as-Richard intends to use and discard Ruina; perhaps unwittingly (for Harriet, though probably not for Rune), it also predicts the next turn of the screw—Rune's betrayal. It is unclear how many viewers penetrate these enigmatic surfaces, but no matter: the installation is a hit.

The time seems ripe for Harriet to rip away the masks. She does so, paradoxically, by donning another. Writing as Richard Brickman, she publishes a letter in an obscure art journal called *The Open Eye* that exposes the truth about *Maskings.* Footnoted and written in a plausible pastiche of academese, Brickman's letter states that Burden explains the hoax thus: "I wanted to see how the reception of my art changed, depending on the persona of each mask" (252). She describes the "masculine enhancement effect" (252) produced by awareness of male genitals that motivated her to resort to a "*mental codpiece.*" Sarcastically, s/he hails "*the fictional rod, the magic wand that opens eyes onto unseen worlds*" (253, italics in original). Brickman notes that critics have read *The Suffocation Rooms* through Eldridge's biography and observes that Harriet "furiously" denies "hard binary [gender] oppositions" (254), a denial partly belied by the contrivance behind *Maskings.* Burden "staunchly maintains" that the masks "allowed her greater fluidity as an artist, an ability to locate herself elsewhere" and to "live out 'a liberating duplicity and ambiguity.'" Each mask becomes a "hermaphroditic self" that belongs to neither participant alone but constitutes a "mingled reality created between them" (255–56). The entire project, then, is a "*performance narrative*" (italics in original) and as such "includes the reviews, notices, ads, and commentary the shows have generated," which she terms "the proliferations" (256). Indeed, this very letter, Brickman acknowledges (without admitting that he doesn't exist) is one of them. As Hess explains later, Brickman is "another character in the larger artwork," a player in the "philosophical comedy" that is *Maskings* (259).

Smash

> To create, I've destroyed myself.
>
> —Bernardo Soares (Fernando Pessoa), *The Book of Disquiet,* Text 299

Like Annette Messager (according to Hustvedt), Harriet believes she has "found [her] identity" through invented characters; and like Pessoa, Harriet turns her art into "a form of theater," a "deadly serious game" (Hustvedt, "Messager" 292, 297). The letter, the philosophy, the provocative works: everything goes as planned. But Harriet forgets an important truth about forgeries and hoaxes—indeed, about all artistic creations—one presented in thesis 12 and enacted repeatedly in this study: that, as (real critic) Jonathon Keats puts it, "out in the world, a fake takes on a life of its own, which even the counterfeiter cannot control" (27). And so Rune steals the credit for *Beneath* and he is believed. Years later, Hess interviews (fictional) critic William Burridge, who inadvertently shows why. Dismissing "Harriet Lord" as a "man-hating flake" (*BW* 258), he deems Rune "dazzling" (260). His vicarious bromance blinds him to whatever doesn't fit his idolatry; hence he never questioned Rune's description of Burden as "*delusional*" (259, italics in original). Proving

Harriet's point, he finds in the work what he expects to find—Rune's ideas and methods, not Harriet's. He adheres to this belief even after Hess reminds him that Harriet described the entire scheme in her private journals: Why would she lie there? Hess maintains that *Beneath* was a collaboration that altered Rune's art and that he could not have created his final work, *Houdini Smash,* without it. Burridge insists that "the woman was not all there," unaware that he is describing her role in *Maskings* (262)—present but invisible, there but not there. This interview bears out Harriet's contention that male critics celebrate the cock and balls, even when they can't see them. Burridge has been infected by the virus of credulity which, in this case, is a sexually transmitted disease. By his lights, Harriet is as crazy as Mad Madge.

Furious and disgusted by Rune's betrayal, Harriet confronts her errant partner. In Notebook O she narrates the encounter in the second person, thereby suggesting how this partnership has alienated her from herself and stripped her even of the power of narration. During the confrontation Rune shows her a video of himself sitting beside Felix. This cruel blow lands with gloves: he assures her that her late husband thought her brilliant (277). Rune then produces the key he had shown Maisie. "I attract you, don't I?" he taunts, before suggesting a new game—"We could play Richard and Felix. . . . Or we could play Rune and Felix. You could be me"—and then dropping his bomb: Felix "liked to watch." "We could pretend he's watching. . . . Did he know your secret? You are Ruina, aren't you, Harry? I was playing you, a repugnant, sniveling, insecure little cunt" (278). A devastated Harriet writes, "I will remember [those words] as long as I live." But Rune isn't finished. He sneers that *Beneath* would have been nothing if her name had been on it, then "pretends" to strangle her. "When he moved his hands to your throat and squeezed gently and said he was just playing around, where was your rage then, Harry?" she asks herself (279). She is a "silent child made of stone"; Rune's name has obliterated hers. He will even use his knowledge of her breakdown after Felix's death to refute her claims of authorship. *Beneath* is "mine now," Rune gloats. "You lift up one mask and you find another. Rune, Harry, then Rune again. I win" (280).

Like Wyatt Gwyon, Harriet has made a "Faustian bargain" in which, according to Bruno, her "great white hope [has] turned into Beelzebub" (288). "He's climbed inside me," she confesses. A superior fakesmith, Rune even trumps the Brickman letter via an interview in the more prestigious *Art Assembly,* where he "generously" states that he "*think[s] of her as a muse,*" while admitting that she is "*a little confused from time to time*" (289, italics in original). Harriet goes berserk with rage, throws furniture, leaves screeching messages on Rune's voice mail. Phineas attests to her creation of *The Suffocation Rooms.* None of this topples Rune's wall of lies. Ironically, Harriet has hidden her authorship so well that not even her assistants know the truth (290). "Her life's work had been ruined," Bruno laments, her carefully laid construction of "one beautiful irony on top of another—which would prove once and for all her theories about sex bias and perception"—has turned to rubble (291). Later he observes Harriet's second confrontation with Rune. When Rune mocks her by playing Harry-as-Ruina and "swishing like a fairy," she knocks him down (293); her violence only bolsters Rune's claim that she is unhinged. Indeed, her entire project seems perversely self-sabotaging. Harriet cannot be blamed for Rune's cruelty, cynicism, and lies. But if Denis Dutton is correct that a forgery is an artistic crime because it misrepresents achievement (181), then Rune has in effect called her out on her own ethical transgression. Having already violated the implicit promise that the name on a work is the actual artist's, she can scarcely claim that her hands are clean. She has made it too easy for him to turn the tables on her: condemnation comes off as hypocrisy. Because of Rune's lies, her project lies in ruins.

Then Rune dies.

In true Runean fashion, his death is captured on video in an artwork about himself. A maze structure akin to the one in *Beneath,* this final work, *Houdini Smash,* looks as if it has "fallen in on itself," like a ruined (or Runed) fragment of the earlier work (303). Rune crawls into a coffin-like space, smokes a cigarette, then downs a handful of pills. Covering his face with a mask identical to those in *Beneath*'s windows, he lies back and gazes into a camera. We watch his transubstantiation into a machine: an immense helmet is fitted over his head, and the metallic limbs protruding from the coffin begin to move, gradually becoming more animated. Multiple cameras record the action from various angles; he sleeps as the recordings continue. The next day Rune is found dead inside the machine. Formerly the monster to Harriet's Frankenstein, Rune has become his own hideous progeny in a "horror narrative in which doctor and monster merge" (304). He even foresaw this development in the interview cited above, when he predicted that "the artist will no longer control his art" (303). According to fictional critic Timothy Hardwick, *Houdini Smash* dramatizes the truth that all art is a "'container' for death" that nonetheless lives on after its creator perishes (304).

Is his death intentional? Hardwick believes that staging his own demise as a sensational exhibit would be entirely in character for Rune. He even trumpets *Houdini Smash* as the advent of the "ego machine," a "technology that will radically transform the meaning of creativity because artists will generate art objects that have self-models" (302–3). But in an interview conducted eight years later, Rune's sister Kirsten aims to set the record straight, to portray her brother as a human rather than an automaton. She recalls that even as a child he lied frequently and forged school excuses; she also remembers that it was he, not his parents, who murdered the kittens (307, 308, 312). When their father died after a fall down the stairs, Rune had asked her, "How do you know I didn't push him?" (314).[10] He protested later that he was only teasing—"You must think I'm the devil. You think I could kill my own father?" (315)—but Kirsten was deeply disturbed and frightened. She is not sure whether he committed suicide but points out that their mother killed herself by taking pills (317). He may have engineered a trap he could not escape, but his defeat is also a victory, for *Houdini Smash* is, indeed, a smash.

Harriet is never mentioned in his obituaries or career retrospectives: her "obliteration [is] total" (298). Like Rune's, her "shining vehicle" has "crashed before it reached its destination." Albeit still a "big, fat, unrecognized nobody," Bruno comments, she "had been more right than she had even known" (298). Harriet realizes that Rune has checkmated her. "He has made the last move, and he has done it in a contraption that steals from *Beneath*, and now he is sanctified" (326). At long last she recognizes her misrecognitions: "I sabotaged myself without knowing it, didn't I? It was as if I had to follow the game to its end, to wind up in that room with Rune and the dead Felix and be threatened, slapped, and humiliated, to be turned back into a cowering, ashamed child who cannot speak up" (326). Rune, she comprehends, was a symbol "of [my] hatred, [my] envy, [my] fury" (327). Felix has won, too, for Rune stands as "the sign of all the boys Felix showed and Felix loved and Felix made famous" (328). A few months after these recognitions, in October 2003, Harriet is diagnosed with stage four ovarian cancer; by April she is dead. A woman named Harry who camouflaged her creative powers behind a cock and balls succumbs, ironically, to a disease of the female reproductive organs. "Well, lady," she writes in Notebook T, "here is your fitting chastisement, the ironical twist in a life lived partly behind male masks" (334). The final words in that notebook read (quoting *Paradise Lost*), "I am multitudes. This earth a spot, a grain an atom. . . . Even my thoughts are not my own anymore" (340).

Monster

> . . . . *Matter* a *Braine* must make;
> Figure must draw a Circle, round, and small,
> Where in the midst must stand a Glassy Ball,
> Without Convexe, the inside a *Concave,*
> And in the midst a round small hole must have,
> That *Species* may passe, and repasse through,
> *Life* the *Prospective* every thing to view.
> —Margaret Cavendish

Beneath is not Harriet Burden's last work. Her final artistic endeavor embodies her evolution beyond the trickery and betrayals of *Maskings* and toward a more empowering brand of hermaphroditic art. Her model is Margaret Cavendish, who in mid-seventeenth-century England wrote a series of innovative works that have recently been rediscovered, analyzed, and celebrated. Cavendish is a striking exemplar of a woman ahead of her time, not only for being one of the world's first female scientists but also for her unorthodox treatment of gender in her life and writings. These latter she called "Paper Bodies"; they are the "breathing works" that most inspire Harry Burden (329).[11] Before the Rune catastrophe, Harriet begins conceiving of a "house-woman" who would "have an inside and an outside, so that we can walk in and out of her." She intends to call her "*The Blazing World* after the duchess" who "made a spectacle of herself" (207). As Harry's health declines in the wake of Rune's betrayal, she returns to this project and fashions a metamorphic monster, a "huge, grinning, naked, heated-up, pregnant mama with her hanging boobs squatting in the studio. . . . This woman had worlds inside her. When you looked up and into her bald, see-through cranium, you saw little people, hoards [*sic*] of busy wax Lilliputians going about their business" (295). The tiny dolls sit at miniature computers, making notes, writing music, creating drawings, formulas, poems, stories; there

Box 5: Mad Madge

Harriet Burden's admiration for Cavendish was not universally shared by the duchess's contemporaries. She was erratic, voluble, and so unconventional that "people judge[d] her to be vain, extravagant, or even mad" (Bowerbank and Mendelson 12). In her memoir, "A True Relation of my Birth, Breeding and Life" (1656), Cavendish admits that she "always took delight in a singularity, even in acoutrements of habits" (60). She frequently appeared in public as a "female cavalier, donning men's clothes or the cavalier hat or resorting to masculine gestures such as bows rather than curtsies" (Battigelli 5). In these and other ways, according to Sylvia Bowerbank and Sara Mendelson, Cavendish fashioned a "personal identity . . . radically different from the [ones accepted in her] world" (9). If her gender-bending behavior was outrageous, her writings compounded the impression of a woman on the verge of a nervous breakdown. Upon reading Cavendish's *Poems and Fancies,* her contemporary, Dorothy Osborne, opined that "there [were] many soberer People in Bedlam"; diarist Samuel Pepys deemed her a "mad, conceited, ridiculous woman" (both qtd. in Battigelli 4). Cavendish purposely encouraged such responses: her attire and behavior were "calculated to engage people while keeping them at a comfortable distance" (Battigelli 7). Yet women such as the distinguished educator and early feminist Bathsua Makin saw through these surfaces, commenting that Cavendish, "by her own Genius, rather than by any timely Instruction, overtops many grave Gown-men" (qtd. in Battigelli 4).[12] As Harriet notes, Cavendish "staged herself as a mask or masque" (*BW* 208); beneath those masks, we find "additional masks" (Battigelli 6). She was, like Harry according to Hustvedt, a monster, a being who eluded, questioned, and violated her culture's most prized categories and conventions: "Like Frankenstein's monster, she [was] always outside looking in" (Becker interview 414).

Cavendish's experiments with multiple selves crop up in many of her writings (Bowerbank and Mendelson 14). She constantly subverts gender orthodoxies, not least by portraying women in "traditionally masculine leadership positions" (Walters 58). Such inversions appear most sweepingly in the Empress of *The Blazing World,* who assumes control of the utopian (or dystopian) society she finds, dominating her husband, interrogating scientists and experts, and bringing in another female—the Duchess of Newcastle!—as her chief adviser. Harriet exults, "The ladies always win in her worlds" (*BW* 208). Her women "refuse to conform to [the] stereotype of female passivity in the face of male aggression . . . and act as arbiters of their own fate" (Mendelson, Introduction 27). In her writings "the category of 'woman' does not stand as a single uncontested constant; its cultural meaning is explored, destabilized, and challenged" (Bowerbank and Mendelson 21).

Moreover, as Harriet explains, "Cross-dressers run rampant in Cavendish" (*BW* 208). Perhaps the most resonant of Cavendish's writings in this regard is her play *The Convent of Pleasure* (1668). This comedy is full of gender transgressions and transformations, of men dressed as women and women behaving (and dressed) as men. Acknowledging that men make "the Female sex their slaves" (101), Lady Happy creates a "convent" for women only, rhetorically asking, "Since there is so much folly, vanity and falshood in Men, why should Women trouble and vex themselves for their sake; for retiredness bars the life from nothing else but Men" (99). The Lady founds a female utopia graced by gardens and accenting natural beauty—sans males. Mr. Take-pleasure and his friends scheme to enter the convent by putting on "Womens apparel" (108). But how can they "frame [their] Eyes and Mouths to such coy, dissembling looks, and pritty simpering Mopes and Smiles, as they do?" (109): Cavendish is well aware that conventional femininity is a performance. Soon a princess visits the convent. We do not learn until later that she is a man dressed as a woman, and for several scenes we witness what seems to be an ardent lesbian love affair between the Princess and the Lady. True to her name, Lady Happy blithely recites this verse: "More innocent Lovers never can there be, / Then [*sic*] my most Princely Lover, that's a She" (111). This relationship becomes even more complicated when the Princess asks to play the part of a male servant (111): a male actor plays a woman who, as a woman, requests to dress and perform as a male servant. One's head begins to spin.

The cloistered women stage a play that, through a series of montage-like vignettes, recounts the myriad ways that men mistreat women, concluding with a coda: *"Marriage is a curse we find, / Especially to Women kind / From the Cobler's Wife we see, / To Ladies, they unhappie be"* (117, italics in original). No longer happy, Lady H, dressed as a shepherdess, is wooed by the Princess wearing male shepherd's clothing (118–23). By lavishly praising Lady H's "wit," the Princess/shepherd wins her, eventually proposing that they "join as one Body and Soul" (122). These women, and the men flexible enough to express their own femininity, gain and sustain power through intimate contact with the natural world, figured as "an infinitely complicated, powerful female body" (Walters 65). When at last the Princess is discovered to be a man, he bows and kisses Lady H's hand, and they marry. Although the conclusion reverts to a heteronormative coupling, the play's gender inversions, stark depictions of male oppression, and flirtations with queer eroticism linger in the mind long after the sappy denouement has faded.

Gender inversions and violations also characterize, in a somewhat different way, Cavendish's *The Description of a New World, Called the Blazing World.* In it, a lady is kidnaped by pirates and transported to an unknown realm called the Blazing World, which seems to be in the arctic. Perceiving her as a goddess, the Emperor falls in love, marries her, and endows her with "an absolute power to rule" as she pleases (*Description* 162). Much of the first half consists of her dialogues with various hybrid humans—bear-men, bird-men, worm-men, and other monsters—that give voice to Cavendish's sophisticated critiques of the science of her day. Another long discourse with the Spirits concerns the relations between body and mind. Are souls immaterial? Can Spirits move without bodies? (If not, the Spirits answer, they must be the "Hermaphrodites of Nature" [202].) Later she befriends the Duchess of Newcastle and the two become inseparable but "Platonick" (it's insisted) friends (210). The Empress enlists the Duchess to help quell the conflict in her own land; what follows is a transparent allegory of the English Civil War. (Staunch royalists, Cavendish and her husband were exiled during the Interregnum and returned with Charles II.) Although Cavendish affirms her belief in monarchy, female power is ascendant throughout, with the Empress as a "hermaphrodized Warrior Queen" (Mendelson 22) who assumes male privileges and exerts "masculine" power. Indeed, the text itself, a strange, complex melange of "romance, science fiction, travelogue, fantasy, satire, philosophical dialogue, surveys of contemporary science and philosophy, biblical criticism, expositions of Cavendish's own scientific theories, political philosophy, biography, blazons and spectacles, and orations and set pieces," has been described not only as heterogeneous, but as "hermaphroditic" (Mendelson 21).

is even a tiny Bruno, drafting the memoir that the fleshly Bruno has just completed. Seven couples (not all heterosexual) copulate in the "female Gulliver's head"; others duel with swords or guns. Nearby are numerous beasts and hybrids resembling those in Cavendish's eponymous fantasy. Emerging from the metamorph's vagina is a throng of humanoids, some suspended in midair, others crawling, walking, or skipping away from the birth canal. This unfinished Margaret mother monster presides like a goddess over the novel's final pages. It supplants the Felix figures, the Rune avatars, even the hermaphroditic doll in *The Suffocation Rooms* as Harriet's monument and supervising spirit; it may permit her to harmonize the strains of influence she has drawn from her collaborators. Hustvedt, who acknowledges the duchess as an "early model for my Harry" (Becker interview 418), incorporates a choir of personae in her novel's "hermaphroditic polyphony" (208), thereby echoing Cavendish, whose "governing interest lies in the relational interplay and tension between multiple voices" (Battigelli 33).

In Cavendish's preface to *The Description of a New World, Called the Blazing World,* she acknowledges that she cannot be "*Henry* the Fifth, or *Charles* the Second" and vows instead "to be *Margaret* the *First.*" Although "Fortune and the Fates" have not endowed her with a monarch's authority, she has "made a World of [her] own: for which no body, [she] hope[s], will blame [her], since it is in every ones power to do the like" (153–54). In the text proper the Spirits similarly remind the fictional Duchess that she "can create [her] self a Celestial World if [she] pleases. . . . For every humane Creature can create an Immaterial World fully inhabited by immaterial Creatures . . . and all this within the compass of the head or scull" (212). By so doing, one may enjoy "as much pleasure and delight as a world can afford" (213). And so the (fictional) Duchess is "converted" from worldly ambitions to the goal of creating a domain "of her own invention" (215). Likewise, at the end, Cavendish, speaking apparently as herself (selves?), concludes that "by this Poetical Description, you may perceive, that my ambition is not onely to be Emperess, but Authoress of a whole World" (250). Why pursue political hegemony when one's imagination can produce and populate any world one desires? Why hide behind a male mask when you possess a creative potency that far exceeds any male's? Harriet Burden answers these questions with her Margaret mother monster metamorph: with it, she can become Empress Harriet I. Her embrace of Cavendish does not mark a reversion to a retrograde feminine role model—a massive mama giving birth—but signals her embrace of the duchess's hermaphroditic, heterogenous experimentalism and her realization that through art she can engender a more authentically creative, and perhaps immortal, Harry. The dying Burden finds further solace in Cavendish's acknowledgment that "if she be slighted now and buried in silence, she may perhaps rise more gloriously hereafter [and] . . . meet with an age where she will be more regarded than she is in this" (qtd. in *BW* 329). Like the duchess, Burden hopes to be raised to "Fames Tower, which is to live by remembrance in after-ages" (Cavendish, "True Relation" 62). Harriet's dolls may escape their confinement after their maker has left the room.

Sweet Autumn Pinkney narrates the final moments of Harriet's life. What at first seems an odd choice by the author actually provides the perfect perspective, for despite her silly argot, Sweet Autumn is a perceptive witness. She senses, for example, that Harry's aura, now that she has accepted death, is "much cleaner. The colors [are] pure" and free of the formerly dominant angry red (355). Months later she visits Harriet's studio, where the Margaret metamorph still resides. Sweet Autumn stands in awe of this "great big statue with no hair, . . . raining numbers and letters and little people from her private parts": it gives her "the sacred feeling" (356). She also notices something nobody else has seen: a tiny Harry abiding inside of Margaret, "minding her own business, looking up at the sky" (356). As Sweet Autumn beholds the doll, it begins to glow. She closes her eyes, then opens them, awed by the "reds and oranges and yellows and greens and blues and violets—blazing hot and bright," and she realizes that each one is "alive with the spirit. For a second there, I could almost hear them breathing" (356). Harriet expires, but her work, no longer suffocated, respires. And inspires.

Like the other fictional and factual forgers we have encountered, Harriet Burden discovers a fresh artistic identity through a form of fakery that expands and enhances her creative powers. Her experiment with male masks is, indeed, too successful. In proving her point that viewers see what they expect to see, she manages simultaneously to amplify and muzzle her own voice. She discovers that although a box may seem to permit an artist to explore nearly infinite possibilities, when one tears down its walls, things fall apart. Yet *Maskings* does enable her to express and ultimately purge the rage that has both charged and choked her muse. Through misrecognizing Harriet, she finally recognizes Harry. Having discarded those factitious cocks and balls, she is free to present herself nakedly as an artist whose true offspring is herself. In order to find out who she is, Harriet Burden must become someone else. That is because, as Hustvedt demonstrates, identity is always relational, social, and multiple, just as artworks always have, in effect, multiple creators.

Although enveloped within Siri Hustvedt's hermaphroditic polyphony, Harriet Burden's *Maskings* also envelopes those voices. That is, just as the reviews of *Maskings* are "embedded in and anticipated by the ideas of the novel itself," so "the reviews of *The Blazing World* by Siri Hustvedt [will] bec[o]me further 'proliferations' of *Maskings* by Harriet Burden" (Becker interview 416). As Rohr elaborates, the text "posthumously constitutes the very last artwork of Harriet Burden, . . . 'Maskings 4'" (252). By borrowing Cavendish's spark, Hustvedt ensures that the duchess's world continues to blaze. Further, by harmonizing with Mary Shelley and Cavendish and conducting a chorus of voices—male and female, queer and straight, cis- and transgender, old and young, dead and living—Hustvedt both honors her predecessors and fashions a plural authorial persona. Her novel reminds us once again (as noted in thesis 7) that an author is always a fictional being. Although Harriet's masks seem to stifle her, they also free her to speak the truth. It is likewise for Hustvedt: the disguise of I. V. Hess and the choir of voices she collates combine to form a heterogeneous, heteronymous, hermaphroditic author who produces a richer, more sophisticated text than the singular author of her previous novels. This author's personae emerge through the interactions among the writer, her masks, and her readers. As with Chatterton and Rowley, Ireland and Shakespeare, Monk Ellison and Stagg Leigh, so here: faking fosters a fresh artistic self. In modeling her artistry after that of Bourgeois, Messager, Shelley, Cavendish, Pessoa, Kierkegaard, and others, Hustvedt prompts us to revisit her ancestors' works. These multiply voiced texts give birth to each other. Which, then, is the parent and which the child?

Epilogue

IT WOULD be entirely in keeping with the spirit of this book if I now confessed that Mark Osteen does not exist and that everything you have just read was actually written by someone else. As a crowning example of misrecognition, such a gambit would certainly dramatize my theses about credulity and gamesmanship. But I won't do that: for better or worse, I am the author of this book. Nevertheless, as you have read these chapters, you have likely conjured up a portrait of their author. That image is not mine; rather, it is a double portrait of you—of what you expected to glean from the book juxtaposed with what, if anything, you have actually taken from it. These gleanings may be quite different from what I aimed to elucidate. Yet that does not matter, because disparities between intentions and consequences are a part of the implicit pact agreed upon by every author and reader, which is: "I, the author, promise not to trick you maliciously; in turn, I ask for your trust." Pseudonyms violate this trust, but such violations are no more than misdemeanors unless the actual creator proffers the false name for a punitive or venal purpose. Such textual games, of which forgery is an extreme case, call out the viewer or reader for making assumptions. At their worst, they are betrayals that epitomize bad faith. At their best, however, they encourage us to examine our expectations, to become more attentive—if more suspicious—consumers and construers of creative artifacts.

I have emphasized that every forgery or hoax requires a story. In that regard they are metaphors for and instances of our creative powers as readers and viewers—and as artists. Forgeries fascinate because we want to believe in stories, to become characters in them, to collaborate with their creators. If the actual creator turns out to be someone else, that twist becomes part of the story, another layer of the painting. Forgeries, because they represent our human capacity for playing, pranking, and creative imitation, force us to view ourselves in the mirror, like Van Eyck in the Arnolfini portrait, to recognize, and re-recognize, how misrecognition can fuel creativity. Whether believers or debunkers, we become part of the story.

While examining each forgery and its fictions in detail, I have also sought to stress what they share by asking and addressing broad questions. Among them are: How much of creative production is solitary and how much is collaborative? How shall we define originality and authenticity, and are they useful measures of aesthetic value? To what degree is identity self-generated, and how much of it is shaped by culture? What is the relationship between selfhood and stories? These chapters, I hope, have also revealed some important truths about the universal human desire for attention and recognition. However, like "authentic" artworks, forgeries also disclose the desires and anxieties of their particular cultures: eighteenth-century Britons' longing to reclaim their literary history and to collaborate with their national poet; Australians' pervasive sense of fraudulence; the erasure of African American history and humanity; the power of late capitalism to shape and distort artistic aims; the challenges of preserving authenticity in a counterfeit society; the obstacles facing female artists.

Perhaps the most resonant theme for today's cultural environment, however, is the persistence of belief, as outlined in thesis 13. The rapid expansion of social media has brought with it a dramatic increase in the dissemination of conspiracy theories, unsourced rumors, bogus news, "alternative facts" (also known as bald-faced lies), malicious hoaxes, pseudo-science, and character assassination. As Kevin Young has written, "forgery . . . has . . . become a metaphor for modern life itself" (256). The erosion of faith in scientific facts in the face of catastrophic climate change and a global pandemic is perhaps the most dangerous of these troubling developments. It is difficult not to be appalled by the gullibility with which the most outrageous prevarications—perpetrated by formerly trusted entities such as the US president—are swallowed by large numbers of people. Our critical intelligence and credulity are tested daily; we often fail the test. These investigations of forgeries and hoaxes have perhaps shed light on these phenomena. What better examples of the now well-known term "confirmation bias" can one find than the Ireland forgeries or the receptions of *My Pafology* or *Maskings*? Even as we marvel at the ingenuity of these con artists, perhaps even root for them, we must also read them as cautionary tales about credulity and not misrecognize the vanity, venality, and self-delusion that impel them, just as these traits motivate the liars and frauds who propagate falsehoods in the mass media. I hope these investigations have accomplished something close to what Harriet Burden aims to do: enabled us to reflect upon ourselves as we gaze into the mirror that is art. We find forgers fascinating, but they undermine the trust necessary to sustain a livable society and a healthy artistic and literary culture. And although we cannot stop reading about them, few of us would want to be them.

NOTES

Prologue

1. The same problem besets Margaret Russett's definition—"a text that lies about its origin" (*Fictions* 15)—which would also fit plagiarism and counterfeit money.
2. For a further analysis of these sources as they apply to Charles Dickens's *Great Expectations* and James Joyce's fiction, see Osteen, "Great Expectations."
3. The earliest citation of the verb "hoax" is from 1796—the year of the Ireland Shakespeare forgeries. The first citation of the noun dates from 1808.
4. Grafton similarly describes mystification as one "extremity" of forgery in which works are "meant to deceive for a short time only, as practical jokes" (5).
5. *Amazons* features a sportswriter named Murray Jay Siskind, who reappears in *White Noise:* thus, anyone reading the novel after 1985 would know that either DeLillo wrote it or that he appropriated the figure. In any case, DeLillo disavows it. When I was preparing a critical edition of *White Noise,* he insisted that I remove *Amazons* from his bibliography. Nonetheless, as Howard notes, *Amazons* sold more copies than any of DeLillo's "own" novels had to that point (59).
6. The editor for Michael Joseph publishing, which had issued Lessing's first novel (under her own name), did note that Somers seemed to be "very much influenced by Doris Lessing" (Lessing, preface vii).
7. In the same collection Margolis rebuts Goodman's distinction, citing as examples Chatterton's Rowley works and James Macpherson's Ossian fabrications (162–64).

1. Thomas Chatterton's Ghosts

1. The "Bridge Narrative" and the dialogue "Elinoure and Juga" (May 1769) were the only two Rowley texts published in Chatterton's lifetime. Donald S. Taylor's *Complete Works* provides an essential chronology of the composition dates. Useful also are appendices 1 and 2 that follow Suarez's chapter in Groom's *Thomas Chatterton and Romantic Culture* (114–18).
2. Chatterton did not imagine these occurrences. The real-life Canynge did become a priest after his wife died. These events are repeated in "Lyfe of W. Canynge—by Rowlie" (*CW* 233).

3. In two of these ghostwritten poems he uses a sixteen-line stanza that anticipates Meredith's "sonnet" form in *Modern Love.* See "To Mr. Powell" and "To Miss Clarke" (*CW* 158, 164).
4. John Dix, whose sympathetic but unreliable biography of Chatterton (1837) influenced Browning and other Victorians, writes that "Walpole, of all men alive, had the least reason to be offended" at Chatterton's trick (qtd. in Smalley 153).
5. Kaplan finds a "desperate sadness beneath his manic braggadocio" (107), but I don't detect any such thing. Her claim carries weight only if one believes Chatterton deliberately killed himself.
6. Kaplan writes that as Rowley, Chatterton spoke "with an honest and noble poetic voice, but when he turned from the false, imagined world to the true, modern world, he produced . . . commonplace and imitative art" (178). The first claim is inaccurate for, as we have seen, "Rowley" was influenced by Chaucer, Spenser, and Shakespeare, among others.
7. It is not clear when the poem was written. It is possible that, having become known to London publishers, Chatterton thought the time ripe to compose another Rowley and offer it to them. Donald Taylor, however, argues that it was written in April/May 1769, with other late Rowley efforts (155).
8. It was probably not gonorrhea; as Kaplan acknowledges, the clap was too common to be regarded as a dread secret or to prompt suicide (208). Given Chatterton's frenetic literary activities in the months before his death, he may have suffered from bipolar disorder. If so, he needed no external reason to fall into a depressive slump.
9. "He took a large dose of opium, some of which was picked out from between his teeth after death, and he was found the next morning a most horrid spectacle, with limbs and features distorted as after convulsions, a frightful and ghastly corpse" (Meyerstein 436).
10. This view lingered into the nineteenth century. Dix, for example, accused Walpole of being an "enemy to his brother authors . . . unjust to the dead, injurious to the living" (qtd. in Smalley 154).
11. Croft came under attack for the dishonest way he had obtained the materials. Only after Sarah, having read the novel, wrote a letter denouncing him for his breach of trust did he reluctantly send her and Mary ££10 (Kaplan 256).
12. Created after Wallis's work is W. B. Morris's painting *Chatterton's Half-Holiday* (1869), in which the youngster, wearing his Colston school garb, pensively examines some papers in a cluttered room. He is not smiling in this picture.
13. See Goodridge for a comprehensive list.

14. Appropriately enough, Wallis's *Chatterton* became involved in a forgery after the artist Joseph Turner bought it; a man named Robinson photographed it for a tableau vivant, then tried to sell the image as Wallis's painting. Turner sued him and won (Cook 201).
15. Diane Johnson comments on the lifelong friendly relations between Wallis and the Peacock family and adduces an advertisement from February 1859 that Wallis placed, in which he sought a furnished apartment for two people (133).
16. Meredith seems to be conflating Mary with her mother, who became severely depressed after her daughter Margaret died as a small child.
17. Mitchell and Benford call this a "caudate" form because the additional two lines function as a "cauda" or tail (xxxiv).
18. For the rules of Forfeits, see Victorian Games, accessed December 15, 2020, https://historicalgames.neocities.org/Victorian/forfeits.html.
19. As John Holmes argues, the narrator and husband move from a biblical understanding of infidelity (hence the snake imagery) to a Darwinian one that views both lovers as subject to natural impulses and forces (533).
20. In the original edition there is more emphasis on wifely infidelity than in the revised 1878 edition (see Lindsay 91). I have used the later version here.
21. *Vala* is, of course, by William Blake, but Wychwood comes to believe that Chatterton wrote Blake's poems.
22. The titles are inside jokes: Ackroyd's two previous novels were *The Great Fire of London* and *The Last Testament of Oscar Wilde.*

2. "What King Forged I?"

1. The younger Ireland's name is often written as "William Henry" in early documents, but the title page of his own *Confessions* has it "William-Henry"; I employ the latter spelling throughout, sometimes shortened to W-H.
2. William-Henry observed that many mulberry trees would have been required to yield so many cups: he knew the relics were fakes (*Confessions* 20).
3. There are five books about the Ireland forgeries. I've relied upon the volumes by Grebanier, Kahan, and D. Stewart for chronology and background. All three largely agree about the facts but interpret them differently. Grebanier's urbane, witty book, while muddling the chronology, expresses compassion for the forger, if not for his father. Kahan's work, the most scholarly and precise about details, is marred by unpersuasive speculations—for example, that the whole Ireland family helped William-Henry execute the forgeries—and by depicting the youthful

hoaxer as a "calculating criminal" (9). Doug Stewart's recent book is the clearest and most crisply told. I have also perused Samuel Ireland's *Miscellaneous papers* (1795), which contains facsimiles of all the forged documents except for *Vortigern,* as well as his rebuttal of Malone. (The pages are unnumbered, except for the preface.) William-Henry's *Authentic Account,* a pamphlet hastily written in late 1795, and his longer *Confessions* (1805), are fascinating texts that furnish (often inconsistent) versions of his motives and thoughts. These documents and the published text of *Vortigern* are housed at the Johns Hopkins University's Milton Eisenhower Library Special Collections. I am grateful to curator Earle Havens for granting access to these extraordinary materials.

4. The real-life victim of the murder was a woman named Martha Ray, who, like Mrs. Freeman, was a former mistress of Lord Sandwich. One can only imagine Mrs. F's emotions as she listened to Samuel read the novel.
5. In imitating Chatterton, William-Henry Ireland thus placed himself in what Radnóti terms a "lineal descent" of English forgers (180): James Macpherson, Chatterton, then himself.
6. The chronology here is a bit unclear. William-Henry writes that he invented the story of Mr. H. after creating the Profession of Faith, but Kahan and others show that the story preceded it. W-H's recollection of the chronology is also inconsistent: he writes in *Confessions* that the Profession of Faith was his second forgery (56), but in the *Authentic Account* he says that it was the third.
7. For a photo of the entire document, see Kahan 69.
8. Kahan contends that Ireland family members helped William-Henry forge the play. But this would mean that each of them kept the secret for several months. Further, W-H's two confessions go to great lengths to absolve his father of blame, and it is difficult to believe that his sisters and Mrs. Freeman would have agreed to the scheme without Samuel's approval. True, they transcribed and edited the play, but they surely believed it was by Shakespeare. Kahan's tracking of the manuscripts and the financial negotiations, however, is most helpful (see 127–44).
9. Samuel Ireland attempts unsuccessfully to rebut this argument as well (*An Investigation* 130).
10. Almost as absurd is Samuel Ireland's rebuttal, which argues that the image's very stupidity proves its authenticity: no faker would be that idiotic (116)!
11. Although Malone's tone is nasty throughout, what truly stirs his indignation is the Shakspeare Papers' suggestion that the MB might have been

a Republican (*Cursory observations* 148–52). Malone's prejudices show here, for there is little in the papers that could be interpreted as political.

12. This is Kahan's conclusion (191). But compare D. Stewart, who argues that Malone's volume "tipped the balance" against *Vortigern* (174). I find unpersuasive Kahan's assertion that Malone and Kemble conspired to undermine *Vortigern.* The play was bad enough to fail on its own, and by this time of the performance, the tide had begun to turn against the papers (see Kahan 169–77, 191).
13. See Kahan for a comparison of "Shakspeare's" play and Holinshed's version (72–73).
14. An incest plot likely drawn from *Pericles* was deleted during the editing.
15. It's not Catagrinus, as Kahan has it (19).
16. William-Henry jokes about this moment in his *Confessions,* writing that the condition of Phillimore "for a dead man was something in the style of Mr. Bannister, jun. in the Critic, who tells Mr. Puff 'that he cannot stay there *dying* all day'" (154).
17. Kahan suggests that Samuel might have known the papers were phony and contends that he insisted that the papers were genuine to protect his son, knowing that he himself would be blamed for them (198). But such a sacrificial gesture would be out of character for this self-important man, and Kahan's claim is belied by numerous documents that he cites.
18. It's worth noting, as Groom does, that the ancient Greek word for fakes is *nothoi,* literally "bastards": thus, "forgery is precisely a bloody bastard way of writing" (*Shadow* 248).
19. Thus, as Phillips intended, the reader detects a "tension between the introduction and the play" (Reilly interview 7).
20. Critical consensus now holds that *Timon of Athens* was a collaboration with George Middleton, who wrote about 900 lines to Shakespeare's 1400. See, for example, Shapiro 257.
21. The Earl of Oxford is one of the most frequently named candidates as the "real" Shakespeare. For a thorough treatment of anti-Stratfordian theories, see Shapiro, particularly 151–219, where he discusses Oxford, and the final chapter, where he dismantles the anti-Stratfordians' theories.
22. This speech echoes the king's soliloquy in *Henry V,* where he considers the difficulties of ruling and observes that a common man is in many ways better off than he. See 4.1.264ff, where the king argues that he sleeps less soundly than the "wretched slave."
23. Editor Arthur sees this is as "a little greeting from my father and proof of Dana's claim that the play is 'about me.'" His footnote prompts a rebuttal from Verre that the date is taken as Shakespeare's birthday and that there

are many better explanations than that "the play was forged to honor a twenty-first-century American novelist" (*Tragedy of Arthur* 280).

24. Contrast this decision with that of Shakespeare's Henry V, who is offered the French princess Katherine and a large dowry as a payment for not invading France. He invades anyway and ends up marrying her, too.
25. So why was it lost? Arthur wonders if its anti-Scottish rhetoric was too inflammatory, given the accession of James I in 1603. But *Henry V*, from 1600, contains a good deal of anti-Scot sentiment and was not suppressed (see 1.2.144ff and esp. l.170). Arthur also notes that this is the motive tendered for the suppression and loss of *Edward III*. But that theory was not proposed until 1990, which means that *Arthur* (which, if forged, was written in the 1970s) benefits fortuitously from a theory that didn't even exist at the time. That would be further evidence of its authenticity (*Tragedy of Arthur* 184).
26. Verre's footnote points out that no such revelation occurs in any other Shakespeare play; the Bard would have placed the revelation *before* Philip introduces himself (if, that is, Arthur is not himself counterfeiting his belief in order to break his pact with Mordred). Such dramatic irony would be more effective. But, like a good Believer, Verre interprets evidence of fraud as proof of authenticity: "I would consider this as an experiment he felt was not worth repeating, or an effect that audiences did not like" (*Tragedy of Arthur* 352).
27. This scholar offers a version of the trace paradigm. These scenes also dramatize Grafton's argument that forgers and critics have always been "entangled like Laocoon and his serpents" (6), generating what Ruthven calls a "never-ending *agon*" (54) in which forgers stimulate scholars to devise increasingly sophisticated methods of detection as well as a richer sense of the past.
28. Phillips evaded this question when Reilly posed it, answering, "If I am the reader, . . . I am prepared to say that Arthur Junior wrote the introduction to a play he believed his father wrote, but one his father did not write. As I said, I am happy to give it to Shakespeare, and no one has explored the possibility that Dana wrote it, or that Dana's mother contributed, or that it resulted from a family project. I would just as soon give it to Shakespeare" (Reilly interview 6).

3. Hideous Progeny

1. *The Darkening Ecliptic* poems are reprinted in D. Brooks 304–24. For the poems themselves I am using the version printed in Brooks, because his edition incorporates an apparently unfinished poem, "So Long," that

McAuley and Stewart included in the packet but that Harris rejected. For the other material regarding the Malley hoax, I use *Ern Malley's Poems* (*EMP*).

2. Meanwhile, Harold Stewart made Malley a visual artist, sending collages he had crafted from *National Geographic* photos and images borrowed from Dalí and Blake (Heyward 137). Malley's visual art, like his poetry and Frankenstein's creature, is a patchwork affair.
3. Herbert Read, likely the hoaxers' ultimate target, wrote to Harris that such fakers must follow procedures that are "akin to, if not identical with, the processes which produced the original work of art." Nor does it matter that they incorporated other sources, for such "mechanical aids to inspiration" are "legitimate" (qtd. in Harris, introduction 10, 11).
4. Much of Judge L. E. Clarke's decision is reproduced in Harris (appendix 45–56).
5. While teaching at Brooklyn College in the 1970s, Ashbery administered an exam in which he presented students with a Malley poem next to one of Geoffrey Hill's Mercian hymns and asked them to determine which one was the spoof. About half got it right (Heyward 288–89). Ashbery has also written two "Ern Malley poems." Koch republished "Boult to Marina" and "Sybilline" in *Locus Solus II,* a journal that he edited, in 1961 (Mead 116).
6. We may wish to add a fifth layer here, for Stewart recalls that the poem was based not on the painting but on a postcard of the painting (*EMP* 17).
7. Although McAuley was probably not aware of this fact, Dürer was one of the most frequently forged of early modern painters. Frank Arnau observes, for example, that there were far more Dürer forgeries than authentic Dürer works circulating during the sixteenth century (119–20).
8. David Brooks cites the *Pericles* allusions as part of what he calls the poems' "signature": clues that, postexposure, allow the forger to say, "See!? How were you deceived?" (71). Among these signatures he also lists "Petit Testament" and the lines from "Sybilline" used as my epigraph.
9. See Vickers (291–332) and Jackson for extensive analyses of *Pericles*' coauthorship. These scholars conclude that George Wilkins wrote acts 1 and 2 and Shakespeare the remainder. The scenes with Boult and Marina, then, were likely written by Shakespeare.
10. Pound's poem begins, "I make a pact with you, Walt Whitman," and proceeds to ask for reconciliation, acknowledging that "We have one sap and one root." D. Brooks also finds allusions to *The Cantos,* especially Canto I, and *Hugh Selwyn Mauberly* (168–72).
11. Lloyd contends that the first voice builds up a sense of readerly engagement "only to be interrupted by a second, contrary, tendency which

introduces ludic comment, deliberately awkward versification, or veiled attacks on *Angry Penguins* personnel." The results alternate between "elevation and hard landings" (28).

12. Musgrave and Kirkpatrick cite Koestenbaum's sentence as part of their argument that *The Darkening Ecliptic*'s body is "continually in a kind of *ekstasis*" that "approximates a fluid multiple identity" characteristic of what Deleuze and Guattari call a "minor literature" (133). They also develop the hints of homosexual desire in the poems, an impulse also noted by Pybus (148), who hypothesizes that the gay Stewart was in love with McAuley.
13. In *Malarky Dry* Malley's poems are written by one Henry Fitzhubert-Ireland, whose name alludes to that of forger William-Henry Ireland. Through the comic misadventures of a drunken former reporter named Bernard Peach, the poems end up being attributed to the deceased Malley. Ian Williams also weaves in allusions to Chatterton's life by having Malley reside in a rented attic room and by giving another character the name Rowley.
14. The piece was performed in 1988. Tahourdin's fascination with Malley has influenced generations of composers: every year, students are assigned to set selected poems from *The Darkening Ecliptic* for voice, solo or unaccompanied ("This story").
15. Tranter, for example, avers that Malley's works are "more interesting than the serious poetry produced by the hoaxers," whose works are "now neglected" ("Malley Variations" online). Brian Elliott similarly opines that the Malley poems are "decidedly superior in some ways to anything they had written independently" (*EMP* 14).
16. For a list of the texts that influenced Shelley, see Ketterer 19–33.
17. In her journal Shelley wrote that she had written "a book in <favor> defence of Polypheme" (Eilenberg 170) (referring to the murderous cyclops in the *Odyssey*), curiously conflating Homer's monster and her own, while transferring namelessness from Odysseus, who fools the one-eyed cannibal by calling himself "Outis" or Nobody.
18. Martinière lists three features that the books share and that are specific to the "myth" of *Frankenstein:* 1) the creature is patched up; 2) it rebels against its creator; and 3) questions of identity and literary creation are superimposed (160).
19. Slater perpetrates a more minor forgery in the novel's present time. When Chubb's threadbare tweed suit is ruined by the hotel dry cleaner, Slater writes a note telling Chubb that the hotel will pay for it and signs it in the manager's name (*MLAF* 113). Slater's position in British intelligence may also be Carey's sly acknowledgment that *Quadrant,* the

literary journal that James McAuley edited for many years, was funded by the CIA (Pybus 149).

20. Carey uses verbatim quotations from the Harris trial (see *MLAF* 50, 56). The crux here also revolves around "Boult to Marina" (47); and Weiss testifies to the "manner in which the hoax itself was both subject and key to the mystery of the poems" (57).
21. The term "resurrectionists" was used for the sort of grave robbers upon whom Frankenstein would have relied for his materials. I'm grateful for this insight to an anonymous reader of an earlier version of this chapter.
22. I have elected to break with convention and use past tense to describe the events in Chubb's story in order to help distinguish the time of his narration (1972) from the time line of those events that took place years earlier.
23. Victor Frankenstein's relationship with his "cousin"/sister/betrothed Elizabeth contains more than a hint of incest, a fact that likely discourages him from marrying her.
24. The raft scene may lead us back to McAuley and Stewart. According to David Brooks they were influenced by a literary hoax in the 1880s contrived by two French poets who parodied the *Symbolistes*. Their invented poet, Adoré Floupette, wrote a book called *Les Déliquescences,* the first poem of which, *Les enervés de Jumièges,* is an ekphrastic work based on a painting of the legend of the two sons of Clovis II, who, after rebelling against their father, were set adrift on a raft in the Seine (Brooks 4–11). Perhaps Carey knew of the hoax poem and had seen this painting, which has for years hung in the Art Gallery of New South Wales in Sydney.
25. The same words are uttered by Victor in David Wickes's adaptation of *Frankenstein* (TNT 1993), just before he kills himself and the creature. McCorkle's words are true in more than one sense here, for by the time Chubb tells his story, he has already been an insurance salesman and a bicycle mechanic—the very occupations he assigned to McCorkle. It's as if he is living in "the sixth circle of his own prank" (*MLAF* 158).

4. *Fuck* It

1. John Brooks has recently discussed *erasure* in somewhat similar terms, analyzing what he calls the novel's "bebop effect," by which he means its "deconstructive sensibility" and capacity to subvert readers' expectations and to "destabilize[ ] the ideas of literary category" (1044, 1043). Brooks's article appeared after I had drafted this chapter; although our readings overlap somewhat, we reached our interpretations independently.
2. Brooks relates Everett's use of multiple forms to the novel's "participation in a sensibility of bebop experimentation" (J. Brooks 1047). His linkage

relies, however, upon a reductive understanding of bebop as chiefly concerned with "rebelling against the idea of the song" (1045). The beboppers did not seek to destroy songs; they used them as launching pads for improvisation and thereby sought to expand the song form.

3. Not Sidney's name provides Everett numerous opportunities for verbal humor. For example, when the protagonist declares to an interlocutor, "I'm Not Sidney Poitier," the response is, "Of course you're not" (193). "'So you're Not Sidney Poitier,' a man says. 'I am,' replies Not Sidney" (193).
4. Turner asks the fictional Everett if he wrote a novel called *erasure* and notes that although he didn't like it overall, he loved "the novel in the novel" (*My Pafology*) because it was "true to life." Everett replies that he "didn't like writing" *erasure* and "didn't like it when [he] was done with it" (225–26).
5. Other episodes revisit *No Way Out* (142), *Lilies of the Field* (170ff), *Buck and the Preacher* (174–75), and *In the Heat of the Night* (206–7).
6. This novel also includes a character called Septic who has written a novel (something like *We's Lives in da Ghetto*) called *Class Ass,* a "no-holds-barred account" (233) of the "gritty, liquidy world of pimps and prostitutes." Her pseudonym notwithstanding, Septic actually resembles Audrey Hepburn and is a "well-spoken" young woman who claims that she "worked summers" while in college as a prostitute and madame (246). The book, she says, is "a kind of ironic mockery of shock fiction" that "tries to be an expose at the same time it makes fun of the conventions of expose writing and the way such sensational stuff is marketed and, well, sensationalized" (246). Doesn't this project sound like *erasure?*
7. Butler has elaborated most fully on the intertextual relation to *Invisible Man,* although many other critics have noted the allusions. Critics who have developed the *Native Son* parallels are listed below in note 12.
8. For a longer list of "I Got Rhythm" contrafacts and an analysis of the legal implications of these compositions, see my "Rhythm Changes."
9. Similarly, Lee Israel describes the signatures on her forged letters as a "riff on the actual signature, a tune played over the melody" (50). She should have written "over the harmony," but she is using "riff" as I use the term here.
10. To further complicate these layers of reference and authorship, one may note that Everett initially wrote this paper as a stand-alone piece (published in *Callaloo*). Curiously, as Barthes himself points out (142), in *Sarrasine* Balzac depicts a castrato who is disguised as a woman: thus, the Balzac text—the source for the parody of the parody—is about masquerading and passing.

11. In his sister's waiting room he is awakened to his own stereotyping when a woman he has written off as ignorant speaks insightfully about Jean Toomer's *Cane* (another text by an African American man who was not "black enough"). Lesson: "I was the stupid one" (21).
12. This scene is based on an incident that happened to Everett himself (Ehrenreich interview 25).
13. Brian Yost is wrong in asserting that Monk writes *My Pafology* for money (1329); as these passages make clear, his motives are primarily emotional, not economic. The large sums of money do, however, mute his later misgivings.
14. Because the affluent Ellison writes in the voice of a lower-class African American, his novella might considered an appropriative or colonizing hoax—what Christopher Miller would call an "intercultural hoax" (25)—like such spurious works as *The Education of Little Tree* (a fake memoir about a Native American written by the white racist Asa Earl Carter), and Danny Santiago's novel *Famous All Over Town* (written by white Yale and Andover alumnus Daniel James [see Miller 22–29]), in which privileged authors disguise themselves as members of marginalized groups in order to elicit favorable responses. Such frauds violate the ethics of ethnicity, the unwritten code stipulating that only members of a minority group may write about that group. Carried to its logical conclusion, however, this code leads to the ghetto.
15. Among the critics who have tallied its debts to Wright's novel are Johns (89), Russett ("Race" 364), Ridley (102), and Gysin, who points out that "it imitates the first book . . . and fragments of the second (par. 10).
16. Larkin (149) outlines the parallels to *Push*, which, in addition to the Down syndrome child, include the protagonists' expulsion from school and obsession with television, among other elements; see also Gysin (par. 17).
17. Brown states that the first Stagolee character in African American literature was Big Boy, the protagonist of Wright's story "Big Boy Leaves Home" (195). Bigger is an expanded version of Big Boy.
18. Compounding the irony is our awareness that Everett originally wrote *My Pafology* as a free-standing novella, only later supplying the parodic frame (Russett, "Race" 359).
19. SF MOMA's digitally enhanced version of *Erased de Kooning* is not blank. Sufficient blots, blurs and faint outlines of the previous work remain for a viewer to perceive that a drawing once existed there. See "Robert Rauschenberg."
20. Everett has asserted that Oprah should "stay the fuck out of literature and stop pretending she knows anything about it" (Shavers interview 64).

21. Brown asserts that this condition is "both the viewing subject and the subject incapable of being viewed . . . [which] creates the powerful energy known as the African-American male" (227). But this is only *one* version of the African American male—and a limiting one.
22. Butler argues that Stagg's appearance reverses the disastrous performances of Go and Tom Wahzetepe and that Monk now "models himself after Ellison's Rinehart, a consummately skilled confidence man who can manipulate people while assuming a fictive identity (145–46). This is only half true. Stagg's performance, though it succeeds in shocking people, is a disaster for Monk because it solidifies Stagg's position as a stereotypical "bad nigger," preventing him from crafting a more flexible persona.
23. Gysin astutely comments: "That the chimera of Stagolee speaks the words of a white betrayer is the ultimate irony" (par. 33).
24. This conceptual shoddiness nearly trapped Everett when Doubleday wished to make *erasure* the first entry of a new imprint devoted to African American writers. He declined, wondering if the editors had actually read the book. "It would be really wonderful," he noted, "to have an imprint inaugurate and invalidate itself with the same book" (Starr interview 23).

5. Original Sins

1. The painting has been variously dated from 1485 to about 1510; current consensus holds that it was completed around 1510.
2. This painting was indeed housed in Spain at the time the novel is set. It is not known how the painting came to be possessed by King Philip II, but it was brought to him in 1574 and remained in the Escorial for centuries thereafter (Büttner 120).
3. Its origins are uncertain. The Prado holds that Bosch himself painted it, while other experts argue that it was a product of Bosch's workshop and assistants. See Büttner 125; s.v. "The Seven Deadly Sins and the Four Last Things," Wikipedia.
4. Klaus Benesch writes that *The Recognitions* is "perhaps the first American novel to deal at length with the quandaries of assessing originality in a cultural environment predicated on an abundance of copies, representations, and simulacra" (30).
5. Because Gaddis frequently employs ellipses in dialogue, when hereafter quoting *The Recognitions* I mark my omissions with bracketed ellipses.
6. Gwyon bought it, he says, from the Conte di Brescia, whose name alludes to Adano di Brescia, a counterfeiter whom Dante consigned to the

eighth circle of his *Inferno* along with alchemists, liars, and impostors (see Comnes 60). I quote translations from this section of Dante's epic later in this chapter.

7. The fictional critic's opinion is at odds with the overwhelming consensus of art historians. Max Friedländer, for example, writes that Memling's work is "imitative and his pictures seem faded" compared to those of his masterly contemporaries (47). Van Eyck's major innovations included using transparent glazes to achieve more complex light effects and employing layered translucent pigments to create richer tones and a more complex surface (Borchert 22; Porras 47).
8. According to Tabbi, these scenes are based on Gaddis's years with a woman named Helen Parker, with whom he lived but never married (*Nobody Grew* 74).
9. Johnston describes him as a "degraded copy or repetition of a series of heroic originals" (132).
10. Leverence (43) proposes that alchemy is the key to interpreting the novel. The introduction to Moore's *Reader's Guide* (11–19) also centers on the novel's use alchemy.
11. Johnston argues that *The Recognitions* registers a transitional stage in which the old regime of clear distinctions between the authentic and inauthentic carries on an unresolved dialogue with this emergent postmodernist realm (21). I think he overstates the degree to which Gaddis overturns these dichotomies, but he is clearly correct that the novel questions and at least partially undermines those categories.
12. Moore reminds us that in Goethe's *Faust* one of Mephistopheles' guises is that of a black poodle (*Reader's Guide* 125).
13. Lenain asserts that fakers "will always *necessarily* betray themselves by a characteristic personal or historic 'accent'" (241). But forger Eric Hebborn challenges this claim: see his list of false "truisms" in the prologue to this work.
14. There is a genuine Van der Goes painting on this subject (see Friedländer plate 96).
15. Valentine says it is in Brussels. Currently it is housed in the Musea Brugge in Bruges (Borchert 161) and is usually dated from about 1475 to 1482. There is also, of course, a famous Van der Goes rendering of the Annunciation, which forms the left panel of the grisaille frontispiece of the Portinari Altarpiece.
16. The other work Wyatt cites, the Steenken *Madonna,* was attributed to Hubert by William Conway, one of Gaddis's sources, but is now believed to be the work of Jan (Knight, *Hints* 74; see also Friedländer 7; and Panofsky 205). Hubert may have begun the altarpiece, but even if he did,

we have no way of determining which portions, if any, are his work (see Pächt 171).

17. Among these innovations were processes for stripping old paintings down to their sizing, methods to maintain the *craquelure* (crack lines in old paintings), and the use of phenol formaldehyde to harden the paint, baking each layer to dry it (see B. Shapiro 135).
18. Knight outlines some parallels between Wyatt's work and Van Meegeren's (*Hints* 70–82). For further information about the Van Meegeren forgeries, see Charney, *Art* 94–100; and Keats 67–92.
19. Perhaps because of its "unprecedented level of realism," this painting possesses the distinction of having been stolen more frequently than any other artwork (Charney, *Art* 53).
20. These blurry lines are also depicted in Dominic Smith's fine recent novel *The Last Painting of Sara de Vos,* in which art restorer Ellie Shipley, while writing her dissertation on sixteenth-century Dutch women painters, begins doing restorations. She then is asked to forge a (fictional) painting by Sara de Vos, the only female member of the Dutch guilds at the time. Similarly, in B. A. Shapiro's novel *The Art Forger,* Claire Roth, who makes her living creating legal reproductions, is drawn into an elaborate forgery scheme by a crooked gallery owner. She soon discerns that the Degas painting she has been assigned to copy is itself a copy—of a painting stolen in a (real-life) heist of the Isabella Gardner Museum.
21. Panofsky writes that they could "clarify the shape and relative location of corporeal things but also . . . shift the interest to phenomena contingent upon the presence of an extracorporeal medium: the way light behaves" (4).
22. When he lived in Greenwich Village in the late 1940s, Gaddis too habitually wore a white Panama suit and a sling on his arm "so that he would write explosively when it was released from its bandage like a bird from a cage," recalls a friend (Kuehl and Moore, introduction 8).
23. For more information in Ninger, see Bloom 44–46; and Osteen, *Economy* 367–68.
24. Ninger followed a peculiarly stringent ethos and refused to write on his bills "Engraved and Printed at the Bureau of Engraving and Printing," which was then printed on all legitimate American currency. Asked why he didn't copy the phrase, he replied, "with devastating logic," "Dey didn't make dem" (Bloom 44).
25. Wolfe contends that Valentine is in love with Wyatt (129). That would make him "queer," which is appropriate, since here queer equals fake. It would also explain why Valentine doesn't draw the pistol he holds in his pocket.

26. The stabbing recalls Faust's mortal wounding of Gretchen's brother Valentine in Goethe's drama, 2.3620–775 (Wolfe 129).
27. Scenes deleted from the final version had Stephen impregnating a woman named Pastora, who gave birth to his child. What remains are scattered references to her and a surprising admission from Stephen that he has a daughter (897).
28. Tony Tanner, for example, asserts that Stephen/Wyatt now embraces a "more comprehensive idea of restoration—namely, the restoring of reality to itself, symbolized by his erasing of the interpositions of art" (398). How does a scraped-off canvas represent "reality," particularly in light of Gaddis's 956-page challenge to conventional realism? Mark Taylor argues that Stephen *becomes* El Greco here: "Paradoxically, by becoming an other, Wyatt becomes himself" (*Rewiring* 52). But that is too pat and contradicts his earlier point that Wyatt has now become Stephen. Attell contends that Stephen is aiming to "recover, or at least discover" the paintings' origins. "And what his restoration work confirms is that the origin is . . . irrecoverable" (286). Not really: he seems quite pleased with the results of his erasures.
29. At a 1974 conference of art historians, this definition was refined to say that restoration should "not falsely modify the known aesthetic, conceptual, and physical characteristics of the cultural property, especially by removing or obscuring original material" (qtd. in Scott 97). By this definition, Stephen's work is not restoration.
30. Magritte also explored this concept in such works as *Le Plagiat* (Plagiary) (1940), in which the outline of a bouquet is partly filled by the image of a tree, as well as in *The Land of Miracles* (1964) and in a 1959 painting also titled *L' Eclair.*
31. "Because de Kooning used erasure heavily in his own drawings, it is possible that some traces made visible through this technology were actually erased by him as part of the original drawing, before it entered Rauschenberg's hands." In other words, erasure is itself part of the process of creation. See "Robert Rauschenberg"; this site also includes an image of the enhanced erasure.
32. Johnston wittily notes that the son is now truly "consubstantial" with his father (97), albeit via a communion that is far from Christian.

6. But Is It Art?

1. Welles first used the trope in *Citizen Kane* (1941), when the protagonist appears in multiple mirrors after he furiously destroys his wife Susan's bedroom. Another example comes from his film *The Immortal Story*

(1968), as the protagonist, Mr. Clay (Welles), dines in solitude, surrounded by mirrors, so that several versions of himself encircle him. The shot is repeated twice later in the film.

2. Conrad similarly notes that *Kane* is a cubist portrait of its protagonist (150), and Thieme points out that *F for Fake*'s editing "reminds one of the cubist collage" (153) but does not develop this idea. McBride also suggests that the film employs cubist techniques (12).
3. Some of the shots in this sequence weren't even of Oja Kodar but of her sister, Nina, wearing the same dress (Rosenbaum 291).
4. This connection becomes even more compelling when we realize that Picasso was inspired by the early cinema of Georges Méliès (Staller 137), particularly the latter's penchant for rending and reassembling human bodies.
5. Welles alluded to cubism in his famous lengthy memo to Universal Pictures executives to justify the "jarring inconsistent angles" he employed in *Touch of Evil* (Conrad 297).
6. Welles's letter to Larry Jackson of the Orson Welles Theatre in Cambridge, Massachusetts, dated September 25, 1974, refers to the film as QUESTION MARK (Welles-Kodar Papers). The film's French title remains *Vérités et Mensonges* (Truths and lies).
7. Radnóti reminds us that there is "something puckish about forging" (10) and traces the link between the forger and the picaro (10–15).
8. In *F for Fake* Irving calls the story of Elmyr's aristocratic roots a "complete fabrication." More recent research has confirmed that he was probably Jewish and middle class. Unless otherwise specified, the account that follows derives from Irving's *Fake!*
9. This is the *Portrait de Jeanne Hebuterne* (1964), reproduced after p. 84 in *Fake!*
10. Later Elmyr, furious at Irving for allegedly reneging on his promise to give him half the proceeds of *Fake!*, sued him for $55 million for slander. Their shared distrust of experts clearly struck a chord with Welles, who resented biographers and critics and may have made *F for Fake* partly as a riposte to Pauline Kael's claim that he had cheated Herman Mankiewicz out of a writing credit for *Kane* (McBride 9).
11. Coincidentally, Welles's first Broadway role was the title part in Marlowe's *Dr. Faustus* (Conrad 77).
12. One of them was François Reichenbach; an art dealer before he was a filmmaker, he admits in *F for Fake* that he purchased several de Hory fakes and then resold them for double the amount. "I didn't want to know," he declares, laughing.
13. After Legros was arrested and extradited from Brazil in 1973, a Paris court convicted him of artistic fraud and attempted financial fraud, and in 1979

he was sentenced to two years in jail and fined $3,000. Most of the sentence was suspended on the basis of psychiatric evidence ("Fernand Legros").

14. Readers might get a chuckle out of Irving's review of *Enigma!* on the book's Amazon webpage, where he disavows the preface allegedly written by himself, describes its reproductions as fakes, and concludes, "Talbot was a dangerous man and if he were still alive I wouldn't dare write these comments. I give this $80 book a second star only because my included text, that of the original FAKE!, is worth reading. FAKE! is for sale at $5.99 on Kindle and Nook" ("Fakes of Fakes," s.v. Ken Talbot, *Enigma!,* Amazon.com).
15. Although purportedly nonfiction, *The Hoax* carries the disclaimer that usually accompanies fictional works. Even so, most of *The Hoax* jibes with the account by Fay et al. It is thus a fake novel about a fake autobiography. Irving published exactly the same book—minus the disclaimer—in 1972 under the title *What Really Happened. The Hoax* is, like *F for Fake,* a repackaging of existing material.
16. Further fakery surrounds this sequence: Welles leads us to believe he is reporting from Beverly Hills and Las Vegas, but the footage was actually shot near Paris (Conrad 357).
17. Irving's fourth novel, *The 38th Floor* (1968), concerns a Black man who becomes Acting Secretary-General of the United Nations. Irving Wallace found it suspiciously similar to his own novel, *The Man* (1964), about the first Black president (Fay et al. 26). It is possible (perhaps likely) that Irving was a plagiarist as well as a forger.
18. In a 1983 interview, Welles added more layers of deception by recanting this self-description: "I didn't want to sound superior to Elmyr, so I emphasized that I was a magician and called it a charlatan which isn't the same thing. And so I was faking even then. Everything was a lie. There wasn't anything that wasn't." McBride wonders parenthetically, "Can *that* statement be believed?" (9).

7. Misrecognizing Harry

1. Shapiro previously made his living by creating copies of old masters' paintings (80). Albeit not exactly a forger, since he doesn't try to pass off these works as originals, he is a faker.
2. For example, Messager's *Les Interdictions* (2014) features a series of small, variously colored doll-like figures posed atop a set of interdicting signs (e.g., a stop sign, a camera inside a red circle with a diagonal line through it, etc.). See https://www.artsy.net/artwork/annette-messager-les-interdictions-the-interdictions.

3. "The Girl Who Was Plugged In" won the Hugo for best novella in 1973; "Love Is the Plan the Plan Is Death" won the Nebula for best short story that year. The novella "Houston, Houston, Do You Read?" garnered both prizes in 1976. Raccoona Sheldon won the Nebula in 1977 for her novelette "The Screwfly Solution" after her real identity had been revealed.
4. "The Women Men Don't See" (1972; republished in *Warm Worlds and Otherwise,* the anthology in which Silverberg argued that Tiptree was a male) is narrated by Don Fenton, who recounts being thrown together with Ruth Parsons and her daughter, Althea, after their chartered plane crashes. When aliens arrive, Don, intent on playing the hero, repeatedly misreads Ruth's motives and actions and believes he must protect the females. Near the end, Ruth announces that "women have no rights . . . except what men allow us" and that when crises arise, males revert to their conventional roles and then blame women (134). Ruth and Althea plead with the aliens to take them away, and they do. The competent, elusive Ruth is clearly a version of Sheldon. In the Nebula and Hugo award-winning novella "Houston, Houston, Do You Read?" (1976), three astronauts—a misogynistic predator (Bud), a patriarchal Christian, and the protagonist, Orren Lorimer, a scientist who struggles with his gender identity ("You shitheads," he thinks, "I'll show you. *I'm not a girl*" [*Her Smoke* 167])—are accidentally thrust into a future in which a virus has wiped out all males. The female astronauts (all clones) who save their lives at first welcome them, but upon witnessing Bud rape one of their crew, they decide there is no place in their society for such violent people. At the end Lorimer, in a sly twist on antifeminist rhetoric, asks, "If you take the risk of giving us equal rights, what could we possibly contribute?" (216).
5. Contributing to Hustvedt's fascination was that Kierkegaard's English translators, Howard and Edna Hong, were her neighbors when she was growing up in Northfield, Minnesota (M. Taylor, "Wounding" 152).
6. S. K.'s life offers some curious parallels with the early life of Wyatt Gwyon, including a harsh religious upbringing meant to "redeem the guilty father's sins" (Taylor, "Wounding" 159).
7. In a striking real-life reenactment of the fictional chests contrived by Chatterton and Ireland, most of Pessoa's works were discovered, posthumously, in a trunk in his Lisbon apartment (Sadlier 8).
8. Later Pessoa gave birth to Bernardo Soares, a "semiheteronym" who authored the unique diary/aphoristic collection entitled *The Book of Disquiet.* For a list of others (including at least one female persona), see "Fernando Pessoa."

9. Images of this work are available at http://www.artnet.com/artists/annette-messager/d%C3%A9sir-d%C3%A9sir-desire-desire-a-bvC370cQTDCLFhW8SMZJEQ2.
10. Recall that in *What I Loved,* Rune-forerunner Teddy Giles is rumored to have killed his own mother by pushing her down the stairs (273).
11. "Paper Bodies" might also describe some of Messager's works. For a mid-career retrospective at the Musée de Grenoble in 1989, she developed *My Little Effigies,* "a series in which she hung photographs of body parts around the necks of stuffed animals, usually arrayed in groups across a wall with a single word inscribed numerous times in crayon on the wall below each" ("Annette Messager," Guggenheim.org).
12. Although Cavendish's treatment of gender is sometimes ambiguous or conventional, as Deborah Boyle argues, she anticipates Mary Wollstonecraft in arguing that women's poor education keeps them subservient: "We are become like worms that onely live in the dull earth of ignorance, winding our selves sometimes out, by the help of some refreshing rain of good educations which seldom is given us" (qtd. in Walters 34; from "To the Two Universities").

WORKS CITED

Abádi-Nagy, Zoltán. "The Art of Fiction: An Interview with William Gaddis." *Paris Review* 105 (Winter 1987): 1–16.

Ackroyd, Peter. *Chatterton*. New York: Ballantine, 1987.

———. Preface to Groom, ed., *Thomas Chatterton and Romantic Culture*, 1–2.

Alberts, Crystal, Christopher Leise and Birger Vanwesenbeeck, eds. *William Gaddis, "The Last of Something": Critical Essays*. Jefferson, NC: McFarland, 2010.

Alighieri, Dante. *Inferno*. Translated by John Ciardi. New York: New American Library, 1954.

"Annette Messager." Guggenheim.org. https://www.guggenheim.org/artwork/artist/annette-messager. Accessed October 28, 2020.

"Annette Messager: motion / emotion." Museum of Contemporary Art. https://www.mca.com.au/artists-works/exhibitions/688-annette-messager-motion-emotion/. Accessed December 31, 2018.

Arnau, Frank. *Three Thousand Years of Deception in Art and Antiques*. Translated by J. Maxwell Brownjohn. London: Cape, 1961.

Arnheim, Rudolf. "On Duplication." In Dutton, ed., *The Forger's Art*, 232–45.

Ashcroft, Bill. "Reading Carey Reading Malley." *Australian Literary Studies* 21 (2004): 28–39.

Attell, Kevin. "The Last Christian Novel: William Gaddis's *The Recognitions*." *Contemporary Literature* 53.2 (2012): 261–91.

Austin, Richard. "George Meredith and Mary Nicolls." *Texas Quarterly* 21 (1978): 127–48.

Ayres, Jackson. "Orson Welles's 'Complicitous Critique': Postmodern Paradox in *F is for Fake*." *Literature Film Quarterly* 40.1 (2012): 6–19.

Baines, Paul. "Chatterton and Johnson: Authority and Filiation in the 1770s." In Groom, ed., *Thomas Chatterton and Romantic Culture*, 172–87.

———. *The House of Forgery in Eighteenth-Century Britain*. Brookfield, VT: Ashgate, 1999.

Baldick, Chris. *In Frankenstein's Shadow: Myth, Monstrosity, and Nineteenth-Century Writing*. Oxford: Clarendon, 1987.

Baldwin, James. "Staggerlee Wonders." 1978. *Poetry Foundation.org*. Accessed July 7, 2019.

Barr, Alan P. "How All Occasions Do Inform: 'Household Matters' and Domestic Vignettes in George Meredith's *Modern Love*." *Victorian Poetry* 42.3 (Fall 2004): 283–93.

Barthes, Roland. "The Death of the Author." 1968. In *Image, Music, Text.* Translated by Stephen Heath, 142–48. New York: Hill and Wang, 1977.

Bataille, Georges. *The Accursed Share: An Essay on the General Economy.* Vol. 1: *Consumption.* 1967. Translated by Robert Hurley. Cambridge, MA: Zone, 1988.

Battigelli, Anna. *Margaret Cavendish and the Exiles of the Mind.* Lexington: University Press of Kentucky, 1998.

Baudrillard, Jean. "Simulacra and Simulations." 1981. In *Selected Writings.* Edited by Mark Poster. Translated by Paul Foss, Paul Patton, and Philip Beitchman, 166–84. Stanford, CA: Stanford University Press, 1988.

Bealer, Alex W. *The Art of Blacksmithing.* Rev. ed. Edison, NJ: Castle, 1995.

Beardsley, Monroe. "Notes on Forgery." In Dutton, ed., *The Forger's Art,* 225–31.

Becker, Susanne. "'Deceiving the Reader into the Truth': A Conversation with Siri Hustvedt about *The Blazing World* (2014)." In Hartmann et al., eds., *Focused Ambiguity in Siri Hustvedt's Works,* 409–22.

Benesch, Klaus. "In the Diaspora of Words: Gaddis, Kierkegaard, and the Art of Recognition(s)." In Tabbi and Shavers, eds., *Paper Empire,* 28–45.

Birdwell, Cleo [Don DeLillo and Sue Buck]. *Amazons: An Intimate Memoir by the First Woman Ever to Play in the National Hockey League.* New York: Holt, 1980.

Bloom, Murray Teigh. *Money of Their Own: The Great Counterfeiters.* New York: Scribner's, 1957.

Böger, Astrid. "'I look and sometimes I see': The Art of Perception in Siri Hustvedt's Novels." In Hartmann et al., eds., *Focused Ambiguity in Siri Hustvedt's Works,* 281–93.

Borchert, Till-Holger. *Van Eyck to Dürer: The Influence of Early Netherlandish Painting on European Art, 1430–1530.* New York: Thames & Hudson, 2011.

Bowerbank, Sylvia, and Sara Mendelson, eds. *Paper Bodies: A Margaret Cavendish Reader.* Peterborough, Ont.: Broadview, 1999.

Boyd, William. *Nat Tate: An American Artist, 1928–1960.* London: Bloomsbury, 2011.

Boyle, Deborah. *The Well-Ordered Universe: The Philosophy of Margaret Cavendish.* Oxford: Oxford University Press, 2018.

Brantlinger, Patrick. "Notes on the Postmodernity of Fake (?) Aboriginal Literature." *Postcolonial Studies* 41.4 (2011): 355–71.

Briefel, Aviva. *The Deceivers: Art Forgery and Identity in the Nineteenth Century.* Ithaca, NY: Cornell University Press, 2006.

Bristow, Joseph, and Rebecca N. Mitchell. *Oscar Wilde's Chatterton: Literary History, Romanticism, and the Art of Forgery.* New Haven, CT: Yale University Press, 2015.

Brooks, David. *The Sons of Clovis: Ern Malley, Adoré Floupette and a Secret History of Australian Poetry.* St. Lucia: University of Queensland Press, 2011.

Brooks, John. "Antiessentialist Form: The Bebop Effect of Percival Everett's *Erasure*." *PMLA* 134.5 (2019): 1042–55.

Brown, Cecil. *Stagolee Shot Billy.* Cambridge, MA: Harvard University Press, 2003.

Browning, Robert. "Fra Lippo Lippi." In *The Norton Anthology of English Literature.* 7th ed. Vol. 2b: *The Victorian Age.* Edited by Carol T. Christ and George H. Ford, 1373–84. New York: Norton, 2000.

Bryden, Inga. "The Mythical Image: Chatterton, King Arthur, and Heraldry." In Groom, ed., *Thomas Chatterton and Romantic Culture,* 64–78.

Butler, Robert J. "Percival Everett's Signifying on Ralph Ellison's *Invisible Man* in *Erasure*." *Canadian Review of Comparative Literature/Revue Canadienne de Littérature Comparée.* 45.1 (March 2018): 141–52.

Büttner, Nils. *Hieronymus Bosch: Visions and Nightmares.* Translated by Anthony Mathews. London: Reaktion, 2016.

Carey, Peter. *Illywhacker.* New York: HarperCollins, 1985.

———. *Jack Maggs.* New York: Knopf, 1998.

———. *My Life as a Fake.* New York: Knopf, 2003.

Carson, James P. "Bringing the Author Forward: *Frankenstein* through Mary Shelley's Letters." *Criticism* 30.4 (Fall 1988): 431–53.

Castle, Robert. "*F for Fake:* The Ultimate Mirror of Orson Welles." *Bright Lights Film Journal* 45 (August 2004). http://brightlightsfilm.com/f-for-fake-the-ultimate-mirror-of-orson-welles/#.WX45NFGQy1s.

Cavendish, Margaret. *The Convent of Pleasure.* In Bowerbank and Mendelson, eds., *Paper Bodies,* 97–135.

———. *The Description of a New World, Called the Blazing World.* In Bowerbank and Mendelson, eds., *Paper Bodies,* 151–251.

———. "Of Many Worlds in *This* World." In Bowerbank and Mendelson, eds., *Paper Bodies,* 252.

———. "A True Relation of My Birth, Breeding and Life." In Bowerbank and Mendelson, eds., *Paper Bodies,* 41–63.

Chambers, Ross. "Adventures in Malley Country: Concerning Peter Carey's *My Life as a Fake*." *Cultural Studies Review* 11.1 (March 2005): 27–51.

Charney, Noah. *The Art of Forgery: The Minds, Motives and Methods of Master Forgers.* New York: Phaidon, 2015.

———. "Bosch's Seven Deadly Sins." *The Secret History of Art.* December 8, 2010. Accessed June 4, 2018. http://secrethistoryofart.blogspot.com/2010/12/boschs-seven-deadly-sins.html.

Chatterton, Thomas. *The Complete Works of Thomas Chatterton.* Edited by Donald S. Taylor and Benjamin B. Hoover. Vol. 1. Oxford: Clarendon Press, 1971.

———. *Poems, supposed to have been written at Bristol in the fifteenth century, by Thomas Rowley, priest, &c., with a commentary in which the antiquity of them is considered and defended, by Jeremiah Milles.* London: Payne, 1782.

———. *Poems supposed to have been written at Bristol, by Thomas Rowley, and others, in the fifteenth century.* Edited by Thomas Tyrwhitt. London: Routledge, 1993.

Cieszkowski, Krzysztof. "The Legend Makers: Chatterton, Wallis and Meredith." *History Today* 32.11 (November 1982). Accessed December 16, 2020. https://www.historytoday.com/archive/legend-makers-chatterton-wallis-meredith.

Ciuraru, Carmela. *Nom de Plume: A (Secret) History of Pseudonyms.* New York: HarperCollins, 2011.

Clingham, Greg. "*Chatterton,* Ackroyd, and the Fiction of Eighteenth-Century Historiography." *Bucknell Review* 42.1 (1998): 35–58.

Combs, Richard. "Orson Welles's *F for Fake* [1976]." In *Imagining Reality: The Faber Book of the Documentary,* edited by Kevin Macdonald and Mark Cousins, 221–24. London: Faber, 1996.

Comnes, Gregory. *The Ethics of Indeterminacy in the Novels of William Gaddis.* Gainesville: University Press of Florida, 1994.

Conrad, Peter. *Orson Welles: Stories of His Life.* London: Faber, 2003.

Conway, William Martin. *Early Flemish Artists: And Their Predecessors on the Lower Rhine.* New York: Macmillan, 1887.

———. *The Van Eycks and Their Followers.* New York: Dutton, 1921.

Cook, Daniel. *Thomas Chatterton and Neglected Genius, 1760–1830.* Houndsmills, UK: Palgrave Macmillan, 2013.

Cowart, David. *Literary Symbiosis: The Reconfigured Text in Twentieth-Century Writing.* Athens: University of Georgia Press, 1993.

Crane, Julie. "'Wandering between Two Worlds': The Victorian Afterlife of Thomas Chatterton." In *Romantic Echoes in the Victorian Era,* edited by Andrew Radford and Mark Sandy, 27–37. Aldershot, UK: Ashgate, 2008.

Croft, Herbert. *Love and madness: a story too true, in a series of letters between parties, whose names would perhaps be mentioned, were they less known, or less lamented; a new edition.* London: Kearsley, 1780.

Däwes, Birgit. "'Openings that can't be closed': Patterns of Surveillance Culture in Siri Hustvedt's Novels." In Hartmann et al. eds., *Focused Ambiguity in Siri Hustvedt's Works,* 295–310.

de Bolla, Peter. "The Stain of the Signature." In *Fiction and Economy,* edited by Susan Bruce and Valeria Wagner, 63–80. Houndsmills, UK: Palgrave Macmillan, 2007.

De Vos, Dirk. *Hans Memling: The Complete Works.* New York: Abrams, 1994.

Dix, John. *The Life of Thomas Chatterton.* London, 1837.

Dunbar, Paul Laurence. "We Wear the Mask." 1895. Poetry Foundation.org. Accessed December 16, 2020. https://www.poetryfoundation.org/poems/44203/we-wear-the-mask.

Dutton, Dennis. "Artistic Crimes." In Dutton, ed., *The Forger's Art*, 172–87.

———, ed. *The Forger's Art: Forgery and the Philosophy of Art.* Berkeley: University of California Press, 1983.

Eckley, Grace. "Exorcising the Demon Forgery, or the Forging of Pure Gold in Gaddis's *Recognitions*." In *Literature and the Occult: Essays in Comparative Literature*, edited by Luanne Frank, 125–36. Arlington: University of Texas at Arlington Press, 1977.

Eco, Umberto. "Forgeries, Originals and Identity." In *Signs of Humanity / L'homme et ses signes*, edited by Michel Balat and Jancie Deledall-Rhodes, 605–18. Vol. 2. Berlin: Mouton DeGruyter, 1992.

Ehrenreich, Ben. "Invisible Man." 2002. Interview in Weixlmann, ed., *Conversations with Percival Everett*, 24–28.

Eilenberg, Susan. "Nothing's Namelessness: Mary Shelley's *Frankenstein*." In Griffin, ed., *Faces of Anonymity*, 167–92.

Eliade, Mircea. *The Forge and the Crucible: The Origins and Structures of Alchemy.* 1962. Translated by Stephen Corbin. New York: Harper & Row, 1971.

Eliot, T. S. *Four Quartets.* New York: Harcourt, Brace, Jovanovich, 1943.

Ellison, Ralph. "Richard Wright's Blues." 1945. In *Shadow and Act*, 77–94. New York: Random House, 1964. Rpt. Vintage, 1972.

Ern Malley. http://www.ernmalley.net/. Accessed Dec. 14, 2020.

Ern Malley's Poems. Introduction by Max Harris. Melbourne: Landsdowne, 1961.

Etching House: Fine Art Works on Paper. https://etchinghouse.com.au/. Accessed May 24, 2016.

Everett, Percival. *erasure.* New York: Hyperion, 2001.

———. *I Am Not Sidney Poitier.* Minneapolis: Graywolf, 2009.

———. *Percival Everett by Virgil Russell.* Minneapolis: Graywolf, 2013.

———. "Signing to the Blind." *Callaloo* 14.1 (1991): 9–11.

Everett, Percival, and James Kincaid. *A History of the African-American People [Proposed] by Strom Thurmond, as Told to Percival Everett and James Kincaid.* New York: Akasic, 2004.

Fairer, David. "Chatterton's Poetic Afterlife, 1770–94: A Context for Coleridge's *Monody*." In Groom, ed., *Thomas Chatterton and Romantic Culture*, 228–52.

Farebrother, Rachel. "'Out of Place': Reading Space in Percival Everett's *Erasure*." *MELUS* 40.2 (Summer 2015): 117–36.

Fay, Stephen, Lewis Chester, and Magnus Linklater. *Hoax: The Inside Story of the Howard Hughes–Clifford Irving Affair.* New York: Viking, 1972.

"Fernand Legros, Dealer in Art." *New York Times*, April 8, 1983.

"Fernando Pessoa." Poets.org. Accessed December 16, 2020. https://poets.org/poet/fernando-pessoa.

Finney, Brian. "Peter Ackroyd, Postmodernist Play, and *Chatterton*." *Twentieth-Century Literature* 38.2 (Summer 1994): 240–61.

Fletcher, Pauline. "'Trifles light as air' in Meredith's 'Modern Love.'" *Victorian Poetry* 34.1 (1996): 87–99.

Fortune, Ron, and Amy E. Robillard. "Life Writing at Cross Purposes: Documentary Forgery and the Reconstruction of Identity." *Life Writing* 10.3 (2013): 277–93.

Foucault, Michel. "What Is an Author?" In *Textual Strategies: Perspectives in Post-Structuralist Criticism,* edited by Josue V. Harari, 141–60. Ithaca, NY: Cornell University Press, 1979.

———. "What Is an Author." In *Language, Counter-memory, Practice: Selected Essays and Interviews,* edited by Donald F. Bouchard. and translated by Donald F. Bouchard and Sherry Simon, 113–38. Ithaca, NY: Cornell University Press, 1977.

Friedländer, Max J. *From Van Eyck to Brueghel.* Ithaca, NY: Cornell University Press, 1981.

Gaddis, William. *The Recognitions.* New York: Harcourt, 1955.

Gates, Henry Louis, Jr. *The Signifying Monkey: A Theory of Afro-American Literary Criticism.* New York: Oxford University Press, 1988.

Gaunt, William. *A Concise History of English Painting.* London: Thames and Hudson, 1964.

George, Lynell. "Parody That's Personal." Interview with Percival Everett. In Weixlmann, ed., *Conversations with Percival Everett,* 10–14.

Gilbert, Sandra. "Horror's Twin: Mary Shelley's Monstrous Eve." In *Critical Essays on Mary Wollstonecraft Shelley,* edited by Mary Lowe-Evans, 39–61. New York: G. K. Hall, 1998.

Goodman, Nelson. "Art and Authenticity." In Dutton, ed., *The Forger's Art,* 93–114.

Goodridge, John. "Rowley's Ghost: A Checklist of Creative Works Inspired by Thomas Chatterton's Life and Writings." In Groom, ed., *Thomas Chatterton and Romantic Culture,* 262–92.

Goux, Jean-Joseph. "Cash, Check, or Charge?" Translated by John Barberet. In *The New Economic Criticism: Studies at the Intersection of Literature and Economics,* edited by Martha Woodmansee and Mark Osteen, 114–27. London: Routledge, 1999.

———. *Symbolic Economies: After Marx and Freud.* Translated by Jennifer Curtiss Gage. Ithaca, NY: Cornell University Press, 1990.

Grafton, Anthony. *Forgers and Critics: Creativity and Duplicity in Western Scholarship.* Princeton, NJ: Princeton University Press, 1990.

Graham, Jenny. *Inventing van Eyck: The Remaking of an Artist for the Modern Age.* New York: Berg, 2007.

Grebanier, Bernard. *The Great Shakespeare Forgery.* New York: Norton, 1965.

Griffin, Robert J., ed. *The Faces of Anonymity: Anonymous and Pseudonymous Publication from the Sixteenth to the Twentieth Century.* Houndsmills, UK: Palgrave Macmillan, 2003.

———. Introduction to Griffin, ed., *Faces of Anonymity,* 1–17.

Groom, Nick. "Foreword: 'Fakelit.'" In *Fakes and Forgeries,* edited by Peter Knight and Jonathan Long, vii–xiii. Amersham, UK: Cambridge Scholars, 2004.

———. *The Forger's Shadow: How Forgery Changed the Course of Literature.* London: Picador, 2002.

———. "*Fragments, Reliques* & MSS: Chatterton and Percy." In Groom, ed., *Thomas Chatterton and Romantic Culture,* 188–209.

———. "'I Am Nothing': A Typology of the Forger from Chatterton to Wilde." In *The Victorians and the Eighteen Century: Reassessing the Tradition,* edited by Francis O'Gorman and Katherine Turner, 203–22. Aldershot, UK: Ashgate, 2004.

———. Introduction to *Thomas Chatterton and Romantic Culture,* 3–14.

———. "Original Copies; Counterfeit Forgeries." *Critical Quarterly* 43.2 (2001): 6–18.

———, ed. *Thomas Chatterton and Romantic Culture.* Houndsmills, UK: St. Martin's/Macmillan, 1999.

Gruber, Michael. *The Forgery of Venus.* New York: Harper, 2008.

Gysin, Fritz. "The Pitfalls of Parody: Melancholic Satire in Percival Everett's *Erasure.*" In *Reading Percival Everett: European Perspectives,* edited by Claude Julien and Anne-Laure Tissut, n.p. Tours, France: Presses Universitaires Francois-Rabelais, 2007. Accessed November 7, 2020. https://books.openedition.org/pufr/5459.

Harris, Max. Introduction and Appendix to *Ern Malley's Poems,* 5–12, 42–56. Melbourne: Landsdowne, 1961

Hartmann, Johanna, Christine Marks, and Hubert Zapf, eds. *Zones of Focused Ambiguity in Siri Hustvedt's Works: Interdisciplinary Essays.* Berlin: De Gruyter, 2016.

Haywood, Ian. *Faking It: Art and the Politics of Forgery.* New York: St. Martin's, 1987.

———. *The Making of History: A Study of the Literary Forgeries of James Macpherson and Thomas Chatterton in Relation to Eighteenth-century Ideas of History and Fiction.* Rutherford, NJ: Fairleigh Dickinson University Press, 1986.

Heyward, Michael. *The Ern Malley Affair.* London: Faber, 1993.

Hickox, Mike. "The Political Background to *The Death of Chatterton* by Henry Wallis." Victorian Web. Accessed December 16, 2020. http://www.victorianweb.org/painting/wallis/paintings/hickox.html.

The Hoax. Directed by Lasse Hallstrom. Performed by Richard Gere, Alfred Molina. Miramax, 2007. Film.

Holmes, John. "Darwinism, Feminism, and the Sonnet Sequence: Meredith's *Modern Love.*" *Victorian Poetry* 48.4 (Winter 2010): 523–38.

Holmes, Richard. "Forging the Poet: Some Early Pictures of Chatterton." In Groom, ed., *Thomas Chatterton and Romantic Culture,* 253–61.

Howard, Gerald. "The Puck Stopped Here." *Bookforum* (December/January 2008): 59.

Hoyle, Brian. "Subversive Montage in Orson Welles' *F for Fake.*" In *Sub/versions: Cultural Critique, Genre and Critique,* edited by Pauline MacPherson, Christopher Murray, Gordon Spark, and Kevin Corstorphine, 149–56. Newcastle: Cambridge Scholars, 2008.

Hughes, Robert. "Afterword: The Well-Wrought Ern." In Heyward, *The Ern Malley Affair,* 299–306.

Hustvedt, Siri. "Annette Messager: Hers and Mine." In *Living, Thinking, Looking,* 290–97.

———. *The Blazing World.* New York: Simon & Schuster, 2014.

———. "Embodied Visions: What Does It Mean to Look at a Work of Art?" In *Living, Thinking, Looking,* 336–54.

———. *The Enchantment of Lily Dahl.* New York: Holt, 1996.

———. "Kierkegaard's Pseudonyms and the Truths of Fiction." In *A Woman Looking at Men,* 487–505.

———. *Living, Thinking, Looking: Essays.* New York: Picador, 2012.

———. "Louise Bourgeois." In *Living, Thinking, Looking,* 245–52.

———. "My Louise Bourgeois." In *A Woman Looking at Men,* 25–33.

———. "Remembering in Art: The Horizontal and the Vertical." In *A Woman Looking at Men,* 452–72.

———. *What I Loved.* New York: Holt, 2003.

———. *A Woman Looking at Men Looking at Women: Essays on Art, Sex, and the Mind.* New York: Simon & Schuster, 2016.

Hutcheon, Linda. *A Theory of Parody: The Teachings of Twentieth-Century Forms.* 1985. Urbana: University of Illinois Press, 2001.

Ireland, Samuel. *An Investigation of Mr. Malone's Claim to the Character of Scholar, or Critic, Being an Examination of his Inquiry into the Authenticity of the Shakspeare Manuscripts etc.* London: Paulder, 1797.

———. *Mr. Ireland's vindication of his conduct, respecting the publication of the supposed Shakspeare MSS., being a preface or introduction to a reply to the critical labors of Mr. Malone.* London: Faulder, 1796.

———. *Miscellaneous papers and legal instruments under the hand and seal of Shakspeare: including the tragedy of* King Lear *and a small fragment of* Hamlet, *from the original MSS. in the possession of Samuel Ireland, of Norfolk Street.* London: Egerton, 1796.

Ireland, William-Henry. *An Authentic Account of the Shaksperian Manuscripts, &c.* London: Debrett, 1796.

———. *Confessions of William Henry Ireland.* London: Goddard, 1805.

———. *Vortigern, an historical tragedy, and Henry the Second, an historical drama, supposed to be written by the author of* Vortigern. London: Barker, 1799.

Irving, Clifford. *Fake! The Story of Elmyr de Hory, the Greatest Art Forger of Our Time.* New York: McGraw Hill, 1969.

———. "Fakes of Fakes. What Next." Review of Ken Talbot, *Enigma.* February 25, 2016. Amazon.com. Accessed Dec. 14, 2020.

———. *The Hoax.* New York: Permanent Press, 1981.

Irving, Clifford, with Richard Suskind. *What Really Happened: His Untold Story of the Hughes Affair.* New York: Grove, 1972.

Israel, Lee. *Can You Ever Forgive Me? Memoirs of a Literary Forger.* New York: Simon & Schuster, 2008.

Jackson, MacD. P. *Defining Shakespeare:* Pericles *as Test Case.* Oxford: Oxford University Press, 2003.

Jarrett, Michael. "Four Choruses on the Tropes of Jazz Writing." *American Literary History* 6.2 (Summer 1994): 336–53.

Johns, Gillian. "Percival Everett's *Erasure:* That Drat Aporia When Black Satire Meets 'The Pleasure of the Text.'" In *Post-Soul Satire: Black Identity after Civil Rights,* edited by Derek C. Maus and James J. Donahue, 85–97. Jackson: University Press of Mississippi, 2014.

Johnson, Barbara. "My Monster / My Self." *Diacritics* 12.2 (1982): 2–10.

Johnson, Diane. *The True History of the First Mrs. Meredith and Other Lesser Lives.* New York: Knopf, 1972.

Johnston, John. *Carnival of Repetition: Gaddis's* The Recognitions *and Postmodern Theory.* Philadelphia: University of Pennsylvania Press, 1990.

Jones, Mervyn. *The Amazing Victorian: A Life of George Meredith.* London: Constable, 1999.

Joyce, James. *Finnegans Wake.* New York: Viking, 1939.

———. *A Portrait of the Artist as Young Man.* 1916. Edited by John Paul Riquelme. Norton Critical Edition. New York: Norton, 2007.

———. *Ulysses.* 1922. Corrected edition. New York: Vintage, 1986.

Kahan, Jeffrey. *Reforging Shakespeare: The Story of a Theatrical Scandal.* Bethlehem, PA: Lehigh University Press, 1998.

Kamuf, Peggy. *Signature Pieces: On the Institution of Authorship.* Ithaca, NY: Cornell University Press, 1988.

Kaplan, Louise J. *The Family Romance of the Impostor-Poet Thomas Chatterton.* New York: Atheneum, 1988.

Karl, Frederick. "Gaddis: A Tribune of the Fifties." In Kuehl and Moore, eds., *In Recognition of William Gaddis,* 174–98.

Keats, Jonathon. *Forged: Why Fakes Are the Great Art of Our Age.* New York: Oxford University Press, 2013.

Keegan, Bridget. "Nostalgic Chatterton: Fictions of Poetic Identity and the Forging of a Self-Taught Tradition." In Groom, ed., *Thomas Chatterton and Romantic Culture,* 210–27.

Keller, Craig. "Question Marks." In DVD booklet for *F for Fake,* 33–38. Masters of Cinema #31. Eureka Video, 2007.

Kelley, Robin D. G. *Thelonious Monk: The Life and Times of an American Original.* New York: Free Press, 2009.

Ketterer, David. *Frankenstein's Creation: The Book, The Monster, and Human Reality.* Victoria, BC: University of Victoria Press, 1979.

Kierkegaard, Søren. [Johannes Climacus]. "Concluding Unscientific Postscript." In *The Essential Kierkegaard,* 186–246.

———. *The Essential Kierkegaard.* Edited by Howard V. Hong and Edna H. Hong. Princeton, NJ: Princeton University Press, 2000.

———. "The Point of View for My Work as an Author: A Direct Communication, Report to History." In *The Essential Kierkegaard,* 455–81.

Knight, Christopher J. "Flemish Art and Wyatt's Quest for Redemption in William Gaddis' *The Recognitions.*" In Kuehl and Moore, eds., *In Recognition of William Gaddis,* 58–69.

———. *Hints and Guesses: William Gaddis's Fiction of Longing.* Madison: University of Wisconsin Press, 1997.

Koenig, David. "The Writing of *The Recognitions.*" In Kuehl and Moore, eds., *In Recognition of William Gaddis,* 20–31.

Koestenbaum, Wayne. *Double Talk: The Erotics of Male Literary Collaboration.* New York: Routledge, 1989.

Kozicki, Henry. "The 'Unholy Battle' with the Other in George Meredith's *Modern Love.*" *Papers on Language and Literature* 23.2 (Spring 1987): 142–60.

Kuehl, John, and Steven Moore, eds. *In Recognition of William Gaddis.* Syracuse, NY: Syracuse University Press, 1984.

LaCapra, Dominick. "The Singed Phoenix and the Gift of Tongues: William Gaddis's *The Recognitions.*" *Diacritics* 4 (Winter 1986): 33–47.

Larkin, Lesley. *Race and the Literary Encounter: Black Literature from James Weldon Johnson to Percival Everett.* Bloomington: Indiana University Press, 2015.

LeClair, Tom. "An Interview with William Gaddis, circa 1980." In Tabbi and Shavers, eds., *Paper Empire,* 17–27.

Lenain, Thierry. *Art Forgery: The History of a Modern Obsession.* London: Reaktion, 2011.

Lessing, Alfred. "What Is Wrong with a Forgery?" In Dutton, ed. *The Forger's Art,* 58–76.

Lessing, Doris. *The Diaries of Jane Somers.* Including *The Good Neighbour* and *If the Old Could. . . .* New York: Vintage, 1984.

———. Preface to *The Diaries of Jane Somers,* v–xi.

Leverence, John. "Gaddis Anagnorisis." In Kuehl and Moore, eds., *In Recognition of William Gaddis,* 32–45.

Lindsay, Jack. *George Meredith: His Life and Work.* London: Bodley Head, 1956.

Lloyd, Brian. "Ern Malley and His Rivals." *Australian Literary Studies* 20.1 (2001): 20–32.

Lolla, Maria Grazia. "'Truth Sacrificing to the Muses': The Rowley Controversy and the Genesis of the Romantic Chatterton." In Groom, ed., *Thomas Chatterton and Romantic Culture,* 151–71.

"Louise Bourgeois." *The Art Story.* Accessed October 27, 2020. https://www.theartstory.org/artist-bourgeois-louise-artworks.htm.

"Louise Bourgeois: *Cell (Eyes and Mirrors)* 1989–93." Tate.org. Accessed October 27, 2020. https://www.tate.org.uk/art/artworks/bourgeois-cell-eyes-and-mirrors-t06899.

"Louise Bourgeois. Structures of Existence: The Cells." Artsy.net. Accessed December 15, 2020. https://www.artsy.net/artwork/louise-bourgeois-in-and-out-1.

Lucas, John. "Meredith as Poet." In *Meredith Now: Some Critical Essays,* edited by Ian Fletcher, 14–33. New York: Barnes & Noble, 1971.

MacFarlane, Robert. "Monstrosity, Fakery, and Authorship in *My Life as a Fake.*" In *Fabulating Beauty: Essays on the Fiction of Peter Carey,* edited by Andreas Gaile, 335–48. Amsterdam: Rodopi, 2005.

MacLeod, Lewis. "'Any Educated Person Would Know': Cosmopolitan Aesthetics, Good Taste, and 'Knowing Better' in Peter Carey's *My Life as a Fake.*" *Ariel* 42.1 (2011): 35–61.

Maier, Michaël. *Atalanta Fugiens.* 1617. http://93beast.fea.st/files/section1/maier/Maier%20-%20Atalanta%20Fugiens.pdf.

Malone, Edmond. *Cursory observations on the poems attributed to Thomas Rowley, a priest of the fifteenth century. 'Second edition, revised and augmented.'* London: J. Nichols, 1782.

———. *An inquiry into the authenticity of certain miscellaneous papers and legal instruments . . . attributed to Shakspeare, Queen Elizabeth, and Henry, Earl of Southampton.* London: Cadell & Davies, 1796.

Margolis, Joseph. "Art, Forgery, and Authenticity." In Dutton, ed., *The Forger's Art,* 153–71.

Martinière, Nathalie. "Setting Free the Monster Within: Self-Authorization in *My Life as a Fake* by Peter Carey." In *Rewriting/Reprising: Plural Intertextualities,* edited by Georges Letissier, 154–66. Newcastle, UK: Cambridge Scholars, 2009.

McBride, Joseph. "'Committing Masterpieces': The Sly Artistry of *F for Fake*." In DVD booklet for *F for Fake*. Masters of Cinema #31. Eureka Video, 2007.

McHale, Brian. "'A Poet May Not Exist': Mock-Hoaxes and the Construction of National Identity." In Griffin, ed., *Faces of Anonymity*, 233–52.

Mead, Philip. "1944, Melbourne and Adelaide: The Ern Malley Hoax." In *The Edinburgh Companion to Twentieth-Century Literatures in English*, edited by Brian McHale and Randall Stevenson, 113–25. Edinburgh: Edinburgh University Press, 2006.

Meiland, Jack W. "Originals, Copies, and Aesthetic Value." In Dutton, ed. *The Forger's Art*, 115–130.

Mellor, Anne K. "Making a 'Monster': An Introduction to *Frankenstein*." In Schor, ed., *Cambridge Companion to Mary Shelley*, 9–25.

Mendelson, Sara H. Introduction to *A Description of a New World, Called the Blazing World*, by Margaret Cavendish. Edited by Sara H. Mendelson, 9–49. Peterborough, Ont.: Broadview, 2016.

Meredith, George. *The Letters of George Meredith*. 3 vols. Edited by C. L. Cline. Oxford: Clarendon Press, 1970.

———. *Modern Love and Poems of the English Roadside, with Poems and Ballads*. Edited by Rebecca N. Mitchell and Criscillia Benford. New Haven, CT: Yale University Press, 2013.

———. *The Ordeal of Richard Feverel*. 1859. New York: Signet, 1960.

———. *The Poems of George Meredith*. Edited by Phyllis B. Bartlett. Vol. 1. New Haven, CT: Yale University Press, 1978.

Meyer, Leonard B. "Forgery and the Anthropology of Art." In Dutton, ed., *The Forger's Art*, 77–92.

Meyerstein, E. H. W. *A Life of Thomas Chatterton*. New York: Russell, 1930.

Miller, Christopher L. *Impostors: Literary Hoaxes and Cultural Authenticity*. Chicago: University of Chicago Press, 2018.

Milton, John. *Areopagitica: A Speech of Mr. John Milton, for the Liberty of Unlicenc'd Printing*. 1644. Accessed October 27, 2020. http://www.dartmouth.edu/~milton/reading_room/areopagitica/text.html.

———. *Paradise Lost*. 1660. Edited by Barbara K. Lewalski. Malden, MA: Blackwell, 2007.

Mitchell, Rebecca N. "George Meredith's Poetry and the Critical Imagination." *Literature Compass* 8.3 (March 2011): 142–50.

Mitchell, Rebecca N., and Criscillia Benford. Introduction to *Modern Love and Poems*, by George Meredith, xxi–xlv.

Moore, Steven. *A Reader's Guide to William Gaddis's* The Recognitions. Lincoln: University of Nebraska Press, 1982.

———. *William Gaddis*. New York: Bloomsbury, 2015.

Morrissey, Ted. "Recognizing a Masterpiece: William Gaddis's Reinterpretation of Flemish Art." Williamgaddis.org. Accessed October 27, 2020. http://williamgaddis.org/critinterpessays/morrisseyrecsart.shtml.

Mulholland, Garry. "Color Me Blind." 2003. Interview with Percival Everett. In Weixlmann, ed., *Conversations with Percival Everett*, 29–34.

Murray, Rolland. "Not Being and Blackness: Percival Everett and the Uncanny Forms of Racial Incorporation." *American Literary History* 29.4 (2017): 726–52.

Musgrave, David, and Peter Kirkpatrick. "Friction as a Social Process: Reading Ern Malley." *Southerly: A Review of Australian Literature* 60.1 (2000): 131–45.

Naremore, James. *The Magic World of Orson Welles*. 1978. Centennial anniversary edition. Urbana: University of Illinois Press, 2015.

O'Hagan, Sean. "The Books Interview: Percival Everett." Interview in Weixlmann, ed., *Conversations with Percival Everett*, 32–34.

Oliver, Lois. "Henry Wallis (1830–1916) *Chatterton* 1855–6." In *Rebels and Martyrs: The Image of the Artist in the Nineteenth Century*, edited by Alexander Sturgis, Rupert Christiansen, Lois Oliver, and Michael Wilson, 84. London: National Gallery, 2006.

Osteen, Mark. *The Economy of* Ulysses: *Making Both Ends Meet*. Syracuse, NY: Syracuse University Press, 1995.

———. "The Great Expectations of Stephen Dedalus." *James Joyce Quarterly* 41.1–2 (Fall 2003/Winter 2004): 169–83.

———. "Introduction: Blue Notes Toward a New Jazz Discourse." *Genre: Forms of Discourse and Culture* 37.1 (Spring, 2004): 1–46.

———. "Rhythm Changes: Contrafacts, Copyright, and Jazz Modernism." In *Modernism and Copyright*, edited by Paul K. Saint-Amour, 89–113. New York: Oxford University Press, 2011.

Osteen, Mark, and Martha Woodmansee. "Taking Account of the New Economic Criticism: An Historical Introduction." In *The New Economic Criticism: Studies at the Intersection of Literature and Economics*, edited by Martha Woodmansee and Mark Osteen, 3–50. New York: Routledge, 1999.

Pächt, Otto. *Van Eyck and the Founders of Early Netherlandish Painting*. Edited by Maria Schmidt-Dengler. Translated by David Britt. London: H. Miller, 1994.

Page, Geoff. "*Urban Myths* by John Tranter." Review. ABC.com. July 30, 2006. Accessed December 19, 2020. https://www.abc.net.au/radionational/programs/archived/bookshow/urban-myths-by-john-tranter-reviewed-by-geoff-page/3318318#transcript.

Panofsky, Erwin. *Early Netherlandish Painting: Its Origins and Character*. 1953. 7 vols. New York: Harper & Row, 1971.

Pessoa, Fernando. *The Book of Disquiet.* Edited and translated by Richard Zenith. New York: Penguin, 2003.

Phillips, Arthur. *The Tragedy of Arthur.* New York: Random House, 2011.

Phillips, Ivan. "A Clash of Harmony: Forgery as Politics in the Work of Thomas Chatterton." *Critical Survey* 24.3 (2012): 23–47.

Phillips, Julie. *James Tiptree, Jr.: The Double Life of Alice B. Sheldon.* New York: Picador, 2006.

Pocock, J. G. A. *The Machiavellian Moment: Florentine Political Thought and the Atlantic Republican Tradition.* Princeton, NJ: Princeton University Press, 1975.

Porras, Stephanie. *Art of the Northern Renaissance: Courts, Commerce, and Devotion.* London: Laurence King, 2018.

Pound, Ezra. "A Pact." Allpoetry.com. Accessed October 27, 2020. http://allpoetry.com/A-Pact.

Pybus, Cassandra. "The Black Swan of Trespass: James McAuley and the Ern Malley Hoax." *Brick* 70 (Winter 2002): 140–49.

Radnóti, Sándor. *The Fake: Forgery and Its Place in Art.* Translated by Ervin Dunai. Lanham, MD: Rowman & Littlefield, 1999.

Rawson, Claude. "Unparodying the Forgery: The Augustan Chatterton." In Groom, ed., *Thomas Chatterton and Romantic Culture,* 15–31.

Reilly, Charlie. "An Interview with Arthur Phillips." *Contemporary Literature* 54.1 (2013): 1–22.

Ridley, Chauncey. "Van Go's *Pharmakon:* 'Pharmacology' and Democracy in Percival Everett's *Erasure.*" *African American Review* 47.1 (Spring 2014): 101–11.

"Robert Rauschenberg, *Erased de Kooning Drawing,* 1953. Overview." SFMOMA.org. Accessed October 27, 2020. https://www.sfmoma.org/artwork/98.298/.

Rogers, Pat. "Chatterton and the Club." In Groom, ed., *Thomas Chatterton and Romantic Culture,* 121–50.

Rohr, Susanne. "'The image makers': Reality and the Role of Autism in Siri Hustvedt's *The Blazing World.*" In Hartmann et al., eds., *Focused Ambiguity in Siri Hustvedt's Works,* 249–61.

Rosenbaum, Jonathan. *Discovering Orson Welles.* Berkeley: University of California Press, 2007.

Russett, Margaret. *Fictions and Fakes: Forging Romantic Authenticity, 1760–1845.* Cambridge: Cambridge University Press, 2006.

———. "Race under *Erasure:* For Percival Everett, 'a Piece of Fiction.'" *Callaloo* 28.2 (2005): 358–68.

Ruthven, K. K. *Faking Literature.* Cambridge: Cambridge University Press, 2001.

Sadlier, Darlene J. *An Introduction to Fernando Pessoa: Modernism and the Paradoxes of Authorship.* Gainesville: University Press of Florida, 1998.

Sagoff, Mark. "The Aesthetic Status of Forgeries." In Dutton, ed., *The Forger's Art,* 131–52.

Salemi, Joseph S. "To Soar in Atonement: Art as Expiation in Gaddis' *The Recognitions.*" In Kuehl and Moore, eds., *In Recognition of William Gaddis,* 46–57.

Sapphire. *Push.* New York: Knopf, 1996.

"Sapphire's Story: How *Push* Became *Precious.*" NPR Online, November 6, 2009. Accessed June 25, 2019. https://www.npr.org/templates/story/story.php?storyId=120176695.

Savu, Laura E. *Postmortem Postmodernists: The Afterlife of the Author in Recent Narrative.* Madison, NJ: Fairleigh Dickinson University Press, 2009.

Schor, Esther, ed. *The Cambridge Companion to Mary Shelley.* Cambridge: Cambridge University Press, 2003.

Schwartz, Hillel. *Culture of the Copy: Striking Likenesses, Unreasonable Facsimiles.* New York: Zone, 1996.

Scott, David A. "Art Restoration and Its Contextualization." *Journal of Aesthetic Education* 51.2 (Summer 2017): 82–104.

Shakespeare, William. *Henry V.* Edited by T. R. Craik. The Arden Shakespeare. London: Routledge, 1995.

———. *Othello.* Edited by George Lyman Kittredge. Waltham, MA: Blaisdell, 1966.

———. *Pericles.* Edited by F. D. Hoeniger. London: Methuen, 1963.

———. *Richard III.* Edited by Thomas Cartelli. Norton Critical Edition. New York: Norton, 2009.

Shapiro, B. A. *The Art Forger.* Chapel Hill, NC: Algonquin, 2013.

Shapiro, James. *Contested Will: Who Wrote Shakespeare?* New York: Simon & Schuster, 2010.

Shavers, Rone. "Percival Everett." 2004. Interview in Weixlmann, ed., *Conversations with Percival Everett,* 57–70.

Shell, Marc. *Money, Language, and Thought: Literary and Philosophical Economies from the Medieval to the Modern Era.* Berkeley: University of California Press, 1982.

Shelley, Mary. *Frankenstein, or, the Modern Prometheus.* 1831. 3rd ed. Edited by Johanna M. Smith. Boston: Bedford/St. Martin's, 2016.

Simmel, Georg. *The Philosophy of Money.* 1907. 2nd ed. Edited by David Frisby. Translated by Tom Bottomore and David Frisby. New York: Routledge, 1990.

Siraganian, Lisa. "'A disciplined nostalgia': Gaddis and the Modern Art Object." In *William Gaddis, "The Last of Something": Critical Essays,* edited by Crystal Alberts, Christopher Leise, and Birger Vanwesenbeeck, 101–14. Jefferson, NC: McFarland, 2010.

Smalley, Donald. *Browning's Essay on Chatterton.* Westport, CT: Greenwood Press, 1948.

Smith, Dominic. *The Last Painting of Sara De Vos.* New York: Farrar, Straus & Giroux, 2016.

Sonnenburg, Hubert von. "A Case of Recurring Deception." *The Metropolitan Museum of Art Bulletin,* New Series 51.3 (Winter 1993–94): 8–19.

Staller, Natasha. *A Sum of Destructions: Picasso's Cultures and the Creation of Cubism.* New Haven, CT: Yale University Press, 2001.

Starr, William W. "'I Get Bored Easily.'" 2002. Interview with Percival Everett. In Weixlmann, ed., *Conversations with Percival Everett,* 18–23.

Stewart, Doug. *The Boy Who Would Be Shakespeare: A Tale of Forgery and Folly.* Cambridge, MA: Da Capo, 2010.

Stewart, Susan. *Crimes of Writing: Problems in the Containment of Representation.* New York: Oxford University Press, 1991.

Suarez, Michael F., SJ. "'This Necessary Knowledge': Thomas Chatterton and the Ways of the London Book Trade." In Groom, ed., *Thomas Chatterton and Romantic Culture,* 96–113.

Swift, Jonathan. *A Full and True Account of the Battel, fought last Friday, between the Ancient and Modern Books in St. James's Library.* 1724. In *The Writings of Jonathan Swift,* edited by Robert A. Greenberg and William B. Piper, 373–96. Norton Critical Edition. New York: Norton, 1973.

Tabbi, Joseph. *Nobody Grew but the Business: On the Life and Work of William Gaddis.* Evanston, IL: Northwestern University Press, 2015.

Tabbi, Joseph, and Roan Shavers, eds. *Paper Empire: William Gaddis and the World System.* Tuscaloosa: University of Alabama Press, 2007.

Tanner, Tony. *City of Words: American Fiction, 1950–1970.* New York: Harper, 1971.

Taylor, Donald. *Thomas Chatterton's Art: Experiments in Imagined History.* Princeton, NJ: Princeton University Press, 1978.

Taylor, Mark C. *Rewiring the Real: In Conversation with William Gaddis, Richard Powers, Mark Danielewski, and Don DeLillo.* New York: Columbia University Press, 2013.

———. "Wounding Words." In Hartmann et al., eds., *Focused Ambiguity in Siri Hustvedt's Works,* 153–81.

Thiemann, Anna. "Portraits of the (Post-)Feminist Artist: Female Authorship and Authority in Siri Hustvedt's Fiction." In Hartmann et al., eds., *Focused Ambiguity in Siri Hustvedt's Works,* 311–25.

Thieme, Claudia. F for Fake *and the Growth in Complexity of Orson Welles' Documentary Form.* Frankfurt, Germany: Lang, 1997.

"This story may even be true." *University of Melbourne Voice* 7.7 (July 11–August 7, 2011).

Thompson, James. *Models of Value: Eighteenth-Century Political Economy and the Novel.* Durham, NC: Duke University Press, 1996.

Thomson, David. *Rosebud: The Story of Orson Welles.* New York: Knopf, 1996.

Thoreau, Henry David. *Walden and Civil Disobedience.* Introduction by Michael Meyer. New York: Penguin, 1986.

Thwaites, Tony. *Joycean Temporalities: Debts, Promises, and Countersignatures.* Gainesville: University Press of Florida, 2001.

Tiptree, James, Jr. *Her Smoke Rose Up Forever.* San Francisco: Tachyon, 2004.

———. "Houston, Houston, Do You Read?" 1976. In *Her Smoke Rose Up,* 163–216.

———. "The Women Men Don't See." 1973. In *Her Smoke Rose Up,* 115–43.

Tougaw, Jason. "The Self Is a Moving Target: The Neuroscience of Siri Hustvedt's Artists." In Hartmann et al., eds., *Focused Ambiguity in Siri Hustvedt's Works,* 113–32.

Tranter, John. "The Malley Variations." *Urban Myths: 210 Poems.* Cambridge: Salt, 2006.

Vickers, Brian. *Shakespeare, Co-Author: A Historical Study of Five Collaborative Plays.* Oxford: Oxford University Press, 2002.

Walsh, John. "The Life and Times of a Master Forger." *The Independent,* April 11, 1998. https://www.independent.co.uk/life-style/interview-the-life-and-times-of-a-master-forger-1155589.html.

Walters, Lisa. *Margaret Cavendish: Gender, Science and Politics.* Cambridge: Cambridge University Press, 2014.

Warton, Thomas. *An enquiry into the authenticity of the poems attributed to Thomas Rowley, in which the arguments of the Dean of Exeter, and Mr. Bryant, are examined.* London: Dodsley, 1782.

Weixlmann, Joe, ed. *Conversations with Percival Everett.* Jackson: University Press of Mississippi, 2013.

Welles, Orson. Letter to Francois Reichenbach, September 5, 1971. Welles-Kodar Papers, University of Michigan Library Special Collections.

———. Letter to Larry Jackson, September 25, 1974. Welles-Kodar Papers, University of Michigan Library Special Collections.

Welles, Orson, director. *F for Fake.* Janus, 1974. Film.

Wendkos, Brad. "Words of Wisdom from Thelonious Monk." Truefire.com, January 19, 2011. https://blog.truefire.com/favorites/words-of-wisdom-from-thelonius-monk/. [Includes a photocopy of Monk's handwritten notes to Steve Lacy.]

Werness, Hope. B. "Han van Meegeren fecit." In Dutton, ed. *The Forger's Art,* 1–53

Westerman, Molly. "Feeling Moved: Emotion and Theory in *Chatterton* and *The English Patient.*" *Soundings* 88.3–4 (2005): 347–69.
Wilde, Oscar. *The Complete Works of Oscar Wilde.* New York: Perennial Library, 1989.
Wilkens, Mathew. "Nothing as He Thought It Would Be: William Gaddis and American Postwar Fiction." *Contemporary Literature* 51.3 (2010): 596–628.
Williams, Ian Kennedy. *Malarky Dry.* Sydney: Hale & Iremonger, 1990.
Williams, John. "Peter Ackroyd's *Chatterton,* Thomas Chatterton, and Postmodern Romantic Identities and Attitudes: 'This Is Essentially a Romantic Attitude.'" *Romanticism* 15.1 (2009): 33–40.
Woideck, Carl, ed. *The John Coltrane Companion: Five Decades of Commentary.* New York: Schirmer, 1998.
Wolfe, Peter. *A Vision of His Own: The Mind and Art of William Gaddis.* Madison, NJ: Fairleigh Dickinson University Press, 1997.
Wolfson, Susan J. "Mary Shelley, Editor." In Schor, ed., *Cambridge Companion to Mary Shelley,* 193–210.
Wood, Michael. Afterword to Groom, ed., *Thomas Chatterton and Romantic Culture,* 259–61.
Woodmansee, Martha. *The Author, Art, and the Market: Rereading the History of Aesthetics.* New York: Columbia University Press, 1994.
Wreen, Michael. "Is, Madam? Nay, It Seems!" In Dutton, ed., *The Forger's Art,* 188–224.
Wright, Elizabeth. "The Significance of the Image Patterns in Meredith's *Modern Love.*" *Victorian Newsletter* 13 (Spring 1958): 1–10.
Yost, Brian. "The Changing Same: The Evolution of Racial Self-Definition and Commercialization." *Callaloo* 31.4 (Fall 2008): 1314–34.
Young, Kevin. *Bunk: The Rise of Hoaxes, Humbug, Plagiarism, Phonies, Post-Facts, and Fake News.* Minneapolis: Graywolf, 2017.
Zenith, Richard. "Table of Heteronyms." In *The Book of Disquiet,* by Fernando Pessoa. New York: Penguin, 2003.

INDEX

Page numbers followed by b *and* f *indicate boxes and figures, respectively.*

CPSIA information can be obtained
at www.ICGtesting.com
Printed in the USA
LVHW042034280722
724653LV00002B/104